Praise for J. R. Ward's Black Dagger Brotherhood series

'Now here's a band of brothers who know how to show a girl a good time'
New York Times bestselling author, Lisa Gardner

'It's not easy to find a new twist on the vampire myth, but Ward succeeds beautifully. This dark and compelling world is filled with enticing romance as well as perilous adventure'
Romantic Times

'These vampires are *hot,* and the series only gets hotter . . . so hot it gave me shivers'
Vampire Genre

'Ward wields a commanding voice perfect for the genre . . . Intriguing, adrenaline-pumping . . . Fans of L.A. Banks, Laurell K. Hamilton and Sherrilyn Kenyon will add Ward to their must-read list'
Booklist

'These erotic paranormals are well worth it, and frighteningly addictive . . . It all works to great, page-turning effect . . . [and has] earned Ward an Anne Rice-style following, deservedly so'
Publishers Weekly

'[A] midnight whirlwind of dangerous characters and mesmerizing erotic romance. The Black Dagger Brotherhood owns me now. Dark fantasy lovers, you just got served'
Lynn Viehl, *USA Today* bestselling author of *Evermore*

J. R. Ward lives in the South with her incredibly supportive husband and her beloved golden retriever. After graduating from law school, she began working in health care in Boston and spent many years as chief of staff for one of the premier academic medical centres in the nation.

Visit her and the Black Dagger Brotherhood at www.jrward.com

Also by J. R. Ward

The Black Dagger Brotherhood series:

Dark Lover
Lover Eternal
Lover Awakened
Lover Revealed
Lover Unbound
Lover Enshrined
Lover Avenged
Lover Mine

The Black Dagger Brotherhood: An Insider's Guide

Fallen Angels series:

Covet
Crave

LOVER UNLEASHED

J. R. WARD

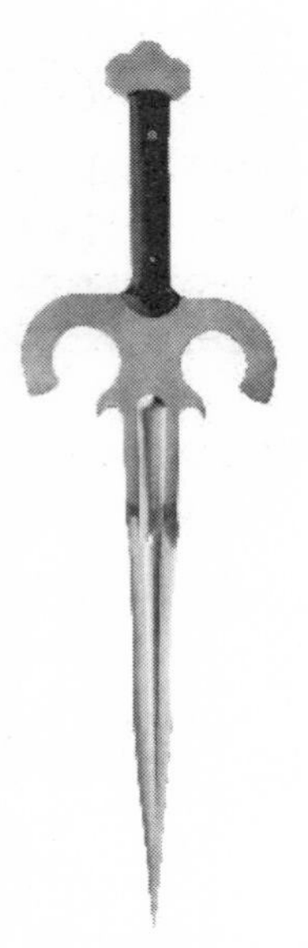

piatkus

PIATKUS

First published in the United States in 2011 by New American Library,
A Division of Penguin Group (USA) Inc., New York
First published in Great Britain as a paperback original in 2011 by Piatkus

All characters and events in this publication, other than those clearly in the public domain, are fictitious and any resemblance to real persons, living or dead, is purely coincidental.

A CIP catalogue record for this book is available from the British Library.

ISBN 978-0-7499-5560-1

Printed and bound in Great Britain by
CPI Mackays, Chatham ME5 8TD

Piatkus
An imprint of
Little, Brown Book Group
100 Victoria Embankment
London EC4Y 0DY

An Hachette UK Company
www.hachette.co.uk

www.piatkus.co.uk

IN LOVING MEMORY OF

MARGARET BIRD

Dedicated to you:

You,
a "brother" indeed.
I think you are right where
you are supposed to be—and
I'm not the only one who feels that way.

lys (n.) Torture tool used to remove the eyes.

mahmen (n.) Mother. Used both as an identifier and a term of affection.

mhis (n.) The masking of a given physical environment, the creation of a field of illusion.

nalla (n., f.) or ***nallum*** (n., m.) Beloved.

needing period (n.) Female vampire's time of fertility, generally lasting for two days and accompanied by intense sexual cravings. Occurs approximately five years after a female's transition and then once a decade thereafter. All males respond to some degree if they are around a female in her need. It can be a dangerous time, with conflicts and fights breaking out between competing males, particularly if the female is not mated.

newling (n.) A virgin.

the Omega (pr. n.) Malevolent, mystical figure who has targeted the vampires for extinction out of resentment directed toward the Scribe Virgin. Exists in a nontemporal realm and has extensive powers, though not the power of creation.

phearsom (adj.) Term referring to the potency of a male's sexual organs. Literal translation something close to "worthy of entering a female."

princeps (n.) Highest level of the vampire aristocracy, second only to members of the First Family or the Scribe Virgin's Chosen. Must be born to the title; it may not be conferred.

pyrocant (n.) Refers to a critical weakness in an individual. The weakness can be internal, such as an addiction, or external, such as a lover.

rahlman (n.) Savior.

rythe (n.) Ritual manner of assuaging honor granted by one who has offended another. If accepted, the offended chooses a weapon and strikes the offender, who presents him- or herself without defenses.

the Scribe Virgin (pr. n.) Mystical force who is counselor to the king as well as the keeper of vampire archives and the dispenser of privileges. Exists in a nontemporal realm and has extensive powers. Capable of a single act of creation, which she expended to bring the vampires into existence.

sehclusion (n.) Status conferred by the king upon a female of the aristocracy as a result of a petition by the female's family. Places the female under the sole direction of her *ghardian*, typically the eldest male in her household. Her *ghardian* then has the legal right to determine all manner of her life, restricting at will any and all interactions she has with the world.

shellan (n.) Female vampire who has been mated to a male. Females generally do not take more than one mate due to the highly territorial nature of bonded males.

symphath (n.) Subspecies within the vampire race characterized by the ability and desire to manipulate emotions in others (for the purposes of an energy exchange), among other traits. Historically, they have been discriminated against and, during certain eras, hunted by vampires. They are near extinction.

the Tomb (pr. n.) Sacred vault of the Black Dagger Brotherhood. Used as a ceremonial site as well as a storage facility for the jars of *lessers*. Ceremonies performed there include inductions, funerals, and disciplinary actions against Brothers. No one may enter except for members of the Brotherhood, the Scribe Virgin, or candidates for induction.

trahyner (n.) Word used between males of mutual respect and affection. Translated loosely as "beloved friend."

transition (n.) Critical moment in a vampire's life when he or she transforms into an adult. Thereafter, he or she must drink the blood of the opposite sex to survive and is unable to withstand sunlight. Occurs generally in the midtwenties. Some vampires do not survive their transitions, males in particular. Prior to their transitions, vampires are physically weak, sexually unaware and unresponsive, and unable to dematerialize.

vampire (n.) Member of a species separate from that of Homo sapiens. Vampires must drink the blood of the opposite sex to survive. Human blood will keep them alive, though the strength does not last long. Following their transitions, which occur in their midtwenties, they are unable to go out into sunlight and must feed from the vein regularly. Vampires cannot "convert" humans through a bite or transfer of blood, though they are in rare cases able to breed with the other species. Vampires can dematerialize at will, though they must be able to calm themselves and concentrate to do so and may not carry anything heavy with them.

south, south, south till the heel of Italy forced them to turn about. And then it was a case of going through those many miles yet anew. And again. And again.

"We leave our provisions herein," Xcor pronounced, pointing to a thick-trunked tree that had fallen over a creek.

Whilst the transfer of their modest supplies was made, there was naught but the sound of creaking leather and the occasional snort from the stallions. When all was stowed under the flank of the downed oak, they remounted and gathered their high-bred horses—which were the only things of value other than the weapons that they possessed. Xcor did not see the usefulness in objects of beauty or comfort—those were naught but weight that bore you down. A strong horse and a well-balanced dagger? Those were priceless.

As the seven of them rode unto the village, they made no effort to mute the pounding of their steeds' hooves. There were no war cries, however. Such was wasted energy, as their enemy needed little invitation to come forth and greet them.

In manner of welcome, a human or two peeked out of doors and then quickly locked themselves back in their abodes. Xcor ignored them. Instead, he scanned the squat stone houses and the center square and the fortified trading shops, searching for a bipedal form that was as pale as a ghost and stank like a corpse coated in treacle.

His father rode up to him and smiled with a vicious edge. "Mayhap afterward we shall enjoy the fruits of the gardens herein."

"Mayhap," Xcor murmured as his stallion tossed its head. Verily, he wasn't much interested in bedding females or forcing males to submit, but his sire was not one to be denied even in whims of leisure.

Using hand signals, Xcor directed three of their band to the left, where there was a small structure with a cross atop its peaked roof. He and the others would take the right. His father would do what he pleased. As always.

Forcing the stallions to remain at a walk was a chore that challenged even the stoutest of arms, but he was used to the tug-of-war and sat solidly in his saddle. With grim purpose, his eyes penetrated the shadows thrown by the moonlight, seeking, probing—

The group of slayers that stepped free from the lee of the smithy had weapons aplenty.

"Five," Zypher growled. "Blessed be this night."

"Three," Xcor cut in. "Two are but humans as yet—although killing that pair . . . 'twill be a pleasure as well."

"Which shall you take, m'lord?" his brother-in-arms said, with a deference that had been earned, not granted as part of some birthright.

"The humans," Xcor said, shifting forward and bracing for the moment he gave his stallion its head. "If there are other lessers *about, that shall draw them out further."*

Spurring on his great beast and melding into his saddle, he smiled as the lessers *stood their ground in their chain mail and weaponries. The two humans beside them were not going to remain as steadfast, however. Although the pair were likewise kitted for fighting, they would turn and run at the first flash of fangs, spooking like plow horses from a cannon blast.*

Which was why he abruptly bore off to the right no more than three strides into the gallop. Behind the farrier's cottage, he hauled up on the reins and threw himself free of his steed. His stallion was a wild cur, but was obedient when it came to a dismount and would await—

A human female burst forth from the back door, her white nightgown a brilliant streak in the darkness as she scrambled to find footing in the mud. The instant she saw him, she froze in terror.

Logical response: He was twice her size, if not three times as large, and dressed not for sleep, as she was, but for war. As her hand rose to her throat, he sniffed the air and caught her scent. Mmm, mayhap his father had a point about enjoying the garden . . .

As the thought occurred, he let out a low growl that galvanized her feet into a panicked run, and at the sight of her fleeing, the predator in him came to the fore. With bloodthirst curling in his gut, he was reminded that it had been a matter of weeks since he'd fed from a member of his species, and though this lass was but human, she could well suffice for tonight.

Unfortunately, there was no time for the diversion the now—although his father would surely catch her afterward. If Xcor needed some blood to tide him over, he would get it from this woman, or another.

Turning his back on her escape, he planted his feet and unsheathed his weapon of choice: Although daggers had their doing, he preferred the scythe, long handled and modified for a holster that strapped upon his back. He was an expert at wielding the heavy weight, and he smiled whilst he worked the vicious, curved blade in the wind, waiting to play net to the pair of fish who were sure to swim—

Ah, yes, how good it was to be right.

Just after a bright light and a popping sound broke out from the main thoroughfare, the two humans came screaming around behind the smithy as if they were being pursued by marauders.

But they got it wrong, did they not. Their marauder was waiting here.

Xcor didn't yell or curse them or even growl. He lunged into a run with the

There was nary a hesitation. The males set upon bended knee, taking out their daggers, and bursting forth with a war cry before burying the blades into the earth at his feet.

Xcor stared at their bowed heads and felt a mantle fall upon his shoulders.

The Bloodletter was dead. No longer living, he was a legend starting this night.

And as is right and proper, the son now stepped into the soles of his sire, commanding these soldiers who would serve not Wrath, the king who would not rule, nor the Brotherhood, who would not deign to lower themselves to this level . . . but Xcor and Xcor alone.

"We go in the direction from whence the female came," he announced. "We shall find her even if it takes centuries, and she shall pay for what she hath wrought this night." Now Xcor whistled loud and clear to his stallion. "I shall take this death out of her hide myself."

Springing up onto his horse, he gathered the reins and spurred the great beast into the night, his band of bastards falling into formation upon his heels, prepared to go to the death for him.

As they thundered out of the village, he put the skull of his father in his leather battle shirt, right over his heart.

Vengeance would be his own. Even if it killed him.

bad attitude and a stride as long as a football field, took immediate advantage of the slowdown, his jockey letting that horse have all its head.

The pair went neck and neck for only a second before the chestnut took control of the race. But it wasn't going to be for long. Manny's girl had picked her moment to weave in between a knot of three horses and come up on his ass tighter than a bumper sticker.

Yup, Glory was in her element, ears flat against her head, teeth bared.

She was going to eat his fucking lunch. And it was impossible not to extrapolate to the first Saturday in May and the Kentucky Derby—

It all happened so fast.

Everything came to an end . . . in the blink of an eye.

On a deliberate sideswipe, the colt slammed into Glory, the brutal impact sending her into the rail. His girl was big and strong, but she was no match for a body check like that, not when she was going forty miles an hour.

For a heartbeat, Manny was convinced she'd rally. In spite of the way she careened and scrambled, he expected her to find her footing and teach that unruly bastard a lesson in manners.

Except she went down. Right in front of the three horses she'd passed.

The carnage was immediate, horses veering widely to avoid the obstacle in their way, jockeys breaking their tight racing curls in hopes of staying on their mounts.

Everyone made it. Except Glory.

As the crowd gasped, Manny shot forward, popping over the box's confines and then vaulting over people and chairs and barricades until he came down to the track itself.

Over the rail. Onto the dirt.

He ran to her, his years of athletics carrying him at breakneck speed to the heartbreaking sight.

She was trying to get up. Bless her big, fierce heart, she was fighting to get up from the earth, her eyes trained on the pack as if she didn't give a shit that she was injured; she just wanted to catch up with the ones who had left her in the dust.

Tragically, her foreleg had other plans for her: As she struggled, that front right flopped around below the knee, and Manny didn't need his years as an orthopedic surgeon to know that she was in trouble.

Big trouble.

As he came up to her, her jockey was in tears. "Dr. Manello, I tried—oh, God . . ."

Manny skidded in the dirt and lunged for the reins as the vets drove up and a screen was erected around the drama.

As the three men in uniforms approached her, her eyes began to go wild from pain and confusion. Manny did what he could to calm her down, allowing her to toss her head as much as she wanted while he stroked her neck. And she did ease up when they shot her with a tranquilizer.

At least the desperate limping stopped.

The head vet took one look at the leg and shook his head. Which in the racing world was the universal language for: *She needs to be put down.*

Manny rode up in the guy's face. "Don't even think about it. Stabilize the break and get her over to Tricounty right now. Clear?"

"She's never going to race again—this looks like a multi—"

"Get my fucking horse off this track and over to Tricounty—"

"She isn't worth it—"

Manny snap-grabbed the front of the vet's jacket, and hauled Mr. Easy Out over until they were nose-to-nose. *"Do it. Now."*

There was a moment of total incomprehension, like being manhandled was a new one to the little snot.

And just so the two of them were really clear, Manny growled, "I'm not going to lose her—but I'm more than willing to drop you. Right here. Right now."

The vet cringed away, as if he knew he was in danger of getting corked a good one. "Okay . . . okay."

Manny was not about to lose his horse. Over the last twelve months, he'd mourned the only woman he'd ever cared about, questioned his sanity, and taken up drinking Scotch even though he'd always hated the shit.

If Glory bit it now . . . he didn't really have much left in his life, did he.

He frowned hard. "What the hell are you talking about? Of course I want you with me."

As his foot got tapping, he wondered how long he had to stay before he could go out for another cigarette. He just couldn't breathe as he sat here, unable to do anything while his sister suffered, and his brain got choked with questions. He had ten thousand whats and whys sitting on the top of his head, except he couldn't ask them. Payne was looking like she could slip into a coma at any moment from the pain, so it was hardly time to kaffeeklatsch it.

Shit, vampires might heal lightning-fast, but they were not immortals by any stretch.

He could well lose his twin from this before he even got to know her.

On that note, he gave a look-see at her vitals on the monitor. The race had low blood pressure to begin with, but hers was hovering close to ground level. Pulse was slow and uneven, like a drum section made up of white boys. And the oxygen sensor had had to be silenced because its warning alarm had been going off continuously.

As her eyes closed, he worried that it would be for the last time, and what had he done for her? All but yell at her when she'd asked him a question.

He leaned in closer, feeling like a schmuck. "You have to hold on here, Payne. I'm getting you what you need, but you've got to hang on."

His twin's lids rose and she looked at him from out of her stationary head. "I have brought too much upon your doorstep."

"You don't worry about me."

"That is all I have ever done."

V frowned again. Clearly this whole brother/sister thing was a news flash only on his end, and he had to wonder how in the hell she'd known about him.

And what she knew.

Shit, here was another chance to wish he'd been vanilla.

"You are so certain of this healer you seek," she mumbled.

Ah, not really. The only thing he was sure of was that if the bastard killed her there was going to be a double funeral tonight—assuming there was anything left of the human to bury or burn.

"Vishous?"

"My *shellan* trusts him."

Payne's eyes drifted upward and stayed there. Was she looking at the ceiling? he wondered. The examination lamp that hung over her? Something he couldn't see?

Eventually, she said, "Ask me how long I have spent at our mother's beckoning."

"You sure you have the strength for this?" When she all but glared at him, he wanted to smile. "How long."

"What is this year for the Earth?" When he told her, her eyes widened. "Indeed. Well, it has been hundreds of years. I was imprisoned by our *mahmen* for . . . hundreds of years of life."

Vishous felt the tips of his fangs tingle in rage. That mother of theirs . . . he should have known what peace he'd found with the female wouldn't last. "You're free now."

"Am I." She glanced down toward her legs. "I cannot live in another prison."

"You won't."

Now that icy stare grew shrewd. "I cannot live like this. Do you understand what I'm saying."

The inside of him went absolutely frigid. "Listen, I'm going to get that doctor here and—"

"Vishous," she said hoarsely. "Verily, I would do it if I could, but I cannot, and there is no one else I have to turn to. Do you understand me."

As he met her eyes, he wanted to scream, his gut roping up, sweat flushing across his brow. He was a killer by nature and training, but that wasn't a skill set he'd ever intended to wield on his own blood. Well, their mother excepted, of course. Maybe their dad, except the guy had died on his own.

Okay, amendment: not something he would ever do to his *sister*.

"Vishous. Do you—"

"Yeah." He looked down at his cursed hand and flexed the goddamn piece of shit. "I get it."

Deep inside his skin, at his very core, his inner string started to vibrate. It was the kind of thing he'd been intimately familiar with for most of his life—and also an utter shock. He hadn't had this sensation since Jane and Butch had come along, and its return was . . . another slice of Fuck Me.

In the past, it had taken him seriously off the rails into the land of hard-core sex and dangerous, on-the-edge shit.

At the speed of sound.

Payne's voice was thready. "And what say you."

Damn it, he'd just met her.

"Yes." He flexed his deadly hand. "I'll take care of you. If it comes to that."

As Payne stared up out of the cage of her dead-lead body, her twin's bleak profile was all she could see, and she despised herself for the position she'd put him in. She had spent the time since she'd arrived on this side trying to tease out another path, another option, another . . . anything.

But what she needed was hardly something one could ask of a stranger.

Then again, he was a stranger.

"Thank you," she said. "Brother mine."

Vishous just nodded once and resumed staring straight ahead. In person, he was so much more than the sum of his facial features and the massive size of his body. Back before she had been imprisoned by their *mahmen*, she had long watched him in the seeing bowls of the sacred Chosen and had known the instant he had appeared in the shallow water who he was to her—all she'd had to do was look at him and she saw herself.

Such a life he had led. Starting with the war camp and their father's brutality . . . and now this.

And beneath his cold composure, he raged. She could feel it in her very bones, some link between them giving her insight beyond that which her eyes informed her of: On the surface, he was collected as a brick wall, his composite components all in order and mortared in place. Inside his skin, however, he seethed . . . and the external clue was his gloved right hand. From underneath its base, a bright light shone . . . and got e'er brighter. Especially after she'd asked him what she had.

This could be their only time together, she realized, her eyes slicking over anew.

"You are mated to the healer female?" she murmured.

"Yeah."

When there was only silence, she wished she could engage him, but it was clear he answered her only out of courtesy. And yet she believed him when he said he was glad she'd arrived herein. He didn't strike her as the type to lie—not because he cared about morality or politeness as such, but rather because he viewed such effort as a waste of time and inclination.

Payne eased her eyes back to the ring of bright fire that hung o'erhead. She wished he would hold her hand or touch her in some way, but she had asked more than plenty of him already.

Lying upon the rolling slab, her body felt all wrong, both heavy and weightless in the same moment, and her only hope was the spasms that tore down her legs and tickled into her feet, causing them to jerk. Surely all was not lost if that was occurring, she told herself.

Except even as she took shelter under that thought, a very small, quiet part of her mind told her that the cognitive roof she was trying to construct would not withstand the rain that hung o'er what was left of her life: When she moved her hands, though she could not see them, she could feel the cool, soft sheeting and the slick chill of the table she was upon. But when she told her feet to do the same . . . it was as though she were in the serene, tepid waters of the bathing pools on the Other Side, cocooned in an invisible embrace, sensing nothing against her.

Where was this healer?

Time . . . was passing.

As the wait went from intolerable to downright agonizing, it was difficult to know whether the choking sensation in her throat was from her condition or the quiet of the room. Verily, she and her twin were alike steeped in stillness—just for very different reasons: She was going nowhere with alacrity. He was on the verge of an explosion.

Desperate for some stimulation, something . . . anything, she murmured, "Tell me about the healer who is coming."

The cool draft that hit her face and the scent of dark spices that tunneled into her nose told her it was a male. Had to be.

"He's the best," Vishous muttered. "Jane's always talked about him like he's a god."

The tone was rather less than complimentary, but, indeed, vampire males did not appreciate others of their persuasion around their females.

Who could it be within the race? she wondered. The only healer that Payne had seen in the bowls was Havers. And surely there would have been no reason to search for him?

Perhaps there was another she had not been witness to. After all, she had not spent a vast amount of time catching up with the world, and according to her twin, there had been many, many, many years transpiring between her imprisonment and her freedom, such as it was . . .

In an abrupt wave, exhaustion cut off her thought process, seeping into her very marrow, dragging her down even harder atop the metal table.

Yet when she closed her eyes, she could withstand the dimness only a moment before panic popped her lids open. Whilst their mother had held her in suspended animation, she had been all too aware of her blank, limitless surroundings and the grindingly slow passage of moments and minutes. This paralysis now was too much alike what she had suffered for hundreds of years.

And that was the why of her terrible request to Vishous. She could not come here to this side only to replicate what she had been so desperate to escape from.

Tears trickled over her vision, causing the bright light source to waver.

How she wished her brother would hold her hand.

"Please don't cry," Vishous said. "Don't . . . cry."

In truth, she was surprised he noticed. "Verily, you are correct. Crying cures naught."

Stiffening her resolve, she forced herself to be strong, but it was a battle. Although her knowledge of the arts of medicine was limited, simple logic spelled out what she was up against: As she was of an extraordinarily strong bloodline, her body had begun repairing itself the moment she had been injured whilst sparring with the Blind King. The problem was, however, the very regenerative process that would ordinarily save her life was making her condition ever more dire—and likely to be permanent.

Spines that were broken and fixing themselves were not likely to achieve a well-ordered result, and the paralysis of her lower legs was testament to that fact.

"Why do you keep regarding your hand?" she asked, still staring at the light.

There was a silent moment. Atop all the others. "Why do you think I am?"

Payne sighed. "Because I know you, brother mine. I know all about you."

When he said not another thing, the quiet was about as companionable as the Old Country inquests had been.

Oh, what things had she set in motion?

And where would they all be when this came to an end?

that not letting her go smacked of cowardice. But he couldn't dwell on that psychobabble bullshit or he'd lose it.

"I can't guarantee anything." The vet went back to staring at the X-rays. "I can't tell you how this is going to go, but I will swear to you—I'll do my best."

God, now he knew how those families felt when he spoke to them. "Thanks. Can I watch in here?"

"Absolutely. I'll get you something to put on, and you know the drill with scrubbing in, Doctor."

Twenty minutes later, the operation started, and Manny watched from her head, stroking her forelock with his latex-gloved hand even though she was out cold. As the head vet worked, Manny had to approve of the guy's methodology and skills—which were just about the only things that had gone right since Glory had fallen. The procedure was over in under an hour, with the bone chips either removed or screwed into place. Then they rolled the leg up and moved her out of the OR and into a pool so she wouldn't break another leg coming out of sedation.

He stayed until she was awake and then followed the vet out into the hall.

"Her vitals are good and the operation went well," the vet said, "but the former can change quick. And it's going to take time until we know what we've got."

Shit. That little speech was exactly what he said to next-of-kins and other relatives when it was time for folks to go home and rest up and wait to see how a patient's postop went.

"We'll call you," the vet said. "With updates."

Manny snapped off his gloves and took out his business card. "In case you don't have it in her records."

"We've got it." The guy took the thing anyway. "If anything changes, you'll be the first to know, and I'll update you personally every twelve hours when I do rounds."

Manny nodded and stuck out his hand. "Thank you. For taking care of her."

"You're welcome."

After they shook, Manny nodded back at the double doors. "Mind if I give her a see-ya-later?"

"Please."

Back inside, he took a moment with his filly. God . . . this hurt.

"You hang on, there, girlie." He had to whisper because he couldn't seem to draw a full breath.

When he straightened, the staff were staring at him with a sadness he knew was going to stick with him.

"We'll take excellent care of her," the vet said gravely.

He believed they would, and that was the only thing that got him back into the hall.

Tricounty's facilities were extensive, and it took him a while to change and then find his way out to where he'd parked by the front door. Up ahead, the sun had set, a rapidly fading peach glow lighting up the sky as if Manhattan were smoldering. The air was cool, but fragrant from spring's early efforts to bring life to winter's barren landscape, and he took so many deep breaths he got light-headed.

God, time had been running at a blur, but now, as the minutes drooled by, clearly the frantic pace had exhausted its energy source. Either that or it had slammed into a brick wall and passed the fuck out.

As he palmed up his car key, he felt older than God. His head was thumping and his arthritic hip was killing him, that flat-out race over the track to Glory's side way more than the damn thing could handle.

This was so not how he'd envisioned this day ending. He'd assumed he'd be buying drinks for the owners he'd beaten . . . and maybe in the flush of victory taking Ms. Hanson up on her generous oral suggestion.

Getting into his Porsche, he started the engine. Caldwell was about forty-five minutes north of Queens, and his car could practically drive the trip back to the Commodore itself. Good thing, too, because he was a goddamn zombie.

No radio. No iPod music. No phoning people, either.

As he got on the Northway, he just stared at the road ahead and fought the urge to turn around and . . . yeah, and do what? Sleep next to his horse?

The thing was, if he could manage to get home in one piece, help was on the way. He had a fresh bottle of Lagavulin waiting for him, and he might or might not slow down to use a glass: As far as the hospital was concerned, he was off until Monday a.m. at six o'clock, and he had plans to get drunk and stay that way.

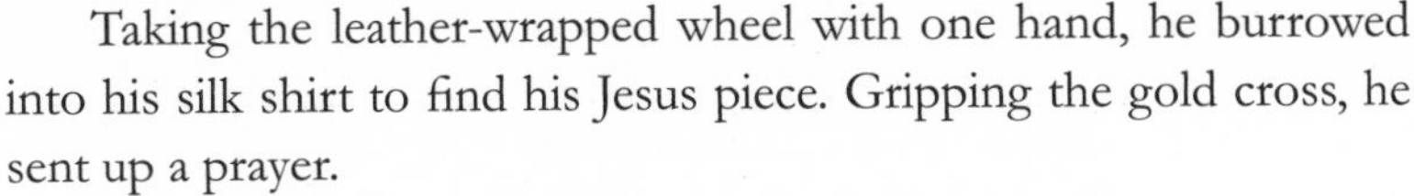

Taking the leather-wrapped wheel with one hand, he burrowed into his silk shirt to find his Jesus piece. Gripping the gold cross, he sent up a prayer.

God . . . please let her be okay.

He couldn't stand losing another one of his girls. Not so soon. Jane Whitcomb had died a whole year ago, but that was just what the calendar told him. In grief time, it had been only about a minute and a half since it had happened.

He didn't want to go through that again.

FOUR

Downtown Caldwell had a lot of tall, windowed buildings, but there were few like the Commodore. At a good thirty floors in height, it was among the taller in the concrete forest, and the sixty or so condos it housed were Trump-tastic, all marble and nickel-plated chrome and designer-everything.

Up on the twenty-seventh floor, Jane walked around Manny's condo, looking for signs of life and finding . . . nothing. Literally. The guy's place was about as much of an obstacle course as a damn dance floor, his furniture consisting of three things in the living room and a huge bed in the master suite.

That was it.

Well, and some leather-seated stools at the counter in the kitchen. As for the walls? The only thing he'd hung anywhere was a plasma-screen TV the size of a billboard. And the hardwood floors had no rugs, just gym bags and . . . more gym bags . . . and athletic shoes.

Which was not to say he was a slob. He didn't own enough to be considered a slob.

With growing panic, she walked into his bedroom and saw half a

Her phone ringing was not exactly good news. She didn't want to tell Vishous that forty-five minutes later she still had nothing to report.

She took out her cell. "Oh . . . God."

That number. Those ten digits that she'd had on speed dial on every phone she'd owned before this one. *Manny.*

As she hit *send*, her mind was blank and her eyes filled with tears. Her dear old friend and colleague . . .

"Hello?" he said. "Ms. Whit?"

In the background, she heard a dim whistle.

"Hello? Hannah?" That tone . . . it was just the same as it had been a year ago: low, commanding. "Anyone there?"

That quiet whistle sounded again.

Jesus Christ . . . , she thought. She knew where he was.

Jane hung up and flashed herself out of his condo, out of downtown, out past the suburbs. Traveling in a blur at the speed of light, her molecules went through the night in a twirling, swirling rush that covered miles as if they were but inches.

Pine Grove Cemetery was the kind of place you needed a map of, but when you were ether in the air, you could case a hundred acres in a heartbeat and a half.

As she came out of the darkness by her grave, she took a halting breath and nearly sobbed. There he was in the flesh. Her boss. Her colleague. The one she'd left behind. And he was standing over a black headstone that had her name carved in its face.

Okay, now she knew she'd made the right decision not to go to her funeral. The closest she had come was reading about it in the *Caldwell Courier Journal*—and the picture of all those surgeons and hospital staff and patients had all but snapped her in half.

This was so much worse.

And Manny looked exactly how she felt: ruined on the inside.

Jesus, that aftershave of his still smelled good . . . and in spite of having lost some weight, he was still handsome as sin, with that dark hair and that hard face. His suit was perfectly tailored and pin-striped—but it had dirt around the cuffs of the precisely pressed slacks. And his loafers were likewise soiled, making her wonder where the hell he'd been. He certainly hadn't picked it up from the grave site. After a year, the soil was packed down and covered with grass—

Oh, wait. Her plot had probably looked like this from day one. She hadn't left behind anything to bury.

As his fingers rested on the stone, she knew he had to have been the one to pick the thing out. Nobody else would have had the sense to get her exactly what she would have wanted. Nothing froufrou or wordy. Short, sweet, to the point.

Jane cleared her throat. "Manny."

His head shot up, but he didn't look over at her—as if he were convinced that he'd heard her speak only in his mind.

Making herself fully corporeal, she spoke louder. "Manny."

Under any other circumstances, the response would have been a laugh riot. He wheeled around, then shouted out, tripped over her headstone, and landed flat on his ass.

"What the . . . hell . . . are you doing here?" he gasped. The expression on his face started as horror, but shifted quickly to utter disbelief.

"I'm sorry."

It was entirely lame, but that was all that came out of her mouth.

And so much for thinking on her feet. Meeting those brown eyes of his, she suddenly had nothing to say.

Manny sprang to his feet, and his dark stare went up and down her body. And up and down. And up . . . to lock on her face.

That was when the anger came. And a headache, evidently, given the way he winced and rubbed his temples. "Is this some kind of joke?"

"No." She wished it were. "I'm so sorry."

His vicious frown was achingly familiar, and what an irony to go nostalgic about a glower like that. "You're *sorry*."

"Manny, I—"

"I *buried* you. And you're *sorry*? What the *fuck* is this?"

"Manny, I don't have time to explain. I need you."

He glared at her for a long moment. "You show up after a year of being *dead* and you *need* me?"

The reality of how much time had passed weighed on her. On top of everything else. "Manny . . . I don't know what to tell you."

"Oh, really? Other than, oh, b.t.w. I'm alive."

He stared at her. Just stared at her.

Then in a hoarse voice, he said, "Do you have any idea what losing you has been like?" He quickly brushed a hand over his eyes. "Do you?"

The pain in her chest made it hard to breathe. "Yes. Because I lost you . . . I lost my life with you and the hospital."

Manny started to pace, going back and forth in front of her headstone. And although she wanted to, she knew not to get too close.

"Manny . . . if there had been a way to come back to you, I would have."

"You did. Once. I thought that was a dream, but it wasn't. Was it."

"No."

"How'd you get into my condo?"

"I just did."

He stopped and looked at her, her gravestone between them. "Why did you do it, Jane? Why fake your death?"

Well, she hadn't, actually. "I don't have time to explain now."

"Then what the fuck are you doing here. How about you explain that."

She cleared her throat. "I've got a patient who's over my head and I want you to come have a look. I can't tell you where I've got to take you and I can't give you a lot of details and I know this is not fair . . . but I *need* you." She wanted to tear her hair out. Fall down weeping. Hug him. But she just kept going because she simply had to. "I've been looking for you for over an hour, so I'm out of time. I know you're pissed off and confused and I don't blame you. But be mad at me later—just come with me now. *Please.*"

All she could do was wait. Manny was not somebody you talked into things, and you couldn't persuade him. He would make the choice . . . or he wouldn't.

And if the latter was the case, unfortunately, she was going to have to call the Brothers. As much as she loved and missed her old boss, Vishous was her man, and she'd be goddamned if she was letting anything happen to his sister.

One way or the other, Manny was going to be operating tonight.

FIVE

Butch O'Neal was not the kind of guy to leave a lady in distress.

It was the old-school in him . . . the cop in him . . . the devout, practicing Catholic in him. That being said, in the case of the phone call he'd just had with the lovely and talented Dr. Jane Whitcomb, chivalry didn't play into his get-up-and-go. Not in the slightest.

As he beat feet out of the Pit, and all but ran through the underground tunnel to the Brotherhood's training center, his interests and hers were totally aligned even without regard to the whole "be a gentleman" thing: They were both terrified that V was going to spin out of control again.

The earmarks were already there: All you had to do was look at him and you could see that the lid on his Crock-Pot was bolting down hard over the heat and turmoil underneath. All that pressure? Had to get let out somehow, and in the past, it had been in the very messiest of ways.

Stepping through the hidden door and emerging into the office, Butch hung a right and barreled down the long corridor that led to the medical facilities. The subtle waft of Turkish tobacco in the air told him exactly where to find his target, but it wasn't as if there had been any doubt.

At the examination room's closed door, he snapped the cuffs of his Gucci shirt into place and jacked up his belt.

His knock was soft. His heartbeat was hard.

Vishous didn't answer with a "come in." Instead, the brother slipped out and closed the door behind himself.

Shit, he looked bad. And his hands shook ever so slightly as he rolled one of his coffin nails. While he was licking the thing closed, Butch dug into his pocket and supplied the lighter, flicking up a flame and holding it forward.

When his best friend leaned into the orange flare, he knew every tell in that cruel, impassive face.

Jane was absolutely right. The poor bastard was humming hard and holding it all in.

Vishous inhaled deep and then settled back against the cinder-block wall, eyes trained straight ahead, shitkickers planted solidly.

Eventually, the guy muttered, "You're not asking how I am."

Butch affected the same lean, right next to his boy. "Don't have to."

"Mind reader?"

"Yup. That's me."

V leaned to the side and tapped his ashes into the bin. "So tell me what I'm thinking, true?"

"You sure you want me to cuss this close to your sister?" When that got a short laugh, Butch stared at V's profile. The tattoos around the guy's eye were especially sinister, given the cloud of control that surrounded him like a nuclear winter.

"You don't want me to guess out loud, V," he said softly.

"Nah. Give it a shot."

This meant V needed to talk but, in characteristic fashion, was wrapped too tight to squeeze it out: The male had always put the *shut it* in relating, but at least he was better than he'd been. Before? He wouldn't have even cracked this door at all.

"She asked you to take care of her if this doesn't work, didn't she," Butch said, voicing what he feared most. "And not in terms of palliative nursing."

V's response was an exhale that lasted aboooooout fifteen minutes past infinity.

"What are you going to do," Butch said, even though he knew the answer.

"I won't hesitate." The *even though it will kill me* went unspoken.

Fucking life. Sometimes the situations it put people in were just too cruel.

Butch closed his eyes and let his head fall back against the wall. Family was everything to vampires. Your mate, the brothers you fought with, your blood . . . that was your whole world.

And along that theory, as V suffered so did he. And Jane. And the rest of the Brotherhood.

"Hopefully, it won't come to that." Butch glanced at the closed door. "Doc Jane is going to find the guy. She's a bulldog—"

"You know what dawned on me about ten minutes ago?"

"What."

"Even if it hadn't been daylight, she would have wanted to go alone to find the guy."

As the male's bonding scent wafted over, Butch thought, Well, duh. Jane and the surgeon had been tight for years, so if there was persuading to do, she'd have better luck on her own—assuming she could get past the whole back-from-the-dead thing. Plus V was a vampire. Hello. Like anyone needed another layer added to this mess?

And on that note, all things considered, it would be great if the surgeon were five feet tall, walleyed, and had bear hair on his back. Fugly was their only friend if V's bonded male side was being triggered.

"No offense," Butch murmured, "but can you blame her?"

"It's my *twin*." The guy raked a hand through his black hair. "Goddamn it, Butch . . . my *sister*."

Butch knew more than a little something about how losing one felt, so yeah, he could feel the male on that front. And man, he was so not leaving the brother's side: He and Jane were the only ones who had a prayer of derailing Vishous when he got like this. And Jane was going to have her hands full with that surgeon and her patient—

The sound of V's cell phone going off made them both jump,

but the Brother recovered fast and there wasn't a second ring before he got it up to his ear.

"Yeah? You did? Thank . . . fuck . . . yeah. Yeah. I'll meet you in the parking garage here. Okay." There was a slight pause and V glanced over like he wished he were alone.

Desperate to make like thin air, Butch looked down at his Dior Homme loafers. The brother was never really into the PDA or talking personal stuff to Jane if there was an audience. But given that Butch was a half-breed, he couldn't dematerialize and where the hell could he run to?

After V muttered a quick "bye," he inhaled deep on his cig and muttered on the exhale, "You can stop pretending not to be next to me."

"What a relief. I suck at it."

"Not your fault you take up space."

"So she got him?" As Vishous nodded, Butch got dead serious. "Promise me something."

"What."

"You won't kill that surgeon." Butch knew exactly what it was like to trip on the outside world and fall into this vampire rabbit hole. In his case, it had worked out, but when it came to Manello? "This is not the guy's fault and not his problem."

V flicked his butt into the bin and glanced over, his diamond eyes cold as an arctic night. "We'll see how it goes, cop."

With that, he pivoted and punched through into where his sister was.

Well, at least the SOB was honest, Butch thought with a curse.

Manny really didn't like other people driving his Porsche 911 Turbo. In fact, short of his mechanic, no one else ever did.

Tonight, however, he'd allowed Jane to get behind the wheel because, one, she was competent and could shift without grinding his transmission into a stump; two, she'd maintained that the only way she could take him where they were going was if she were doing the ten-and-two routine; and three, he was still reeling from seeing someone he'd buried pop out of the bushes to hi-how're-ya him.

So maybe operating heavy machinery going seventy miles an hour was not a good idea.

He could *not* believe he was sitting next to her, heading north, in his car.

But of course he'd said yes to her request. He was a sap for women in distress . . . and he was also a surgeon who was an OR junkie.

Duh.

There were a lot of questions, though. And a lot of pissed off. Yeah, sure, he was hoping to get to a place of peace and light and sunshine and all that namby-pamby bullshit, but he wasn't holding his breath for the kumbaya-all-cools. Which was ironic. How many times had he stared up at his ceiling at night, all nestled in his beddy-bye with his new Lagavulin habit, praying that by some miracle his former chief of trauma would come back to him?

Manny glanced over at her profile. Illuminated in the glow of the dash, she was still smart. Still strong.

Still his kind of woman.

But that was never happening now. Aside from the whole liar-liar-pants-on-fire about her death, there was a gunmetal gray ring on her left hand.

"You got married," he said.

She didn't look at him, just kept driving. "Yes. I did."

That headache that had sprouted the instant she'd made her appearance instantly went from grouchy to gruesome. And meanwhile, shadowy memories Loch Nessed below the surface of his conscious mind, tantalizing him, and making him want to work for the full reveal.

He had to cut that cognitive search-and-rescue off, though, before he popped an aneurysm from the strain. Besides, he wasn't getting anywhere with it—no matter how hard he tried, he couldn't reach what he sensed was there, and he had a feeling he could do permanent damage if he kept struggling.

As he looked out the car window, fluffy pine trees and budding oaks stood tall in the moonlight, the forest that ran around Caldwell's edges growing thicker as they traveled away from the city proper and its choking knot of population and buildings.

"You died out here," he said grimly. "Or at least pretended you did."

A biker had found her Audi in and among the trees on a stretch of road not far from here, the car having careened off the shoulder. No body, though—and not because of the fire, as it had turned out.

Jane cleared her throat. "I feel like all I've got is 'I'm sorry.' And that just sucks."

"Not a party on my end, either."

Silence. Lots of silence. But he wasn't one to keep asking when all he got in return was *I'm sorry.*

"I wish I could have told you," she said abruptly. "You were the hardest to leave."

"You didn't dump your job, though, did you. Because you're still working as a surgeon."

"Yes, I am."

"What's your husband like?"

Now she winced. "You're going to meet him."

Great. Joy.

Slowing down, she took a right-hand turn off onto . . . a dirt road? What the hell?

"FYI," he muttered, "this car was built for racetracks, not roughing it."

"This is the only way in."

To where? he wondered. "You're so going to owe me for this."

"I know. And you're the only one who can save her."

Manny flashed his eyes over. "You didn't say it was a 'her.'"

"Should it matter?"

"Given how much I don't get about all of this, *everything* matters."

A mere ten yards in and they went through the first of countless puddles that were as deep as frickin' lakes. As the Porsche splashed through, he felt the scrape on its tender belly, and gritted out, "Screw this patient. I want payback for what you're doing to my undercarriage."

Jane let out a little laugh, and that made the center of his chest ache—but get real. It wasn't like the pair of them had ever been together. Sure, there had been attraction on his part. Big attraction. And, like, one kiss. That was it, however.

And now she was Mrs. Someone Else.

As well as back from the goddamn dead.

Christ, what kind of life was he in? Then again, maybe this was a dream . . . which kind of cheered him up, because maybe Glory hadn't gone down, either.

"You haven't told me what kind of injury," he said.

"Spinal break. Between T6 and T7. No sensation below the waist."

"Shit, Jane—that's a tall order."

"Now you know why I need you so badly."

About five minutes later, they came up to a gate that looked like it had been erected during the Punic Wars—the thing was hanging at Alice in Wonderland angles, the chain link rusted to shit and broken in places. And the fence it bisected? That POS was hardly worth the effort, nothing more than six feet of barbed cattle wire that had seen better days.

The damn thing opened smoothly, however. And as they went past it, he saw the first of the video cameras.

While they progressed at a snail's pace, a strange fog rolled in from nowhere in particular, the landscape blurring until he couldn't see more than twelve inches ahead of the car's grille. For chrissakes, it was like they were in a *Scooby-Doo* episode out here.

And then there was a curious progression: The next gate was in slightly better condition, and the one after that was even newer, and number four looked only a year old, tops.

The last gate they came to was spit-and-shine sparkling, and all about the Alcatraz: Fucker reached twenty-five feet off the ground and had high-voltage warnings all over it. And that wall it cut into? It was nothing for cattle, more like velociraptors; and what do you want to bet that its concrete face fronted a solid twelve or even twenty-four inches of horizontal stone.

Manny swiveled his head around to Jane as they passed through and began a descent into a tunnel that could have had a "Holland" or "Lincoln" sign tacked on it for its fortification. The farther down they went, the more that big question that had been plaguing him since he'd first seen her loomed: Why fake her death? Why cause the kind of chaos she had in his life and the lives of the other people she'd worked with at St. Francis? She'd never been cruel, never been a liar, and had no financial problems and nothing to run from.

Now he knew without her saying a word:

U.S. government.

This kind of setup, with this sort of security . . . hidden on the outskirts of what was a big enough city, but nothing so huge as New York, LA, or Chicago? Had to be the government. Who else could afford this shit?

And who the hell was this woman he was treating?

The tunnel terminated in an underground parking garage that was standard-issue, with its pylons and little yellow-painted squares—and yet as large as it appeared to be, the place was empty except for a couple of nondescript vans with darkened windows and a small bus that also had blackouts for glass.

Before she even had his Porsche in park, a steel door was thrown open and—

One look at the huge guy who stepped out and Manny's head exploded, the pain behind his eyes getting so intense he went limp in the bucket seat, his arms falling to the sides, his face twitching from the agony.

Jane said something to him. A car door was opened. Then his own was cracked.

The air that hit him smelled dry and vaguely like earth . . . but there was something else. Cologne. A very woody spice that was at once expensive and pleasing, but also something he had a curious urge to get the fuck away from.

Manny forced his lids to open. His vision was wonky as hell, but it was amazing what you could pull out of your ass if you had to—and as the man in front of him came into focus, he found himself staring up at the goateed motherfucker who had . . .

On a fresh wave of fucking-OW, his eyes rolled back and he nearly threw up.

"You've got to release the memories," he heard Jane say.

There was some conversating at that point, his former colleague's voice mixing with the deep tones of that man with the tattoos at his temple.

"It's killing him—"

"There's too much risk—"

"How the hell is he going to operate like this?"

There was a long silence. And then all of a sudden, the pain lifted as if it were a veil drawn back, all that pressure gone within the blink of an eye. In its place, memories flooded his mind.

Jane's patient. From back at St. Francis. The man with the goatee and . . . the six-chambered heart. Who had shown up in Manny's office and taken the files on that cardiac anomaly of his.

Manny popped open his lids and lasered in on that nasty-looking face. "I know you."

"You get him out of the car," was the only response from Goatee. "I don't trust myself to touch him."

Hell of a welcome wagon.

And there was someone else behind the big bastard. A man Manny was one hundred percent sure he'd seen before . . . Must have been only in passing, though, because he couldn't call up a name or remember where they'd met.

"Let's go," Jane said.

Yeah. Great idea. At this point, he needed something to focus on other than all this say-what?.

As Manny's brain struggled to process what was happening, at least his feet and legs got with the program. After Jane helped him out of the car and onto the vertical, he followed her and the Goateed Hater into a facility that was as nondescript and clean as any hospital: Corridors were uncluttered, fluorescent lights were in panels on the ceiling, everything smelled like Lysol.

And there were also the bubbled fixtures of security cameras at regular intervals, like the building was a monster with many eyes.

While they walked along, he knew better than to ask any questions. Well, that and his head was so scrambled, he was pretty fucking sure ambulation was the extent of his capabilities at this point. And then there was Goatee and his death stare—not exactly an opening for chitchat.

Doors. They passed many doors. All of which were closed and no doubt locked.

Happy little words like *undisclosed location* and *national security* hopscotched through his cranial park, and that helped a lot, making him think maybe he could forgive Jane for ghosting out on him—eventually.

When she stopped outside a pair of double flappers, her hands fidgeted with the lapels of her white coat and then the stethoscope in her pocket. And didn't that make him feel like he had a gun to his head: In the OR, in countless trauma messes, she'd always kept her cool. It was her trademark.

This was personal, though, he thought. Somehow, whatever was on the other side of these doors hit close to home for her.

"I've got good equipment here," she said, "but not everything. No MRI. Just CAT scans and X-rays. The OR should be adequate, however, and not only can I assist, but I've got an excellent nurse."

Manny took a breath and reached down deep, pulling himself together. By force of will, he shut off all the questions and the lingering ow-ow-ow in his head and the strangeness of this descent into 007-land.

First thing on his to-do list? Ditch the pissed-off peanut gallery.

He glanced over his shoulder at Goatee. "You need to back off, my man. I want you out in the hall."

The response he got in return was . . . just fang-tastic: The bastard bared a pair of canines as long as his arm and growled, natch, like a dog.

"Fine," Jane said, getting in between them. "That's fine. Vishous will wait out here."

Vishous? Had he heard that right?

Then again, this boy's baby mama sure hit the nail on the head, considering that little dental show. But whatever. Manny had a job to do, and maybe the bastard could go chew on a rawhide or something.

Pushing into the examination room, he—

Oh . . . dear God.

Oh . . . Lord above.

The patient on the table was lying still as water and . . . she was probably the most beautiful anything he'd ever seen: Hair was jet-black and braided into a thick rope that hung free next to her head. Skin was a golden brown, as if she were of Italian descent and had recently been in the sun. Eyes . . . her eyes were like diamonds, both colorless and brilliant, with nothing but a dark rim around the iris.

"Manny?"

Jane's voice was right behind him, but he felt as if she were miles away. In fact, the whole world was somewhere else, nothing existing except for the stare of his patient as she looked up at him from out of her immobilized head.

It finally happened, he thought as he burrowed under his shirt and took hold of his heavy cross. All his life he'd wondered why he'd never fallen in love, and now he knew: He'd been waiting for this moment, this woman, this time.

The female is mine, he thought.

And even though that made no sense at all, the conviction was so strong, he couldn't question it.

"Are you the healer?" she said in a low voice that stopped his heart. "Are you . . . here for me?"

Her words were heavily accented, gorgeously so, and also a little surprised.

"Yeah. I am." He wrenched off his suit's coat and threw it into a corner, not giving a shit where the thing landed. "I'm here for you."

As he approached, her stunning icy eyes slicked with tears. "My legs . . . they feel as though they are moving, but I suspect they do not."

"Do they hurt?"

"Yes."

Phantom pain. Not a surprise.

Manny stopped by her side and glanced at her body, which was covered with a sheet. She was tall. Had to be at least six feet. And she was built with sleek power.

This was a soldier, he thought, measuring the strength in her bare upper arms. This was a fighter.

And, God, the loss of mobility in someone like her took his breath away. Even if you were a couch potato, life in a wheelchair was a bitch and a half, but to somebody like this, it would be a death sentence.

Manny reached out and gathered her hand into his own—and the instant he made contact, his whole body went wakey-wakey on him, as if she were the socket to his inner plug.

"I'm going to take care of you," he said as he looked her right in the eye. "I want you to trust me."

She swallowed hard as one crystal tear slipped out to trail down her temple. On instinct, he reached forward and caught it on his fingertip—

The growl that percolated up from the doorway was the countdown to an ass-kicking if he'd ever heard it. Except as he glanced over at Goatee, he felt like snarling right back at the son of a bitch. Which, yet again, made no sense.

Still holding his patient's hand, he barked at Jane, "Get that miserable bastard out of my operating room. And I want to see the goddamn scans and X-rays. *Now.*"

He was going to save this woman even if it killed him.

And as Goatee's eyes flashed with pure hatred, Manny thought, Well, shit, it might just come down to that. . . .

SIX

Qhuinn was out alone in Caldwell.

For the first time in his frickin' life.

Which, when he thought about it, was nearly a statistical impossibility. He'd spent so many nights fighting and drinking and having sex in and around the clubs downtown that surely one or two had to have been solo flights. But nope. As he walked into the Iron Mask, he was without his two wingmen for the very first time.

Things were different now, however. Times had changed. People, too.

John Matthew was now happily mated, so when he had a shift off, like this evening, he was staying home with his *shellan*, Xhex, and giving their bed one hell of a workout. And yeah, sure, Qhuinn was the guy's *ahstrux nohtrum* and all, but Xhex was a *symphath* assassin more than capable of watching out for her male, and the Black Dagger Brotherhood's compound was a fortress not even a SWAT team could break into. So he and John had come to an agreement—and kept it quiet.

And as for Blay . . .

Qhuinn wasn't going to think about his best friend. Nope. Not at all.

Scanning the inside of the club, he put his fuck filter on and began weeding through the women and the men and the couples. There was one and only one reason he'd come here, and it was the same for the other Goths in the place.

This was not for a relationship. This was not even for companionship. This was all about the in and out, and when that was over, it would be a case of, *Thank you, ma'am*—or *sir*, depending on his mood—*I'm ghost.* Because he was going to need someone else. Or someones else.

No way this was going to be a one-shot deal tonight. He felt like peeling his own skin off, his body all but chattering from the need to release. Man, he'd always liked the fucking, but in the last couple of days, his libido had gone Godzilla on him—

Was Blay even his best friend anymore?

Qhuinn paused and briefly looked for a plate-glass window to put his head through: For fuck's sake, he wasn't five years old. Grown males didn't have best friends. Didn't need them.

Especially if said male was banging someone else. All day long. Every single day.

Qhuinn marched over to the bar. "Herradura. Double. And make it the Selección Suprema."

The woman's eyes heated up behind her heavy liner and fake lashes. "You starting a tab?"

"Yeah." And going by the way she ran her hand down her tight stomach and over her hip, clearly he could have ordered a shot of her as well.

When he held out his black AmEx, she breast-iculated wildly to accept the damn thing, bending over so far she might as well have been trying to pick a swizzle stick off the floor with her nipples.

"I'll be right back with your drink."

What a surprise. "Great."

As she hipped her way off, she was so wasting her time: not at all what he was looking for tonight—not even close. Wrong sex, for one thing. And he wasn't going for anything dark haired. Matter of fact, he couldn't believe what he wanted.

Being color-blind had its limitations, but when you only wore black and worked at night, it wasn't a big deal most of the time. Besides, his mismatched eyes were so acute and sensitive to variants of gray that he actually perceived "colors"—it was all about the gradient. For example, he knew who the blondes in the club were. Knew the difference between the brunettes and the black-hairs. And yeah, he might misread it if one of the fidiots had gotten a whacked-out dye job, but even then, he could usually tell something was up because the skin tone never looked right.

"Here you go," the bartender said.

Qhuinn reached over, picked up the shot glass, downed the tequila, and put the empty back on the bar. "Let's try that a couple more times."

"Right away." She flashed her double-Ds again, no doubt hoping he'd do a grab. "You're my number one customer. 'Cuz clearly you can handle the juice."

Uh-huh. Right. Like the ability to gullet up four ounces of liquor on a oner was a BFD. God, the idea someone with that value system was allowed to vote made him want to look for that sheet of glass again.

Humans were pathetic.

Although, as he turned back to look at the crowd, he thought maybe dialing down the attitude might be a good call. He was pretty fucking pathetic himself tonight. Especially as he caught sight of two men off in a corner, the pair of them separated only by the leathers they were wearing. Naturally, one was blond. Just like his cousin was. So naturally, hypotheticals of Blay with Saxton played through his inner polo field, marking up his proverbial grass with hoofprints and horseshit.

Except they weren't hypotheticals, were they: At the end of every night, as the table at the Brotherhood's mansion broke up after Last Meal and people went off to do their thing, Blay and Saxton always discreetly headed for the grand staircase and disappeared down the upstairs hall to their bedrooms.

They never held hands. Never kissed in front of anyone. And there were no covert hot glances, either. But then again, Blay was a gentleman. And Saxton the Classy Slut put on a good show.

His cousin was a straight-up whore—

No, he is not, a small voice pointed out. *You just hate him because he's balling your boy.*

"He is *not* my boy."

"What did you say?"

Qhuinn shot a glare at the kibitzer—and then pulled back on the hard-ass. Bingo, he thought.

Standing next to him was a human male, about six feet–ish tall with great hair, a good face, and very nice lips. Clothes were not totally Gothed out, but he had some chains on his hip and a couple of hoops in one of his ears. But it was the hair color that really did it.

"I was talking to myself," Qhuinn murmured.

"Ah. I do that a lot." The smile was brief and then the guy went back to nursing his . . .

"What are you drinking?" Qhuinn asked.

A half-empty glass was held up. "Vodka-'n'-tonic. I can't stand the fruity shit."

"Neither can I. I'm tequila. Straight up."

"Patrón?"

"Never. I'm HD."

"Ah." The guy pivoted around and stared ahead at the crowd. "You like the real stuff."

"Yup."

Qhuinn wanted to ask whether Mr. V&T was checking out the guys or the chicks, but he kept that one on ice. Man, that hair was amazing. Thick. Curled at the ends.

"You looking for someone in particular?" Qhuinn said in a low voice.

"Maybe. You?"

"Definitely."

The guy laughed. "Lot of hot women here. You can have your pick."

Mother. Fucker. Just his luck: a hetero. Then again, maybe they could share something and take things from there.

The man leaned in and offered his palm. "I'm . . ."

As the two looked at each other full-on, the guy let the sentence trail off, but that didn't matter. Qhuinn didn't give a shit what the name was.

"Are your eyes different colors?" the man asked softly.

"Yup."

"That's really . . . cool."

Well, yeah. Unless you were a vampire born into the *glymera.* Then it was a physical defect that meant you were genetically broken and therefore an embarrassment to your bloodline and utterly unmate-able.

"Thanks," Qhuinn said. "What color are yours?"

"You can't tell?"

Qhuinn tapped the tattooed tear underneath his eye. "Color-blind."

"Ah. Mine are blue."

"And you're a redhead, aren't you."

"How do you know that?"

"Your skin tone. Plus you're pale and have freckles."

"That's amazing." The guy glanced around. "It's dark in here— I wouldn't think you could tell."

"Guess I can." To himself, he added, *And how about I show you some of my other tricks.*

Qhuinn's new buddy smiled a little and went back to checking out the crowd. After a minute, he said, "Why're you looking at me like that."

Because I want to fuck you. "You remind me of someone."

"Who?"

"Someone I lost."

"Oh, shit, sorry."

"It's okay. It was my fault."

Little pause. "So you're gay, huh."

"No."

The guy laughed. "Sorry. I just figured . . . Guess it was a good friend, then."

No comment. "I'm about to get a refill. Why don't I hook you up, too."

"Thanks, man."

Qhuinn turned around and signaled the bartender. As he waited for her to hopscotch over, he planned out his approach. Little more liquor. Then add some females to the mix. Step three was to go back into one of the bathrooms and fuck the girl(s).

Then . . . more eye contact. Preferably when one or both of them were inside a woman. Because as much as this redhead with the great hair appeared to be into chicks, the SOB had felt the connection when the two of them had looked at each other—and *hetero* was a relative term.

Kind of like *virgin.*

Which made two of them, didn't it. After all, Qhuinn never, ever nailed redheads.

But tonight was going to be an exception.

SEVEN

As Payne lay on her metal slab beneath the odd chandelier of illumination, she couldn't believe her healer was a human.

"Do you understand what I'm saying?" His voice was quite deep and his accent was strange to her, but not one she hadn't heard before: Her twin's mate had the same intonation and inflection. "I'm going to go in and . . ."

While he spoke to her, he leaned down into her field of vision, and she liked when he did that. His eyes were a brown color, but not that of oak bark or old leather or the coat of a stag. They were a lovely reddish shade, like mahogany that had been polished—and just as luminous, she would venture to say.

There had been such a flurry of activity since his arrival, and one thing had become clear: He was well versed in the giving of orders and very confident in his job. Actually, there was something else, too. . . . He didn't care that her brother had taken an instant hatred to him.

If Vishous's bonding scent got any stronger, it would be visible upon the air.

"Do you understand?"

"Her ears are just fucking fine."

Payne glanced over as far as she could toward the doorway. Vishous had returned and was baring his fangs like he was of half a mind to attack. Fortunately, by his side, a male stood tight upon him, rather like a leash with stout legs: If her twin were to lunge for it, that male with the dark hair was obviously poised to encompass Vishous bodily and drag him from the room.

This was good.

Payne refocused on her healer. "I understand."

The human's eyes narrowed. "Then tell me what I said."

"Whatever for?"

"This is your body. I want to make sure you know what I'm going to do to it, and I'm concerned about a language barrier."

"She knows what the fuck you're say—"

Her healer glared over his shoulder. "Are you *still* here?"

The dark-haired male beside her twin locked an arm around Vishous's chest and muttered something on a hiss. Then he addressed her healer, speaking with a slightly different accent. "You need to chill, my man. Or I'm going to let him turn you into beef jerky for taking that tone. *Capisce?*"

She had to approve of the way her healer met the aggression head-on: "You want me to operate, it's on my terms and in my way. So he's out in the hall or you're getting yourself another scalpel. What's it gonna be."

There was a lot of consternated arguing at that point, with Jane rushing over from where she had been at a window that played pictures upon its pane. She spoke softly at first until finally her voice was as loud as the rest of theirs were.

Payne cleared her throat. "Vishous. *Vishous. Vishous!*"

Getting nowhere, she put her two lips together and whistled loud enough to shatter glass.

As a flame would be snuffed out, so too were the lot of them, although the angry energy lingered about in the air like smoke from atop a wick.

"He shall treat me now," she said weakly, the tension in the room a form of fever that took o'er her body, making her even more lethargic. "He shall . . . treat me. It is my wish." Her eyes went to her healer. "You shall endeavor to rebreak my fused spinal vertebrae, as you call them, and it is your hope that my spinal cord is not severed but merely injured. You state further that you cannot predict the outcome, but that when you are 'in there,' you may be able to assess the damage more clearly. Yes?"

Her healer looked at her in a powerful way. Deeply. Gravely. With an edge that she was confused about . . . and yet not threatened by. Fates, hardly that—in fact, something in his eyes made her . . . uncurl on the inside.

"Have I recalled it all correctly?" she prompted him.

Her healer cleared his throat. "Yes. You have."

"Then operate . . . as you call it."

Over by the doorway, she heard the dark-haired man say something to her twin, and then Vishous lifted his arm and pointed his gloved finger at the human. "You will not live through this if she does not."

Cursing, Payne closed her eyes and wished anew that what she had sought for so long had not been gained. Better to have gone unto the Fade than cause the death of some innocent human—

"Deal."

Payne's lids popped open. Her healer stood unbowed before her twin's size and strength, accepting the burden laid upon his head.

"But you leave," the human said. "You need to get the fuck out of here and stay out. I'm not going to be distracted by your shit."

Her twin's massive body twitched in the shoulders and the chest, but then he inclined his head once. "Deal."

And then she was alone with her healer, except for Jane and the other nurse.

"One last test." Her healer leaned to the side and got a thin stick off one of the counters. "I'm going to run this pen up your foot. I want you to tell me if you feel anything."

When she nodded, he moved out of her range of sight and she closed her eyes to concentrate, straining for some kind of sensation to register. Anything.

Surely if there was a response, however dim, that was a good sign—

"I feel something," she said with a surge of energy. "On my left side."

There was a pause. "How about now."

She begged her legs for a similar reception and had to breathe deeply before she could answer. "No. Nothing."

The sound of the soft sheets being repositioned was the only confirmation she got that she was covered once again. But at least she had felt something.

Except instead of addressing her, her healer and her twin's mate conversed quietly, just out of earshot.

"Verily," Payne said, "mayhap you will include me in the discussion." The pair of them came over and it was curious that neither looked pleased. "It is good that I felt aught, no?"

Her healer came closer to her head, and she felt the warm strength of his palm take her own. As he stared at her, she was yet anew captivated: His lashes were very long. And across his strong jaw and his cheeks, a shadow of beard was showing. His thick, dark hair was shiny.

And she really liked the way he smelled.

But he hadn't replied to her, had he? "Is it not, healer?"

"I wasn't touching you on your left foot at that time."

Payne blinked through an unexpected upset. And yet, after all this time being immobile, she should be prepared for information like that, shouldn't she.

"So are you going to begin the now?" she asked.

"Not yet." Her healer glanced over at Jane, and then looked back. "We're going to have to move you for the operation."

"This hallway ain't far enough away, buddy."

As Butch's reasonable voice registered, V wanted to bite the guy's head off. And the urge got even stronger as the bastard continued. "How 'bout heading over to the Pit?"

Logical advice, true. And yet . . . "You're starting to piss me off, cop."

"Like that's a news flash? And P.S., I don't care."

The door to the exam room opened and his Jane slipped out. As she looked at him, her forest green eyes were not happy.

"Now what," he barked, unsure whether he could handle any more bad news.

"He wants to move her."

After a moment of blinking like a cow, V shook his head, convinced he'd gotten his languages confused. "Excuse me?"

"To St. Francis."

"No. Fucking. Way—"

"Vishous—"

"That's a human hospital!"

"V—"

"Have you lost your mind—"

At that moment, the godforsaken human surgeon came out, and to his credit, or his insanity, he got right up into V's grille. "I can't work on her here. You want me to try it and paralyze her for good myself? Use your goddamned head—I need an MRI, microscopes, equipment, and staff you don't have here. We're out of time, and she can't be transported far—besides, if you're the U.S. government, you can bury her records and make sure this doesn't get picked up by the press, so the exposure will be minimal with my help."

U.S. government? What the— Yeah, whatever with that. "She's not going to a human hospital. Period."

The guy frowned over the "human" thing, but then seemed to shake it off. "Then I'm not operating—"

V launched himself at the man.

It was a total blink-of-the-eye kind of thing. One minute, he was planted in his shitkickers; the next he was all fly-be-free—at least until he slammed into the good doctor and velvet-Elvised the bastard onto the corridor's concrete wall.

"Get in there and start cutting," V growled.

The human could barely draw a breath, but hypoxia didn't stop him from manning up. He met V right in the eyeball. Unable to speak, he mouthed, *Won't. Do. It.*

"Let him go, V. And let him take her where he needs to go."

As Wrath's voice cut through the drama, the urge to go pyrotechnic became nearly irresistible. Like they needed another kibitzer? And *fuck-that* on the command.

V squeezed the surgeon's collar trash-bag tight. "You are not taking her anywhere—"

The hand on V's shoulder was heavy, and Wrath's voice had an edge like a dagger. "And you're not in charge here. She's my responsibility, not yours."

Wrong thing to say. On so many levels.

"She is my blood," he snarled.

"And I'm the one who put her on that bed. Oh, and I'm also your cocksucking king, so you will do as I command, Vishous."

Just as he was about to say and do something he would later regret, Jane's sanity reached him. "V, at this moment, you are the problem. Not your twin's condition, or Manny's decision. You need to step back, get some clarity, and think, not react. I will be with her the whole time, and Butch will come with me, won't you."

"Abso," the cop replied. "And I'll get Rhage, too. She won't be left alone for an instant."

Dead silence. During which V's rational side fought for his steering wheel . . . and that human refused to back down. In spite of the fact that he was one stab through the heart away from a coffin, that son of a bitch just kept glaring right back.

Christ, you could almost respect him for it.

Jane's hand on V's biceps was nothing like Wrath's. Her touch was light, soothing, careful. "I spent years in that hospital. I'm familiar with all the rooms, all the people, all the equipment. There is not one square inch of that facility that I don't know like the back of my hand. Manny and I will work together and make sure that she gets in and gets out fast—and that she's protected. He's got ultimate power there as chief of surgery, and I will be with her every step of the way . . ."

Jane continued talking but he heard nothing more, a sudden vision coming down through him like a signal received from some external transmitter: With crystal clarity, he saw his sister astride a horse, going at a gallop on the edge of a forest. There was no saddle, no bridle, and her hair was unfurled and streaming behind her in the moonlight.

She was laughing. With complete and utter joy.

She was free.

Throughout his life, he had always seen pictures of the future—so he knew this was not one of them. His visions were exclusively of deaths—those of his brothers and Wrath and their *shellans* and children. Knowing how those around him would pass was part of his reserve and all of his madness: He was privy only to the means, never the time, and therefore he couldn't save them.

So what he saw now was not the future. This was what he wanted for the twin he had found far too late and was in danger of losing far too early.

V, at this moment, you are the problem.

Not trusting himself to speak to any of them, he dropped the doc like a dime and pulled back. As the human caught his breath, V didn't look at anyone but Jane.

"I can't lose her," he said in a weak voice, even though there were witnesses.

"I know. I'll be with her every step of the way. *Trust me.*"

V closed his eyes briefly. One of the things that he and his *shellan* had in common was that they were both very, very good at what they did. Devoted to their jobs, they existed in parallel universes of their own creation and focus: the fighting for him, the healing for her.

So this was the equivalent of him swearing he would kill someone for her.

"Okay," he croaked. "All right. Gimme a minute with her, though."

Pushing through the double doors, he approached his twin's bed, and was very aware this could be the last time he spoke with her: Vampires, like humans, could die during operations. Did die.

She looked even worse than before, lying all too motionless, her eyes not just closed but squeezed shut as if she were in pain. Shit on a shingle, his *shellan* was right. He was the slow-up here. Not that f'n surgeon.

"Payne."

Her lids lifted slowly, like they weighed as much as I beams. "Brother mine."

"You're going to a human hospital. Okay?" As she nodded, he hated that her skin was the color of the white bedsheet. "He's going to operate on you there."

When she nodded again, her lips parted and her breath hitched like she was having trouble breathing. "'Tis for the best."

God . . . now what? Did he tell her he loved her? He guessed he did, in his own fucked-up way.

"Listen . . . you take care," he mumbled.

Lame-ass. Fucking lame-ass little bitch. But it was all he could manage.

"You . . . too," she groaned.

Of its own volition, his good hand reached out and slowly slid against hers. As he tightened his grip slightly, she didn't move or respond, and he had a sudden panic that he'd missed his opportunity, that she was already gone.

"*Payne.*"

Her lids fluttered. "Yes?"

The door opened and Jane put her head in. "We have to get going."

"Yeah. Okay." V gave his sister's palm a final squeeze; then he left the room in a hurry.

When he got out into the hall, Rhage had arrived, and so had Phury and Z. Which was good. Phury was especially proficient at hypnotizing humans—and he'd done it at St. Francis before.

V went up to Wrath. "You're going to feed her, true. When she comes out of the operation, she's going to need to feed, and your blood's the strongest we've got."

As he put the demand on the table, it would have been great if he'd given a shit that Beth, the queen, might have a problem with sharing her mate like that. But, selfish bastard that he was, he didn't care.

Except Wrath just nodded. "My *shellan* was the one who suggested it first."

V's eyes squeezed shut. Damn, that was a female of worth right there. Straight up.

Before he took off, he grabbed a last glance at his *shellan*. Jane was as steady as a house on solid ground, her face and her eyes strong and sure.

"I have no words," he said hoarsely.

"And I know exactly what you're telling me."

V stood three feet from her, stuck to the floor, wishing he were a different kind of male. Wishing . . . so much about everything was different.

"Go," she whispered. "I've got this."

V took a last look over at Butch, and when the cop nodded once, the decision was final. Vishous nodded at his boy and then he strode off, out of the training center, into the underground tunnel, and up to the Pit.

Where he promptly realized that the physical distance didn't do shit for him. He still felt he was in the midst of all the drama . . . and didn't really trust himself not to end up back down there "to help."

Out. He needed out and away from them all.

Breaking through the heavy front door, he marched into the courtyard . . . and ended up parked and going nowhere, just like the cars that were lined up side by side opposite the fountain.

As he stood like a planker, a strange, flicking noise got his attention. At first he couldn't place it, but then he looked down. His gloved hand was shaking and hitting his upper thigh.

From beneath the lead-lined leather, the glow was bright enough to leave him squinting.

Goddamn it. He was so close to the edge of losing it, he might as well have already been in midair.

With a curse, he dematerialized and headed for the place he always went when he got like this. He didn't want the destination or the drive that sent him into the night . . . but like Payne, his destiny was out of his hands.

EIGHT

OLD COUNTRY
PRESENT

The dream was an old one. Centuries old. And yet its images were fresh and clear as the night all had changed so many aeons ago.

Deep within his sleep, Xcor saw before him the apparition of a female of rage, the mist swirling about her white robes and frothing them up into the chilly air. Upon her appearance, he knew immediately why she had come out of the thick forest—but her target was as yet unaware of her presence or her purpose.

His father was too busy riding his steed down upon a human woman.

Except then the Bloodletter saw the ghost.

Thereafter, the sequence of events was as set as the lines in Xcor's brow: He yelled an alarm and spurred on his stallion whilst his sire dropped the human female he had caught and went gunning for the spirit. Xcor never made it in time. Always, he watched in horror as the female sprang up from the earth and took his father down.

And then the fire . . . the fire the female wrought upon the

Bloodletter's body was brilliant and white and instantaneous and it consumed Xcor's sire within moments, the stench of burning flesh—

Xcor bolted upright, his dagger hand gripping his chest, his lungs pumping and yet drawing no air.

Planting his palms onto his pallet of blankets, he propped himself up and was damned glad for being alone in his own quarters. No one needed to see him like this.

As he sought to come back unto reality, his breathing echoed and rebounded, the sounds bouncing off the barren walls and multiplying until they seemed like screams. In a rush, he willed the candle beside him on the floor to light. That was of aid. And then he got up to stretch his body, the process of pulling out his bones and muscles and resettling them into proper alignment helping his brain as well.

He needed food. And blood. And a fight.

Then he would be fully himself.

After dressing in well-worked leather, and putting a dagger into his belt, he went out of his room and into the drafty hallway. In the distance, deep voices and the clanking of pewter plates told him that First Meal had been served down below in the great hall.

The castle he and his band of bastards lived in was the one he had come upon that night his father had been killed, the one that overlooked the sleepy medieval hamlet that had matured into a preindustrial village and then grown in modern times into a small city of about fifty thousand humans.

Which, given the prevalence of Homo sapiens, was naught but a fern in a forest of oaks.

The stronghold suited him perfectly—and for the reasons that had first attracted him to the place. The stout walls of stone, and the moat with the bridge, were still very much in place, and they functioned well to keep people out. Added upon them were plenty of bloody fictions and full truths that cast a whispered pall over his lands and his home and his males. Indeed, for the last hundred years, he and his soldiers had done their duty to propagate the bullshit vampire myths by "haunting" the roads in the area from time to time.

Which was easy to do when you were a killer and you could dematerialized at your will.

Boo! had never been so fucking effective.

And yet there were issues. Having single-handedly decimated the *lesser* population in the Old World, they had had to find ways to keep their killing skills sharp. Fortunately, humans had stepped into the void—although, of course, he and his brothers had to remain in secret, with their true identities protected.

Enter the human urge for retaliation.

There was but a single laudable characteristic of humans and that was their wrath when it came to those among them who committed atrocities. By the vampires' hunting down only rapists and pedophiles and murderers, their "crimes" were tolerated far better. Fate knew that if you went for the moral types, humans were like bees streaming out of a hive to protect their turf, but the violators?

Eye for an eye, their Bible said.

And with that, his band of bastards had their target practice.

It had been thus for two decades, always with the hope that their true enemy, the Lessening Society, would send more appropriate foes for them. None had come, however, and the conclusion forming within him was that there were no more *lessers* left in Europe and none due to arrive. After all, he and his males had traveled hundreds of miles in all directions each night on their hunts for human villains, so they would have run across slayers somewhere, somehow.

Alas, there were none.

The absence was logical, however. The war had changed continents long ago: Back when the Black Dagger Brotherhood had left for the New World, the Lessening Society had followed them like dogs, leaving the dregs behind for Xcor and his bastards to clean up. For a long while it had been enough of a challenge, the slayers continuing to make themselves available and the battles proceeding apace and the fighting good. But that time had passed and humans were no true match.

At least *lessers* could be an amusing challenge.

A feeling of dense dissatisfaction crowded him as he descended the rough-honed stairwell, his boots crushing an ancient, threadbare runner that should have been replaced generations ago. Down below, the huge space that unfolded was a cave of stone, with naught but a tremendous oak table set afore a hearth that was big as a mountain. The humans who had built this fortress had lined its coarse walls with tapestries, but the scenes of warriors astride steeds of worth had aged no better than any of the rugs had: The shredded, faded fibers hung dejected from their pinnings, the bottom hems growing e'er longer until surely they would be floor coverings soon as well.

In front of the blazing fire, his band of bastards sat upon carved chairs, eating stag and grouse and pigeon that had been hunted upon the grounds of the estate and cleaned in the field and cooked in the hearth. They drank ale they steeped and fermented themselves in the root cellars beneath the earth, and they ate upon those pewter plates with hunting knives and stabbing forks.

There was little electricity in the manse—no need for it in Xcor's mind a'tall, but Throe had different thoughts. The male had insisted that there be a room for his computers and that required pesky wiring of descriptions that were neither very interesting nor terribly relatable. But there was a point to the modernization. Although Xcor didn't know how to read, Throe did, and humans were not only endless propagators of gore and depravity; they were fascinated by it as well—which was how prey was located throughout Europe.

The seat at the head of the table was open for him, and the second he sat down the others stopped eating, lowering their hands.

Throe was at his right, in the position of honor, and the vampire's pale eyes were alight. "How fare thee?"

That dream, that godforsaken dream. In truth, he was scattered in his skin, not that the others would e'er know. "Well enough." Xcor reached forward with his fork and speared a thigh. "By your expression, I would venture to say that you are with purpose."

"Aye." Throe proffered a thick print out of what seemed to be a compilation of newspaper articles. On the top, there was a prominent black-and-white photograph and he pointed to it. "I want him."

The human male depicted was a dark-haired tough fist with a broken nose and the low, heavy brow of an ape. The script under the photo and the columns of print were nothing but a pattern to Xcor's eyes; however, he understood clearly the malevolence in that visage.

"Why this particular man, *trahyner*?" Even though he knew.

"He killed women in London."

"How many?"

"Eleven."

"Not a square dozen then."

Throe's frown smacked of disapproval. Which was a delight, really. "He cut them up while they were alive and waited until they were dead to . . . take them."

"Fuck them, you mean?" Xcor ripped the flesh from the bone with his fangs, and when there was no reply, he cocked a brow. "Do you mean that he fucked them, Throe."

"Yes."

"Ah." Xcor smiled with an edge. "Dirty little fool."

"There were eleven. Women."

"Yes, you mentioned. So he's a rather horny little perverted fool."

Throe took the papers back and flipped through them, staring down at the faces of the worthless human women. No doubt he was praying to the Scribe Virgin at this very moment, hoping to be granted the opportunity to perform a public service for a race that was nothing but an induction ceremony away from being their enemy.

Pathetic.

And there would be no solo traveling for him—which was why he looked so put upon: Alas, the oath these five males had taken the night of the Bloodletter's incineration tied them to Xcor with iron cables. They went nowhere without his consent and approval.

Although when it came to Throe, that male had been bound to him far earlier than that, hadn't he.

In the silence, tendrils of Xcor's dream resurged in his mind—as did the burn of knowing that he had never found that wraith of a female. Which was not right. Although he was more than willing to be the backbone of myths within human minds, he did not believe in ghosts or hauntings or spells and curses. His father had been taken by something of flesh and blood, and the hunter in him wanted to find it and kill it.

"What say you?" Throe demanded.

So like him. Such a hero. "Nothing. Or I would have spoken, yes?"

Throe's fingers started to tap against the old stained wood of the table, and Xcor was pleased to let him sit and play drummer boy. The others simply ate, content to wait for this battle to be resolved one way or the other. Unlike Throe, the rest did not care which targets were chosen—provided they were fed, watered, and well sexed, they were content to fight whenever and wherever were chosen for them.

Xcor stabbed another strip of meat and eased back into his massive oak chair, his eyes drawn to the decrepit tapestries. Within the faded folds, those images of humans going off to war on stallions that he approved of and weapons he could appreciate irked the shit out of him.

The sense that he was in the wrong place tingled along his shoulders, making him as twitchy as his number two.

Twenty years of no *lessers* and eradicating mere humans to keep up their skills was no kind of existence for his crew or himself. And yet there were some vampires who had stayed in the Old Country, and he had lingered on this continent in hopes of finding among them what he saw only in his dreams.

That female. Who had taken his father.

Where had all this tarrying gotten him, however?

The decision he had long toyed with crystallized in his mind once again, forming shape and structure, angles and arches. And whereas previously, the impetus had always faded, now, the nightmare gave it the kind of stay-power that turned mere idea into action.

"We shall go unto London," he pronounced.

Throe's fingers immediately stilled. "Thank you, my liege."

Xcor inclined his head and smiled to himself, thinking Throe might get a chance to off that human man. Or . . . perhaps not.

Travel plans were indeed afoot, however.

NINE

ST. FRANCIS HOSPITAL
CALDWELL, NEW YORK

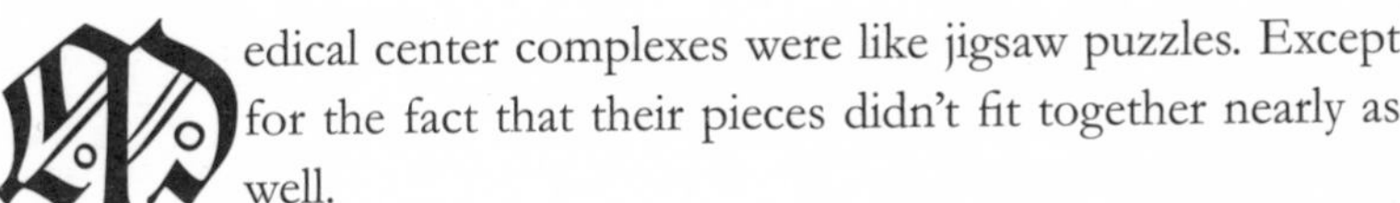

Medical center complexes were like jigsaw puzzles. Except for the fact that their pieces didn't fit together nearly as well.

But that was not a bad thing on a night like tonight, Manny thought as he scrubbed in.

On some level, he was amazed it had all gone so easily. The thugs who had driven him and his patient here had parked in one of the thousand dark corners of St. Francis's outer edge, and then Manny had called the head of security himself, stating that he had a VIP patient coming in the back who required total discretion. Next ring-a-ding-ding had been to his nursing staff and the line was the same: Special patient coming in. Ready the third-floor OR on the far end and have the MRI techs ready for a quickie. Final dial had been to transport, and what do you know, they had shown up lickety-split with a gurney.

Within fifteen minutes of finishing the MRI, the patient was here in OR VII, getting prepped.

"So who is she?"

The question came from the nurse in charge, and he'd been waiting for it. "An Olympic equestrian. From Europe."

"Well, that explains it. She was mumbling something and none of us could understand the language." The woman flipped through some paperwork—which he was going to make sure he snagged after all this was through. "Why all the secrets?"

"She's royalty." And wasn't that the truth. As he'd ridden along with her, he'd spent the entire trip staring at her regal features.

Sap. Stupid-ass sap.

His head nurse glanced out into the corridor, her eyes wary. "Explains the security detail—my God, you'd think we were bank robbers."

Manny leaned back for a peek as he scrubbed under his nails with a stiff brush. The three who had come in with him stood in the hall about ten feet away, their huge bodies dressed in black with a lot of bulges.

Guns, no doubt. Maybe knives. Possibly a flamethrower or two, who the fuck knew.

Kinda cured a guy of the whole government-is-just-full-of-paper-pushing-pencil-necks idea.

"Where're her consent forms?" the nurse asked. "There's nothing in the system."

"I've got all those," he lied. "You have the MRI for me?"

"Up on the screen—but the tech says that it's with errors? He really wants to redo."

"Let me look at it first."

"Are you sure you want to be listed as the responsible party for all this? Doesn't she have money?"

"She has to be anonymous, and they'll reimburse me." At least, he was assuming they would—not that he really cared.

Manny rinsed the brown blush of Betadine off his hands and forearms and shook them off. Keeping his arms up, he hit the swinging door with his back and entered the OR.

Two nurses and an anesthesiologist were in the room, the former double-checking the rolling trays of instruments set on blue surgical drapes, the latter calibrating the gases and equipment that would be used for keeping his patient asleep. The air was cool to discourage bleeding and smelled like astringent, and the computer equipment hummed quietly along with the ceiling lights and the operating chandelier.

Manny beelined for the monitors—and the instant he saw the MRI, his heart jumping-jacked on him. Going slowly, he reviewed the digital images carefully until he couldn't stand it anymore.

Looking to the windows in the flap doors, he remeasured the three men standing right outside the room, their hard faces and cold eyes locked on him.

They were not human.

His stare slipped to his patient. And neither was she.

Manny went back to the MRI and leaned in closer to the screen, like that was somehow going to magically fix all the anomalies he was seeing.

Man, and he'd thought the Goateed Hater's six-chambered heart was odd?

As the double doors opened and shut, Manny closed his lids and took a deep one. Then he turned around and confronted the second doctor who had come into the room.

Jane was scrubbed in so that all you could see was her forest green eyes from behind a plexi-surgical mask, and he'd covered her presence by telling the staff she was a private doctor for the patient—which was not a lie. The little ditty that she knew everyone here as well as he did he kept to himself. And so did she.

As her eyes shifted to his and locked on without apology, he wanted to scream, but he had a goddamn job to do. Refocusing, he pushed the things that weren't immediately helpful out of his mind, and reviewed the damage to the vertebrae to plan his approach.

He could see the area that had fused following a fracture: Her spine was a lovely pattern of perfectly placed knots of bone interspersed between dark cushioning disks . . . except for the T6 and T7. Which explained the paralysis.

He couldn't see whether the spinal cord was compressed or cut through completely, and he wouldn't know the true extent of the damage until he got in there. But it didn't look good. Spinal compressions were deadly to that delicate tunnel of nerves, and irreparable damage could be done in a matter of minutes or hours.

Why the hurry to find him? he wondered.

He looked over at Jane. "How many weeks since she was injured?"

"It was . . . four hours ago," she said so quietly no one else could have heard.

Manny recoiled. "What?"

"Four. Hours."

"So there was a previous injury?"

"No."

"I need to talk to you. Privately." As he drew her over to the corner of the room, he said to the anesthesiologist, "Hold up, Max."

"No problem, Dr. Manello."

Angling Jane into a tight huddle, Manny hissed, "What the fuck is going on here?"

"The MRI is self-explanatory."

"That is not human. Is it."

She just stared at him, her eyes fixed on his and unwavering.

"What the hell did you get pulled into, Jane?" he demanded under his breath. "What the hell are you doing to me?"

"Listen to me carefully, Manny, and believe every word I say. You are going to save her life and, by extension, save mine. That's my husband's sister, and if he . . ." Her voice hitched. "If he loses her before he gets a chance to even know her, it's going to kill him. Please—stop asking questions I can't answer and do what you do best. I know this isn't fair and I would do anything to change that—except lose her."

Abruptly, he thought of the screaming headaches that he'd gotten over the past year—every time he'd thought about the days leading up to her car accident. That damn stinging pain had come back the instant he'd seen her . . . only to lift and reveal the layers of recollection he had sensed but been unable to call forward.

"You're going to make it so that I don't remember anything," he said. "And neither will any of them. Aren't you." He shook his head, well aware that this was far, far bigger than just some U.S. government special-agent spy shit. Another species? Coexisting with humans?

But she wasn't going to come clean with him on that, was she.

"Goddamn you, Jane. Seriously."

As he went to turn away, she caught his arm. "I owe you. You do this for me, I owe you."

"Fine. Then don't *ever* come for me again."

He left her in the corner and went over to his patient, who had been oriented on her stomach.

Bending down beside her, he said, "It's . . ." For some reason, he wanted to use his first name with her, but given the other staff, he kept it professional. "It's Dr. Manello. We're going to start now, okay? You're not going to feel a thing, I promise you."

After a moment, she said weakly, "Thank you, healer."

He closed his eyes at the sound of her voice. God, the effect on him of just three words from her mouth was epic. But what exactly was he attracted to? What was she?

An image of her brother's fangs filtered through his mind—and he had to lock it out. There would be time to Vincent Price it after this.

With a soft curse, he stroked her shoulder and nodded at the anesthesiologist.

Showtime.

Her back had been Betadined by the nurses, and he palpated her spine with his fingers, feeling his way along as the drugs went to work and put her out.

"No allergies?" he said to Jane, even though he'd already asked.

"None."

"Any special issues we need to be aware of when she's under?"

"No."

"All right then." He reached over and swung the microscope closer into position, but not directly over her.

He had to cut into her first.

"Do you want music?" the nurse asked.

"No. No distractions on this case." He was operating like his life depended on it, and not just because this woman's brother had threatened him.

Even though it made no sense, losing her . . . whatever she was . . . would be a tragedy the likes of which he couldn't put into words.

TEN

The first thing Payne saw when she came awake was a pair of male hands. She was evidently sitting upright and in some kind of sling mechanism that supported her head and neck. And the hands in question were on the edge of the bed beside her. Beautiful and capable, with their nails trimmed down tight to the quick, they were on papers, quietly flipping through many pages.

The human male they belonged to was frowning as he read and used a scribing utensil to make occasional notations. His beard growth was heavier than when she'd seen it last, and that was how she guessed that hours had passed.

Her healer looked as exhausted as she felt.

As her consciousness surged forth e'er further, she became aware of a subtle beeping next to her head . . . and of a dull pain in her back. She had a feeling that they had given her potions to numb sensation, but she didn't want that. Better to be alert—as it was, she felt encased in cotton-wool batting and that was strangely terrifying.

Unable to speak as yet, she looked around. She and the human male were alone, and this was not the room she had been held within previously. Outside, various voices in that odd human accent vied for prominence against a constant stream of footsteps.

Where was Jane? The Brotherhood—

"Help . . . me. . . ."

Her healer snapped to attention and then tossed his pages onto a rolling table. Surging to his feet, he leaned down to her, his scent a glorious tingle in her nose.

"Hey," he said.

"I feel . . . nothing. . . ."

He took her hand, and when she could sense neither warmth nor touch, she became downright o'erwrought. But he was there for her: "Shh . . . no, no, you're okay. It's just the pain medications. You're okay and I'm here. Shh . . ."

His voice soothed her as surely as a stroking palm would have.

"Tell me," she demanded, her voice reedy. "What . . . transpired?"

"Things went satisfactorily in the OR," he said slowly. "I reset the vertebrae, and the spinal cord wasn't completely compromised."

Payne hitched her shoulders up and tried to resettle her heavy, aching head, but the contraption about her kept her right where she was. "Your tone . . . speaks more than your words."

She got no immediate reply to that. He just kept soothing her with his hands that she could not feel. His eyes conversed with her own, however—and the news was not good.

"Tell. Me," she bit out. "I deserve naught else."

"It was not a failure, but I don't know where you'll end up. Time is going to tell us more than anything else."

She closed her eyes for a moment, but the darkness terrified her. Throwing her lids open, she clung to the sight of her healer . . . and hated the self-blame in his handsome, grim face.

"'Tis not your fault," she said roughly. "It is what is meant to be."

Of that, at least, she was sure. He had tried to save her and done his level best—the frustration at himself was so very clear.

"What is your name?" he said. "I don't know your name."

"Payne. I am Payne."

When he frowned again, she was fairly sure that the nomenclature did not please him, and she found herself wishing she had been birthed to other syllables. But there was another reason for his displeasure, wasn't there. He had seen her from the inside and had to know she was different from him.

He had to know she was an "other."

"What you suppose to be true," she murmured, "is not wrong." Her healer drew in a vast breath and seemed to hold it for a day. "What goeth on in your mind? Speak to me."

He smiled a bit, and ah, how lovely that was. So lovely. 'Twas a shame it was not from humor, however.

"Right now . . ." He drew a hand through his thick, dark hair. "I'm wondering whether I should just let it all go and play dumb like I don't know what's going. Or get real."

"Real," she said. "I do not have the luxury of even a moment of falsity."

"Fair enough." His eyes locked on her. "I think that you—"

The door to the room opened a bit and a fully draped figure peered inside. Going by the delicate, pleasing scent, it was Jane, hidden beneath blue robing and a mask.

"It's almost time," she said.

Payne's healer's face became positively volcanic. "I do not agree with this."

Jane came inside and shut them all in. "Payne, you're awake."

"Indeed." She tried to smile and hoped that her lips moved. "I am."

Her healer put his body betwixt them, as if he sought to protect her. "You can't move her. It's about a week too soon for that."

Payne glanced over at the curtains that hung from the ceiling to the floor. She was nearly certain there were glass windows on the other side of the pale bolts of fabric, and very sure that if that were the case, every one of the sun's rays would pierce through when dawn came.

Now her heart pounded and she did feel it behind her ribs. "I must go. How long?"

Jane checked a timepiece on her wrist. "About an hour. And Wrath is on his way here. Which will help."

Perhaps that was why she felt so weak. She needed to feed.

As her healer seemed on the verge of speech, she cut him off to address her twin's *shellan*. "I shall handle this here. Please leave us."

Jane nodded and backed out the door. But no doubt stayed close by.

Payne's human rubbed his eyes as if he were hoping that doing so would change his perception . . . or perhaps this reality they were stuck in.

"What name would you want me to have?" she asked quietly.

He dropped his hands and considered her for a moment. "Screw the name thing. Can you just be honest with me?"

Verily, she doubted that was a promise she could give him. Although the technique of burying memories was easy enough, she was not overly familiar with the repercussions of doing it, and her concern was that the more he knew, the more there was to hide and the more damage that could be rendered upon him.

"What do you wish to know."

"What are you."

Her eyes returned to the closed curtains. As sheltered as she had been, she was aware of the myths that the human race had constructed around her species. Undead. Killers of the innocent. Soulless and without morals.

Hardly something to crow about. Or waste their last few precious moments on.

"I cannot be exposed to sunlight." Her gaze shifted back to him. "I heal far, far faster than you. And I need to feed before I am moved—after I do, I shall be stable enough to travel."

As he looked down at his hands, she wondered if he was wishing that he hadn't operated on her.

And the silence that stretched out between them became as treacherous as a battlefield, and just as dangerous to cross. Yet she heard herself say, "There is a name for what I am."

"Yeah. And I don't want to say it out loud."

A curious ache began in her chest, and with supreme effort, she dragged her forearm upward until her palm rested over the pain. Odd that her whole body was numb, but this she could feel. . . .

Abruptly, the sight of him became wavy.

Immediately, his expression gentled and he reached forward to brush her cheek. "Why are you crying?"

"Am I?"

He nodded and lifted his forefinger so she could see it. On the pad, a single crystal drop glistened. "Do you hurt?"

"Yes." Blinking quickly, she sought and failed to have him come into focus. "These tears are rather irritating."

The sound of his laughter and the sight of his white, even teeth lifted her, even as she stayed upon the bed. "Not one for crying, are you, then," he murmured.

"Never."

He leaned to the side and brought forth a square tissue that he used to blot what ran down her face. "Why the tears."

It took her a while to say it. And then she had to: "Vampire."

He eased back down into the chair beside her and took elaborate care folding up the square and then tossing it into a squat bin.

"I guess that's why Jane disappeared a year ago, huh," he said.

"You do not appear shocked."

"I knew there was something big doing." He shrugged. "I've seen your MRI. I've been inside of you."

For some reason, that phraseology heated her up. "Yes. You have."

"You're just similar enough, though. Your spine was not so different that I didn't know what I was doing. We were lucky."

For truth, she did not share that opinion: After years of caring naught for males, she felt a mystical pull toward this one, and it was the sort of thing she would have liked to explore had they not been where they were.

But as she had learned long ago, fate was rarely concerned with what she wanted.

"So," he pronounced, "you're going to handle me, right? You're going to make this whole thing go away." He waved his arm in a vague manner. "I won't recall this at all. Just like when your brother came through here a year ago."

"You shall perhaps have dreams. Nothing more."

"Is that how your kind have stayed hidden."

"Yes."

He nodded and glanced around. "You going to do it now?"

She wanted more time with him, but there was no reason for him to see her feed from Wrath. "Soon enough."

He glanced back at the door and then looked her straight in the eye. "Will you do me a favor."

"But of course. It would be a pleasure to serve you."

One of his brows flicked and she could have sworn his body threw off more of that delicious scent of his. But then he became utterly grave. "Tell Jane . . . I get it. I understand why she did what she did."

"She is in love with my brother."

"Yeah, I saw it. Back . . . wherever we were. Tell her it's cool. Between her and me. After all, you can't help who you fall for."

Yes, Payne thought. Yes, that was so very true.

"You've been in love?" he asked.

As humans did not read minds, she realized she'd spoken out loud. "Ah . . . no. I . . . no. I have not."

Although even this short time with her healer was informing. He fascinated her, from the way he moved to how he filled out his white coat and blue dressings, to the scent of him and his voice.

"Are you mated?" she asked, fearing his answer.

He laughed in a hard burst. "Hell, no."

Her breath left her on a relieved sigh, even as it was strange to think that his status mattered as much as it did. And then there was nothing but silence.

Oh, the passing of time. How regrettable it was. And what should she say to him in these final minutes they had left? "Thank you. For caring for me."

"My pleasure. I hope you recover well." He stared at her as if trying to memorize her, and she wanted to tell him to stop trying. "I'm always here for you, okay? If you need me to help you . . . come and find me." Her healer took out a small, stiff card and wrote something on it. "That's my cell. Call me."

He reached forward and slipped the thing into the weak hand that rested o'er her heart. As she gripped what he'd given her, she thought of all the repercussions. And implications.

And complications.

With a grunt, she tried to shift herself around.

The healer was instantly on his feet. "You need repositioning?"

"My hair."

"Is it pulling?"

"No . . . please unbraid my hair."

Manny froze and just stared down into his patient's face. For some reason, the idea of unraveling that thick rope seemed pretty goddamned close to getting her naked, and what do you know, his sex drive was all over it.

Jesus . . . he had a frickin' hard-on. Right under his surgical scrubs.

See, he thought, this was the unpredictable law of attraction at work, right here, right now: Candace Hanson offered to blow him and he'd been about as interested as he was in wearing a dress. But this . . . female? woman? . . . asked him to unveil her hair and he was all but panting.

Vampire.

In his head, he heard the word spoken in her voice with her accent . . . and the thing that shocked him most was his lack of reaction to the news flash. Yeah, if he considered the implications his motherboard started to spark and fizzle: Fangs are not just for Halloween and horror flicks anymore?

And yet the freaky thing was the unfreaky.

That and this sexual-attraction thing he had going on.

"My hair?" she said.

"Yeah . . ." he whispered. "I'll take care of it."

His hands did not tremble ever so slightly. Nope. They did not.

They shook like a motherfucker.

The end of the braid was tied with a length of the softest fabric he'd ever felt. It wasn't cotton; it wasn't silk. . . . It was something he'd never seen before, and his keen surgeon's fingers seemed sloppy and too rough on the stuff as he worked at the winding knot. And then her hair . . . good God, her wavy black hair made that cloth feel like nettles in comparison.

Inch by inch, he separated the tripart weave, the waves both slick and clinging. And because he was a bastard, all he could think about was the shit falling over his bare chest . . . his abs . . . his cock—

"That's far enough," she said.

Damn straight it was. Yanking his inner manwhore back to the land of polite conversating, he forced his hands to stop. Even halfway undone, the reveal was astounding. If she was beautiful all tied up, she was utterly resplendent with those waves curling around her waist.

"Braid it in, please," she said, holding his card out with her lax hand. "That way no one will find it."

He blinked and thought, Well, duh. There was no way in hell the

Goateed Hater would be cool with his sister reaching out and touching her surgeon—

Not touching, he corrected himself.

Well, maybe a *little* touching. Like he could just do her. Er . . . touch her.

Time to shut it, Manello, even though you're not talking out loud.

"You are brilliant," he said. "Altogether smart."

That got her to smile, and file that under Holy Shit. Those incisors of hers were sharp and white and long . . . and evolutionarily designed for striking at the throat.

An orgasm tingled in the tip of his arousal—

And at that moment a frown passed over her face.

Oh, mannnn. "Ah . . . can you read minds?"

"When I am stronger, yes. But your scent just grew more intense."

So she was making him sweat and somehow knew it. Except . . . he got the feeling she was clueless as to the why, and wasn't that as tantalizing as the rest of her: She was utterly guileless as she stared up at him.

Then again, she might well not think of him sexually because he was a human. And hello, she'd just gotten out of the OR, so this was hardly spring break on Myrtle Beach.

Manny cut off his second interior convo and folded his business card in half. The good news about all her hair was that it was the work of a moment to camo his info in the braid. When he was finished, he rewrapped the cloth and tied a bow; then he carefully set the length down beside her on the bed.

"I hope you use it," he said. "I really do."

Her smile was so sad that it told him his chances were not all that hot, but come on. Contact between the two species was obviously not on their hit list or the term *blood bank* would have totally different connotations.

But at least she had his info.

"What do you think will happen?" she asked, nodding down at her legs.

His eyes followed her lead. "I don't know. The rules are obviously different with you . . . so anything is possible."

"Look at me," she said. "Please."

He cracked a smile. "Never thought I'd say this . . . but I don't want to." He braced himself, but couldn't make the shift up to her face quite yet. "Just promise me something."

"What may I grant you?"

"Call me if you can."

"I shall."

She didn't mean it, however. He wasn't sure how he knew that, but he was damn certain. Why she was keeping the card, though? Not a clue.

He glanced at the door and thought of Jane. Shit, he should apologize in person for being a little bitch about all this. "Before you do it, I need to go—"

"I wish I could leave something of myself behind. With you."

Manny snapped back around and locked his eyes on her. "Anything. I want anything you can give me."

The words were a dark growl, and he was very aware that he was talking sexually—and how much of a pig did that make him?

"Except anything tangible . . ." She shook her head. "It would be of harm to you."

He stared at her strong, beautiful face . . . and lingered on her lips. "I have an idea."

"Whatever would you like?" The innocence in her stare gave him pause. And lit up his libido like a bonfire.

Not like it needed the help.

"How old are you?" he asked abruptly. He might be a letch, but he didn't do underage anything. She was sure as hell built like an adult, but who knew what their maturity rate was—

"I am three hundred and five years of age."

Blink. Blink. Annnnnnd one more for good measure. Sure as shit that had to be of age, he thought. "So you're marriageable?"

"I am. I am not with a male, however."

So there was a God. "I know what I want, then." Her. Naked. All over him. But he'd settle for a hell of a lot less.

"What?"

"A kiss." He held up his hands. "Doesn't have to be all hot and heavy. Just . . . a kiss."

When she didn't reply, he wanted to kick his own ass. And thought seriously of turning himself in to that brother of hers for the beating he deserved.

"Show me how?" she whispered.

"Does your kind not . . . kiss?" God only knew what they did. But if any parts of the legend held true, sex was in the repertoire big-time.

"They do. I just never have before— Are you ill?" She reached out with her hand. "Healer?"

He opened his eyes . . . which evidently had slammed shut. "Let me ask you something. Have you ever been with a man?"

"Never with a human man. And . . . not with a male, either."

Manny's cock just about blew its top off. Which was nuts. It had never mattered to him before whether a woman had been with someone . . . or not. Actually, the kind of chicks he usually went for had lost their virginity in their early teens—and never looked back.

Payne's clear, pale eyes stared up at him. "Your scent is even stronger."

Probably because he'd broken out in a sweat trying not to orgasm.

"I like it," she added in a deeper voice.

There was an electric moment between them, one that he could not believe would be erased by any mind-over-gray-matter parlor trick. And then her lips parted and her pink tongue came out to wet her mouth . . . as if she were imagining something that made her thirsty.

"I think I want to taste you," she said.

Right. Fuck kissing. If she wanted to eat him raw he was down for it. And that was before he watched the tips of her white fangs drop even farther from her upper jaw.

Manny could feel himself panting, but he couldn't hear a thing as the blood roared in his ears. Goddamn it, he was on the verge of losing control—and not in a metaphoric sense. He was literally a heartbeat away from stripping the blankets off her body and mounting her. Even though she was in traction. And had never been with anyone before. And wasn't his kind.

It took all he had in him to stand up and step back.

Manny cleared his throat. Twice. "I think I'd better take a rain check."

"Rain check?"

"Later."

Instantly, her face changed, the lovely lines tightening up and hiding the fragile passion that had bled through her features. "But . . . of course. Indeed."

He hated hurting her, but there was no way to explain how badly he wanted her without making it pornographic. And she was a virgin, for God's sake. Who deserved better than him.

He took one last lingering look at her and told his brain to remember it. Somehow, he needed to not lose her. "Do what you have to. Now."

Her eyes drifted down the length of him and lingered at his hips. When he realized she was looking at his sex, which was standing at attention and then some, he discreetly hid what was going on beneath his scrubs with his hands.

His voice got hoarse. "You're killing me here. I can't be trusted with you right now. So you've got to do it. Please. God, just do—"

ELEVEN

R*avasz. Sbarduno. Grilletto. Trekker.*

The word *trigger* banged around V's skull in all the languages he could put it into, his brain spicin' his vocabulary up for shits and giggles—because it was either that or the thing would cannibalize itself.

As he rocked his Google Translate, his feet took him through his penthouse at the Commodore over and over again, his relentless pacing turning the place into a multimillion-dollar hamster-wheel equivalent.

Black walls. Black ceiling. Black floor. Night view of Caldwell that was never what he came here for.

Through the kitchen, through the living room, through the bedroom and back.

Again. And again.

In the light of black candles.

He'd bought the condo about five years ago, when the building was still under construction. As soon as the skeleton had risen down by the river, he'd been determined to own one-half of the top of the skyscraper. But not as some kind of home—he'd always had a place away from where he slept. Even before Wrath had consolidated the Brotherhood into Darius's old mansion, V had been in the habit of keeping where he crashed and stashed his weapons separate from his . . . other activities.

On this night, feeling as he did, the fact that he had come here was both logical and ludicrous.

Over the decades and centuries, he'd developed not only a reputation in the race, but a stable of males and females who needed what he had to give. And as soon as he'd taken possession of this unit, he'd brought them here to this black hole for a very specific kind of sex.

Here, he'd shed their blood.

And he'd made them scream and cry out.

And he'd fucked them or had them fucked.

V paused by his worktable, the old wood battered and marked not just from the tools of his trade, but from blood and orgasms and wax.

God, sometimes the only way to know how far you'd come was to return to where you once had been.

Reaching forward with his gloved hand, he took hold of the thick leather bindings he used to keep his subs where he wanted them.

Had used, he corrected himself. As in past tense. Now that he had Jane, he didn't do those things anymore—hadn't had the impulse.

Glancing over at the wall, he measured his collection of toys: Whips and chains and barbed wire. Clamps and ball gags and razor blades. Floggers. Lengths of chain.

The games he played—*had* played—were not for the faint of heart or the beginners or the casually curious. For hard-core subs, there was such a fine line between sexual release and death—both got you off, but the latter was your last shot. Literally. And he was the ultimate master, capable of taking others where they needed to go . . . and one thin inch past that.

Which was why they all came for him.

Had come for him—

To him, he corrected.

Fuck.

And that was why his relationship with Jane had been a revelation. With her in his life, he hadn't felt the burning need for any of this. Not for the relative anonymity, not for the control he exerted over his subs, not for the pain he enjoyed inflicting on himself, not for that sense of power or the pounding releases.

After all this time, he'd thought he'd been transformed.

Wrong.

That internal switch was still with him, and it had been flipped to the "on" position.

Then again, the urge to commit matricide was stressful as shit—when you couldn't act on it.

V leaned in and fingered a leather flogger that had stainless-steel balls tied on its ends. As the lengths filtered through the fingers of his ungloved hand, he wanted to throw up . . . because standing here, he would have given anything for a slice of what he'd had before—

No, wait. As he stared at his table, he revised that. He wanted to *be* what he once had had. Before Jane, he'd had sex as a Dom because it was the only way he'd felt safe enough to get through the act—and part of him had always wondered, especially as he was cracking the whip, so to speak, why his subs had wanted what he'd given them.

Now he had a pretty good idea: What was banging around his inner skin was so toxic and violent, it needed a release valve that was cut from its own cloth. . . .

He walked over to one of his black candles without being aware that his shitkickers were crossing the floor.

And then the thing was against his palm before he even knew he was gripping it.

His craving brought the flame upward . . . and then he tipped the lit tip toward his chest, hot black wax hitting his collarbone and rivering down to streak under his muscle shirt.

Closing his eyes, he let his head fall back as a hiss sucked through his fangs.

More wax on his bare skin. More sting.

As he got hard, half of him was on board and the other half felt like a total skeez. His gloved hand had no problems with a split personality, however. It went for the button fly on his leathers and sprang his cock.

In the candlelight, he watched himself bring the candle down and hold it over his erection . . . and then tilt the lit wick toward the floor.

A black tear slipped free of the heat source and went into a free fall—

"Fuck . . ."

When his lids loosened enough so that he could open them, he looked down to see the hardened wax on the rim of his head, the little line of it paving the way to where it had dropped off.

This time he moaned deep in his throat as he lowered the candle tip—because he knew what was coming.

More moaning. More wax. A loud curse that was followed by another hiss.

There was no need to go pneumatic. The pain was enough, the rhythmic drop on his cock shooting electric shocks into his balls and the muscles of his thighs and ass. Periodically, he moved the flame up and down his shaft to get clean shots at fresh flesh, his arousal leaping every time it got hit . . . until there had been enough foreplay.

Sweeping his free hand under his sac, he went vertical with his sex.

The wax hit right on the sweet spot, and the sharp agony was so intense, he nearly went down on the floor—but the orgasm was what saved his legs from going loose, the power of the release stiffening him from head to foot as he came hard.

Black wax everywhere.

Come all over his hand and his clothes.

Just like the good ol' days . . . except for one thing: It was really fucking hollow. Oh, wait. That had been part of the GOD, too. The difference was that back then, he hadn't known there was something else out there. Something like Jane—

The sound of his phone chiming made him feel like he'd been shot through the head, and even though it wasn't loud, the quiet shattered like a mirror, the shards of it showing him a reflection of himself he didn't want to see: Happily mated, he was nonetheless here in his chamber of perversion, getting himself off.

He hauled back and Curt Schillinged the candle across the room, the flame extinguishing in midflight—which was the only reason the whole fucking place didn't get burned down.

And that was before he saw who the call was from.

His Jane. No doubt with a report from the human hospital. For fuck's sake, a male of worth would have been outside the OR, waiting for his sister to come around, supporting his mate. Instead, he'd been banished for being out of control, and had come here to spend quality time with his black wax and his hard-on.

He hit *send* as he stuffed his still-hard cock back in his leathers. "Yeah."

Pause. During which he had to remind himself that she couldn't read minds, and thank fuck for it. Christ, what had he just done?

"Are you okay?" she said.

Not in the slightest. "Yeah. How's Payne?" Please let this not be bad news.

"Ah . . . she made it through. We're en route back to the compound. She did well and Wrath fed her. Her vitals are stable and she seems to be relatively comfortable, although there's no telling what the long term result is going to be."

Vishous closed his eyes. "At least she's still alive."

And then there was a whole lot of silence, broken only by the quiet whir of the vehicle she was traveling in.

Eventually, Jane said, "At least we're over the first hurdle, and the operation went as smoothly as it could—Manny was brilliant."

V judiciously ignored that comment. "Any problems with the hospital staff?"

"None. Phury worked his magic. But in case there's someone or something we missed, it's probably a good idea to monitor the record systems for a while."

"I'll take care of that."

"When are you coming home?"

Vishous had to grit his teeth as he did up the buttons of his fly. In about a half hour, he was going to have a ball so blue it was a U of K fan: Once was never enough for him. It took five or six times to get him what he needed on an average night—and there was nothing even close to average doing right now.

"Are you at the penthouse?" Jane said quietly.

"Yeah."

There was a tense pause. "Alone?"

Well, the candle was an inanimate object. "Yeah."

"It's okay, V," she murmured. "You're allowed to think like you are right now."

"How do you know what's on my mind."

"Why would there be anything else?"

Jesus . . . what a female of worth. "I love you."

"I know. And right back at you." Pause. "Do you wish . . . you were there with someone else?"

The pain in her voice was nearly eclipsed by composure, but to him the emotion was bullhorn clear. "That's in the past, Jane. Trust me."

"I do. Implicitly. You would cut off your good hand first."

Then why did you ask, he thought as he squeezed his eyes shut and hung his head. Well, duh. She knew him too well. "God . . . I don't deserve you."

"Yes, you do. Come home. See your sister—"

"You were right to tell me to go. I'm sorry I was an asshole."

"You're allowed to be. This is stressful stuff—"

"Jane?"

"Yes?"

He attempted to form words and failed, the silence stretching out between them once more. Fucking hell, no matter how much he tried to put sentences together, he found that there was no magical combination of syllables to properly phrase what was in him.

Then again, maybe it was less a function of vocabulary, and more a case of what he'd just done to himself: He felt like he had something to confess to her, and he couldn't quite do it.

"Come home," Jane cut in. "Come see her, and if I'm not in the clinic, find me."

"All right. I will."

"It's going to be okay, Vishous. And you need to remember something."

"What's that?"

"I know what I married. I know who you are. There's nothing that's going to shock me—now hang up the phone and get home."

As he told her good-bye and hit *end*, he wasn't sure about the no-shock thing. He'd surprised himself tonight, and not in a good way.

Putting his phone away, he rolled up a cigarette and patted his pockets for a lighter before remembering he'd tossed his Bic POS back at the training center.

His head cranked around and he looked at one of those goddamn black candles. With no other option, he went over and leaned in to light his hand-rolled.

The idea of going back to the compound was the right idea. A good, solid plan.

Too bad it made him want to scream until he lost his voice.

After he finished his smoke, he meant to extinguish the candles and go straight home. He honestly did.

But he didn't make it.

Manny was dreaming. Had to be.

He was dimly aware that he was in his office, lying facedown on the leather couch that he regularly crashed on for REM catch-ups. As always, there was a set of surgical scrubs wadded under his head for a pillow, and he'd kicked off his Nikes.

All this was normal, business as usual.

Except then his little nap warped on him . . . and suddenly he wasn't alone. He was on top of a woman—

As he reared back in surprise, she stared up at him with icy eyes that were blazing hot.

"How did you get in here?" he asked hoarsely.

"I am in your mind." Her accent was foreign and sexy as hell. "I am inside of you."

And then it dawned on him that beneath his body, she was so very naked, and warm—and holy Christ, even with his confusion, he wanted her.

It was the only thing that made any sense.

"Teach me," she said darkly, her lips parting, her hips rolling under his own. "Take me."

Her hand moved between the two of them and found his erection, rubbing at it, making him moan.

"I am empty without you," she said. "Fill me. *Now.*"

With an invitation like that, he didn't give anything else a second thought. Fumbling around, he shoved his scrubs down his thighs and then . . .

"Oh, fuck," he groaned as his hard cock slipped up her slick core.

One shift over and he would be buried deep, but he forced himself not to breach her sex. He was going to kiss her first, and more to the point, he was going to do that right because . . . she'd never been kissed before—

Why did he know that?

Who the fuck cared.

And her mouth wasn't the only place he was going to go with his lips.

Pulling away a little, he ran his eyes down her long neck to her collarbone . . . and went even lower—or at least tried to.

Which was his first clue that something was off. Although he could see every detail of her strong, beautiful face and her long, braided black hair, the sight of her breasts was hazy and staying that way: No matter how much he frowned, there was no clarity coming. But whatever, she was perfect to him no matter what she looked like.

Perfect *for* him.

"Kiss me," she breathed.

His hips jerked at the sound of her voice, and as his erection slid against the very heart of her, the friction made him groan. God, the feel of her pressed up tight to him, with the head of his cock having parted her and burrowed in, searching for that sweetest spot. . . .

"Healer," she gritted as she arched back, her tongue coming out and dragging over her lower lip—

Fangs.

Those two white tips were fangs, and he froze: What was underneath him and ready for him was not human.

"Teach me . . . take me . . ."

Vampire.

He should have been shocked and terrified. But he wasn't. If anything, what she was made him want inside her with a desperation that left him in a sweat. And there was something else . . . it made him want to mark her.

Whatever the hell that meant.

"Kiss me, healer . . . and don't stop."

"I won't," he moaned. "I'm not ever going to stop."

As he dipped his head to bring his lips to hers, his cock went off in an explosion, the orgasm shooting out of him and going all over her—

Manny came awake on a gasp that was loud enough to rouse the dead.

And oh, shit, he was coming hard, his hips grinding into the sofa as delicious, hazy memories of his virgin lover made him feel like her hands were all over his skin. Fucking A; even though the dream was clearly over, the orgasm kept coming until he had to lock his teeth and jack one of his knees up tight, the jerking pumps of his cock fisting the heavy muscles of his thighs and chest until he couldn't breathe.

When it was all over, he sagged face-first into the cushions and did his best to grab for some oxygen, because he had a feeling round two was going to get its groove on soon. Tendrils of the dream tantalized him and made him want to go back into that moment that had not existed and yet felt as real as the consciousness he had now. Reaching into his memory banks, he tugged at the filaments of where he'd been, bringing the female back into—

The headache that plowed into his temples all but knocked him out—sure as hell, if he hadn't already been horizontal, he would have landed on the damn floor.

"Fuuuuck . . ."

The pain was astounding, like someone had nailed him on the skull with a lead pipe, and it was a while before he had the strength to shove himself onto his back and try to sit up.

The first attempt at vertical didn't go well. The second was successful only because he braced his arms on either side of his torso to keep from pulling a down-and-out again. As his head hung like a deflated balloon off his shoulders, he stared at the Oriental rug and waited until he felt like he could make a beeline for the bathroom and fire back some Motrin.

He'd had these headaches a lot. Right before Jane had died—

The thought of his former chief of trauma brought on a new wave of someone-please-shoot-me-between-the-eyeballs.

Breathing shallowly and purposely thinking of absolutely, positively, fucking nothing somehow got him through the attack. When the agony had mostly passed, he lifted his head experimentally . . . just in case a minute change in altitude brought on another pounder.

The antique clock behind his desk read four sixteen.

Four a.m.? What in the hell had he done all night since leaving the horse-pital?

As he thought back, he remembered driving out of Queens after Glory had come around and his intention had been to go home. Clearly, that hadn't happened. And he had no clue how long he'd been asleep in his office. Looking at his scrubs, there were drops of blood here and there . . . and his kicked-off Nikes were in the blue booties he always operated in. Apparently, he'd worked on a patient—

A fresh flare of pain burst into his mind, causing him to brace every muscle in his body and fight for control. Knowing that biofeedback was his only friend, he let all cognitive processes go lax as he breathed slowly and evenly.

Focusing on the clock, he watched the hands click to seventeen . . . then eighteen . . . then nineteen. . . .

Twenty minutes later, he was finally able to stand up and lurch over to his bathroom. Inside, the private room was Ali Baba gorgeous, with enough marble, crystal and brass to be castle-worthy—or in the case of tonight, make him curse at all the bright-brights.

Reaching in through the glass door of the shower, he cranked the faucets on and then he headed to the sink to pop open the mirror and grab the bottle of Motrin. Five tablets at once was more than the recommended dosage, but he was a doctor, damn it, and he was advising himself to take more than just two.

The hot water was a blessing, rinsing away not only the remnants of that incredible release, but also the strain of the last twelve hours. God . . . Glory. He hoped like hell she was doing well. And that female he'd op—

As he felt another stinger coming on, he dropped whatever thought had been about to take root like it was poison and focused only on the way the spray hit the nape of his neck and split off his shoulders, falling down his back and his chest.

His cock was still hard.

Rock-hard.

The irony that the damn thing remained all wakey-wakey, in spite of the fact that his other head was totally scrambled, was no laughing matter. The last thing he felt like doing was more palm aerobics, but he had a feeling this arousal he was rocking was going to be like lawn sculpture: there for the duration unless he took care of it.

When the soap slipped off the brass holder and landed on his foot like an anvil, he cursed and hopped around . . . then bent down and picked the bar up.

Slippery. Oh, so slippery.

After putting the Dial back where it belonged, he let his hand go south to grip his shaft. As he drew his palm up and back, the warm water and the slick, soapy routine were effective, but still a poor substitute for what it had felt like to be against that woman's—

Sharp. Shooter. Right through his frontal lobe.

God, it was like there were armed guards surrounding any thoughts of her.

With a curse, he shut his brain down because he knew he had to finish what he'd started. Bracing an arm against the marble wall, he let his head drop while he pumped himself. He'd always had a tremendous sex drive, but this was something else entirely, a hunger that punched through any veneer of civility and ran down deep to some core of himself that was a total news flash.

"Shit . . ." As the orgasm hit, he gritted his teeth and let loose against the flushed walls of the shower. The release was just as strong as the one on the couch had been, sacking his body until his cock wasn't the only thing twitching uncontrollably: Every muscle he had seemed to be involved in the release, and he had to bite his lip to keep from yelling.

When he finally surfaced from the rock-'em, sock-'em, his face was mashed up against the marble and he was breathing like he'd sprinted from one side of Caldwell to the other.

Or maybe all the way to Canada.

Turning into the spray, he rinsed off again and stepped out, nabbing a towel and . . .

Manny looked down at his hips. "Are. You. Kidding."

His cock was just as erect as it had been the first time: Undaunted. Proud and strong as only a dumb handle could be.

Whatever. He was done servicing it.

Worse came to worst, he could just disappear the damn thing in his pants. Obviously, the "relief" method wasn't working, and he was out of energy. Hell, maybe he was coming down with the flu or some shit? God knew, working in a hospital you could pick up a lot of things.

Including amnesia, evidently.

Manny wrapped a towel around himself and walked out into his office—only to stop dead. There was a strange scent lingering in the air . . . something like dark spices?

Wasn't his cologne, that was for certain.

Striding across the Oriental in his bare feet, he opened his door and leaned out. The administrative offices were dark and empty, and the smell wasn't anywhere around.

With a frown, he looked back at his couch. But he knew better than to allow himself to think of what had just happened on it.

Ten minutes later, he was dressed in fresh scrubs and had had a shave. Mr. Happy, who was still making like the Washington Monument, was tucked up in his waistband and tied in place like the animal it was. As he picked up his briefcase and the suit he'd worn to the track, he was beyond ready to put the dream, the headache, the whole godforsaken evening behind him.

Walking out through the surgical department's offices, he took the elevator down to the third floor, where the ORs were. Members of his staff were doing their thing, operating on emergency cases, dealing with patient setup or transport, cleaning, prepping. He nodded to folks, but didn't say much—so as far as they knew, it was business as usual. Which was a relief.

And he almost made it to the parking lot without losing it.

His exit strategy came to a screeching halt, however, when he got to the recovery suites. He meant to go steaming past them, but his feet just stopped and his mind churned—and abruptly, he felt compelled to go into one of the rooms. As he followed the impulse, his headache was Johnny-on-the-spot with a return to life, but he let it roll as he pushed into the isolated bay that was all the way over by the fire exit.

The bed against the wall was neat as a pin, the sheets tucked in so tight they were all but ironed flat across the mattress. There were no staff notations on the dry-erase board; no beeping of machines; and the computer wasn't logged into.

But the scent of Lysol lingered in the air. And so did some kind of perfume . . . ?

Someone had been in here. Someone he'd operated on. Tonight.

And she had—

Agony overwhelmed him, and Manny pulled another sag-and-grab, latching onto the doorjamb and leaning in to keep standing. As his migraine, or whatever it was, got worse, he had to bend over—

Which was how he saw it.

Frowning against the pain, he stumbled over to the bedside table and got down on his haunches. Reaching underneath, he patted around until he found the folded, stiff card.

He knew what it was before he looked at the thing. And for some reason, as he held it against his palm, his heart broke in half.

Flattening the crease, he stared at the engraving of his name and title and the hospital's address, phone, and fax. In his handwriting, in the white space to the right of the St. Francis logo, he'd written his cell phone number.

Hair. Dark hair in a braid. His hands undoing—

"Mother . . . fucker." He threw out a palm to the floor, but went down anyway, hitting the linoleum hard before rolling over onto his back. As he cradled his head and strained against the agony, he knew his eyelids were bolted open, but damned if he could see anything.

"Chief?"

At the sound of Goldberg's voice, the sharpshooter at his temples faded a little, as if his brain had reached out for the auditory lifesaver and been dragged away from the sharks. At least temporarily.

"Hey," he moaned.

"Are you all right?"

"Yup."

"Headache?"

"Not at all."

Goldberg laughed briefly. "Look, there's something going around. I've had four nurses and two admins take to the floor just like you have. I've called in for extra staff and sent the others home to bed."

"Wise of you."

"Guess what."

"Don't say it. I'm going, I'm going." Manny forced himself to sit up, and then, when he was ready, he pulled his sorry ass off the floor by using the rails of the hospital bed.

"You were supposed to be gone this weekend, Chief."

"I came back." Fortunately, Goldberg didn't ask about the horse race results. Then again, he didn't know there were any to be shared. Nobody had a clue about what Manny did outside the hospital, mostly because he'd never thought it was important enough compared to the work they did here.

Why did his life feel so empty all of a sudden?

"You need a ride?" his chief of trauma asked.

God, he missed Jane.

"Ah . . ." What was the question? Oh, right. "I took some Motrin—I'll be fine. Page me if you need me." On the way out, he clapped Goldberg on the shoulder. "You're in charge until tomorrow at seven a.m."

Goldberg's response didn't register.

Turned out that was a theme. Manny wasn't tracking at all as he found the north bank of elevators and took one down into the parking garage—it was almost as if that last round of the owies had TKO'd everything but his brain stem. Stepping out, he put one foot in front of the other until he got to his designated space. . . .

Where the fuck was his car?

He looked around. The chiefs of service all had assigned parking spots, and his Porsche was not in its slot.

His keys were not in his suit pocket, either.

And the only good news was that as he became royally incensed, the headache backed off completely—although that was obviously the result of the Motrin.

Where. The. Hell. Was. His. Goddamn car.

For shit's sake, you couldn't just bust a window, roll start it with the clutch, and head out. You needed the pass card he kept in his—

Wallet was gone, too.

Great. Just what he needed: a stolen billfold, a Porsche on the way to an illegal chop shop, and a go-around with the cops.

The security office was down where you checked out of the garage, so he hoofed it along instead of calling because gee-frickin'-whiz, his cell phone had been taken, too, natch—

He slowed. Then stopped. Halfway to the exit, in the row where patients and families parked, there was a gray Porsche 911 Turbo. Same year as his. Same NYRA sticker on the back window.

Same license plate.

He approached the thing like there was a bomb taped to its undercarriage. The doors were unlocked, and he was cautious as he popped the driver's side open.

His wallet, keys, and cell phone were under the front seat.

"Doc? You all right?"

Okaaay. Apparently, there were two theme songs of the night: no memories and people asking him the one question he was guaranteed not to answer truthfully.

Looking up, he wondered what exactly he could say to the security guard: Hey, has someone turned my marbles in to Lost and Found?

"What you doing parked down here?" the guy in the blue uni asked.

I don't have a clue. "Someone was in my spot."

"Damn, you should have called, my man. We'd have fixed that quick."

"You're the best." At least that wasn't a lie.

"Well, take care—and get some rest. You don't look so hot."

"Excellent advice."

"I shoulda been a doctor." The guard lifted his flashlight on a wave. "Night."

"G'night."

Manny got into his phantom Porsche, started the engine, and threw her into reverse. As he drove over to the garage's exit, he took out his pass card and used it without a problem to open up the gate. Then on St. Francis Avenue, he hung a louie and headed downtown for the Commodore.

Driving along, he was certain about one and only one thing.

He was losing his ever-loving mind.

TWELVE

V should be home by now, Butch thought, as he stared into space at the Pit.

"He should be here," Jane said behind him. "I talked to him nearly an hour ago."

"Great minds, great minds," Butch muttered as he checked his watch. Again.

Getting off the leather couch and walking around the coffee table, he went over to his best friend's computer setup. The Four Toys, as those high-tech bastards were called, were worth a good fifty grand—and that was about all Butch knew about them.

Well, that and how to use a mouse to locate the GPS chip in V's phone.

No reason to zero in. The address told him everything he needed to know . . . and also gave his gut a whirl. "He's still down at the Commodore."

When Jane said nothing, he glanced up over the monitors. Vishous's *shellan* was standing by the Foosball table, her arms crossed over her chest, her body and profile translucent so that he could see the kitchen on the far side of her. After a year, he'd gotten more than used to her various forms, and this one usually meant she was thinking hard about something, her concentration consumed by things other than making herself corporeal.

Butch was willing to bet they were thinking the same thing: V's staying late at the Commodore when he knew his sister had been operated on and was safely here at the compound was sketchy—especially given the brother's mood.

And his extremes.

Butch went over to the closet and got out his suede coat.

"Is there any way you could—" Jane stopped and laughed a little. "You read my mind."

"I'll bring him back. Don't worry about it."

"Okay. All . . . right. I think I'll go and stay with Payne."

"Good idea." His quick response was about more than just the clinical benefits to V's sister's doctor staying on site—and he wondered if Jane knew it. Then again, she wasn't stupid.

And God only knew what he was going to find at V's place. He'd hate to think of the guy cheating with some skank, but people made mistakes, especially when they snapped from stress. And better that someone other than Jane get an eyeful of what might be doing.

On his way out, he gave her a quick hug—which she immediately returned, solidifying herself and squeezing him back.

"I hope . . ." She didn't finish the sentence.

"Don't worry," he told her, lying through his teeth.

A minute and a half later, he was behind the wheel of the Escalade and driving like a bat out of hell. Although vampires could dematerialize, as a half-breed, that handy *I Dream of Jeannie* trick was not in his repertoire.

Good thing he didn't have a problem with breaking the speed limit.

Into pieces.

Downtown Caldwell was still in sleep mode when he got to it, and unlike on a weekday, when the delivery trucks and the early-bird commuters would start streaming in before sunrise, the place was going to stay a ghost town. Sunday was a day of rest—or collapse, depending on how hard you worked. Or drank.

When he'd been a homicide detective with the Caldwell PD, he'd gotten very familiar with the daily—and nightly—rhythms of this maze of alleys and buildings. He knew the places where bodies tended to get dumped or hidden. And the criminal elements that made either a profession or a recreation out of killing folks.

He'd made so many trips into town like this, at a dead run, with no clue what he was getting into. Although . . . when he put it like that, his new job inhaling *lessers* with the Brotherhood? Old frickin' hat when it came to the adrenaline rush and the grim knowledge that death was waiting for him.

And on that note, he was a mere two blocks from the Commodore when his sense of impending whatever sharpened into something specific . . . *lessers.*

The enemy was close by. And there were a number of them.

This was not instinct. This was knowledge. Ever since the Omega had done its thing with him, he'd been a divining rod for the enemy, and though he hated that evil was inside of him, and purposely didn't grind on that bone very often, it was one hell of an asset in the war.

He was the *Dhestroyer* prophecy made manifest.

With the back of his neck going hair-shirt wild on him, he was cuffed between two polars: the war and his brother. After a good stretch of the Lessening Society chilling out, there were slayers popping up everywhere in the city, the enemy having pulled a Lazarus and revived itself with new members. So it was entirely possible that some of his brothers were pulling an end-of-the-night special with the enemy—in which case he was probably going to be hit up soon to come do his thing.

Hell, maybe it was V? Which would explain the late routine.

Shit, perhaps this wasn't as dire as they'd all thought. It sure as hell was close enough to the Commodore to justify the GPS reading, and when you were going hand-to-hand, it wasn't like you could hit a *pause* button and text an update on your ETA.

As Butch rounded the corner, the Escalade's headlights swung around into a long, narrow alleyway that was the urban equivalent of a colon: The brick buildings that formed its walls were grungy and sweaty, and the asphalt lane was pocked with filthy puddles—

"What the . . . fuck?" he breathed. Taking his foot off the accelerator, he leaned into the wheel . . . like maybe that would change what he was seeing.

At the far end, a fight was in progress, three *lessers* going hand-to-hand with a single opponent.

Who wasn't fighting back.

Butch threw the SUV into park and broke out of the driver's side, hitting the pavement at a dead run. The slayers had triangled Vishous, and the motherfucking idiot was slowly turning in the circle—but not to kick ass or to watch his own back. He was letting each of them have a go at him . . . and they had chains.

In the permaglow of the city, red blood was flowing on black leather as V's massive body absorbed the licking strikes of the links that flew around him. If he'd wanted to, he could have snagged the ends of those chains, pulled the slayers in, and dominated his attackers—they were nothing but new recruits who still had their own hair and eye colors, street rats who had been inducted an hour and ten minutes ago.

Christ, given V's self-control, he could have focused himself and dematerialized out of the ring if he'd wanted to.

Instead, he was standing with his arms out at the shoulders so there was no barrier between the impacts and his torso.

Bitch-ass bastard was going to look like a car-crash victim if he kept this up. Or worse.

Coming up to the ass whipping, Butch pulled a run and jump and pancaked the nearest slayer. As the pair of them hit the pavement, he grabbed onto a fist of dark hair, yanked back, and sliced deep across its throat. Black blood exploded out of the thing's jugular and it flopped around, but there was no time to roll the slayer over and inhale its essence down into his lungs.

Time for cleanup later.

Butch leaped to his feet and caught the ripcord end of a flying length of chain. Giving a good pull, he leaned back and rocked a spin of his own that whipped the *lesser* out of V's flagellation zone and Tasmanian-deviled it into a Dumpster.

As the undead saw stars and made like a welcome mat for future garbage hauls, Butch pivoted around, and was ready to end this thing—except surprise, surprise, V had decided to wake up and take care of biz. Even though the brother was clearly injured, he was a force to be reckoned with as he spun out a kick and then attacked with his fangs bared. Closing the distance with his incisors, he bit into the *lesser's* shoulder and locked on like a bulldog; then he black-daggered the fucker in the gut.

While the thing's intestinal tract hit the pavement in a sloppy mess, V cut the Colgate hold and let the slayer slump down and sprawl.

And then there was nothing but raw breathing.

"What the hell . . . were you . . . doing?" Butch bit out.

V bent at the waist and braced his palms on his knees, but clearly that wasn't enough relief from the agony he was in: Next thing Butch knew, the brother went down on his knees next to the slayer he'd gutted and just . . . breathed.

"Answer me, asshole." Butch was so pissed, he was of half a mind to kick the SOB in the head. "What the *fuck* are you doing?"

As cold rain began to fall, red blood dripped out of V's mouth, and he coughed a couple of times. That was it.

Butch dragged a hand through his dampening hair and turned his face up to the sky. As dappling drops hit his forehead and cheeks, the cooling benediction calmed him down some. But did absolutely nothing to relieve the pit in his stomach.

"How far were you going to let it go, V?"

He didn't want a reply. Wasn't even talking to his best friend. He was just looking up at the night sky with its washed-out stars and vast, answerless expanse hoping for some strength. And then it dawned on him. The weak sparkles up above were not just about the city's ambient light—they were because the sun was about to flex its brilliant biceps and go Lite-Brite all over this part of the world.

He had to move fast.

As Vishous spit another load of plasma onto the asphalt, Butch snapped into focus and got his dagger in hand. No time for inhaling the slayers, but that was beside the point: After he was finished with his *Dhestroyer* shit, he had to be healed by V or he wallowed in the land of dry heaves with the Omega's sooty remains consuming him. Right now? He barely trusted himself to sit next to the brother on the trip home.

For fuck's sake, V wanted a good beating?

Well, he was feeling like just the bastard to give him one.

As Butch stabbed the *lesser* with the intestinal leaks back to the Omega, Vishous didn't blink at the pop and flash that went off next to him. And he didn't seemed to track as Butch went over and disappeared the one who had the neck slice.

Last slayer left was Dumpster Boy, who had just enough strength to pull himself up against the car-sized bin and hang off the edge like a zombie.

Jogging over, Butch raised the hilt of his dagger above his shoulder, so ready to get this—

Just as he was about to strike, a scent drifted into his nose, one that was not just *eau d'*enemy . . . but something else. Something he was all too familiar with.

Butch followed through on the stab, and as the flare faded, he looked at the top of the Dumpster. One-half of the lid was closed. The other part was hanging cockeyed off to the side, as if it had been peeled by a passing truck, and the dim light that shone in was enough for him to go by. Apparently, the building serviced by the bin had some kind of metal-working thing going on because there were countless curls of thin metal in it, like crazy-ass Halloween wigs—

In and among them, there was a dirty, pale hand that had small, thin fingers . . .

"Shiiiiiiit," he whispered.

Years of training and experience shot him right into detective mode, but he had to remind himself that there was no time left for him in this alleyway. Dawn was coming, and if he didn't get his groove on and go back to the compound, he was up in smoke.

Besides, his days as a cop had long passed.

This was human business. Not his anymore.

In an absolutely foul mood, he raced over to the SUV, put the cocksucking engine in drive, and floored the gas even though he had to cover only about twenty yards. When he slammed on the brake, the Escalade screeched and fishtailed on the damp pavement, stopping a mere foot from V's bent form.

As the vehicle's automatic wipers swept back and forth, Butch punched the passenger-side window down.

"Get in the car," he ordered, staring straight ahead.

No response.

"Get in the *motherfucking* car."

Back at the Brotherhood's place of healing, Payne was in a room other than the one she'd started out in, and yet everything seemed the same:

She was lying motionless on a bed that was not her own in a state of impotent agitation.

The only difference was that her hair was loose now.

As thoughts of her last moments with her healer barged into her mind, she let them run amok, too tired to fight the surge. Whatever state had she left him in? Covering up his memories had felt like an act of robbery, and his blank stare afterward had terrified her. What if she had done harm to him . . .

He was utterly innocent in this—they were using him and then all but discarding him, and he deserved so much better. Even if he hadn't fixed her, he had done his level best, of that she was certain.

After she had sent him off to wherever he was most likely to go at that time of night, she had been racked with regret—and very aware that she could not be trusted with any information on how to contact him. Those electric moments between them were too much temptation to turn away from, and the last thing she wanted was to have to steal more memories from him.

With strength that had come from fear, she'd unbraided what he had plaited for her . . . until his little card had fallen to the floor.

And now she was here.

Verily, the only course for the pair of them was to cut off communication. If she survived . . . if she had indeed been made whole by him . . . she would seek him out . . . and for what purpose?

Oh, whoever was she kidding. The kiss that had never happened. That was why she would seek him out. And they wouldn't stop there.

Thoughts of the Chosen Layla came forth, and she found herself wishing she could go back to the conversation the two of them had had at the reflecting pool mere days ago. Layla had found a male with whom she wished to mate, and Payne had thought she'd gone daft in the head—a stance forged in ignorance, as it had turned out. In less time than it took to have a meal, her human healer had taught her that she could feel for the opposite sex.

Fates, she would never forget what he looked like, standing o'er her bed, his body so thickly aroused and ready to take hers. Males were magnificent like that, and what a surprise to learn such a thing.

Well, her healer was magnificent. She didn't imagine she would feel the same if it had been anyone else. And she wondered what it would have felt like, to have his mouth upon hers. His body within hers—

Ah, what fantasies could be spun when one was alone and feeling morose.

For truth, what future could they have? She was a female who didn't fit in anywhere, a warrior stuck within the tepid skin of a Chosen's body—to say nothing of the paralysis problem. Meanwhile, he was a vibrant, sexual male of a species different from her own.

Fate would ne'er see fit to put them together, and mayhap that was a good thing. It would be too cruel for them both, because there could never be any mating—of the ceremonial or the physical kind: She was ensconced here in the Brotherhood's secret enclave, and if the king's protocol didn't keep them apart, her brother's violent streak certainly would.

They were not to be.

As the door swung open and Jane walked in, it was a relief to focus upon something, anything else, and Payne tried to summon a smile at the ghostly mate of her twin.

"You're awake," Jane said, coming over.

Payne frowned at the female's tense expression. "How fare thee?"

"More important, how are you?" Jane set a hip on the bed, her eyes tracing the mechanicals that monitored every pump of blood and draw of lung. "Are you resting comfortably?"

Not at all. "Indeed. And I thank you for all that has been done on my behalf. Tell me, though, wherever is my brother?"

"He is . . . not home yet. But he will be soon. He's going to want to see you."

"And I he."

V's *shellan* seemed to run out of words at that point. And the silence said so much.

"You do not know where he is, do you," Payne murmured.

"Oh . . . I know the place. All too well."

"So you are worried about his predilections, then." Payne winced a little. "Forgive me. I am e'er too blunt."

"It's all right. Actually, I do better with blunt than polite." Jane's eyes shut briefly. "So you know . . . about him?"

"Everything. All of it. And I loved him afore I e'er met him."

"How do you . . . did you—"

"Know? 'Tis the work of a moment when you are a Chosen. The seeing bowls have allowed me to watch him through all the seasons of his life. And I daresay that this time, with you, is by far the best."

Jane made a noncommittal noise. "Do you know what happens next?"

Ah, always the question—and as Payne thought of her legs, she found herself wondering along similar lines. "Alas, I cannot say, as 'tis only the past that is shown, or the very nearest moment-to-moment of the present."

There was a long silence. And then Jane said, "I find Vishous so hard to reach sometimes. He's right in front of me . . . but I can't get to him." Dark green eyes flashed over. "He hates emotion. And he's very independent. Well, I'm the same way. Unfortunately, in situations like this, I feel like the pair of us are not so much together as side by side, if that makes sense? God, listen to me. I'm rambling . . . and I sound like I've got problems with him."

"On the contrary, I know how much you adore him. And I am not at all unversed with his nature." Payne thought of the abuse wrought upon her twin. "Has he e'er spoken of our father?"

"Not really."

"I am unsurprised."

Jane's eyes held hers. "What was the Bloodletter like?"

What to reply to that? "Let us just say . . . I killed him for what he did to my brother—and we shall leave it at that."

"God . . ."

"More like the devil, if you apply human traditions."

Jane's frown was deep enough to wrinkle her forehead. "V never talks about the past. Ever. And he mentioned only once what happened to his—" She stopped there. In truth, however, there was no reason to go on as Payne knew too well that to which the female referred. "Maybe I should have pressed him, but I didn't. Talking about deep stuff upsets him, so I've left it alone."

"You know him well."

"Yeah. And because I do, I'm worried about what he did tonight."

Ah, yes. The bloodied lovers he favored.

Payne reached out and brushed the healer's translucent arm—and was surprised to see that where she touched became corporeal. As Jane started, she apologized, but her twin's mate shook her head.

"Please don't. And it's funny . . . only V can do that with me. Everyone else just passes through."

And wasn't there a metaphor in that.

Payne spoke clearly: "You are the right *shellan* for my twin. And he loves only you."

Jane's voice cracked. "But what if I can't give him what he needs."

Payne had no easy answer for that one. And before she could formulate some kind of response, Jane said, "I shouldn't be talking to you like this. I don't want you to worry about him and me, or put yourself in an awkward position."

"We both love him and we know who he is so there is naught to be awkward about. And before you ask, I shall tell him nothing. We became sisters of one blood the moment you mated him, and I shall e'er hold your confidence close to my heart."

"Thank you," Jane said in a low voice. "Thank you a million times over."

In that moment, an accord was reached between them, the kind of wordless tie that was the strength and foundation of all family whether they be united by birthright or circumstance.

Such a strong female of worth, Payne thought.

Which reminded her. "My healer. What do you call him?"

"Your surgeon? You mean Manny—Dr. Manello?"

"Ah, yes. He gave me a message for you." Jane seemed to stiffen. "He said he forgives you. For everything. I can only guess you know that to which he refers?"

Vishous's mate exhaled, her shoulders easing. "God . . . Manny." She shook her head. "Yes, yes, I do. I really hope he comes out of this okay. There've been a lot of memories erased in that head of his."

Payne couldn't agree more. "May I inquire . . . however do you know of him?"

"Manny? He was my boss for years. The best surgeon I ever worked with."

"Is he mated?" Payne asked in a voice she hoped read as casual.

Now Jane laughed. "Not at all—although God knows there are always women around him."

As a subtle growl pumped through the air, the good doctor blinked in surprise, and Payne quickly silenced the possessiveness she had no right to feel. "What . . . what kind of female does he favor?"

Jane rolled her eyes. "Blond, leggy, and busty. I don't know if you're familiar with Barbie, but that was always his type."

Payne frowned. She was neither blond nor particularly busty . . . but leggy? She could do leggy—

Why was she even thinking like this?

Closing her eyes, she found herself praying that the male never, ever met the Chosen Layla. But how ridiculous was that—

Her twin's mate gently patted her arm. "I know you're exhausted so I'm going to let you rest. If you need me, just hit the red button on the rail and I'll come right to you."

Payne forced her lids up. "Thank you, healer. And worry not about my twin. He shall return to you afore the dawn's call of light."

"I hope so," Jane said. "I really do. . . . Listen, you rest and then later this afternoon, we'll start some PT on you."

Payne bid the female good day and closed her eyes once more.

Left by herself, she found herself understanding how the female felt about the idea of Vishous being with another. Images of her healer around the likes of the Chosen Layla made her sick to her stomach—even though there was no cause for the indigestion.

What a mess she was in. Stuck upon this hospital bed, her mind tangled in thoughts of a male she had no right to on so many levels . . .

And yet the idea of his sharing that sexual energy with anyone but her made her downright violent. To think that there were other females around her healer, seeking what he had seemed prepared to give her, wanting that straining length at his hips and the pressure of his lips against their mouths—

When she growled again, she knew it was for the best that she had let that card with his information go. Else she would have wrought carnage upon the lovers he took.

After all, she had no problems killing.

As history had well proven.

THIRTEEN

Qhuinn entered the mansion through the vestibule. Which was a mistake.

He should have gone into the mansion through the garage, but the truth was, those coffins stacked up in the corner freaked him out. He always expected their lids to open and some kind of *Night of the Living Dead* to whassup the ever living crap out of him.

He so needed to get over being a pussy, however.

Courtesy of his case of the nancys, the instant he pushed his way into the foyer, he got a clear shot at Blaylock and Saxton coming down the grand staircase, the two of them all *GQ*'d up for Last Meal. Both wore slacks, not jeans, and sweaters, not sweatshirts, and loafers, not shitkickers. They were clean-shaven, cologned, and coiffed, but they were not she-males in the slightest.

Frankly, that would have made things a lot easier.

For fuck's sake, he wished one of the SOBs would RuPaul their shit and go all feather boa and fingernail polish. But no. They just kept looking like two too-hot males who knew how to spend their money at Saks . . . while he, on the other hand, gutter-snaked it up in his leathers and his muscle shirts—and in the case of tonight, sported hair styled by rough sex, and cologne, if you could call it that, from the same line of slut-care products.

Then again, he was willing to bet all that separated them from the state he was in was a hot, soapy shower and a visit to the ol' closet: Dollars to licks they'd been in a clinch all night. They were looking far too satisfied as they headed for a meal they were no doubt starved for.

As they hit the mosaic depiction of an apple tree in full bloom, Blay's set of blues shifted over and pulled a head-to-heel on Qhuinn. The guy's face didn't show any reaction. Not anymore.

That old flare of pain was nowhere in sight—and not because Qhuinn's recreations weren't perfectly frickin' obvi.

Saxton said something and Blay looked away . . . and there it was. A blush on that lovely pale skin as blue eyes met gray ones.

I can't do this, Qhuinn thought. *Not tonight.*

Avoiding the whole dining room scene, he headed for the door beneath the stairs and put the thing to good use. The instant it closed behind him, the chatty patter of people talking was cut off and silent darkness rushed up to greet him. Which was more like it.

Down the shallow stairs. Through another coded door. Into the underground tunnel that ran from the main house to the training center. And now that he was alone, he ran out of gas, making it only about two feet before his legs stopped working and he had to lean against the smooth wall. Letting his head fall back, he closed his eyes . . . and wanted to put a gun to his temple.

He'd had that redhead back at the Iron Mask.

Had that hetero good and hard.

And it had happened exactly the way he'd predicted, starting with the pair of them yakking it up at the bar and checking out the chicks. Not long after, a set of double-Ds had gone trolling by on black platform boots. Talked to her. Drank with her . . . and her friend. Hour later? The four of them were in a bathroom, squeezed in tight.

Which had been part two of the plan. Hands were hands in cramped spaces, and when there was a lot of moving and pawing going down, you could never be sure who was touching you. Stroking you. Feeling you up.

The whole time they'd been with the chippies, Qhuinn had been strategizing on how to get rid of the females, and it had taken waaay longer than he'd wanted. After the sex, the girls had wanted to hang out some more—trade numbers, kibitz, ask if they wanted to go out for a bite.

Yeah, right. He didn't need no digits, because he was never going to call them; he wasn't into kibitzing even with people he liked; and the sort of bite he could offer them had nothing to do with greasy-ass diner food.

After filing the requests under Bitch, Please in his head, he'd been forced to brainwash them into leaving—which had led him to a rare moment of pity for human males who didn't have that luxury.

And then he and his prey had been alone, the human male recovering against the sink; Qhuinn pretending to do likewise against the door. Eventually there had been eye contact, casual on the human's side, very serious on Qhuinn's.

"What?" the man had asked. But he'd known . . . because his eyelids had grown heavy.

Qhuinn had reached behind himself and turned the lock so they wouldn't be disturbed. "I'm still hungry."

Abruptly, the redhead had stared at the door like he'd wanted to leave . . . but his cock had told a different story. Behind the button fly of those jeans . . . he got hard.

"No one will ever know," Qhuinn had said darkly. Hell, he could have made it so the redhead didn't remember—although as long as the guy hadn't tweaked to the whole vampire thing, there'd been no reason to pull out the skull Swiffer and clean things up.

"I thought you said you weren't gay. . . ." The tone had been on the plaintive side, as if the man hadn't felt entirely comfortable with what his body wanted.

Qhuinn had closed the distance between them, putting his chest against the redhead's. And then he'd grabbed the back of the guy's neck and yanked him over to his mouth. The kiss had done what it was designed to do: get all that thinking out of the bathroom and leave nothing but sensation behind.

Shit had gone from there. Twice.

When it was over, the guy hadn't offered his number. He'd gotten off spectacularly, but it was clear that it had been a first-and-only experimental thing on his end—which was just fine with Qhuinn. They'd parted without a word, each going on about his life, with the redhead heading back to the bar . . . and Qhuinn leaving to go wander the streets of Caldwell alone.

Only dawn's imminent arrival had made him return here.

"Fucking hell . . ." he said to himself.

The whole night had been a lesson in scratching poison ivy—yes, there were times in life when proxies worked: at a council meeting, for example, when you sent someone else to give your vote. Or when you needed something from a supermarket and you gave your list to a *doggen*. Or when you'd promised to play pool, but were too drunk to hold your stick, so you got someone else to snap your balls.

Unfortunately, the proxy theory most certainly did not work when you wished you had been the one to take someone's virginity, but you hadn't, and your best follow-up idea was to go to a club, find someone with a similar physical trait, like . . . oh, say . . . hair color . . . and fuck them instead.

In that proxy situation, you ended up feeling hollow, and not because you'd come your brains out and were floating on a little postcoital cloud of *ahhhhh, yeah*.

Standing in this tunnel, all by himself, Qhuinn was utterly empty in his own skin. Ghost-towned from the inside out.

Too bad his libido was far from out of bright ideas. In the quiet solitude, he started to imagine what it would be like if it were him instead of his cousin coming down with Blay for dinner. If he was the one sharing not just a bed, but a bedroom with the guy. If he stood up to everyone and said, Hey, this is my mate—

The mental lockdown that followed that little ditty was so complete, he felt like he'd been punched in the head.

And that was the problem, wasn't it.

As he rubbed his mismatched eyes, he thought back on how much his family had hated him: He'd been raised to believe his genetic defect of having one blue and one green iris meant he was an abnormal freak, and they'd treated him as an embarrassment to the bloodline.

Well, actually it had been worse than that. They'd ended up kicking him out of house and sending an honor guard to teach him a lesson. Which was how he'd ended up a *wahlker*.

To think they'd never known about the other "abnormalities" he harbored.

Like wanting to be with his best friend.

Christ, he so didn't need a mirror to see himself for the coward and the fraud he was . . . but there was nothing he could do about it. He was locked in a cage with no key that he could find, years of his family's derision boxing him in and cramping him: The truth behind his wild side was that he was a straight-up pussy. Blay, on the other hand, was the strong one. Tired of waiting around, he'd declared who he was and found somebody to be with.

Fucking hell, this hurt . . .

With a curse, he cut off the premenstrual monologue and forced himself to get walking. With each footfall, he tightened himself up, duct-taping his messy inner workings together and fortifying his leaky pipes.

Life was about change. Blay had changed. John had changed.

And he was next on the list, apparently, because he couldn't keep going like this.

As he entered the training center through the back of the office, he decided that if Blay could turn over a new leaf, so could he. Life was what you determined it to be; regardless of where fate put you, logic and free will meant you could make your cabbage patch anything the fuck you wanted.

And he didn't want where he was: Not the anonymous sex. Not the desperate stupidity. Not the burning jealousy and nagging regrets that got him nowhere.

The locker room was empty, as there were no training classes going on, and he changed by himself, getting naked before pulling on black running shorts and a pair of black Nikes. The workout room was likewise an echo chamber, and that was just as well.

Firing up the sound system, he flipped through the shit with the remote. When Gorillaz's "Clint Eastwood" came on, he went over to a treadmill and got on the thing. He hated working out . . . just despised the mindless gerbil nature of it all. Better to fuck or fight, he'd always said.

However, when you were stuck indoors because of the dawn, and were determined to try to give celibacy a shot, running to get nowhere seemed pretty frickin' viable as an energy suck.

Juicing up the machine, he hopped on and sang along.

Focusing on the white-painted concrete across the way, he pounded one foot after another, again and again and again, until there was nothing to his mind or his body except the repetitive footfalls and the beat of his heart and the sweat that formed on his bare chest and stomach and back.

For once in his life, he did not go for breakneck: The speed was calibrated so that his pace was a steady churn, the kind of thing he could sustain for hours.

When you were trying to get away from yourself, you gravitated to the loud and obnoxious, to the extremes, to the reckless, because it forced you to scramble and hang on with your clawing nails to cliffs of your own self-invention.

Just as Blay was who he was, Qhuinn was the same: Even though he wished he could be out and with the . . . male . . . he loved, he couldn't make himself go there.

But by God, he was going to stop running from his cowardice. He had to own his shit—even if it made him hate himself to the core. Because maybe if he did, he'd stop trying to distract himself with sex and drinking, and figure out what he *did* want.

Apart from Blay, that was.

FOURTEEN

Sitting beside Butch in the Escalade, V was a six-foot-six, two-hundred-fifty-pound contusion.

As they sped back to the compound, every inch of him was pounding, the pain forming a haze that calmed the screaming inside of him.

So he'd gotten something of what he'd needed.

The trouble was, the relief was beginning to fade already, and didn't that get him pissed off at the Good Samaritan behind the wheel. Not that the cop seemed to care. He'd been dialing that cell phone of his and hanging up and dialing again and hanging up, like the fingers on his right hand had a case of Tourette's.

He was probably calling Jane and thinking better of it. Thank fuck—

"Yeah, I'd like to report a dead body," he heard the cop say. "No, I'm not giving my name. It's in a Dumpster in an alley off Tenth Street, two blocks over from the Commodore. Looks to be a Caucasian female, late teens, early twenties . . . No, I'm not giving my name. . . . Hey, how about you get down the address and stop worrying about me. . . ."

As Butch got into it with the operator, V shifted his ass in the seat and felt the broken ribs on his right side howl. Not bad. If he needed another hit to chill him out, he could just do some sit-ups and get back on the agony-go-round—

Butch tossed his cell onto the dash. Cursed. Cursed again.

Then decided to share the wealth: "How far were you going to let it go, V? Until they stabbed you? Left you for the sun? What was going to be far enough?"

V talked around his swollen lip. "Don't front, true."

"Front?" Butch swung his head around, his eyes positively violent. "Excuse me?"

"Don't pretend . . . you don't know what this is like. I've seen you on a bender. . . . I've seen—" He coughed. "I've seen you drunk on your feet with a glass in both hands. So do *not* go holier-than-thou on me."

Butch refocused on the road. "You are a miserable son of a bitch."

"Whatever."

Yup, that was about it for the convo.

By the time Butch tooled up in front of the mansion, both of them were wincing and blinking like they'd been hit in the puss with Mace: The sun was still buried on the far side of the horizon, but it was close enough to put a blush in the sky that was only a few megawatts south of deadly to a vampire.

They didn't go into the big house. No fucking way. Last Meal was about to get its knife and fork on, and given both their moods, there was no reason to feed the gossip mill.

Without saying another word, V walked into the Pit and beelined for his bedroom. There was no seeing Jane or his sister looking like this, for real. Hell, given what his mug felt like, there might be no seeing them even after a shower.

In the bath, he started the water and disarmed in the dark—which involved all of taking his one dagger out of the belt holster around his waist and putting it on the counter. His clothes were filthy, covered with blood and wax and other shit, and he let them fall on the floor, unsure what he was going to do with them.

Then he got under the spray before it was warm. As the cold water hit his face and pecs, he hissed, the shock shooting down into his cock and hardening him—not that he felt any interest in doing something about the erection. He just closed his eyes as his blood and the blood of his enemy sluiced off his body and got sucked down the drain.

Man, after he got his shit washed up, he was so going to put a turtleneck on. His face was fucked-up, but maybe that could be explained away by his having been in a fight with the enemy. Turning himself into a black-and-blue canvas from head to foot?

Not so much.

Hanging his head and letting the water run off his nose and chin, he tried desperately to go back to the numb floats he'd had in the car, but with the pain fading, his drug of choice was losing its grip on him and the world was getting too clear again.

God, the sense of being out of control and pissed off choked him sure as if there were hands around his throat.

Fucking Butch. Do-gooder, nosy-ass, interfering son of a bitch.

Ten minutes later, he stepped out, grabbed a black towel, and stemmed-to-sterned the terry cloth as he walked into the bedroom. Popping open his closet, he willed a black candle on and . . . got an eyeful of wife-beaters. And leathers. Which was what happened to your wardrobe when you fought for a living and slept naked.

Not a turtleneck in sight.

Well, maybe the damage wasn't so bad—

A quick pivot to the mirror on the back of the door and even he had to pause. He looked like he'd been clawed by Rhage's beast, great stripes of angry red welts wrapping around his torso and pouring over his shoulders and his pecs. His face was a fucking joke, one eye so swollen that the lid was nearly inoperable . . . his lower lip split deep . . . his jaw looking like he was a squirrel stashing nuts.

Great. He was like one of Dana White's boys.

After he grabbed his dirty clothes and stuffed them into the back of the closet, he stuck his swollen balloon head out in the hall, and took a listen. ESPN was chattering away down on the left. Something liquid was pouring to the right.

He headed for Butch and Marissa's room buck-ass naked. No reason to hide the bruising from Butch—SOB had seen it happen.

As he stepped into the doorway, he found the cop sitting on the end of his bed, elbows on his knees, glass of Lag in his palms, bottle between his loafers.

"You know what I'm thinking about right now?" the guy said without looking up.

V could guess it was a hell of a list. "Tell me."

"The night I watched you throw yourself off the balcony at the Commodore. The night I thought you'd died." Butch took a swig from his glass. "I assumed we were over that."

"If it's any consolation . . . so did I."

"Why don't you go see your mom. Talk this shit out with her."

Like there was anything that female could say at this point? "I'd kill her, cop. I don't know how I'd do it . . . but I'd kill the bitch for this. She leaves me to that sociopath of a father—being precisely aware of what he's like, because, hello, she sees all. Then she keeps herself a secret from me for three hundred years, before she turns up on my birthday and wants to put me out to stud for her stupid-ass religion. But I could have punted on that shiz, true? My sister, my twin, though? She put Payne away, cop. Held her against her will. For centuries. And never told me I even had a sibling? That's too fucking much. I'm done." V stared at the Lag. "You got some juice to spare there?"

Butch corked the bottle and tossed the thing. As V caught it in his palm, the cop said, "Waking up dead is not the answer, though. And neither is getting your ass kicked like that."

"You volunteering to do it for me, then? Because I'm going crazy and it needs out, Butch. For real. I'm dangerous over here. . . ." V took a pull on the booze and cursed as the slice in his lip made it feel like he'd sucked on the wrong end of a hand-rolled. "And I can't think of any way to get it out of me—because I sure as fuck am not going to fall into my old habits."

"Not tempted at all?"

V braced himself and then went for another drink. Through his grimace, he said, "I want the release, but I'm not going to be with anyone except Jane. No way I'm coming back to our mated bed with the stank of some slut all over my cock—it would ruin everything, not just for her but for me. Besides, what I need right now is a Dom, not a sub—and there's no one I can trust." Except maybe Butch, but that would cross too many lines. "So I'm caught. I got a screaming harpy in my head and nowhere to go with it . . . and it's making me fucking mental."

Jesus . . . he'd said it. All of it.

Go, him.

And the reward was another suck on the bottle. "Goddamn, my lip hurts."

"No offense, but good—you deserve it." Butch's hazel eyes lifted, and after a moment, he smiled a little, flashing that cap on his front tooth as well as his fangs. "You know, I was really getting into hating you for a minute there, I truly was. And before you ask, the turtlenecks are down at the far end of that rack. Take some sweatpants, too. Your legs look like they've been hit with a clawhammer, and that ball of yours is clearly about to explode."

"Thanks, man." V walked down the lineup of clothes that were suspended on fine cedar hangers. One thing you could say about Butch was that his wardrobe was full of options. "Never thought I'd be glad that you're a clothes whore."

"I believe the term is sharp dresser."

With that Boston accent of his, the words came out *shahhp dressah*, and V found himself wondering if there'd ever been a time when he hadn't heard that Southie twang in his ear.

"What are you going to do about Jane?"

V put the bottle on the floor, pulled a cashmere turtleneck over his head, and was pissed to find it barely covered his navel. "She's got enough on her plate. No *shellan* needs to hear her male went out for a good beating—and I don't want you to tell her."

"How're you going to explain your puss, smart-ass?"

"The swelling's going to go down."

"Not fast enough—you go to see Payne like this—"

"She doesn't need the viewing pleasure, either. I'm just going to stay scarce for a day. Payne's in recovery and is stable—at least, that's what Jane told me, so I'm going to go to my forge."

Butch held out his glass. "If you don't mind?"

"Roger that." V poured some for his boy, took another drink for himself and then yanked on some bottoms. Holding his arms out, he did a turn. "Better?"

"All I see are ankles and wrists—and FYI, you're pulling a Miley-frickin'-Cyrus with that belly flash. Not attractive."

"Fuck off." As V grabbed another hit from the bottle, he decided that getting drunk was his new plan. "I can't help it that you're a goddamn midget."

Butch barked a laugh and then got back to serious. "If you pull this shit again . . ."

"You asked me to take your clothes."

"That's *not* what I'm talking about."

V tugged at the turtleneck's sleeves and got absolutely nowhere with them. "You're not going to have to step in, cop, and I'm not going to get myself killed. That's not the point. I know where the line is."

Butch cursed, his face going grim. "You say that, and I believe you think it's true. But situations can spiral—especially that kind. You can be riding that wave of . . . whatever it is you need . . . and the tide can turn against you."

V flexed his gloved hand. "Not possible. Not with this—and I really don't want you talking to my girl about this, true. Promise me. You need to stay out of this."

"Then you have to speak with her."

"How can I tell her . . ." His voice broke, and he had to clear his throat. "How the fuck can I explain this to her?"

"How can you not. She loves you."

V just shook his head. He couldn't imagine telling his *shellan* he wanted to be hurt physically. It would kill her. And he absolutely didn't want her to see him like this. "Look, I'm going to take care of this myself. All of it."

"That's what I'm afraid of, V." Butch swallowed the rest of his Scotch on a oner. "That's . . . our biggest problem."

Jane was watching her patient sleep when her cell phone went off in her pocket. It wasn't a call, but a text from V: *Am home & goin 2 forge 2 wrk. Hw P? & u?*

Her exhale was not about relief. He'd come back about ten minutes before full-on sunrise, and he wasn't seeing her or his sister?

Screw this, she thought, as she stood up and walked out of the recovery suite.

After doing a handoff to Ehlena, who was in the clinic's exam room updating the Brothers' files, Jane marched down the corridor, hung a left into the office, and went out the back of the supply closet. No reason to futz around with the lock codes; she just ghosted through—

And there he was, about twenty yards down the tunnel, walking away from her . . . having passed the training center on his way to go even deeper into the mountain.

The fluorescent ceiling lights illuminated him from over his head, hitting his huge shoulders and his heavy lower body. Going by the gloss, his hair looked wet, and the lingering scent of the soap he always used was the confirmation that he'd just showered.

"Vishous."

She said his name once, but the tunnel was an echo chamber that batted the syllables back and forth, multiplying them.

He stopped.

That was the only response she got.

After waiting for him to say something, to turn around . . . to acknowledge her, she discovered something new about her ghostly state: Even though she wasn't technically alive, her lungs could still burn sure as if she were suffocating.

"Where did you go tonight," she said, not expecting an answer.

And she didn't get one. But he'd halted right under a ceiling fixture, so even from a distance she could see his shoulders tightening up.

"Why aren't you turning around, Vishous."

Dear God . . . what had he done at the Commodore? Oh, Jesus . . .

Funny, there was a reason that people "built" lives together. Although the choices you made as husband and wife were not bricks, and time was not mortar, you were still constructing something tangible and real. And right now, as her *hellren* refused to come over to her—hell, even show her his face—an earthquake was rumbling under what she had thought was solid ground.

"What did you do tonight," she choked out.

At that, he pivoted on his heel and took two long steps toward her. But it wasn't to get close. It was to step out of the direct light. Even still . . .

"Your *face*," she gasped.

"I got into a fight with some *lessers*." As she went to move forward, he held up his palm. "I'm fine. I just need some space right now."

Something about this was off, she thought. And she hated the question that jumped into her mind—to the point where she refused to let it out.

Except then all they had was silence.

"How's my sister?" he said abruptly.

Through a closed throat, she replied, "She's resting comfortably still. Ehlena's with her."

"You should take some time off and have a rest."

"I will." Uh-huh, right. With things like this between them, she was never going to sleep again.

V dragged his gloved hand through his hair. "I don't know what to say right now."

"Were you with someone else?"

He didn't even hesitate: "No."

Jane stared at him . . . and then slowly exhaled. One thing that was true about her *hellren*, one thing you could always take to the bank, was that Vishous didn't lie. For all the faults he had, that was not one of them.

"All right," she said. "You know where to find me. I'll be in our bed."

She was the one who turned away and started walking in the opposite direction. Even though the distance between them broke her heart, she wasn't going to badger him into something he wasn't capable of, and if he needed space . . . well, she would give it to him.

But not forever, that was for sure.

Sooner or later, that male was going to talk to her. He had to or she was going to . . . God, she didn't know what.

Her love wasn't going to survive forever in this vacuum, though. It just couldn't.

FIFTEEN

The fact that José de la Cruz hit a Dunkin' Donuts drive-through on the way into downtown Caldwell was one hell of a cliché. Collective wisdom had all homicide detectives drinking coffee and eating doughnuts, but that wasn't always the truth.

Sometimes there wasn't time to stop.

And man, screw the television shows and the detective novels, the reality was, he functioned better on caffeine and with a little sugar in his bloodstream.

Plus he lived for the honey dips. So sue him.

The call that had woken him and his wife up had come in at close to six a.m., which considering the number of nighttime ring-a-dings he got was almost civilized: Dead bodies, like live ones with medical problems, didn't play by nine-to-five rules—so the nearly decent hour had been a novel benediction.

And that wasn't the only thing going his way. Courtesy of it being a Sunday morning, the roads and highway were bowling-alley empty, and his unmarked made excellent time in from the burbs—so his coffee was still pipin' hot as he piloted himself down into the warehouse district, pulling rolling stops at the red lights.

The lineup of squad cars announced the location where the body had been found even better than the yellow warning tape that had been wound around everywhere like ribbon on some fucked-up Christmas present. With a curse, he parked parallel to the brick wall of the alley and got out, sipping and walking his way over to the knot of grim-looking blue unis.

"Hey, Detective."

"S'up, Detective."

"Yo, Detective."

He nodded at the boys. "Mornin' all. How we doing?"

"We didn't touch her." Rodriguez nodded over to the Dumpster. "She's in there and she's had initial photographs taken by Jones. Coroner and the CSI types are on the way. So's the man-sogonist."

Ah, yes, their faithful photog. "Thanks."

"Where's your new partner?"

"Coming."

"He ready for this?"

"We'll see." No doubt this grungy alley was plenty familiar with people tossing their cookies. So if the greenhorn lost his proverbial lunch, s'all good.

José ducked under the tape and walked over to the Dumpster. As always when he approached a body, he found his sense of hearing grew almost unbearably acute: The soft chatter of the men behind him, the sound of the soles of his shoes on the asphalt, the whistling breeze off the river . . . everything was too loud, like the volume of the whole damn world was cranked up into the red zone.

And of course, the irony was that the purpose of his being here, on this morning, in this alley . . . the purpose of all the cars and the men and the tape . . . was perfectly silent.

José gripped his Styrofoam cup as he peered over the rusted lip of the bin. Her hand was the first thing he saw, a pale lineup of fingers with nails that were split and had something brown under them.

She'd been a fighter, whoever she was.

As he stood over yet another dead girl, he wished like hell his job would go through a slow month or week . . . or for shit's sake, even a night. Hell, a career slump was what he was really gunning for: When you were in his line of work, it was hard to take satisfaction in what you did. Even if you solved a case, someone was still burying a loved one.

The cop next to him sounded like he was on the business end of a bullhorn: "You want me to open the other half?"

José almost told the guy to pipe down, but chances were good he was talking like he was in a library. "Yeah. Thanks."

The officer used a nightstick to push the lid up far enough for the light to stream in, but the guy didn't look inside. He just stood there like one of those stiffs in front of Buckingham Palace, staring out across the alley while focusing on nothing.

As José rose up onto the balls of his feet and got a look, he didn't blame the uni for his reticence.

Lying in a bed of metal curls, the female was naked, her gray, mottled skin strangely luminous in the dawn's diffused light. Going by her face and body, she looked to be in her late teens, early twenties. Caucasian. Hair had been cut off at the roots, so close in places that the scalp was lacerated. Eyes . . . had been removed from their sockets.

José took a pen out of his pocket, stretched downward, and carefully pushed her stiff lips apart. No teeth—not a one left in the ragged gums.

Moving to the right, he upped one of her hands so he could see the underside of the fingertips. Sheered clean off.

And the defacement didn't end at the head and hands. . . . There were gouges in her flesh, one at the top of her thigh, another down her upper arm, and two on the insides of her wrists.

Cursing under his breath, he was certain she'd been dumped here. Not enough privacy to do this kind of work—this shit required time and tools . . . and restraints to keep her put.

"What do we have, Detective?" his new partner said from behind him.

José glanced over his shoulder at Thomas DelVecchio, Jr. "Have you had breakfast yet?"

"No."

"Good."

He stepped back so Veck could have a look. As the guy was taller by nearly six inches, he didn't have to arch up to see in; all he did was tilt at the hips. And then he just stared. No lurching over to the wall and throwing up. No gasping. No real change in expression, either.

"The body was dumped here," Veck said. "Had to be."

"Her."

Veck looked over, his dark blue eyes smart and unfazed. "I'm sorry?"

"*She* was dumped here. That's a person. Not a thing, DelVecchio."

"Right. Sorry. She." The guy leaned in again. "I think we've got ourselves a trophy keeper."

"Maybe."

Dark brows shot up. "There's a lot missing . . . on her."

"You watch CNN lately?" José wiped his pen on a tissue.

"I don't have time for TV."

"Eleven women have been found like this in the past year. Chicago, Cleveland and Philly."

"Shiiiiiit." Veck popped a piece of gum in his mouth and chewed hard. "So you're wondering if this is the beginning for us?"

As the guy ground his molars, José rubbed his eyes against memories that bubbled up. "When did you quit?"

Veck cleared his throat. "Smoking? 'Bout a month ago."

"How's it going?"

"Sucks ass."

"I'll bet."

José put his hands on his hips and refocused. How the hell were they going to find out who this girl was? There were a countless number of missing young women in the state of New York—and that was assuming the killer hadn't done this in Vermont or Massachusetts or Connecticut and driven her here.

One thing was for sure: He'd be damned if some motherfucker was going to start picking off Caldie's girls. Wasn't going to happen on his watch.

As he turned away, he clapped his partner on the shoulder. "I give you ten days, buddy."

"Till what."

"Till you're back in the saddle with the Marlboro Man."

"Don't underestimate my willpower, Detective."

"Don't underestimate what you're going to feel like when you go home and try to sleep tonight."

"I don't sleep much, anyway."

"This job ain't gonna help."

At that moment, the photographer arrived with her click-click, flash-flash, and her bad attitude.

José nodded in the opposite direction. "Let's back off and let her do her thing."

Veck glanced over and his eyes popped as he got glared at but good. The fuck-off reception was no doubt a news flash for the guy—Veck was one of those types women gravitated to, as the last two weeks had proven: Down at HQ, the females were all over him.

"Come on, DelVecchio, let's start casing this joint."

"Roger that, Detective."

Ordinarily, José might have had the guy call him de la Cruz, but none of his "new" partners had lasted much longer than a month, so what was the point. "José" was out of the question, of course—only one person had called him that on the job, and that bastard had disappeared three years ago.

It took about an hour for him and Veck to nose around and learn absolutely nothing material. There were no security cameras on the outsides of the buildings and no witnesses who had come forward, but the CSI guys were going to crawl all around with their headgear and their little plastic baggies and their tweezers. Maybe something would turn up.

The coroner showed at nine and did his thing, and the body was cleared for removal another hour or so after that. And when folks needed a hand with the body, José was surprised to find that Veck snapped on a pair of latex specials and jumped right in that Dumpster.

Just before the coroner took off with her, José asked about the time of death and was told about noontime the day before.

Great, he thought as the cars and vans started to pull out. Nearly twenty-four hours dead before they found her. She could well have been driven in from out of state.

"Database time," he said to Veck.

"I'm on it."

As the guy turned away and headed for a motorcycle, José called out, "Gum is not a food group."

Veck stopped and glanced over his shoulder. "Are you asking me for breakfast, Detective."

"Just don't want you passing out on the job. It would embarrass you and give me another body to step over."

"You're all heart, Detective."

Maybe he used to be. Now he was just hungry himself and he didn't feel like eating alone. "I'll meet you at the twenty-four in five."

"Twenty-four?"

That's right; he wasn't from here. "Riverside Diner on Eighth Street. Open twenty-four hours a day."

"Got it." The guy put on a black helmet and swung a leg over some kind of contraption that was mostly engine. "I'm buying."

"Suit yourself."

Veck slammed the kick start down and juiced the motor. "I always do, Detective. Always."

As he tore off, he left a wake of testosterone in the alley, and José felt like a middle-aged minivanner in comparison as he schlepped over to his oatmeal-colored unmarked. Sliding behind the wheel, he put his nearly empty and totally cold Dunkin' Donuts fister into the cup holder and looked past the tape to that Dumpster.

Nabbing his cell phone out of his suit jacket, he dialed into HQ. "Hey, it's de la Cruz. Can you patch me over to Mary Ellen?" The wait was less than a minute. "M.E., how you be? Good . . . good. Listen, I want to hear the call that came in about the body over by the Commodore. Yup. Sure—just play it back. Thanks—and take your time."

José shoved the key into the slot at the steering wheel. "Great, thanks, M.E."

He took a deep breath and cranked the engine over—

Yeah, I'd like to rahport a dead bahdy. Nah, I'm not giving my name. It's in a Dumpstah in an alley off Tenth Street, two blocks ova from th' Commahdore. Looks to be a Caucasian female, late teens, early twenties . . . Nah, I'm not giving my name. . . . Hey, how 'bout you get down the address and stahp worrying 'bout me. . . .

José gripped his phone and started to shake all over.

The South Boston accent was so clear and so familiar it was like time had gotten into a car wreck and whiplashed backward.

"Detective? You want to hear it again?" he heard Mary Ellen say in his ear.

Closing his eyes, he croaked out, "Yes, please . . ."

When the recording was finished, he listened to himself thank Mary Ellen and felt his thumb hit the *end* button to terminate the call.

Sure as water down a sink drain, he was sucked into a nightmare from about two years ago . . . when he'd walked into a shitty, run-down apartment that was full of empty Lagavulin bottles and pizza boxes. He remembered his hand reaching out to a closed bathroom door, the damn thing quaking from palm to fingertips.

He'd been convinced he was going to find a dead body on the other side. Hanging from the showerhead by a belt . . . or maybe lying in the tub soaking in blood instead of bubble bath.

Butch O'Neal had made hard living as much of a professional pursuit as his job in the homicide department. He'd been a late-night drinker, and not just a relationship-phobe, but completely incapable of forming attachments.

Except he and José had been tight. As tight as Butch had ever gotten with anyone.

No suicide, though. No body. Nothing. One night he'd been around; the next . . . gone.

For the first month or two, José had expected to hear something—either from the guy himself or because a corpse with a busted nose and a badly capped front tooth turned up somewhere.

Days had slid into weeks, however, and in turn had dumped into seasons of the year. And he supposed he became something like a doctor who had a terminal disease: He finally knew firsthand how the families of missing persons felt. And God, that dreaded, cold stretch of Not Knowing was nothing he'd ever expected to wander down . . . but with his old partner's disappearance, he didn't just walk it; he bought a lot, put up a house, and moved the fuck in.

Now, though, after he'd given up all hope, after he no longer woke up in the middle of the night with the wonders . . . now this recording.

Sure, millions of people had Southie accents. But O'Neal had had a telltale hoarseness in his voice that couldn't be replicated.

Abruptly, José didn't feel like going to the twenty-four, and he didn't want anything to eat. But he put his unmarked in drive and hit the gas.

The moment he'd looked into the Dumpster and seen those missing eyes and that dental job, he'd known that he was going in search of a serial killer. But he couldn't have guessed he'd be on another search.

Time to find Butch O'Neal.

If he could.

SIXTEEN

One week later, Manny woke up in his own bed with a stinger of a hangover. The good news was that at least this headache could be explained: When he'd come home, he'd hit the Lag like a punching bag and it had done its job, smacking him back and knocking him flat on his ass.

The first thing he did was reach over and get his phone. With blurry eyes, he called the vet's cell. The pair of them had a little early-morning ritual going, and he thanked God that the guy was also an insomniac.

The vet answered on the second ring. "Hello?"

"How's my girl?" The pause told him everything he had to know. "That bad?"

"Well, her vitals remain good, and she remains as comfortable as she can be in her suspension, but I'm worried about the foundering. We'll see."

"Keep me posted."

"Always."

At that point, hanging up was the only thing he could do. The conversation was over, and it wasn't like he was a shoot-the-shit kind of guy—although even if he had been, chitchat wasn't going to get him what he wanted, which was a healthy fucking horse.

Before his alarm went off at six thirty and put paid on the shot-through-the-head routine, he slapped his radio clock into perma-silence and thought, Workout. Coffee. Back to the hospital.

Wait. Coffee, workout, hospital.

He definitely needed caffeine first. He wasn't fit to run or lift weights in this condition—and shouldn't be operating heavy machinery like an elevator, either.

As he shifted his feet to the floor and went vertical, his head had a heartbeat of its own, but he revolted against the idea that maybe, just maybe, the pain wasn't about the liquor: He was not sick, and he wasn't cooking up a brain tumor—although if he was, he'd still go in to St. Francis. It was in his nature. Hell, when he'd been young, he'd fought to go to school when he was ill—even when he'd had the chicken pox and had looked like a connect-the-dots canvas, he'd insisted on heading for the bus.

His mother had won that particular one. And bitched that he was just like his father.

Not a compliment, and something he'd heard all his life—also something that didn't mean shit because he'd never met the guy. All he had was a faded picture that was the only thing he'd ever put in a frame—

Why the hell was he thinking about that this morning?

Coffee was Starbucks Breakfast Blend. Workout clothes went on while it was brewing, and two mugs were downed over the sink as he watched the superearly traffic snake around the Northway's curves in the dim light of dawn. The last thing he did was grab his iPod and put it in his ears. He was not a chatter to begin with, but Lord help some chipper chick with a motormouth today.

Downstairs in the workout room, the place was fairly empty, which was a huge relief, but not something that was going to last. Hopping on the treadmill closest to the door, he turned off the CNBC newscast on the overhead TV and got huffing.

Judas Priest carried his feet, and his mind unplugged, and his stiff, aching body got what it needed. All things considered, he was better than he had been coming out of the previous weekend. The headaches were still hanging in, but he was keeping up with his work and patient load, and functioning all right.

It made him wonder, though. Right before Jane had hit that tree, she'd had headaches, too. So if they'd been able to do an autopsy on the body, would they have found an aneurysm? Then again, what were the chances of the two of them both having one within—

Why did you do it, Jane? Why fake your death?

I don't have time to explain now. Please. I know this is asking a lot. But there's a patient who needs you, desperately, and I've been looking for you for over an hour, so I'm out of time—

"Fuck—" Manny quickly popped his feet off onto the side gunwales and gritted his teeth against the agony. Draping his upper body over the machine's instrument panel, he breathed slow and steady—or as much as someone who'd been running a six-minute-mile pace could.

Over the last seven days, he'd learned through trial and error that when the pain struck, the best call was to blank out his mind and focus on nothing at all. And the fact that the simple cognitive trick worked was reassuring on the whole aneurysm front: If something was going to blow a hole in the wall of a cerebral artery, ain't no yoga-two-part-breath shit going to make a difference.

There was a pattern, however. The onset seemed to follow thoughts either about Jane . . . or that wet dream he kept having.

Fucking hell, he'd had enough orgasms in his sleep to lame out even his libido. And, sick bastard that he was, the near-guarantee of being back with that female in his fantasies made him look forward to hitting the pillow for the first time in his life.

Although he couldn't explain why certain cognitions would bring on the headaches, the good news was that he *was* getting better. Each day after that bizarre black hole of a weekend, he felt a bit more like himself.

When there was little but a dull ache remaining, Manny got back on the treadmill and finished the workout. On his way to the exit, he nodded to the early-morning stragglers who'd come in, but took off before anyone could Oh-my-God-are-you-okay him if they'd seen him take his breather.

Up in his place, he showered, changed into clean scrubs and his white jacket, and then grabbed his briefcase and hit the elevators. To beat the traffic, he took the surface roads through the city. The Northway was invariably jammed this time of day, and he made great time while he listened to old-school My Chemical Romance.

"I'm Not Okay" was a tune he couldn't get enough of for some reason.

As he turned into the St. Francis Hospital complex, dawn's early light had yet to break through fully, which suggested they were going to have clouds. Not that it mattered to him. Once he was inside the belly of the beast, short of a tornado, which had never happened in Caldwell, the weather didn't affect him in the slightest. Hell, a lot of days, he came to work when it was dark and left when it was dark—but he'd never felt like he was missing out on life just because he wasn't all *I've seen sunshine, I've seen rain. . . .*

Funny. He felt out of the loop now, though.

He'd come here from Yale Medical School after his surgical residency, and he'd meant to go on to Boston, or Manhattan, or Chicago. Instead, he'd made his mark here, and now it was over ten years later and he was still where he'd started. Granted, he was at the top of the heap, so to speak, and he'd saved and improved lives, and he'd taught the next generation of surgeons.

The trouble was, as he went down the ramp into the parking garage, all that seemed hollow, somehow.

He was forty-five years old, with at least half of his useful life in the bin, and what did he have to show for it? A condo full of Nike shit and a job that had taken over all his nooks and crannies. No wife. No kids. Christmases and New Years and Fourths of July were spent at the hospital—with his mother finding her own way for the holidays and no doubt pining for grandchildren she'd better not be holding her breath for.

Christ, how many random women had he fucked over the years? Hundreds. Had to be.

His mother's voice shot through his head: *You're just like your father.*

Too true. His dad had also been a surgeon. With a wandering streak.

It was actually why Manny had picked Caldwell. His mother had been here at St. Francis as an ICU nurse, working to put him through his years and years of schooling. And when he'd graduated from med school? Instead of pride, there had been distance and reserve in her face. . . . The closer he'd become to what his father had been, the more often she'd gotten that faraway look in her eye. His idea had been that if they were in the same city, they'd start relating or some shit. Hadn't worked out that way, though.

But she was okay. She was down in Florida now in a house on a golf course that he'd paid for, playing rounds of scramble with ladies her age, having dinner with the bridge brigade and arguing over who snubbed who on the party circuit. He was more than happy to support her, and that was the extent of their relationship.

Dads was in a grave in Pine Grove Cemetery. He'd died in 1983 in a car accident.

Dangerous things, cars.

Parking the Porsche, he got out and took the stairs instead of the elevators for the exercise; then he used the pedestrian walkway to enter the hospital on the third floor. As he passed by doctors and nurses and staff, he just nodded at them and kept going. Usually, he went to his office first, but no matter what he told his feet to do, that was not where he ended up today.

He was heading for the recovery suites.

He told himself it was to check on patients, but that was a lie. And as his head became fuzzier and fuzzier, he studiously ignored the fog. Hell, it was better than the pain—and he was probably just hypoglycemic from working out and not eating anything afterward.

Patient . . . he was looking for his patient. . . . No name. He had no name, but he knew the room.

As he came up to the suite closest to the fire escape at the end of the hall, a flush shot through his body and he found himself making sure his white coat was hanging smoothly from his shoulders and then doing a hand-pass through his hair to neaten it up.

Clearing his throat, he braced himself, stepped inside, and—

The eighty-year-old man in the bed was asleep, but not at rest, tubes going in and out of him like he was a car in the process of being jump-started.

Dull pain thumped in Manny's head as he stood there staring at the guy.

"Dr. Manello?"

Goldberg's voice from behind him was a relief, because it gave him something concrete to grab onto . . . the lip of the pool, so to speak.

He turned around. "Hey. Good morning."

The guy's brows popped and then he frowned. "Ah . . . what are you doing here?"

"What do you think. Checking on a patient." Jesus, maybe everyone was losing their minds.

"I thought you were going to take a week off."

"Excuse me?"

"That's . . . ah . . . that's what you told me when you left this morning. After we . . . found you in here."

"What are you talking about?" But then Manny waved a hand in dismissal. "Listen, let me get some breakfast first—"

"It's dinnertime, Dr. Manello. Six o'clock at night? You left here twelve hours ago."

The flush that had heated him up whirlpooled out of him and was instantly replaced by a cold wash of something he never, ever felt.

Icy fear bowled him over and sent his pins spinning.

The awkward silence that followed was broken by the hustle and bustle out in the corridor, people rushing by in soft-soled shoes, hurrying to patients or rolling bins of laundry along or taking meals . . . dinner, natch . . . from room to room.

"I'm . . . going to go home now," Manny said.

His voice was still as strong as ever, but the expression on his colleague's face revealed the truth in and around him: No matter what he told himself about feeling better, he was not what he once had been. He looked the same. He sounded the same. He walked the same.

He even tried to convince himself he was the same.

But something had changed that weekend, and he feared that there was no going back from it.

"Would you like someone to drive you?" Goldberg asked tentatively.

"No. I'm fine."

It took all the pride he had not to start running as he turned to leave: By force of will, he kicked back his head and straightened his spine and put one foot calmly in front of the other.

Oddly, as he went out the way he'd come in, he thought of his old surgery professor . . . the one who'd been "retired" by the school admin when he'd turned seventy. Manny had been a second-year med student at the time.

Dr. Theodore Benedict Standford III.

The guy had been a straight-up hard-ass prick in class, the kind of fucker who liked it best when the students gave the wrong answer, because it provided him with an opportunity to dress people down. When the school had announced his departure at the end of the year, Manny and his classmates had thrown a going-away party for the sorry bastard, all of them getting drunk in celebration that they were the last generation to be subjected to his bullshit.

Manny had been working as a custodian at the school that summer for cash, and he'd been mopping the hallway when the last of the movers had taken the final boxes from Standford's office . . . and then the old man himself had turned the corner and wing-tipped it out for the last time.

He'd left with his head high, walking down the marble stairs and leaving through the majestic front entrance with his chin up.

Manny had laughed at the arrogance of the man, undying even in the face of age and obsolescence.

Now, walking that same way, he wondered if that had been true.

More likely, Standford had felt as Manny did now.

Discarded.

SEVENTEEN

Jane heard the tearing sound all the way down in the training center's office. The ripping woke her up, yanking her head off the pillow of her forearms and snapping her spine straight from its curl over the desk.

Ripping . . . and flapping . . .

At first, she thought it was a gust of wind, but then her brain clicked on. No windows here underground. And it would take a damn thunderstorm to create that much of a disturbance.

Bolting up from the chair and scrambling around the desk, she hit the corridor outside in a run as she gunned for Payne's room. All doors were open for precisely this reason: She had only one patient, and although Payne was mostly quiet, if something happened—

What the *hell* was all that noise? There was grunting, too—

Jane skidded around the doorjamb of the recovery room and just about screamed. Oh, God . . . the *blood.*

"Payne!" She rushed for the bed.

V's twin was going wild, her arms flailing around, her fingers clawing at the sheets and also at herself, her sharp nails biting into the skin of her upper arms and shoulders and collarbones.

"I can't feel it!" the female yelled, her fangs flashing, her eyes so wide there was white all around them. "I can't feel anything!"

Jane lunged forward and grabbed one of those arms, but her grip slipped the instant contact was made, snapping off all those slick scratches. "Payne! Stop it!"

As Jane fought to still her patient, bright red blood spackled her face and white coat.

"Payne!" If this kept up, those wounds were going to be deep enough to show bone. "Stop—"

"I can't feel it!"

The Bic pen appeared in Payne's hand from out of nowhere—except, no, it wasn't magical. . . . The thing was Jane's, the one she kept in the side pocket of her white coat. The instant she saw it, all the furious flapping morphed into a surreal slow-mo as Payne's hand lifted up.

Her stabbing swipe was so strong and sure that there was no stopping it.

The sharp point pierced through the female's heart, dead on, and her torso jerked upward, a death gasp shooting in through her open mouth.

Jane screamed, "*Noooooo*—"

"Jane—wake up!"

The sound of Vishous's voice made no sense. Except then she opened her eyes . . . to complete darkness. The clinic and the blood and Payne's hoarse breathing were replaced by a black visual shroud that—

Candles flared to life, and the first thing she saw properly was Vishous's hard face. He was right beside her, even though they hadn't gone to bed at the same time.

"Jane, it was only a dream. . . ."

"I'm okay," she blurted, shoving her hair out of her face. "I'm . . ."

While she propped herself up on her arms and panted, she wasn't sure what was dream and what was real. Especially given that Vishous was next to her. Not only had they not been going to bed together; they hadn't been waking up together either. She assumed he was sleeping down in his forge, but maybe that hadn't been the case.

She hoped it hadn't.

"Jane . . ."

In the dim quiet, she heard in the word all the sadness that V never would have let out in any other situation. And she felt the same way. The days without them talking much, the stress of Payne's recovery, the distance . . . the goddamn distance . . . it was so damned sad.

Here in the candlelight, in their mated bed, though, all that faded some.

With a sigh, she turned into his warm, heavy body and the contact changed her: Without having to turn herself solid, she became corporeal, the heat flowing between them and magnifying and making her as real as he was. Looking up, she stared at his fierce, beautiful face with its tattoo at the temple and the black hair that he always shoved back and the slashing eyebrows and those icy pale eyes.

Over the past week, she'd played and replayed that night when things had gotten so rough. And though a lot of it was disappointing and anxious-making, there was one thing that just didn't make sense.

When they'd met up in the tunnel, Vishous had been wearing a turtleneck. And he never wore turtlenecks. He hated them because he found them confining—which was ironic, given what sometimes got him off. Typically, he wore muscle shirts or went naked, and she wasn't stupid. He might be a hard-core hard-ass, but his skin bruised as easily as anyone else's did.

He'd said he'd gotten into a fight, but he was a master at hand-to-hand combat. So if he was pulling a head-to-toe black-and-blue it happened for only one reason: because he allowed it.

And she had to wonder who had done it to him.

"You all right?" V asked.

She reached up and put her palm on his cheek. "Are you?" Were they?

He didn't blink. "What was the dream about?"

"We're going to have to talk about things, V."

His lips thinned out. And got even tighter as she waited. Finally, he said, "Payne is where she is. It's only been a week and—"

"Not about her. About what happened that night you were out alone."

Now he eased back, sinking into the pillows and linking his two hands over his tight abs. In the dim light, the tight bands of muscle and ropes of vein that ran up his neck threw sharp shadows.

"You accusing me of being with someone else? I thought we went through this."

"Stop deflecting." She stared at him steadily. "And if you want to pick a fight, go find some *lessers*."

In any other male, her hitting back like that might have guaranteed a flat-out argument, with all the attendant dramatics.

Instead, Vishous turned to her and smiled. "Listen to you."

"I'd rather you talked to me."

The sexual light that she was so familiar with, but hadn't seen in a week, boiled up in his eyes as he rolled over toward her. Then his lids lowered and he looked at her breasts underneath the simple Hanes T-shirt she'd fallen asleep in.

She put her face in the way, but she was smiling, too. Things had been so stiff and strained between them. This felt normal. "I'm not going to be distracted."

As heat poured out of his big body in waves, her mate took his fingertip and trailed it along her shoulder. And then he opened his mouth, the white tips of his fangs making an appearance and getting even longer as he licked his lips.

Somehow, the sheet that was covering him got tugged down his ribbed abdomen. Lower. Lower still. It was his gloved hand doing the duty, and with every inch exposed, her eyes had more trouble going anywhere else. He stopped right before his massive erection was revealed, but he gave her a show: The tattoos around his groin stretched and righted themselves as his hips curled and relaxed, curled and relaxed.

"Vishous . . ."

"What."

His gloved hand dipped under the black satin, and she didn't have to see where it went to be well aware he'd gripped himself: The fact that he arched back told her everything she needed to know. That and the way he bit down on his lower lip.

"Jane . . ."

"What."

"Are you just going to watch, true?"

God, she remembered the first time she'd seen him like this, all laid out on a bed, erect, ready. She'd been giving him a sponge bath, and he'd read her like a book: As much as she hadn't wanted to admit it, she'd been desperate to watch him get off.

And she'd made sure he had.

Feeling heated herself, she leaned over to him, dropping her mouth so that it almost touched his. "You're still deflecting—"

In a flash, his free hand snapped up and clasped the back of her neck, trapping her. And didn't that power in him go straight down between her thighs.

"Yes. I am." His tongue came out and flicked across her lip. "But we can always talk after we're through. You know I never lie."

"I thought the line was more like . . . you're never wrong."

"Well, that's true, too." A pumping growl came out of him. "And right now . . . you and I need this."

That last part was said with none of the passion and all of the seriousness she needed to hear. And what do you know, he was right. The pair of them had been circling for the last seven days, stepping carefully, avoiding the land mine in the center of their relationship. Connecting like this, skin-to-skin, was going to help them get through to the words that had to be spoken.

"So what do you say?" he murmured.

"What are you waiting for?"

The laugh he let out was low and satisfied, and his forearm tightened and released as he started to stroke himself. "Pull the sheet back, Jane."

The command was husky, but clear, and it got to her. As it always did.

"Do it, Jane. Watch me."

She put her hand on his pec and drifted it downward, feeling the ribs of his chest and the hard ridges of his abdominals, hearing the hiss as he drew a sharp breath in through his teeth. Lifting the sheet, she had to swallow hard as the head of him breached the top of his fist, breaking free and offering itself with a single, crystal tear.

When she reached out for him, he snapped a hold on her wrist and held her back.

"Look at me, Jane . . ." came the groan. "But don't touch."

Son of a bitch. She hated when he did this. Loved it, too.

Vishous didn't let go of his hold on her as he worked his erection with his gloved hand, his body so beautiful as it found a rhythm with the pump of his palm. Candlelight turned the whole episode into something mysterious, but then . . . it was always like that with V. With him, she never knew what to expect, and not just because he was the son of a deity. He was sex on the edge all the time, hard-cornered and crafty, twisted and demanding.

And she knew that she merely got the watered-down version of him.

There were deeper caves in his underground maze, ones that she had never visited and could never go to.

"Jane," he said roughly. "Whatever you're thinking about, drop it. . . . Stay with me here and now and don't go there."

She closed her eyes. She'd known what she was mating and what she loved. Back when she'd committed to him for eternity, she'd been well aware of the men and the women and the way he'd had them. She'd just never have guessed that that past would come between them—

"I wasn't with anyone else." His voice was strong and sure. "That night. I swear to it."

Her lids lifted. He'd stopped working himself out and was lying still.

Abruptly, the sight of him was obscured by tears. "I'm so sorry," she croaked. "I just needed to hear that. I trust you, I honestly do, but I—"

"Shh . . . it's okay." His gloved hand reached out and brushed the tear from her cheek. "It's all right. Why wouldn't you question what's doing with me?"

"It's wrong."

"No, I'm wrong." He took a deep breath. "I've spent the last week trying to force things to come out of my mouth. I've hated this shit, but I didn't know what the hell to say that wouldn't make it worse."

On some level, she was surprised at the compassion and the understanding. The two of them were so very independent and that was why their relationship worked: He was reserved and she didn't need much emotional support, and usually that math added up beautifully.

Not this week, however.

"I'm sorry, too," he murmured. "And I wish I were a different kind of male."

Somehow, she knew he was talking about so much more than his reserved nature. "There's nothing you can't talk to me about, V." When all she got back was a "Hmm," she said, "There's a lot of stress right now for you. I know that. And I would do anything to help you."

"I love you."

"Then you've got to talk to me. The one thing guaranteed not to work is silence."

"I know. But it's like looking into a dark room. I want to tell you shit, but I can't . . . I can't see anything I feel."

She believed that—and recognized it as something that victims of child abuse tended to struggle with in adulthood. The early survival mechanism that got them through everything was compartmentalization: When things got too much to handle, they fractured their inner selves and stashed their emotions far, far away.

The danger, of course, was the pressure that invariably built up.

At least the ice between them was broken, though. And they were in this quiet, semi-peaceful space now.

Of their own volition, her eyes drifted down to his arousal, which lay flat up his stomach, stretching even beyond his navel. Suddenly, she wanted him so badly she couldn't speak.

"Take me, Jane," he growled. "Do whatever the fuck you want to me."

What she wanted to do was suck on him and so she did, bending over his hips, taking him into her mouth, drawing him down to the back of her throat. The sound he made was all animal, and his hips jerked up, pushing the hot length of him farther into her. Then one of his knees abruptly bent up so that he wasn't just prone, but sprawled, as he gave himself over to her completely, cupping the back of her head while she found a rhythm that drove him—

The shift of her body was both fast and smooth.

With his tremendous strength, V repositioned her in the blink of an eye, pivoting her around and shoving the sheets out of the way so he could lift her hips up and over his torso. Her thighs were split over his face and—

"Vishous," she said around his erection.

His mouth was slick and warm and right on target, fusing with her sex, latching on and sucking before his tongue snaked out and licked inside of her. Her brain didn't so much turn off as explode, and with nothing left to think with, she was blissfully lost in what was happening and not what had gone before. She had a feeling V was the same. . . . He was all about the stroking, lapping at her and sucking on her, his hands digging into her thighs as he moaned her name against her core. And it was damn hard to concentrate on what he was doing to her at the same time she was doing it for him, but what a problem to have. His erection in her mouth was hot and hard, and he was pure velvet between her legs, and the sensations were proof that even though she was a ghost, her physical reactions were just the same as when she'd been "alive"—

"Fuck, I need you," he cursed.

On another quick burst of power, Vishous lifted her as if she didn't weigh more than the sheet did, and the shift was not a surprise. He always preferred to come inside her, deep inside of her, and he spread her legs before settling her on top of his hips, his blunt head nudging into her . . . *and slamming home.*

The invasion was not just about sex, but him staking his claim, and she loved it. This was the way it should be.

Falling forward and bracing herself against his shoulders, she stared into his eyes as they moved together, the rhythm pounding until they came at the same time, both of them going rigid as he jerked inside of her and her sex milked him. And then V flipped her onto her back and shot down her body, going back to where he'd been, his mouth fusing on her, his palms locking on her thighs as he ate at her.

As she came hard, there was no break or pause. He surged forward, stretching up both her legs and swording in, entering her on a solid stroke and taking over. His body was a massive, pistoning machine on top of her, his bonding scent roaring in the room as he orgasmed hard, the week of abstinence getting dusted in one glorious session.

While his orgasm rocked through him, she watched him as he came, loving all parts of him, even the ones that she sometimes struggled to understand.

And then he kept going. More sex. And still more.

Nearly an hour later, they were finally sated, lying still and breathing deep in the candlelight.

Vishous rolled them over, keeping them joined, and his eyes roamed her face for a long moment. "I have no words. Sixteen languages, but no words."

There was both love and despair in his voice. He was truly handicapped when it came to emotions, and falling in love hadn't changed that . . . at least, not when things were as stressful as they were right now. But that was okay—after this time together it was okay.

"It's all right." She kissed his pec. "I understand you."

"I just wish you didn't have to."

"You get me."

"Yeah, but you're easy."

Jane propped herself up. "I'm a frickin' ghost. In case you haven't noticed. Not something a lot of men would be psyched about."

V pulled her to his mouth for a quick, hard kiss. "But I get you for the rest of my life."

"That you do." Humans, after all, didn't last a tenth of what vampires did.

When the alarm went off beside them, V glared at the thing. "Now I know why I sleep with a gun under my pillow."

As he reached out to silence the clock, she had to agree. "You know, you could just shoot it."

"Nah, Butch would get his ass in here, and I don't want a weapon in my palm if he ever sees you naked."

Jane smiled and then lay back as he got out of bed and walked over to the bathroom. At the door, he paused and looked over his shoulder. "I came to you, Jane. Every night this week, I came to you. I didn't want you to be alone. And I didn't want to sleep without you."

On that note, he ducked into the bath, and a moment later she heard the shower come on.

He was better at words than he thought.

With a satisfied stretch, she knew she had to get up and moving, too—time to relieve Ehlena from her day shift in the clinic. But man, she would love to lie here all night. Maybe just a little longer . . .

Vishous left ten minutes later to go to meet with Wrath and the Brotherhood, and he kissed her on the way to the exit. Twice.

Getting out of bed, she hit the bathroom for a while, and then went to their closet and opened the double doors. Hanging from the rod there were leathers—his; plain white T-shirts—hers; white coats—hers; biker jackets—his. The weapons were all locked up in a fire safe; shoes were down on the floor.

Her life was in many ways incomprehensible. Ghost married to a vampire? Come on.

But looking at this closet, so nice and arranged with their crazy lives at rest among these carefully placed clothes and footwear, she felt good about where they were. "Normal" was not a bad thing in this lunatic world; it really wasn't.

No matter how it happened to be defined.

EIGHTEEN

Down in the training center's clinic, Payne was doing her exercises, as she'd come to think of them.

Lying in the hospital bed with the pillows pushed to the side, she crossed her arms over her chest and tightened her stomach, pulling her torso upright on a slow rise. When she was perpendicular to the mattress, she extended her arms straight out and held them there while she eased back down. After even one round, her heart was pounding and her breath was short, but she gave herself only a brief recovery and repeated. And repeated. And repeated.

Each time the effort grew progressively more strenuous, until sweat beaded on her forehead and her stomach muscles strained into pain. Jane had shown her how to do this, and she supposed it was a benefit—although compared to what she had been capable of, it was a spark measured against a bonfire.

Indeed, Jane had tried to get her to do so much more . . . had even wheeled in a chair for her to sit in and ambulate, but Payne couldn't bear the sight of the thing, or the idea of spending her life rolling from place to place.

In the past week, she had summarily closed off all avenues of accommodation in the hopes of a singular miracle . . . that had never materialized.

It felt like centuries since she'd fought with Wrath . . . since she had known the coordination and strength of her limbs. She had taken so much for granted, and now she missed who she had once been with a grief that she'd assumed one had only for the dead.

Then again, she supposed she had died. Her body just wasn't smart enough to stop working.

With a curse in the Old Language, she collapsed back and left herself lying there. When she was able, she found the leather strap that she had cranked down over her thighs. The thing was so tight, she knew it was cutting off circulation, but she felt neither the constriction of the binding nor any sweet release as she sprang the clasp and the leather popped loose.

It had been thus since the night she had returned herein.

No change.

Closing her eyes, she reentered into an inner war whereupon her fears drew swords against her mind, and the results were e'er more tragic. After seven cycles of night and day, her army of rationality was suffering from a sorry lack of ammunition and deep fatigue amongst its troops. Thus, the tide was turning. First, she had been buoyed by optimism, but that had faded, and then there had been a period of resolved patience, which had not lasted long. Since then, she had tarried along this barren road of baseless hope.

Alone.

Verily, the loneliness was the worst part of the ordeal: For all the people who were free to come and go, in and out of her room, she was utterly separate even when they sat and talked to her or attended to her very basic needs. Confined to this bed, she was on another plane of reality from them, separated by a vast, invisible desert that she could see clearly o'er, but was unable to cross.

And it was strange. All that she had lost became most acute whenever she thought of her human healer—which was so often she could not count the times.

Oh, how she missed that man. Many were the hours she had spent remembering his voice and his face and that last moment between them . . . until her memories became a blanket with which to warm herself during the long, cold stretches of worry and concern.

Unfortunately, however, much like her rational side, that blanket was fraying from overuse, and there was no repairing it.

Her healer was not of her world and ne'er to return—nothing but a brief, vivid dream that had disintegrated into filaments and fragments now that she had awoken.

"Cease," she said to herself out loud.

With the upper-body strength she was trying to maintain, she turned to the side for the two pillows, fighting against the deadweight of her lower body as she strained to—

Her balance failed in a flash, and sent her careening even in her prone position, her arm knocking the glass of water from the table next to her.

And alas, it was not an object well suited for impact.

As it shattered, Payne closed her mouth, which was the only way she knew to keep her screams in her lungs. Otherwise, they would breach the seal of her lips and ne'er stop.

When she thought she had enough self-control, she looked over the side of the bed at the mess on the floor. Ordinarily, it would be so simple—something spilled and one would clean it up.

Previously, all she would have done was bend over and mop it up.

Now? She had two choices: Lie here and call for help like an invalid. Or prethink and strategize and make an attempt to be independent.

It took her some time to figure out the bracing points for her hands and then judge the distance to the floor. Fortunately, she was unplugged from all the tubing that had been running into her arm, but a catheter remained . . . so mayhap trying to do this herself was a bad idea.

Yet she could not bear the indignity of just lying here. No soldier was she; now she was a child incapable of caring for herself.

It was no longer supportable.

Snapping out squares of "Kleenex," as people called them, she lowered the railing on the bed, gripped the top of it, and curled herself over onto her side. The torsion caused her legs to flop around like those of a puppet, all motion without grace, but at least she could reach downward to the smooth floor with the white fluff on her palm.

As she stretched whilst trying to maintain a precarious balance on the ledge of the bed, she was tired of being done for, tended to, washed and wrapped like a young newly born unto the world—

Her body went the way of the glass.

Without warning, her grip slipped off the smooth rail, and with her hips so far off the mattress, she fell headfirst toward the floor, the grab of gravity too strong for her to overcome. Throwing out her hands, she caught herself on the wet flooring, but both palms shot from under her and she took the force of impact on the side of the face, breath exploding out of her lungs.

And then there was no movement.

She was trapped, the bed buttressing her useless limbs so that they remained directly over her head and torso, cramming her into the floor.

Dragging air down her throat, she called out, "Help . . . *hellllp* . . ."

With her face squeezed, her arms starting to go numb, and her lungs burning from suffocation, rage lit up within her until her body trembled—

It started as a squeak. Then the noise turned into movement as her cheek began to skid on the tile, the skin stretching so thin, she felt like it was being peeled off her skull. And then pressure grew on the nape of her neck, her thick braid pulling her head in one direction at the same time her strange position drove her forward.

Summoning all her strength, she focused her rage and maneuvered her arms so that her palms were back flat to the floor. After a tremendous inhale, she shoved hard, pushing herself up and flipping herself on her back—

Her rope of hair fell in and among the railing's supports and locked in tight, the thick length keeping her in place, whilst wrenching her neck to her shoulder. Trapped and going nowhere, she could see only her legs from her vantage point, her long, slender legs that she had never before given any particular thought to.

As the blood gradually pooled into her torso, she watched the skin on her calves get paper white.

Fists curling, she willed her toes to move.

"Damn you . . . *move*. . . ." She would have closed her eyes to concentrate, but she didn't want to miss the miracle if it happened.

It did not.

It had not.

And she was coming to realize . . . it would not.

As the pads of her toenails went from pink to gray, she knew she had to come to terms with where she was. And was not there a fine analogy to her current physical position.

Broken. Useless. Deadweight.

The breakdown that finally ensued carried with it no tears or sobs. Instead, the snap was demarcated by a grim resolve.

"Payne!"

At the sound of Jane's voice, she closed her eyes. This was not the savior she wanted. Her twin . . . she needed her twin to do right by her.

"Please get Vishous," she said hoarsely. "Please."

Jane's voice got very close. "Let's get you up off the floor."

"Vishous."

There was a click and she knew that the alarm she had not been able to reach had been sounded.

"Please," she groaned. "Get Vishous."

"Let's get you—"

"Vishous."

Silence. Until the door was thrown open.

"Help me, Ehlena," she heard Jane say.

Payne was aware that her own mouth was moving, but she went deaf as the two females hefted her back upon the bed and resettled her legs, lining them up parallel to each other before covering them with white sheeting.

Whilst various and sundry cleaning endeavors occurred both upon the bed and the floor, she focused across the room at the white wall she had stared at for the eternity since she had been moved into this space.

"Payne?"

When she didn't reply, Jane repeated, "Payne. Look at me."

She shifted her eyes over and felt nothing as she stared into the worried face of her twin's *shellan*. "I need my brother."

"Of course I'll get him. He's in a meeting right now, but I'll have him come down before he leaves for the night." Long pause. "Can I ask you why you want him?"

The even, level words told her clearly that the good healer was no imbecile.

"Payne?"

Payne shut her eyes and heard herself say, "He made me a promise when this all started. And I need him to keep it."

* * *

In spite of the fact that she was a ghost, Jane's heart was still capable of stopping in her chest.

And as she eased down onto the edge of the hospital bed, there was nothing moving behind her sternum. "What promise was that," she said to her patient.

"It is a matter betwixt the pair of us."

The hell it was, Jane thought. Assuming that she was guessing right.

"Payne, there might be something else we can do."

Although what that was, she hadn't a clue. The X-rays were showing that the bones had been aligned properly, Manny's skills having fixed them perfectly. That spinal cord, though—that was the wild card. She'd had a hope that some regeneration of nerves might be possible—she was still learning about the vampire body's capabilities, many of which seemed like pure magic compared to what humans could do in terms of healing.

But no luck. Not in this case.

And it didn't take an Einstein extrapolation to figure out what Payne was looking for.

"Be honest with me, *shellan* of my twin." Payne's crystal eyes locked on hers. "Be honest with yourself."

If there was one thing that Jane hated about being a doctor, it was the judgment call. There were a lot of incidents when decisions were clear: Some guy presented at the ER with his hand in an ice cooler and a tourniquet around his arm? Reattach the appendage and run those nerves back where they needed to be. Woman in labor with a preemergent cord? C-section her. Compound fracture? Open it up and set it.

But not everything was that "simple." On a regular basis, the gray fog of maybe-this, maybe-that rolled in, and she had to stare into the cloudy and the murky—

Oh, who was she kidding.

The clinical side of this equation had reached its correct sum. She just didn't want to believe the answer.

"Payne, let me go get Mary—"

"I did not wish to speak with the counseling female two nights ago, and I shan't speak unto her now. This is over for me, healer. And as much as it pains me to call upon my twin, please go and get him. You are a good female and you should not be the one."

Jane looked at her hands. She had never once used them to kill. Ever. It was antithetical not just to her calling and her commitment to her profession, but her as a person.

And yet as she thought about her *hellren* and the time they'd spent together when she'd woken up with him, she knew she couldn't let him come here and do what Payne wanted him to: He'd taken a small step back from the precipice he'd been about to jump off of, and there was nothing Jane wouldn't do to keep him from that ledge.

"I can't go get him," she said. "I'm sorry. I just won't put him in that position."

The moan that rose from Payne's throat was despair from the heart given wings and released. "Healer, this is my choice. *My* life. Not yours. You wish to be a true savior, then make it look accidental, or get me a weapon and I'll do it. But leave me not in this state. I cannot bear it, and you have done no good for your patient if I continue thus."

On some level, Jane had known this was coming. She had seen it clear as the pale shadows in the dark X-rays, the ones that told her everything should be working right—and if it wasn't, the spinal cord had been irreparably injured.

She stared at those legs that lay under the sheet so still and thought of the Hippocratic oath she had taken years ago: "Do no harm" was the first commandment.

It was hard not to see Payne as having been harmed if she were left like this—especially because she hadn't wanted the procedure in the first place. Jane had been the one urging the salvation, pushing it on the female for her own reasons—and V had been the same.

"I shall find a way," Payne said. "Somehow, I shall find a way."

Hard not to believe that.

And there was a greater chance of safe success if Jane helped in some manner—Payne was weak, and any weapon in her hand would be a disaster waiting to happen.

"I don't know if I can do this." The words left Jane's mouth slowly. "You're his sister. I don't know if he'd ever forgive me."

"He need never know."

God, what a bind. If she were stuck in that bed, she would feel exactly as Payne did, and she would want someone to help her execute her final wish. But the burden of keeping something like that from V? How could she do that?

Except . . . the only thing worse would be his not coming back from that dark side of himself. And killing his sister? Well, that was an express train right into that part of his neighborhood, wasn't it.

The hand of her patient found her own. "Help me, Jane. Help me. . . ."

As Vishous left the nightly meeting with the Brotherhood and headed for the training center's clinic, he was feeling more like himself—and not in a bad way. The sex with his *shellan* had been mission critical for them both, a kind of reboot that hadn't just been physical.

God, it had felt good to be back with his female. Yeah, sure, there were problems still waiting for him . . . and, well, shit, the closer he got to the clinic, the more the mantle of stress returned, hitting his shoulders like a pair of cars: He had seen his sister at the beginning of every evening and then again at dawn. For the first few days, there had been a lot of hope, but now . . . that had mostly passed.

Whatever, though. She needed to get out of that room, and that was what he was going to do tonight. He was off rotation, and he was going to take her to the mansion and show her there was something other than that white cage of a recovery room to live for.

She wasn't getting better physically.

So the mental was going to have to carry her through. It just had to.

Bottom line? He was not prepared to lose her now. Yeah, he'd been around her for a week, but that didn't mean he knew her any better than he had when this had all started—and he was thinking they both needed each other. No one else was the offspring of that goddamn deity mother of theirs, and maybe together they could sort out the crap that came with their birthright. For shit's sake, it wasn't like there was a twelve-step for being the Scribe Virgin's kid:

Hi, I'm Vishous. I'm her son and I've been her son for three hundred years.

HI, VISHOUS.

She's done a head job on me again, and I'm trying not to go to the Other Side and scream bloody murder at her.

WE UNDERSTAND, VISHOUS.

And on the bloody note, I'd like to dig up my father and kill him all over again, but I can't. So I'm just going to try to keep my sister alive even though she's paralyzed, and attempt to fight the urge to find some pain so I can deal with this Payne.

YOU'RE A STRAIGHT-UP PUSSY, VISHOUS, BUT WE SUPPORT YOUR SORRY ASS.

Pushing his way out of the tunnel and into the office, he crossed over to the glass door and then strode down the corridor. As he went by the workout room, someone was running like their Nikes were on fire, but otherwise, there was a whole lot of no one around—and he had a feeling Jane might still be back in their bed, lounging after he'd done her right.

Which the bonded male in him took a fuckload of satisfaction from. For real.

When he came to the recovery room, he didn't knock, but—

As he stepped inside, the first thing he saw was the hypodermic needle. The next thing was that it was about to change hands, going from his *shellan*'s to his twin's.

No therapeutic reason for that.

"What are you doing?" he breathed, abruptly terrified.

Jane's head whipped around, but Payne didn't look at him. Her stare was fixated on that needle like it was the key to the lock on her jail cell.

And sure as shit it was going to help her out of that bed . . . right into a coffin.

"What the *fuck* are you doing." Not a question. He already knew.

"My choice," Payne said grimly.

His *shellan* met him in the eye. "I'm sorry, V."

A whitewash cut his vision off, but did nothing to slow his body down as he lunged forward. Just as he reached the bedside, his eyes cleared and he saw his gloved hand latch onto his *shellan's* wrist.

His death grip was the only thing keeping his twin from death. And he addressed her, not his mate. *"Don't you fucking dare."*

Payne's eyes were violent as they met his own. "And do not you dare!"

V recoiled for a moment. He had stared into the faces of bested enemies and discarded subs and forgotten lovers both male and female, but he had never seen such depths of hatred before.

Ever.

"You are not my god!" she screamed at him. "You are but my brother! And you will not chain me unto this body any more than our *mahmen* will!"

Their fury was so well matched that for the first time in his life, he was at a loss. After all, it made no sense to enter into conflict if your opponent was equal.

Trouble was, if he left now, he was coming back to a funeral.

V wanted to pace to dial down his pissed-off, but he'd be damned if he was looking away for even a split second. "I want two hours," he said. "I can't stop you, but I can ask you to give me one hundred and twenty minutes."

Payne's eyes narrowed. "Whatever for."

Because he was going to do something that would have been inconceivable when this whole thing had started. But this was a type of war, and accordingly, he didn't have the luxury of picking his weapons—he had to use what he had, even if he hated it.

"I'll tell you *exactly* why." V took the needle from Jane's hold. "You're going to do it so this doesn't haunt me for the rest of my fucking life. How 'bout that for a reason. Good enough?"

Payne's lids sank down and there was a whole lot of silence. Except then she said, "I will give you what you ask, but my mind will not be changed if I remain in this bed. Assure yourself of your expectations afore you depart—and be forewarned if you attempt to reason with our *mahmen*. I will not trade this prison for one on her side, in her world."

Vishous shoved the needle in his pocket and unsheathed the hunting knife that was perm-attached to the belt on his leathers. "Give me your hand."

When she offered it, he sliced her palm with the blade and did the same to his own flesh. Then he clasped the wounds together.

"Vow it. On our shared blood, you take a vow to me."

Payne's mouth twitched as if, once again, she would have smiled under different circumstances. "Trust me not?"

"Nope," he said roughly. "Not in the slightest, sweetheart."

A moment later, her hand gripped his and a slick of tears formed over her eyes. "I so vow."

Vishous's lungs loosened and he drew a deep breath. "Fair enough."

He dropped his hold, turned around, and strode for the door. As soon as he was in the corridor, he didn't waste time heading for the tunnel.

"Vishous."

At the sound of Jane's voice, he wheeled around and wanted to curse. Shaking his head, he said, "Don't follow me. Don't call me. Nothing good is going to come out of my being within earshot of you right now."

Jane's arms crossed over her chest. "She's my patient, V."

"She's my blood." In frustration, he slashed the air with his hand. "I don't have time for this. I'm out of here."

At that, he took off at a run. Leaving her behind.

NINETEEN

When Manny got back to his place, he closed the door, locked it . . . and stood there. Like a piece of furniture. With his briefcase in his hand.

It was amazing how, when you'd lost your mind, you were kind of out of options for what to do next. His will hadn't changed; he still wanted to get control of himself and this . . . whatever it was that was going on in his life. But there was nothing to grab at, no reins to this beast.

Shit, this had to be how Alzheimer's patients felt: Their personality was intact and so was their intellect . . . but they were surrounded by a world that no longer made sense because they couldn't hold on to their memories and associations and extrapolations.

It was all tied to that weekend—or at least, it had started then. But what exactly had changed? He'd lost at least some of one night, as far as he could tell. He remembered the racetrack and Glory's fall and the vet afterward. Then the trip back to Caldwell, where he went to . . .

The forewarning of another blooming headache had him cursing and giving up.

Walking over to the kitchen, he dropped his briefcase and ended up staring at the coffee machine. He'd left it on when he'd headed off for the hospital. Great. So his morning java had actually been nighttime joe, and it was a miracle he hadn't burned his fucking condo down.

Sitting on one of the stools at the granite counter, he stared out the wall of glass in front of him. The city on the far side of his terrace was glowing like a lady heading to the theater with all her diamonds on, the lights in the skyscrapers twinkling and making him feel really and truly alone.

Silence. Emptiness.

The condo was more like a coffin.

God, if he couldn't operate, what did he have—

The shadow appeared from out of nowhere on his terrace. Except it wasn't a shadow. . . . There was nothing translucent about the thing. It was as if the lights and the bridges and the skyscrapers were a painting that had had a hole cut in them.

A hole in the shape of a large man.

Manny rose off the stool, his eyes fixated on the figure. In the back of his mind, at the seat of his brain stem, he knew that this was the cause of everything, his "tumor" upright and walking . . . and coming for him.

As if bidden, he went over and opened the sliding glass door, the wind hitting him hard in the face, his hair stripping back from his forehead.

It was cold. Oh, so cold . . . but the frigid shock wasn't just the chilly April night. A deep freeze was rolling out from the figure standing so still and deadly mere feet away from him; he got the very distinct impression the arctic blast was because this fucker in black leather hated his ass. But Manny wasn't afraid. The answer to what was doing with him was tied to this huge man who had appeared from out of nowhere, some twenty stories up off the pavement—

A female . . . one with braided dark hair . . . this was her—

The headache slammed into him, tackling him on the nape of the neck and shooting forward over his dome to pound the shit out of his frontal lobe.

As he sagged, he caught himself on the slider, and lost his patience. "For fuck's sake, don't just stand there. Talk to me or kill me, but *do* something."

More wind on the face.

And then a deep voice. "I shouldn't have come here."

"Yeah, you should have," Manny groaned through the pain. "Because I'm losing my fucking mind and you know that, don't you. What the fuck did you do to me?"

That dream . . . about the woman he wanted, but couldn't have . . .

Manny's knees started to buckle, but to hell with that. "Take me to her—and don't fuck with me. I know she exists . . . I see her every night in my dreams."

"I don't like any of this."

"Yeah, and I'm having a party over here." The *motherfucker* went unsaid. As did the fact that if this dark bastard decided to act on all the aggression he was stewing in, Manny was going to bust out the fists and do some damage of his own. He was going to get creamed for sure, but fucked in the head or not, he didn't go down without a fight.

"Come on," Manny spat. "Do it."

There was a tight laugh. "You remind me of a friend of mine."

"You mean there's another son of a bitch lost in his own life because of you? Great. We'll start a support group."

"Fucking hell . . ."

The guy raised a hand and then . . . memories exploded in Manny's mind and flowed through his body, the sights and sounds of his lost weekend returning with a vengeance.

Stumbling back, he put his hands to his head.

Jane. Secret facility. Operation.

Vampire.

An iron grip on his biceps was all that kept him off the hardwood, his patient's brother grabbing on. "You have to come and see my sister. She's going to die if you don't."

Manny breathed through his mouth and swallowed a lot. The patient . . . *his patient* . . .

"Is she still paralyzed?" he moaned.

"Yes."

"Take me," he bit out. "Now."

If it was a case of that spinal cord being permanently damaged, there was nothing he could do for her clinically, but that didn't matter. He had to see her.

"Where's your car?" the goateed fucker asked.

"Downstairs."

Manny broke free and beelined for his briefcase and the keys he'd left on the kitchen counter. As he tripped and fell about his place, his brain felt fuzzy in a way that terrified him. Any more of this in-and-out shit with his motherboard and he was going to be permanently damaged. But that was a discussion for another time.

He had to get to his female.

When he got to the front door, the vampire was right behind him, and Manny switched his stuff to his left hand.

A quick pivot and he threw out his right fist, snapping it up in an arc perfectly calculated to catch the guy's jaw.

Crack. The impact was solid and the bastard's head knocked back.

As the vampire releveled his stare and lifted the corner of his mouth in a snarl, Manny was having none of it. "That's for fucking with me."

The male dragged the back of his hand across his bloody mouth. "Nice hook."

"You're welcome," Manny said as he stepped out of his place.

"I could have stopped that at any moment. Just so we're clear."

Undoubtedly, that was true. "Yeah, but you didn't, did you." Manny marched over to the elevator, punched the *down* button, and glared over his shoulder. "So that makes you a chump or a masochist. Your choice."

The vampire got in close. "Careful, human—you're only alive because you're useful to me."

"She's your sister?"

"Don't forget it."

Manny smiled by baring all his teeth. "Then there's something you need to know."

"What."

Manny rose up on his toes and met the fucker eye-to-eye. "If you think you want to kill me now, this ain't nothin' compared to how you're going to feel when I see her again."

He was practically hard just thinking about the female.

With a ding, the double doors opened and he stepped off, stepped in and turned around. The vampire's eyes were spears looking for a target, but Manny shrugged off the aggression. "Just letting you know where I stand. Now get in or ghost down to the street and I'll pick your ass up."

"You must think I'm an idiot, true," the vampire growled.

"Actually, not at all."

Pause.

After another moment, the vampire muttered under his breath and slipped in just as the sliders started to shut. And then the pair of them just stood side by side, watching the numbers count down over the double doors . . .

Five . . . four . . . three . . . two . . .

Like the countdown to an explosion.

"Be careful, human. I'm not someone you want to push too hard."

"And I've got nothing to lose." Except for this big bastard's sister. "Guess we'll just have to see where this ends up."

"You got that right."

Payne was a grim block of ice as she stared at the clock by the door to her room. The circular face was as plain as the white wall behind it, marked by nothing but twelve black numbers separated by black lines. The hands of the thing, two black, one red, lolled their way around as if they were as bored with their job as she was with watching them work.

Vishous had to have gone to see their mother. Where else would he turn?

So this was a waste of time; for certain, he would come back with nothing. It was sheer arrogance to think that She Who Could Not Be Swayed would be affected in the slightest by the perils of her birthed children.

Mother of the race. What piffle—

Payne frowned. The sound started off as nothing save a dim rhythm, but it quickly grew louder. Footsteps. Heavy footsteps traveling over a hard floor at a fast clip, and there were two sets of them. Perhaps it was naught but her twin's Brothers coming in for a check—

When the door swung open, all she could see was Vishous, standing so tall and uncompromising. "I brought you something."

He didn't so much step aside as he was pushed. . . .

"Dearest Scribe Virgin . . ." Payne mouthed as tears rushed to her eyes.

Her healer burst into the room, and oh, he was just as she had remembered . . . so broad at the chest and long of limb, with a flat stomach and a sharp jawline. His dark hair was sticking straight up, as if he had been running many fingers through it, and he was breathing hard, his mouth slightly parted.

"I *knew* you were real," he blurted. "Goddamn it, I knew it!"

The sight of him rocketed through her, energy lighting her up from the inside and tripping her emotions into a free fall. "Healer," she said hoarsely. "My healer . . ."

"Fucking hell," she heard her brother say.

Her human spun around on Vishous. "Give us some privacy. Now—"

"Watch your fucking mouth—"

"I'm her doctor. You brought me here to assess her clinically—"

"Don't be ridiculous."

There was a pause. "Then why the fuck am I here?"

"For precisely the reason I hate you!"

That ushered in a lot of silence—along with a sob on her part. She was just so glad to see her healer in his strength and his flesh. And her single sniffle whipped both their heads around, her healer's face changing instantly, going from flat-out fury to driving concern.

"Shut the door behind you," he barked over his shoulder as he came to her.

Passing her hands across her eyes, she cleared her tears and looked past her healer as he sat on the side of her bed. Vishous had turned away and was going for the exit.

He knew, she thought. More than anything their mother could have done for her, he had brought her the one thing guaranteed to make her want to live.

"Thank you, brother mine," she said, eyes locked on him.

Vishous stopped. The tension in him was so great, both of his fists were curled in tight, and as his head slowly cranked around, his icy eyes burned.

"I would do anything for you. Anything."

With that, he pushed his way out . . . and as the door eased shut, she realized that *I love you* could indeed be said without actually uttering the phrase.

Actions did mean more than words.

TWENTY

As the pair of them were left alone together, Manny couldn't get enough of looking at his patient. His stare just kept going over her face and her throat and her long, lovely hands. Jesus, she smelled the same, that perfume of hers burrowing into his nose and going straight to his cock.

"I knew you were real," he repeated. Christ, it probably would have been better to say something else, anything else, but that was all he had, evidently: The relief at the fact that he wasn't going crazy was just overwhelming.

At least until the luminous sheen of tears in her eyes registered . . . along with bottomless lack of hope in her stare.

He'd done all he could for her, and yet he had failed. Totally.

Although it wasn't as if he hadn't guessed her condition before now. That brother of hers hadn't come into the human world again because shit was going so frickin' well on this side.

"How are you doing?" he asked.

As he stared into her eyes, she slowly shook her head. "Alas . . . I am . . ."

When she didn't finish, he reached for her hand and held on to it. God, her skin was soft. "Talk to me."

"My legs . . . are no better."

He cursed under his breath. He wanted to do an exam on her and look at her newest X-rays . . . maybe make arrangements to get her into St. Francis for another MRI.

But, as critical as all that assessment stuff was, it could wait. Right now, she was fragile emotionally, and he needed to help her deal with that first.

"No feeling still?" he said.

When she shook her head, a tear escaped and slid down her cheek. He hated that she was crying, but as God was his savior, he had never seen anything so beautiful as those eyes of hers.

"I am . . . e'er to be thus," she said on a shudder.

"And 'thus' to you means precisely what?"

"Here. Upon this bed. Stuck." Her eyes didn't just hold his, but reached out and grabbed them. "I cannot countenance this torture. Not for a night more."

She was dead fucking serious, and for a split second, he felt a terror that cut right through to his soul. Maybe in another female . . . or male, for that matter . . . a statement like that might have been an emotional release of despair. For her? It was a plan.

"You got Internet around here?" he asked.

"Internet?"

"A computer with access to the Web."

"Ah . . . I believe there is one in the larger room beyond. Through that other door."

"I'll be right back. Stay here."

That got a half smile. "Wherever shall I go, healer?"

"That's what I'm going to show you."

As he stood up, he had to resist the urge to kiss her, and he hurried out to make sure he didn't. It took no time at all to find the Dell in question and get signed in with the help of a rather attractive blond nurse who introduced herself as Elena. Ten minutes later, he came back to Payne's room and paused in the doorway.

She was fixing her hair, her hands trembling as she smoothed the crown of her head and felt down the length of her braid as if searching for defects.

"You don't have to do that," he murmured. "You look perfect to me."

Instead of replying, she blushed and grew flustered—which was just about the best thing she couldn't say. "Verily, you tie my tongue."

Well, now, didn't that take his mind into places it shouldn't be going.

Staring across at her, he forced his head to change gears. "Payne, I'm your doctor, right?"

"Yes, healer."

"And that means that I'm going to tell you the truth. No sandbagging, no hiding anything. I'm going to tell you exactly what I think and I'll let you make up your own mind—and I need you to hear me on that, okay? The truth is all I've got, nothing more, nothing less."

"Then you need not utter a thing, for I know too well where I sit."

He glanced around the room. "Have you been out of here since you came back from the operation."

"No."

"So you've been staring at these four empty walls for a week, trapped on a bed, having other people feed you, bathe you, and deal with your bodily functions."

"I do not need the reminder," she said drily. "Thank you kindly—"

"How do you know where you're at, then."

Her frown was deep and dark . . . and sexy as hell. "That's ridiculous. I am here." She pointed to the mattress under her. "I have been *here*."

"Exactly." As she glared up at him, he closed the distance between them. "I'm going to pick you up and carry you, if you don't mind?"

Now her brows popped. "Wherever to?"

"Out of this godforsaken cage."

"But . . . I can't. I have a—"

"I know." Of course she would be worried about her catheter, and to save any embarrassment, he snagged a clean white towel off the bedside table. "I'll be careful with it and you."

After he made sure her equipment was secure, he untucked the top sheet that covered her and scooped her up. Her weight was solid against his upper body, and he took a moment just to hold her, her head on his shoulder, her long, long legs draped over his arm. Her perfume or soap or whatever it was reminded him of sandalwood and something else.

Oh, right . . . orgasms.

The ones he'd had when he'd dreamed about her.

Great, now he was pulling the blush-and-flush.

Payne cleared her throat. "Do I weigh too much? I am large for a female."

"You are perfect for a female."

"Not where I come from," she muttered.

"Then they're using the wrong standard."

Manny carried his precious load through the door into the exam room. The place was empty, at his request—he'd asked the nurse—Elina? Elaina?—to give them some privacy.

No telling how this was going to go.

Keeping her in his hold, he sat down in front of the computer, and angled them so she could see the monitor. When she seemed more interested in staring at him, he didn't mind in the slightest—but it was hardly conducive to concentration. Or the reason he'd gotten her out of that bed.

"Payne," he said.

"What?"

Christ, that husky voice of hers. The damn thing was capable of ripping through him like a knife and making him like the bite of pain that came along with the wounding: To want her as he did and restrain himself was an agonizing pleasure that was somehow better than the best sex he'd ever had.

It was an antici-gasm at its finest.

"You're supposed to be looking at the monitor," he said as he brushed her cheek.

"I'd rather stare at you."

"Oh, yeah . . . ?" As his voice grew as husky as hers, he knew it was time for some internal dialogue along the lines of oh-no-you-don't-big-boy.

But *damn.*

"You make me feel something all over my body. Even in my legs."

Well, sexual attraction would do that to someone. His circuits were sure as hell lit up like Manhattan at midnight.

Except there was a larger purpose to this Santa's-lap routine, something that was so much more important than a quickie . . . or even a session that lasted a week, or a month, or God save them both, a year. It was about a lifetime. Hers.

"How about you look at the computer for a little bit, and then you can stare at me all you like?"

"All right."

When she didn't glance away from his face, he cleared his throat. "The computer, *bambina*."

"Italian?"

"On my mother's side."

"And as for your father's?"

He shrugged. "Never met him, so I couldn't tell you."

"Your sire was unknown?"

"Yup, pretty much." Manny put his forefinger under her chin and tilted her head toward the computer. "Look."

He tapped the monitor and knew when she focused properly because she frowned, her dark brows going down low over her diamond eyes.

"This is a friend of mine—Paul." Manny did nothing to keep the pride out of his voice. "He was also a patient of mine. He kicks ass . . . and he's been in that wheelchair for years."

At first, Payne was not sure exactly what the image was. . . . It was moving; that was for certain. And it appeared to be— Wait. That was a human, and he was sitting in some kind of contraption that rolled o'er the ground. To ambulate, he pumped with his great arms, his face in a grimace, his concentration as fierce as any warrior's would be in the height of battle.

Behind him, there was a field of three other men in similar mechanicals, and they were all fixated on him as if trying to close the e'er-widening distance betwixt them and their leader.

"Is it . . . a race?" she asked.

"That's the Boston Marathon, wheelchair division. Paul's coming up Heartbreak Hill, which is the hardest part."

"He's ahead of the others."

"Wait for it—he's only getting started. He didn't just win that race. . . . He snapped it in half on his knee and lit it on fire."

They watched the man win by a tremendous margin, his huge arms going like the wind, his chest pumping, the crowd on either side of the road roaring in support. As he broke through a ribbon, a stunning woman ran up and the pair embraced.

And in the human female's arms? A babe with the same coloring as the man.

Payne's healer leaned forward and moved a little black instrument around on the desk to change the picture on the screen. Gone was the moving image. . . . In its place was a static portrait of the man smiling. He was very handsome and glowed with health, and by his side were the same red-haired woman and that young with his blue eyes.

The man was still sitting down, and the chair he was on was more substantial than that which he had competed in—in fact it was much like the one Jane had brought in. His legs were out of proportion to the rest of him, small and tucked away beneath the seat, but you didn't notice that—or even his rolling apparatus. You only saw the fierce strength and intelligence.

Payne reached out to the screen and touched the face of the man. "How long . . . ?" she asked hoarsely.

"Has he been paralyzed? About ten years or so. He was on his touring bike when he was hit by a drunk driver. I did seven operations on his back."

"He is still in the . . . chair."

"You see that woman next to him?"

"Yes."

"She fell in love with him after the accident."

Payne whipped her head around and stared up into her healer's face. "He . . . sired young?"

"Yup. He can drive a car . . . he can have sex, obviously . . . and he lives a fuller life than most people who have two working legs. He's an entrepreneur and an athlete and a hell of a man, and I'm proud to call him friend."

As he spoke, her healer moved that black thing around and the pictures changed. There were ones of the man in other athletic contests, and then smiling by some kind of large building construction, and then with him seated before a red ribbon with a big pair of golden scissors in his hand.

"Paul is the mayor of Caldwell." Her healer gently turned her face back to his. "Listen to me . . . and I want you to remember this. Your legs are part of you, but not all of you or what you are. So wherever we go after tonight, I need you to know that you are no less for the injury. Even if you are in a chair, you still stand as tall as you ever did. Height is just a vertical number—it doesn't mean shit when it comes to your character or the kind of life you live."

He was dead serious, and if she were to be truthful with herself, she fell a little in love with him in that moment.

"Can you move the . . . that thing?" she whispered. "So that I may see more?"

"Here—you work the mouse." He took her hand and placed it on the warm, oblong scooter. "Left and right . . . up and down . . . See? It shifts the arrow on the screen. Click this when you want to see something."

It took her a couple of tries, but then she got the knack of it . . . and it was absurd, but just making her way around the different areas on the screen and choosing what she wanted to look at gave her a dizzy sense of energy.

"I can do this," she said. Except then she got embarrassed. Considering how simple it was, it was too small a victory to crow over.

"That's the point," her healer said in her ear. "You can do *anything*."

She shivered at that. Or likely it was because of more than merely his words.

Refocusing on the computer, she liked the pictures of the man in the races best. His expression of agonized effort and indomitable willpower was something she had long felt burning in her own chest. But then the one of the family together was also among her favorites. They were humans, but the bonds seemed so strong between them. There was love, such love there.

"What do you say?" her healer murmured.

"I think you came at the perfect time. That's what I say."

She shifted in his strong arms and stared up at him. As she sat in his lap, she wished she could feel more of him. All of him. But from the waist down there was only a nonspecific warmth, one that was better than the chill that had persisted since the operation, yes . . . but there was so much more to be had.

"Healer . . ." she whispered, her eyes going to his mouth.

His lids lowered and he seemed to stop breathing. "Yeah . . . ?"

"May I . . ." She licked her lips. "May I kiss you?"

He seemed to wince, as if in pain, but that scent he carried roared, so she knew that he wanted what she did.

"Jesus . . . Christ," he bit out.

"Your body wants this," she said, bringing her hand up to the soft hair at the nape of his neck.

"And that's the problem." At her look of confusion, he leveled a hot stare right at her breasts. "It wants a hell of a lot more than just a kiss."

Suddenly, there was a shift inside her body, one so subtle it was hard to pin down. But she felt something different throughout her torso and all her limbs. A tingling? She was too wrapped up in the sexual energy between them to worry about defining it.

Snaking another arm around his neck, she said, "What else does it want."

Her healer groaned deep in his throat, and the sound gave her the same shot of power as when she'd a weapon in her hand. To feel that again? It was like a drug.

"Tell me, healer," she demanded. "What else does it want."

His mahogany eyes were on fire as they locked on her own. "Everything. It wants every square inch of you—outside . . . and on the inside. To the point where I'm not sure you're ready for how much I'm after."

"I decide," she countered, a strange, pounding need taking root in her gut. "I decide what I can and cannot handle, yes?"

His half smile was all evil. In a good way. "Yes, ma'am."

As a low, rhythmic sound filled the air, she was surprised to realize it was her. Purring. "Do I have to ask again, healer?"

There was a pause. And then he slowly shook his head back and forth. "Nope. I'll give you . . . exactly what you want."

TWENTY-ONE

When Vishous pushed open the door to the exam room, he got a gander at the kind of seating arrangement that made him think fondly of castration.

Which, considering his own experience with the knife-on-the-'nads routine, was saying a lot.

Then again, his sister was all but straddling that ass-wipe human's Mr. Happy, the man's arms around her, their heads all nestled in. Except they weren't looking at each other—and that was the only reason he didn't break up the party: They were staring at the computer screen . . . at a man in a wheelchair racing a bunch of other guys.

". . . Height is just a vertical number—it doesn't mean shit when it comes to your character or the kind of life you live."

"Can you move the . . . that thing?"

For some reason, V's heart pounded as the human showed his sister how to work a mouse. And then he heard something that gave him reason for hope:

"I can do this," she said.

"That's the point," Manello said softly. "You can do *anything*."

Well, shit—the gamble had come up aces, hadn't it: V had been willing to throw that human back into the mix briefly, just to get her past the suicidal impulse. Except he'd never once thought the guy would give her anything more than a case of puppy love.

And yet, here the motherfucker was . . . showing her so much more than how to kiss.

V had wanted to be the one to save her—and he supposed by bringing in Manello, he might have, but why hadn't he done more sooner? Why hadn't Jane? They should have gotten her out of this place, taken her to the mansion . . . had meals and talked with her.

Shown her that her future was different, but not disappeared.

V rubbed his face as anger tackled him to the ground. Goddamn Jane . . . how could she not know that patients required more than pain meds and sponge baths? His twin had needed a fucking horizon—anyone would go mad stuck in that room.

Fucking hell.

He glanced back at his sister and the human. The pair of them had locked eyes and it was looking like it would take a crowbar to get their heads apart.

Kinda got V back to wanting to kill the bastard.

As his gloved hand went into his pocket for a hand-rolled, he had half a mind to clear his throat loudly. Either that or take his dagger and end-over-end it at the human's head. Trouble was, that surgeon was a tool to be used until he wasn't needed anymore—and they hadn't reached that point yet.

V forced himself to back out of the doorway—

"How're they doing?"

As he wheeled around, he dropped his fucking cigarette.

Butch picked it up. "Need a light?"

"Try a knife." He took the thing back and got out his new Bic, which actually frickin' worked. After he inhaled, he let the smoke drift from his mouth. "We going out for a drink?"

"Not yet. I think you need to go talk to your female."

"Trust me. I don't. Not right now."

"She's packing up a bag, Vishous."

The bonded male in him went crazy, but nonetheless, he forced himself to stand there in the hall and keep smoking. Thank God for his nicotine addiction: Sucking on the hand-rolled was the only reason he wasn't cursing.

"V, my man. What the hell is going on?"

He could barely hear the guy for the scream inside of his head. And couldn't come close to a full explanation. "My *shellan* and I have had a difference of opinion."

"So talk it out."

"Not right now." He put the tail end of the cig out on the sole of his shitkicker and deep-sixed the butt. "Let's go."

Except . . . well, when it came down to it, he somehow couldn't walk off to the parking garage where the Escalade had been getting its oil changed. He was literally incapable of leaving, his feet having glued themselves to the floor.

As he glanced down toward the office, he mourned the fact that just an hour ago it had looked like things were back on track. But no. It was almost as if the shit before had been nothing except a warm-up for where they were now.

"I got nothing to say to her, true." As always.

"Maybe it'll come to you."

Doubt that, he thought.

Butch clapped him on the shoulder. "Listen to me. You have the fashion sense of a park bench and the interpersonal skills of a meat cleaver—"

"Is this supposed to be helping?"

"Let me finish—"

"What's next? The size of my cock?"

"Hey, even pencils can get the job done—I've heard the moaning from your room to prove it." Butch gave him a shake. "I'm just telling you—you need that female in your life. Don't fuck that shit up. Not now—not ever, feel me?"

"She was going to help Payne kill herself." As the guy winced, V nodded. "Yeah. So this ain't about some he-said, she-said argument about the cap on the fucking toothpaste."

After a moment, Butch murmured, "There must have been a pretty damn good reason."

"There is no reason. Payne's the only blood I've got and she was going to take that away from me."

With the situation boiled down to its basics like that, the buzzing at the base of V's brain got so much stronger and louder, he had to wonder if he was going to stroke out—and in that moment, for the first time in his life, he was scared of himself and what he was capable of. Not hurting Jane, of course—no matter how fried he was, he would never touch her in anger—

Butch took a step back and raised his palms. "Hey. Easy there, roomie."

V looked down. In his hands were both of his daggers . . . and his fists were so tight he wondered whether the grips were going to have to be surgically removed from his palms.

"Take these," he said numbly, "away from me."

In a rush, he gave all of his weapons to his best friend, disarming himself completely. And Butch accepted the load with quick, grim efficiency.

"Yeah . . . maybe you're right," the guy muttered. "Talk to her later."

"She's not the one you need to worry about, cop." 'Cuz apparently suicidal impulses ran the fuck all over his family tonight.

Butch caught his arm as he went to turn away. "What can I do to help."

V had a quick, shocking picture filter through his brain. "Nothing you could handle. Unfortunately."

"Don't do my thinking for me, motherfucker."

V stepped in close, bringing their faces to within an inch of each other. "You don't have the stomach for it. Trust me."

Those deep hazel eyes held his and didn't blink. "You'd be amazed what I would do to keep you alive."

Abruptly, V's mouth opened, his breath growing tight. And as the two of them stood chest-to-chest, he knew every inch of his body, felt all of it at once.

"What are you saying, cop."

"Do you honestly think *lessers* are a better option," Butch muttered hoarsely. "At least I can make sure you aren't dead at the end of it."

Images flickered through his mind, graphically detailed and appallingly perverted. And all of them with him in a starring role.

After a moment of neither saying a word, Butch stepped off. "Go see your female. I'll be waiting for you at the Escalade."

"Butch. You don't mean it. You can't."

His best friend regarded him coolly. "The fuck I don't." Turning away, he strode down the corridor. "Come find me. When you're ready."

As V watched the guy go, he wondered whether that was about them going out to drink tonight . . . or the pair of them walking through the dangerous door the cop had just opened.

In his heart of hearts, he knew it was both.

Holy. Shit.

Back in the exam room, as Manny stared into Payne's eyes, he was dimly aware that someone was smoking somewhere close by. Knowing his luck, it was her cocksucking brother, and the big bastard was getting nicotined up right before he came in here to mop the floor with Manny's piehole.

Whatever, though. Payne's mouth was mere inches from his own, and her body was warm against him, and his cock was bursting at the seams. He was a man of willpower and self-determination, but stopping what was about to happen was waaaaaaay beyond even his skill set.

Reaching up, he cupped the side of her face. As contact was made, her lips parted and he knew he should say something, but his voice had packed its bags and taken a bus out of town, evidently—along with his brain.

Closer. He drew her closer and met her halfway, their mouths fusing. And even though his body had all the patience of an unfed tiger, he was careful as the contact was made. God, she was soft . . . oh, so soft . . . in a way that made him want to spread her wide and penetrate her with everything he had, his fingers, his tongue, his sex.

But none of that was happening right now. Or tonight. Or even the day after. He hadn't had a lot of experience with virgins, but he was pretty damn sure that even if she was having a sexual response, how it was taken care of could be overwhelming—

"More," she said with husky demand. *"More . . ."*

For a split second, his heart stopped and he rethought the go-easy routine: That tone of voice was so not little-girl-lost. It was all woman, ready for a lover.

And gee whiz, under the she-didn't-need-to-ask-twice theory, he took over, stroking her mouth with his own before sucking in her lower lip. As his hand wound around her nape, he wanted to undo that braid and get into that hair of hers . . . but that was too close to undressing her, and this was far from private.

And he was close enough to coming already, thank you very much.

He slipped his tongue into her and groaned, his arms tightening around her—before he told them to loosen up or he was going to break them both off below the shoulder. Man, she was pure octane in his blood, his body in full gear and roaring. And he'd thought those dreams were hot? The real thing made that shit feel room-temperature compared to the surface of Mercury.

More with the tongue, more getting into her and pulling out, more of everything, until he had to force himself back. His hips were grinding against her tight ass in his lap—and that hardly seemed fair, given that she couldn't feel it.

Taking a deep breath, he didn't last long before dropping down to her neck to suck along the column of her throat—

Her nails bit so hard into his shoulders, he knew that if he'd been naked, she'd have drawn blood—and that fucking turned him on. Shit, the idea that there could be even more than just sex, that she could lock herself on his neck, and take him into her in more than just one way—

With a sharp hiss, Manny yanked himself off her skin and let his head fall back, breath shooting up and out of his lungs. "I think we need to slow it down."

"Why," she said, her eyes missing nothing about him. Leaning in, she growled, "You want this."

"Oh, fuck . . . yeah."

Her hands went to the front of his shirt. "Then let's keep going—"

He snapped a hold on her wrists as an orgasm tingled at the tip of his erection. "You have to stop that. Right now."

God, he could barely breathe.

Abruptly, she pulled herself out of his grip and ducked her head. Clearing her throat, she said roughly, "Verily, I am sorry."

The shame she had made his chest raw. "No, no . . . it's not you."

When she didn't respond, he tilted her chin up, and had to wonder if she had any clue what the male body did when it was this turned on. Christ, did she even know what an erection was?

"Listen carefully," he all but growled. "I want you. Here. Back in your room. On the floor out in the hall. Up against the wall. Any way, anywhere, anytime. Clear?"

Her eyes flared. "But then why don't—"

"I think your brother's out in the hall, for one thing. For another, you've told me you've never been with anyone before. I, on the other hand, know exactly where this could lead, and the last thing I want to do is freak you out by going too fast."

Their eyes stayed locked. And then after a moment, her lips lifted into a smile so far and wide that a dimple popped out on one side and her perfect white teeth gleamed—

Jesus . . . her fangs were longer. Much longer. And oh, so very sharp.

Manny couldn't help himself: All he could do was imagine what it would feel like to have one of them dragging up the underside of his cock.

The orgasm in his shaft made yet another bid to break free.

And that was before Payne's pink tongue came out and did a lingering sweep over the sharp points. "You like?"

Manny's chest pumped hard. "Yeah. Fuck, yeah . . ."

All at once, the lights went off, the room plunging into darkness. And then there were two clicks . . . locks? Could it be the locks on the doors?

In the glow of the computer screen, he saw her face change. Gone was any remnant of shy, innocent passion. . . . In its place was a raw, strapping hunger that reminded him she was not human. She was a beautiful predator, a gorgeous, powerful animal that was just human enough for him to forget who and what she really was.

Moving without thought, Manny brought one of his hands up to his white coat. In the process of his sitting down with her, the stiff lapels had popped up and now he pulled them down, exposing his neck.

He was panting. Straight-up panting.

"Take me," he ground out. "Do it . . . I want to know what it's like."

Now she was the one in control, her strong hands coming up to his face and dragging down his neck to his collarbone. She didn't have to tilt his head back. He did that without direction, his throat bared and inviting.

"Are you certain," she said, her accent rolling those Rs.

He was breathing so hard he wasn't sure he could choke out a reply, so he nodded. And then, worried that wasn't enough, he put his hands over hers, pressing her hold into him.

She took over from there, focusing on his jugular, her eyes seeming to light up like stars in the night. When she closed in, she did it slowly, disappearing the inches between her fangs and his flesh with aching delay.

The brush of her lips was nothing but velvet, except the anticipation of what was to come had him hyper-focusing so everything was magnified. He knew precisely where she was—

The scrape was viciously soft as she nuzzled him.

Then her hand snaked around to his nape and clamped on, holding him in place so hard, he realized she could snap his neck if she wanted.

"Oh, God," he moaned, giving himself over completely. "Oh—*fuck*!"

The strike was strong and sure, two points going in deep, the sweet pain robbing him of sight and sound until all he knew was the sucking draw at his vein.

That and the massive orgasm that rolled through his balls and pumped out the head of his cock, his hips jacking up against her as his erection kicked and jerked . . . and kept going.

He wasn't sure how long the release lasted. Ten seconds? Ten minutes? Or was it hours? All he knew was that with every drawing pull she took from him, he came some more, the pleasure so intense he was ruined by it. . . .

Because he knew he wasn't going to find this with anyone but her. Vampire or human.

Palming the back of her head, he pushed her down tighter, holding her to him, not caring whether she drank him dry. What a way to die—

Too soon, she went to pull away, but he was desperate for her to keep going, and tried to force her to stay at his throat. It was no contest, though. She was so strong physically, it was as if he had put up no protest at all. And didn't that make him come again.

As overrun as his nervous system was, he still felt the retraction of her fangs from his neck and knew the exact moment she was out of him. Then the biting pain was replaced with a soft, lapping stroke, as if she were sealing him closed.

Falling into a semi-trance, Manny's lids lowered and his head lolled on the top of his spine like a deflated balloon. From out of the corner of his eye, he looked at her perfect profile, the illumination from the monitor giving him plenty of light to watch her lick her lower lip—

Except it was not the computer.

The screen saver had come on and all that was showing was a black background with a Windows logo.

She was glowing. All over. From head to foot.

He guessed they did that, and how . . . extraordinary.

Except she was frowning. "Are you all right? Mayhap I took too much. . . ."

"I'm . . ." He swallowed. Twice. His tongue felt numb in his mouth. "I am . . ."

Panic set into her beautiful face. "Oh, fates, what have I done—"

He forced his head upright. "Payne . . . the only way it could have been better is if I'd come inside of you."

She was momentarily relieved. And then she asked, "What is coming?"

TWENTY-TWO

Up at the Pit, Jane was moving fast through her bedroom. Opening the closet's double doors, she started pulling white shirts out and throwing them over her shoulder onto the bed. In her haste, hangers flipped off the rod and bounced on the floor, or twisted around and got pinned at the back of the closet—and she couldn't have cared less.

There were no tears. Which she was proud of.

On the other hand, her whole body was shaking so badly it was all she could do to keep her hands corporeal.

As her stethoscope slipped off her neck and landed on the carpet, she stopped only so she didn't step on it. "God . . . damn it—"

Straightening after she picked the thing up, she glanced at the bed and thought, right, maybe it was time to quit with the white shirts. There was a mountain of them on the black satin sheets.

Backing across the room, she sat down next to her Mount Hanesmore and stared at the closet. V's muscle shirts and leathers were still all arranged; her side was a train wreck.

Wasn't that a perfect metaphor.

Except . . . he was a mess, too, wasn't he.

God . . . what the hell was she doing? Moving down to the clinic, even temporarily, was not the answer. When you were married, you stayed and worked it out. That was how relationships survived.

She left now? No telling where they were going to end up.

God, they'd had what, all of two hours of back-to-normal? Great. Frickin' great.

Taking out her phone, she called up a blank text and stared at the screen. Two minutes later, she flipped the cell shut. It was hard to put everything she had to say into 160 characters. Or even six pages of 160s.

Payne was her patient, and she had a duty to her. Vishous was her mate, and there was nothing she wouldn't do for him. And V's twin had not been prepared to give her any time whatsoever.

Although apparently that was something she was willing to grant her brother. And obviously, Vishous had gone to their mother.

God only knew what was going to come of that.

Staring at the mess she'd made of the closet, Jane ran through the situation over and over again, and kept coming to the same conclusion: Payne's right to choose her destiny superseded anyone's right to trap her in her own life. Was that harsh? Yes. Was it fair on those who loved her? Absolutely not.

Would the female have hurt herself worse if there hadn't been a humane way of doing it? One hundred percent, yes.

Jane didn't agree with the female's thinking or of her choice. But she was clear on the ethics, as tragic as they were.

And she was determined that Vishous hear her side of it.

Instead of running, she was going to stay put so that when he came home, she would be waiting for him and they could see if there was anything left of their life together. She wasn't fooling herself. This might well not be something they could work through, and she didn't blame him if that was the case. Family was family, after all. But she had done what the situation had called for according to the duty she had to her patient. Which was what doctors did, even when it cost them . . . everything they had.

Getting up, she picked hangers off the floor until she got to the closet. There were a lot of them in and around the boots and shoes, so she bent down, reaching into the back—

Her hand hit something soft. Leather—but it was not shitkicker.

Sitting back on her heels, she brought whatever it was with her.

"What the hell?" V's fighting leathers didn't belong shoved behind the shoes—

There was something on the cowhide— Wait. It was wax. It was black wax. And . . .

Jane put her hand over her mouth and let the pants slip out of her grip.

She'd given him enough orgasms to know what they looked like on his leathers. And that wasn't the only stain. There was blood. Red blood.

With a dreadful sense of inevitability, she reached into the closet once more and patted around until she felt a shirt. Pulling it out, she found more blood and wax.

The night he'd gone to the Commodore. It was the only explanation: These were not ancient, forgotten relics, the dusty remnant of a life he'd previously led. Hell, the scent of the wax still clung to the fibers and hide.

She knew the instant Vishous walked into the doorway behind her.

Without looking up, she said, "I thought you weren't with anyone else."

His response was a long time coming. "I wasn't."

"Then can you explain these?" She held up the leathers, but come on, like there was anything else in the room?

"I was not with anyone else."

She threw them back into the closet and tossed the muscle shirt in there as well. "To coin a phrase you yourself have used, I have nothing to say right now. I truly don't."

"You honestly think I could fuck something on the side."

"What the hell are those clothes, then?"

He didn't respond. He just stood there looming over her, so tall and strong . . . and strangely foreign, even though she knew his body and face as well as her own.

She waited for him to speak. Waited some more. And to pass the time, she reminded herself that his upbringing had been a bitch and that remaining stoic and unyielding had been the only way to survive.

Except that rationale simply wasn't enough. At some point, the love they had deserved better than silence that was grounded in the past.

"Was it Butch?" she said, hoping that was the case. At least if it was V's best friend, she knew that any release had been incidental. Butch was a totally faithful guy to his mate and he would do any Domming only because it was the strange, dark medicine V needed to keep level. As bizarre as it sounded, *that* she could understand and get past.

"Was it?" she said. "Because I can deal with that."

Vishous seemed momentarily surprised, but then he shook his head. "Nothing happened."

"Then are you telling me I'm blind?" she croaked. "Because unless you give me a better explanation, all I have are these leathers . . . and the pictures in my mind that are making me sick."

Silence, only silence.

"Oh, God . . . how could you?" she whispered.

V just shook his head, and said in the same tone, "Right back at you."

Well, at least she had a reason for what had happened with Payne. And she hadn't lied about it.

After a moment, V stepped into the room and picked up a duffel bag that was empty of his gym clothes. "Here. You're going to need this."

With that, he tossed it over . . . and walked away.

TWENTY-THREE

Down in the exam room, Payne's healer was looking half-dead, but entirely happy with his partial demise.

As she waited for him to answer her question, she was rather more concerned with his condition than he was. His blood had been shockingly rich on her tongue, the dark wine slipping to the back of her throat and tunneling into her, flooding not just her gut but her whole body.

It was the first time she'd ever taken a vein at the neck. Chosen, when they were in the Sanctuary, required not the sustenance of blood, nor did they cycle through their needings. And that was when one wasn't in suspended animation, as she had been.

And she barely remembered feeding from Wrath's wrist.

Strange . . . the two bloods had tasted much the same, though the flavor of the king's had been bolder.

"What is this coming?" she repeated.

Her healer cleared his throat. "It's . . . ah, what happens when you're into someone and you're with them."

"Show me."

The laughter that came out of him was velvety and deep. "I would love to. Trust me."

"Is it something I . . . can make you do?"

He coughed a little. "You already have."

"Really?"

Her healer nodded slowly, his eyelids dropping low. "You most certainly did. So I need a shower."

"And then you will show me." It wasn't a request; it was a demand. And as his arms tightened up on her, she had the sense he was aroused. "Yes," she growled. "You shall show me everything."

"I'll so fucking do that," he said darkly. *"Everything."*

When he stared at her as if he knew secrets she couldn't begin to guess at, she realized, even with the paralysis, that this was worth living for. This connection and excitement were worth more than her legs, and she had a sudden, stark terror that she had nearly missed this.

She had to thank her twin properly. But however could she balance this gift?

"Let me take you back to your room." Her healer stood up smoothly, in spite of her weight. "After I'm cleaned off, we'll start with a sponge bath for you."

Her nose crinkled in distaste. "How clinical."

There was more of that secret smile of his. "Not the way I'm going to do it. Trust me." He paused. "Hey, any chance you can hit the lights for me so I don't bump us into something? You're glowing, but I'm not sure it's enough to go by."

Payne had a moment of confusion—until she lifted her arm. Her healer was right. She was softly aglow, her skin casting a faint phosphorescence. . . . Perhaps this was her sexual response?

Logical, she thought. For the way he made her feel on the inside was as uncontainable as happiness and as luminous as hope.

When she willed the lights back on and unlocked the doors, he shook his head and started walking. "Damn. You've got some fancy tricks there, woman."

Perhaps, but not the ones she wanted. She would love to give him back what he had shared with her . . . but she had no secrets to teach him and no blood to gift him with, as not only did humans not require such a thing, but it was capable of killing them.

"I wish I could repay you," she murmured.

"For what?"

"Coming herein and showing me . . ."

"My buddy? Yeah, he's an inspiration."

For truth, 'twas more about the man in the flesh than the one on the screen. "Indeed," Payne demurred.

Back in the recovery room, he took her to the bed and laid her out with such care, arranging the sheeting and blankets so that no part of her was bare . . . taking the time to resettle the equipment that dealt with her bodily functions . . . plumping the pillows behind her head.

Whilst he worked, he always covered his hips with something. A part of the bedding. The two halves of his coat. And then he stood on the far side of the rolling table.

"Comfortable?" When she nodded, he said, "I'll be right back. Holler if you need me, okay?"

Her healer disappeared into the bathroom and the door shut most of the way—but not completely. A shaft of light pierced through into the stall of the falling water and she saw clearly his white-coated arm reach in, turn a handle, and call forth the warm rain.

Clothes were removed. All of them.

And then there was a brief glimpse of glorious flesh as he stepped under the spray and closed the glass partition. As the auditory rhythm of the water changed, she knew his naked form was breaking up the free fall.

What did he look like, sluiced with water, slick and warm and so very male?

Pushing herself up off the pillows, she leaned to the side . . . and leaned a little more . . . and leaned more still until she was all but hanging off. . . .

Ah, yeeees. His body was in profile, but she saw plenty: Carved with musculature, his chest and arms were heavy over tight hips and long, powerful legs. A dusting of dark hair sat upon his pectorals and formed a line that went o'er his abdomen and down, down . . . so far down. . . .

Damn it, she could not see enough, and her curiosity was too desperate and driving to ignore.

What did his sex look like? Feel like . . .

With a curse, she awkwardly shuffled herself around so that she was on the end of the bed. Angling her head, she made the very best of the limited exposure of that crack in the doorway. But as she had moved, so had he, and he was now facing away from her, his back and his . . . lower body . . .

She swallowed hard and stretched upward to see even more. As he unwrapped the cleansing bar, water streamed across his shoulder blades and rivered o'er his spine, flowing onto his buttocks and the backs of his thighs. And then his hand appeared on the nape of his neck, the frothy suds he had called up in his palms going the way of the water as he washed his body.

"Turn about . . ." she whispered. "Let me see all of you. . . ."

The desire for her eyes to get greater access only increased as his soapy ministrations went below his waist. Lifting one leg, and then the other, his hands were tragically efficient as they went o'er his thighs and calves.

She knew when he tended to his sex. Because his head fell back and his hips curled up tight.

He was thinking of her. She was sure of it.

And then he spun around.

It happened so fast that as their eyes met, both of them recoiled.

Even though she had been caught and then some, she shambled back against the pillows, and resumed her former position, restraightening the blankets he had been so careful with. With her face aflame, she wanted to hide—

A sharp squeak echoed through the room, and she glanced up. He had burst forth from the bathroom, the shower left open and running, soap still clinging to his abdominals and dripping from off . . .

His sex was a magnificent shock. Standing out from his body, the rod of him was hard and thick and proud.

"You . . ."

He said something further, but she was too captivated to care, too enthralled to notice. Deep within her, a wellspring was released, her sex swelling and preparing itself to accept him.

"Payne," he demanded, covering himself with his hands.

Instantly, she was ashamed and put her palms to her hot cheeks. "Verily, I am sorry I spied upon you."

Her human gripped the edge of the doorway. "Not that . . ." He shook his head as if to clear it. "Are you aware of what you were doing?"

She had to laugh. "Yes. Believe in this, my healer—I was totally aware of what I was regarding so thoroughly."

"You were sitting up, Payne. You were up on your knees at the end of the bed."

Her heart stopped. Surely she could not have heard him right. Surely.

As Payne frowned, Manny lurched forward—and then realized he was really fucking naked. Which was a condition that occurred when a guy didn't just have his ass in the breeze, but was totally and completely, ball-numbingly erect as he pulled a birthday suit. Reaching into the bathroom, he snagged a towel, wrapped it around his hips, and *then* went over to the bed.

"I . . . no, you must be wrong," Payne said. "I couldn't have—"

"You did—"

"I had merely stretched upon—"

"How did you get to the end of the bed, then. And how did you get back where you are?"

Her eyes went to the short footboard, confusion drawing her brows in tight. "I do not know. I was . . . watching you and you were all I knew."

The man in him was astounded and . . . strangely transformed. To be wanted that much by someone like her?

But then the physician in him took over. "Here, let me see what's doing, okay?"

He untucked the sheets and blanket from the end of the bed and rolled them up to the tops of her thighs. Using his finger, he ran it across the sole of her pretty foot.

He expected it to twitch. It didn't.

"Anything?" he said.

When she shook her head, he repeated on the other side. Then he moved higher, wrapping his palms around her slender ankles. "Anything?"

Her eyes were tragic as they met his. "I feel nothing. And I do not understand what you think you saw."

He moved higher, to her calves. "You were on your knees. I swear to it."

Higher still, to her taut thighs.

Nothing.

Christ, he thought. She had to have had some control over her legs. There was no other explanation. Unless . . . he'd been seeing things.

"I do not understand," she repeated.

Neither did he, but he was going to damn well figure it out. "I'm going to go review your scans. I'll be right back."

Out in the exam room, he got some help from the nurse and accessed Payne's medical record via the computer. With practiced efficiency, he went through everything: vitals, exam notes, X-rays—he even found the stuff he'd done to her at St. Francis, which was a surprise. He hadn't a clue how they'd gotten access to that original MRI—he'd erased the file nearly as soon as it had gone into the medical center's system. But he was glad to see it again, that was for sure.

When he was finished, he sat back in the chair, and the band of coldness that shot across his shoulder blades reminded him he was in nothing but a towel.

Kind of explained that nurse's walleyed look when he'd spoken with her.

"What the hell," he muttered, staring at the latest X-ray.

Her spine was perfectly in order, the vertebrae lined up nice and square, their ghostly glow against the black background giving him a perfect snapshot of what was going on down her back.

Everything, from the medical record to the exam he'd just given her on the bed, suggested that his original conclusion upon seeing her again was the correct one: He'd done the best technical work of his life, but the spinal cord had been irreparably damaged and that was that.

And abruptly, he remembered the expression on Goldberg's face as it had become obvious that the difference between night and day had escaped his notice.

Rubbing his eyes, he wondered if he was, yet again, going crazy. He knew what he'd seen, however. . . . Didn't he?

And then it dawned on him.

Twisting around, he looked to the ceiling. Sure enough, all the way up in the corner there was a pod attached to a panel. Which meant the security camera inside could see every square inch of the place.

Had to be one in the recovery room. Had to be.

Getting to his feet, he went over to the door and peered out into the corridor, hoping that nice blond nurse was somewhere to be found. "Hello?"

His voice echoed down the hall, but there was no reply, so he had no choice except to barefoot it around. Without an instinct as to which way to head, he choose "right" and walked fast. At all of the doors, he knocked and then tried to open them. Most were locked, but those that weren't revealed . . . classrooms. And more classrooms. And a huge, professional-size gym.

When he got to one marked WEIGHT ROOM, he heard the pounding of someone trying to break a treadmill with some Nikes and decided to keep going. He was a half-naked human in a world of vampires, and somehow he doubted that nurse would be marathoning it if she were on duty.

Besides, going by how hard and heavy that footfall was? He was liable to open up a can of whoop-ass, instead of just a door—and whereas he was suicidal enough to fight anything that rode up on him, this was about helping Payne, not his ego or his boxing skills.

Doubling back, he headed in the opposite direction. Knocking. Opening when he could. The farther he went, the less classroom-y it was and the more police-station-interrogation-y shit became. Down at the far end, there was a massive door that was right out of the movies, with its reinforced, bolted panels.

Outside world, he thought.

Going right up to it, he threw his weight against the bar, and—surprise! He burst out into the parking garage, where his Porsche was parked at the curb.

"What the fuck do you think you're doing?"

His eyes snapped over to a blacked-out Escalade: windows, rims, grille, everything was tinted. Standing next to it was the guy he'd seen that first night, the one he'd thought he'd recognized . . .

"I've seen you somewhere," Manny said as the door shut behind him.

From his pocket, the vampire took out a baseball cap and put it on. Red Sox. Of course, given the Boston accent.

Although the big question was, how in the hell did a vampire end up sounding like he was from Southie?

"Nice Jesus piece," the guy muttered, glancing at Manny's cross. "Are you looking for your clothes?"

Manny rolled his eyes. "Yeah. Someone stole them."

"So they could impersonate a doctor?"

"Maybe it's your Halloween—how the fuck do I know?"

From under the dark blue brim, a smile cranked into place, revealing a cap on one of his front teeth . . . as well as a set of fangs.

As Manny's brain cramped, the conclusion it struggled with was unassailable: He'd been a human once, this guy. And how did that happen?

"Do yourself a favor," the male said. "Stop thinking, go back to the clinic, and get dressed before Vishous shows up."

"I know I've seen you, and eventually I'm going to put it all together. But whatever—right now, I need access to the feeds from the security cameras down here."

That snarky half smile evaporated. "And why the hell is that."

"Because my patient just sat herself up—and I'm not talking about her raising her torso off the damn pillows. I wasn't there when she did it and I need to see how it happened."

Red Sox seemed to stop breathing. "What . . . I'm sorry. What the fuck are you saying."

"Do I need to reenact it in charades or some shit?"

"I'll pass on that—I so don't need you on your knees in front of me with only a towel on."

"Which makes two of us."

"Wait, are you serious?"

"Yeah. I'm really not interested in blowing you, either."

There was a pause. And then the bastard barked out a laugh. "You've got a smart mouth on you, I'll give you that—and yeah, I can help you, but you got to get your clothes on, my man. V catches you like that around his sister and you're going to need to operate on your own legs."

As the guy started to walk back to the door, Manny put it together. It wasn't from the hospital. "St. Patrick's. That's where I've seen you. You sit in the back pews during the midnight Masses alone, and you always wear that hat."

The guy threw open the entrance and stood to the side. No telling where his eyes were because of that brim, but Manny was willing to bet they weren't on him.

"Don't know what you're talking about, buddy."

Bull. Shit, Manny thought.

TWENTY-FOUR

Welcome to the New World.

As Xcor stepped out into the night, everything was different: The smell was not of the woods around his castle, but a city's musk of smog and sewer, and the sounds were not of distant deer soft-footing about the underbrush, but of cars and sirens and shouted talk.

"Verily, Throe, you have found us stellar accommodations," he drawled.

"The estate should be ready tomorrow."

"And am I to think it shall be an improvement?" He glanced back at the row house they'd spent the day holed up in. "Or will you surprise us with even lesser grandeur."

"You will find it more than suitable. I assure you."

In truth, considering all the variables of getting them over here, the vampire had done a superb job. They had had to take two overnight flights to ensure that no daylight problems occurred, and once they finally arrived in this Caldwell, Throe had somehow arranged everything: That decrepit house nevertheless had a solid basement, and there had been a *doggen* to serve them meals. The permanent solution to their residence had yet to make its appearance, but it was likely going to be what they needed.

"It had better be out of this urban filth."

"Worry not. I know your preferences."

Xcor did not like being in cities. Humans were stupid cows, but a stampede with no brains was more dangerous than one with intelligence—you could never predict the clueless. Although there was one benefit: He wanted to case the city before announcing his arrival to the Brotherhood and his "king," and there was no greater proximity than the one they had.

The house was in the thick of the downtown.

"We walk this way," he said, striding off, his band of bastards falling into formation behind him.

Caldwell, New York, would no doubt offer few revelations. As he had learned from both olden times and this well-lit present, cities at night were all the same, regardless of geography: The people out were not the plodding law abiders, but the truants and misfits and malcontents. And sure enough, as they progressed block by block, he saw humans sitting on the pavement in their own excrement, or packs of scum striding with aggression, or seedy females seeking even seedier males.

None thought to take on his group of six strong backs, however—and he almost wished they would. A fight would burn off their energy—although with luck, they would come upon the enemy and face a worthy opponent for the first time in two decades.

As he and his males turned a corner, they came upon a human infestation: Several barlike establishments set on either side of the road were lit up brightly and had lines of half-dressed people waiting to get into their confines. He could not read the signs that o'erhung the openings, but the way the men and women stamped their feet and twitched and talked, it was obvious that temporary oblivion waited on the far side of their hapless patience.

He was of a mind to slaughter them all, and he became acutely aware of his scythe: The weapon was at rest upon his back, folded in two, nestled in its harness and hidden under his floor-length leather duster.

To keep it in its place, he mollified the blade with the promise of slayers.

"I'm hungry," Zypher said. Characteristically, the male was not talking about food, and his timing was not a mistake: The cue for sex was in the lineup of human females they walked past. Indeed, the women presented themselves for using, painted eyes locking on the males they mistakenly believed were of their race.

Well, locking on the faces of the males who were other than Xcor. Him they took one look at and glanced away with alacrity.

"Later," he said. "I shall see that you get what you need."

Although he doubted he would partake, he was well aware that his soldiers required sustenance of the fucking variety, and he was more than willing to grant it—fighters fought better if they were serviced; he had learned that long ago. And who knew, mayhap he would take something himself if his eye was caught—assuming she could get past what he looked like. Then again, that was what they made money for. Many was the time he had paid for females to put up with his being within their sex. 'Twas far better than forcing them to submit, which he hadn't the stomach for—though he would admit such weakness to no one.

Such dalliances would not be until the end of the night, however. First, they needed to survey their new environment.

After they passed through the choked thicket of clubs, they came out into precisely what he had hoped to find . . . utter urban emptiness: whole blocks of buildings that were unoccupied for the evening, or perhaps even longer; roads that were bereft of traffic; alleys that were dark and cloistered with good space to fight in.

The enemy would be herein. He just knew it: The one affinity among both parties to the war was secrecy. And here, fights could happen with less fear of interruption.

With his body itching for a conflict and the sounds of the heels of his band of bastards behind him, Xcor smiled into the night. This was going to be—

Rounding yet another corner, he halted. A block up on the left, there was a gaggle of black-and-white cars parked in a loose circle around the opening of an alley . . . rather as if they were a necklace about the throat of a female. He couldn't read the patterns on the doors, but the blue lights atop their roofs told him they were human police.

Inhaling, he caught the scent of death.

Fairly recent killing, he decided, but not as juicy as an immediate one.

"Humans," he sneered. "If only they were more efficient and would kill each other off completely."

"Aye," someone agreed.

"Onward," he demanded, proceeding forth.

As they stalked by the crime scene, Xcor looked into the alley. Human men with queasy expressions and fidgety hands stood around a large box of some kind, as if they expected something to jump out at any moment and seize them by the cocks with a taloned grip.

How typical. Vampires would be delving in and dominating—at least, any vampire worth his nature. Humans only seemed to find their mettle when the Omega interceded, however.

Standing over a cardboard box that was stained through in places and big enough to fit a refrigerator in, José de la Cruz flicked his flashlight on and ran the beam over another mutilated body. It was hard to get much of an impression of the corpse, given that gravity had done its job and sucked the victim down into a tangle of limbs, but the savagely shaved-off hair and the gouged patch on the upper arm suggested that this was number two for his team.

Straightening, he glanced around the empty alley. Same MO as the first, he was willing to bet: Do the work elsewhere, dump the remains in downtown Caldwell, go trolling for another victim.

They had to catch this motherfucker.

Clicking off his beam, he checked his digital watch. Forensics had been doing their nitpicking job, and the photographer had clicked her shit, so it was time to take a good look at the body.

"Coroner's ready to see her," Veck said from behind him, "and he'd like some help."

José pivoted on his heel. "Have you got gloves . . ."

He paused and stared over his partner's broad shoulder. On the street beyond, a group of men walked by in triangular formation, one in the lead, two behind him, three behind them. The arrangement was so precise and their footfalls in such synchronization that at first, all José noticed was the militarylike marching and the fact that they were all wearing black leather.

Then he got a sense of their size. They were absolutely huge, and he had to wonder what kind of weapons they were packing under their identical long coats: The law, however, forbade police officers from strip-searching civilians just because they looked deadly.

The one in the lead cranked his head around and José took a mental snapshot of a face only a mother could love: angular and lean, with hollowed cheeks, the upper lip malformed by a cleft palate that hadn't been fixed.

The man resumed looking straight ahead and the unit continued onward.

"Detective?"

José shook himself. "Sorry. Distracted. You got gloves?"

"I'm holding them out to you."

"Right. Thanks." José took the set of latex and snapped them on. "You've got the—"

"Bag? Yup."

Veck was grim and focused, which, José had learned, was the man's cruising speed: He was on the young side, only in his late twenties, but he handled shit like a veteran.

Verdict thus far: He did not suck as a partner.

But it had been only a week and a half since they'd really started working together.

At any crime scene, who moved the bodies depended on a host of variables. Sometimes Search and Rescue handled it. With others, like this sitch, it was a combination of whoever was around who had a strong stomach.

"Let's cut open the front of the box," Veck said. "Everything's been dusted and photographed, and it'll be better than trying to tip it forward and have the bottom rip free."

José glanced over at the CSI guy. "You sure you got everything?"

"Roger that, Detective. And that's what I was thinking, too."

The three of them worked together, Veck and José holding the front side while the other man used a box cutter—natch. And then José and his partner carefully lowered the panel.

She was another young woman.

"Damn," the coroner muttered. "Not again."

More like *damned*, José thought. The poor girl had been done just as the others had, which meant she'd been tortured first.

"Fucking hell," Veck muttered under his breath.

The three of them were careful with her, as if even in her deceased state, her battered body registered the rearrangement of her limbs. Carrying her a mere two feet, they placed her in the opened black bag so the coroner and photographer could do their things.

Veck stayed crouched down with her. His face was utterly composed, but he nonetheless gave off the vibe of a man who was angered by what he saw—

The brilliant flare of a camera flash broke out through the dim alley, sure as a scream through a church. Before the shit even faded, José's head ripped around to see who the hell was taking pictures, and he wasn't the only one. The other officers who were standing about all snapped to attention.

But Veck was the one who exploded up and took off at a hard run.

The camera guy didn't stand a chance. In a totally brazen move, the bastard had ducked under the police tape and taken advantage of the fact that everyone had been focusing on the victim. And in his escape, he got snared in what he'd violated, tripping and falling before he recovered and gunned for the open door of his car.

Veck, on the other hand, had the legs of a sprinter and way more lift than your average white boy: No scurrying under the yellow for him; he vaulted over the bitch and launched himself onto the hood of the sedan, pulling his weight up by the lip of the hood. And then everything went slow-mo. While the other officers rushed forward to help, the photographer floored it, and the tires squealed as he panicked and tried to peel off—

Right in the direction of the crime scene.

"Fuck!" José yelled, wondering how in the hell they were going to protect the body.

Veck's legs fishtailed around as the car snapped through the yellow tape and came arrowing right for the cardboard box. But that son of a bitch DelVecchio not only stayed put like glue; he managed to reach in through the open window, grab the wheel, and crash the sedan into a Dumpster four feet in front of the goddamned victim.

As the air bags exploded and the engine let out a vicious hiss, Veck was thrown up and over the trash bin—and José knew he was going to remember the sight of that man airborne for the rest of his life, the guy's suit jacket blown open, his gun on one side and his badge on the other flashing as he flew without wings.

He landed flat on his back. Hard.

"Officer down!" José hollered as he ran for his partner.

But there was no telling that SOB to stay still or even a chance to help him up. Veck jumped onto his feet like the fucking Energizer bunny and lurched over to the knot of officers who had surrounded the driver with guns drawn. Shoving the others out of the way, he ripped open the driver's-side door and pulled out a partially conscious photo poacher who was one last pastrami and rye away from a heart attack: The bastard was as fat as Santa Claus and had the ruddy coloring of an alkie.

He was also having trouble breathing—although it wasn't clear whether that was from inhaling the powder of the air bag or the fact that he'd made eye contact with Veck and clearly knew he was about to get a beat-down.

Except Veck just dropped him and dived into the car, pawing his way through the deflated bags. Before he could get hold of the camera and bust it to dust, José jumped in.

"We need that for evidence," he barked, as Veck outted himself and lifted his arm over his head like he was going to slam the Nikon down on the pavement.

"Hey!" José two-handed the guy's wrist and threw all his weight into his partner's chest. Christ, the fucker was a big bastard—not just tall, but jacked—and for a split second, he had to wonder whether he was going to get anywhere with this manhandling bullshit.

Momentum turned the tide, however, and Veck's back slammed into the side of the car.

José kept his voice calm in spite of the fact that he had to use all his strength to keep the guy in place. "Think about it. You kill the camera, we can't use the picture he took against him. You hear me? Think, damn you . . . *think*."

Veck's eyes shifted over and locked on the perp, and frankly, the lack of crazy in them was a little disturbing. Even in the midst of manic, physical exertion, DelVecchio was strangely relaxed, utterly focused . . . and undeniably deadly: José got the sense that if he let the other detective go, the camera wasn't the only thing that was going to be irreparably damaged.

Veck looked entirely capable of killing in a very calm, competent way.

"Veck, buddy, snap out of it."

There was a moment or two of nothing-doing, and José knew damn well that everyone in the alley was as unsure as he was about how this was going to go. Including the photog.

"Hey. Look at me, my man."

Veck's baby blues slowly shifted over and he blinked. Gradually, the tension in that arm loosened and José escorted the thing down until he could take the Nikon—no way of knowing whether the storm was truly over.

"You okay?" José asked.

Veck nodded and pulled his jacket back into place. When he nodded a second time, José stepped back.

Big mistake.

His partner moved so fast there was no stopping him. And he cocked that photog so hard, he probably broke the fucker's jaw.

As the perp sagged in the hold of the other policemen, no one said a thing. They'd all wanted to do it, but given Veck's little car ride, he'd earned the right.

Unfortunately, the payback move was probably going to get the detective suspended—and maybe the CPD sued.

Shaking out his punching hand, Veck muttered, "Someone give me a cigarette."

Shit, José thought. There was no reason to keep trying to find Butch O'Neal. It was like his old partner was right in front of him.

So maybe he should give up trying to trace that 911 call from last week. Even with all the resources available down at headquarters, he'd gotten nowhere and the cold trail was probably a good thing.

One wild card with a self-destructive streak was more than he could handle on the job, thank you very much.

TWENTY-FIVE

Down in the training center at the compound, Butch kind of wanted to hate the surgeon out of loyalty to V. Especially given the guy's Chippendale, half-naked routine with that towel.

God, the idea that piece of meat had been near Payne all undressed? Wicked bad idea on so many levels.

It would have been different if he'd been built like a chess player, for instance. As it was, Butch felt like John Cena had been macking on V's little sister. How the hell was a surgeon built like that?

Still, there were two things that saved the guy: The bastard had put on the fresh scrubs Butch had given him—so no more ladies' night. And, as they'd sat down in front of the Dell in the exam room, the guy seemed honestly concerned about Payne and her welfare.

Not that they were getting anywhere on that front. The pair of them were staring at the computer screen like two dogs watching Animal Planet: very focused, but incapable of turning up the volume or changing the channel.

Ordinarily? Butch would phone or text Vishous. But that was not going to happen, given the showdown that was going on up at the Pit.

God, he hoped V and Jane got their act back together.

"So now what," the surgeon asked.

Butch shook himself back into focus and put his palm on the mouse. "We pray I pull the security files out of my ass. That's what."

"And you were bitching about my towel."

Butch cracked a smile. "Smart-ass."

As if on cue, the two of them leaned in closer to the screen—like that was somehow going to magically help the mouse find the stuff they were looking for.

"I suck at this shit," the surgeon muttered with disgust. "I'm better with my hands."

"Me, too."

"Go to the start menu."

"I'm going, going. . . ."

"Shit," they said together as they got a load of all the files or programs or whatever it was.

Naturally, there was nothing named "Security," "Cameras," or "Click here, dummy, to find what you two losers are looking for."

"Wait, would it be under 'videos'?" the surgeon said.

"Good idea."

They both inched even closer, until the tips of their noses were all but polishing the damn monitor.

"Can I help you guys?"

Butch snapped his head around. "Thank God, Jane. Listen, we need to find the security camera's digital files—" He stopped himself. "Are you okay?"

"Fine, fine."

Uh-huh, right. Standing in the doorway, she wasn't fine. Not even close to fine. To the point where he knew not to ask where V was—or expect the brother to show up anytime soon.

"Hey, Doc," Butch said, as he casually got to his feet, "can I talk to you a sec?"

"Ah—"

He cut off the protest she was about to put up. "Thanks. Just outside in the corridor. Manello, you try and find your way around the comp."

"I'll get right on that," the guy said drily.

When he and Jane were outside the room, Butch dropped his

voice. "What's going on? And yes, it's none of my business. But I want to know anyway."

After a moment, Jane crossed her arms over her white coat and just stared ahead. But not to shut him out, it seemed. More like she was replaying something in her mind.

"Talk to me," he murmured.

"You know why he went for Manny, right?"

"Not the particulars. But . . . I can guess." The female had been looking pretty suicidal, frankly.

"As a doctor, I get pulled in different directions. If you can extrapolate . . ."

Oh, God, it was worse than he'd thought. "I can. Shit."

"That's not all," she continued. "When I went up to pack, I found a set of his leathers in the back of the closet. There's black wax all over them. Along with blood and . . ." She took a shuddering breath. "Something else."

"Christ," Butch groaned.

As Jane went silent, he knew she didn't want to put him in the middle and wasn't going to ask out loud. But she was good like that.

Fucking hell . . . so much for honoring V's stay-out-of-it demand. Except he just couldn't watch the two of them fall apart.

"He didn't cheat on you," he said. "That night, a week ago? He let himself get beaten, Jane. By *lessers*. I found him surrounded by three of them and they were whipping him raw with chains."

She let out a gasp, which she covered with her hands. "Oh . . . God . . ."

"I don't know what you found of his, but he wasn't with anyone else. He told me himself."

"But what about the wax? And the . . ."

"Did it ever occur to you he might have done it himself."

Jane was momentarily speechless. "No. Although why couldn't he just say so."

Wasn't that the theme song of the night. "No guy wants to admit to his wife he was jacking off alone. It's too pathetic—and he probably thought it was cheating in a way. He's that devoted to you."

As tears speared into Jane's forest green eyes, Butch was momentarily nonplussed. The good doctor was as buttoned up as her *hellren*—and that reserved strength was why she was so damned useful as a doctor. It didn't mean that she was without feelings, though, and here they were.

"Jane . . . don't cry."

"I just don't know how we're going to get through this. I really don't. He's upset. I'm upset. And then there's Payne." Abruptly, she put her hand on his arm and squeezed. "Can you please . . . can you help him. With what he needs. Maybe it's the crack in the ice that will help us."

As the two of them stared at each other, he wondered if they were really on the same level. But how could he bring that up judiciously: So do you want me to work him over instead of the *lessers*?

What if they weren't on the same page. And she was already tearing up.

"I can't do it," Jane said roughly. "And not just because we've got issues at the moment. I just don't have it in me. He trusts you—I trust you . . . and he needs it. I'm worried that if he doesn't break through this wall he's got going on that he and I aren't going to make it—or worse. Take him to the Commodore, please."

Well, that settled one issue.

He cleared his throat. "I've been thinking the same thing, frankly. And, actually, I just . . . offered it to him."

"Thank you." She cursed and wiped her eyes. "You know him as well as I do. He needs to get unfrozen—somehow, some way."

"Yeah." Butch reached out and stroked her cheek. "And I'll take care of him. You don't worry about it."

She put her hand on his. "Thank you."

They embraced for a moment, and as they did, he thought there was nothing he wouldn't do to keep Jane and V together.

"Where is he now?" he asked.

"I have no idea. He gave me a bag and I just packed it and left. I didn't see him in the Pit, but then I wasn't looking for him."

"I'm on it. Will you help Manello?"

When she nodded, he gave her a lingering squeeze and then took off, hitting the underground tunnel and rocketing down to the last stop in the thing: the Pit.

With no idea what he was walking into, he put in the pass code and stuck his head in through the reinforced door. No smoke, so nothing was on fire. No screaming. No scent of anything but the fresh bread his Marissa had baked earlier.

"V? You here?" No answer.

God, it was too fucking quiet.

Down the hall, he found V and Jane's room empty and in a mess. The closet door was open and there were things gone from the hangers, but that was not what really got his attention.

He went over to the leathers and picked them up. Nice Catholic boy like him didn't know much about BDSM, but it looked like he was going to be learning firsthand.

Taking out his cell phone, he hit V, but didn't expect an answer. He guessed GPS was going to have to come in handy once again.

"Seems like old times."

Manny focused on the computer screen as he spoke. Hard to say what was the most awkward part of sitting next to his former colleague. With so much to choose from, the silence between them was an Easter-egg hunt for three-year-olds, everything badly hidden, ready to be found and captured.

"Why do you want to review the digital files?" she asked.

"You'll see when we get there."

Jane had no problem locating the right program, and a moment later the live image of Payne's room came up on the screen. Wait, the bed was empty . . . except for a duffel bag.

"Wrong one. Here it is," Jane murmured.

And there she was. His Payne. Lying against the pillows, the tail end of her braid in her hands, her eyes locked on the bathroom as if maybe she were imagining him still in the shower.

Damn . . . she was beautiful.

"You think," Jane said softly.

Okay, now would be a great time for his mouth to stop working independently.

He cleared his throat. "Can we go back about a half hour?"

"No problem."

The image reversed, the little counter in the lower right-hand corner draining down in milliseconds.

As he saw himself checking her over in that towel, it was too frickin' obvious that they were attracted to each other. Oh, God . . . that fucking hard-on so gave him another reason not to look at Jane.

"Wait . . ." He sat forward. "Slow down. Here it is."

He watched himself back into the bath in a rush. . . .

"Holy . . . crap," Jane breathed.

And there it was: Payne up on her knees at the bottom of the bed, her body long and lean and balanced perfectly as her eyes focused on the bathroom door.

"Is she glowing?"

"Yeah," he murmured, "she is."

"Hold on. . . ." Jane hit *forward*, running the images in proper order. "You're testing her sensations here?"

"Nothing. She felt nothing. And yet—go back again . . . thanks." He pointed at Payne's legs. "Here, though, she clearly has muscle control."

"This isn't logical." Jane played and replayed the file. "But she did it . . . oh, my God . . . she does it. It's a miracle."

Sure the fuck looked like one. Except . . . "What's the impetus," he muttered.

"Maybe it's you."

"No way. My operation clearly didn't do the ticket or she would have been kneeling before tonight. Your own exams showed she remained paralyzed."

"I'm not talking about your scalpel."

Jane reversed the file back to the moment Payne rose up, and froze the frame. "It's you."

Manny stared at the image, and tried to see something other than the obvious: Sure as hell, it seemed that as Payne had looked at him, the glow in her had gotten brighter and she was able to move.

Jane forwarded the file frame by frame. As soon as he came out of the bathroom and she was lying back, the glow was gone . . . and she had no feeling.

"This makes no sense," he muttered.

"Actually, I think it does. It's her mother."

"Who?"

"God where to start with that." Jane indicated her own body. "I'm what I am because of the Scribe Virgin."

"Who?" Manny shook his head. "I don't understand any of this."

Jane smiled a little bit. "You don't have to. It's happening. You just need to stay with Payne and . . . see how she changes."

Manny resumed staring at the monitor. Well, shit, it seemed like that Goateed Hater had made the right call. Somehow, the motherfucker had known this was what would happen. Or maybe the guy had merely hoped. Either way, it looked like Manny was a kind of medicine for that extraordinary creature lying on that bed.

So damn right he was going to hang in.

But he wasn't fooling himself. This wasn't going to be about love or even sex; it was about getting her up and moving so she could live her life again—no matter what it took. And he knew he wasn't going to be allowed to stay with her at the end of it. They were going to discard him like an empty orange bottle from the pharmacy—and yeah, sure, she might get attached to him, but she was a virgin who didn't know any better.

And she had a brother who was going to force her to make the right choices.

As for him? He wasn't going to remember any of this, was he.

Gradually, he became aware of Jane's stare on his profile. "What," he said without taking his eyes off the screen.

"I've never seen you like this about a female."

"I've never met anyone like her before." He put up his palm to stop any conversating. "And you can save the don't-go-there. I know what's coming at the end of this."

Hell, maybe those bastards were going to kill him and roll him into the river. Make it look like an accident.

"I wasn't going to say that, actually." Jane shifted in her seat. "And believe me . . . I know how you feel."

He glanced over at her. "Yeah?"

"It's how I was when I first met Vishous." Her eyes watered, but she cleared her throat. "Back to you and Payne—"

"What's going on, Jane. Talk to me."

"Nothing's going—"

"Bullshit—and right back at you. I've never seen you like this before. You look ruined."

She drew in a great breath. "Marital problems. Plain and not so simple."

Clearly, she didn't want to go into it. "Okay. Well, I'm here for you . . . for as long as I'm allowed to be."

He rubbed his face. It was a total waste of time to worry about how long this was going to last, how much time he had. But he couldn't help it. Losing Payne was going to kill him even though he barely knew her.

Wait a minute. Jane had been human. And she was here. Maybe there was—

What. The. Fuck.

"Jane . . . ?" he said weakly as he looked at his old friend. "What . . ."

Words deserted him at that point. She was sitting in the same chair, in the same position, wearing the same clothes . . . except he could see the wall behind her . . . and the steel cabinets . . . and the door across the way. And not "see" as in on the far side of her shoulders. He was looking *through* her.

"Oh. Sorry."

Right before his eyes, she went from translucent to . . . back to normal.

Manny jumped out of his chair and pinwheeled back until the examination table bit into his ass and stopped him.

"You need to talk to me," he said hoarsely. "Jesus . . . Christ . . ."

As he grabbed for the cross that hung around his neck, Jane's head dropped and one of her hands tucked some of her short hair behind her ear. "Oh, Manny . . . there's a lot you don't know."

"So . . . tell me." When she didn't reply, the screaming in his head got way too loud. "You'd better fucking tell me, because I'm really done with feeling like a lunatic."

There was a long silence. "I died, Manny, but not in that car wreck. That was staged."

Manny's lungs got tight. "How."

"A gunshot. I was shot. I . . . died in Vishous's arms."

Okay, he so could not breathe over here. "Who did it?"

"His enemies."

Manny rubbed his crucifix, and the Catholic in him suddenly believed in the saints as so much more than examples of good behavior.

"I'm not who you once knew, Manny. On so many levels." There was such sadness in her voice. "I'm not even actually alive. That was why I didn't come back to see you. It wasn't about the vampire/human thing . . . it's because I am not really here anymore."

Manny blinked. Like a cow. A number of times.

Well . . . the good news in all this, he supposed, was that finding out his former trauma surgeon was a ghost? Barely a blip on his radar. His mind had been blown too many times to count, and like a joint that had been dislocated, it had total and complete freedom of movement.

Of course, its functionality was fucked.

But who was counting.

TWENTY-SIX

Alone in downtown Caldwell, Vishous stalked the night by himself, traversing the underbelly stretch beneath the city's bridges. He'd started out at his penthouse, but that hadn't lasted more than ten minutes, and what an irony that all those glass windows had felt so confining. After launching himself into the air from the terrace, he'd coalesced down by the river. The other Brothers would be out in the alleys looking for *lessers* and finding them, but he didn't want to be around the peanut gallery. He wanted to fight. Solo.

At least, that was what he told himself.

It dawned on him, however, after about an hour of aimless wandering, that he wasn't really looking for some kind of hand-to-hand showdown. He wasn't actually looking for anything.

He was utterly empty, to the point where he was curious where the ambulation routine was coming from, because he sure as fuck wasn't doing anything consciously.

Stopping and staring across the sluggish, stinking waters of the Hudson, he laughed cold and hard.

In all the course of his life, he'd accumulated a body of knowledge to rival the Library of frickin' Congress. Some of it was useful, such as how to fight, how to make weapons, how to get information and how to keep it secret. And then there was some that was relatively useless on a day-to-day basis, like the molecular weight of carbon, Einstein's theory of relativity, Plato's political shit. There were also thoughts that he ruminated on once and never again, and their polar opposites, the ideas that he took out at regular intervals and played with like toys when he was bored. There were also things he never, ever let himself think of.

In and among those various cognitive outposts was a huge stretch of cerebellum that was nothing but a dump yard of bullshit that he didn't believe in. And given that he was a cynic? It was miles and miles of rotting, metaphorical Hefty bags full of trash along the lines of . . . fathers were supposed to love their sons . . . and mothers were gifts beyond measure . . . and blah, blah, blah.

If there was a mental equivalent of the EPA, that part of his brain would have been cited, fined, and closed down.

But it was funny. Tonight's little stroll in this underpass of God-and-awful by the river had him ruminating through that landfill and pulling something out of the pile:

Bonded males were nothing without their females.

So bizarre. He'd always known he'd loved Jane, but being the tight-ass that he was, he had stitched up his feelings without realizing a needle and thread were in his proverbial hand. Shit, even when she'd come back to him after she'd died, and he'd known for that brief moment what the term *overjoyed* not just meant, but felt like . . . he hadn't truly let himself go.

Sure, his permafrost had slicked over on its top layer from the warmth she brought to him, but the inside, the deep inside, had stayed the same. Good God, they'd never even gotten properly mated. He'd just moved her into his room and loved every minute of having her there as they'd gone about their nights separately.

He'd fucking wasted those hours.

Criminally wasted them.

And now here they were, separated by rifts that, in spite of his intelligence, he had no clue how to cross.

Christ, when she'd been holding those leathers in her hands and waiting for him to talk, it was like someone had stapled his lips together—probably because he'd felt guilty about what he'd done at his place, and how fucked-up was that? His own hand hardly counted as cheating.

The trouble was, however, that even being drawn to the type of release he'd once had so much of had felt wrong. But that was because sex had always been a part of it.

Naturally, this made him think of Butch. The solution the guy had suggested was so obvious, V was surprised he hadn't realistically considered it sooner himself—but then again, asking his best friend to beat the shit out of him wasn't exactly a casual idea to have.

He wished he'd had that option a week ago. Maybe it would have helped things . . . Except that scene in the bedroom wasn't his and Jane's only issue, was it. She should have come to him first about the sitch with his sister. He should have been briefed and decided what to do with the two of them.

As anger rose like a stench inside of him, he feared what was on the other side of this emptiness. He wasn't like other males, never had been, and not just because of the *Mommie Dearest* deity crap: Knowing his luck, he'd be the one bonded male on the face of the planet who got past these purposeless numbs at losing his *shellan* . . . and went somewhere oh, so much darker.

Insanity, for instance.

Wait, he wouldn't be the first, would he. Murhder had gone mad. Absolutely and irrevocably.

Maybe they could start a club. And the handshake could involve daggers.

Emo-ass motherfuckers that they were—

With a snarl, V pivoted in the direction of the prevailing wind, and he would have offered up a prayer of thanks if he didn't hate his mother so much: In and among the tendrils of fog, riding upon the vapors of gray and white humidity, the sweet smell of the enemy gave him purpose and a definition that his numb state had not just lacked, but seemed likely to reject.

His feet started to walk and then jog and then run. And the faster he went, the better he felt: To be a soulless killer was far, far, far better than to be a breathing void. He wanted to maim and murder; he wanted to tear with his fangs and claw with his hands; he wanted the blood of slayers on him and in him.

He wanted the screams of those he killed to ring in his ears.

Following the sickly stench, he cut over into the streets and weaved in and out of alleys and straightaways, tracking the scent as it grew stronger and stronger. And the closer he got, the more relieved he became. There had to be a number of them—and even better news? No sign of his brothers, which meant first come . . . first served.

He was saving this for himself.

Rounding the last corner of the quest, he plowed into a short, squat stretch of urban armpit and skidded to a halt. The alley had no outlet on the other side, but like a chute system for livestock, the buildings on either side were directing the wind that came off the river outward, the herd of molecules scrambling and picking up the smells on their hooves and galloping it straight into his sinuses.

What . . . the . . . hell . . . ?

The stench was so strong, his nose filed relocation papers—but there weren't a bunch of those pale-ass fools standing around, stroking each other's knives. The place was empty.

Except then he noticed the sound of dripping. As if a faucet hadn't been quite turned off.

After throwing up some *mhis*, he pulled his glove free of his glowing hand and used his palm to light the way. Walking forward, the illumination formed a shallow pool of clear-and-visi right in front of him, and the first thing he came to was a boot . . . which was attached to a camo'd calf . . . and a thigh and hip. . . .

That was it.

The slayer's body had been cut in half, sure as if it had been deli sliced, the cross section leaking portions of the intestinal tract, the stump of the spine showing bright white in and among all the greasy black.

A resonant scratching drew him over to the right.

This time he saw a hand first . . . a pale hand that was digging its nails into the damp asphalt and retracting like it was trying to hoe up the ground.

The *lesser* was just torso, but it was still alive—although that wasn't a miracle; it was how they worked: Until you stabbed them through the heart with something that was made of steel, they hung around, no matter what state their bodies were in.

As V slowly moved his palm-light upward, he got a load of the thing's face. Its mouth was stretching wide, the tongue clicking as if it were trying to speak. Typical of the current crop of killers, this one was a new recruit, his dark skin and hair having yet to turn floury white.

V stepped over the bastard and kept going. A couple of yards over, he found the two halves of a second one.

As the back of his neck went ants-all-over in warning, he passed his glowing hand around, moving outward from the bodies in a concentric circle.

Well, well, well . . . wasn't this a blast from the past.

And so not in a good way.

Back at the Brotherhood's compound, Payne lay in her bed, waiting.

She was not good at patience at the best of times, and she felt as though ten years passed before her healer finally came back to her. When he did, he brought with him a thin booklike panel.

As he sat down on the bed, there was tension in his strong, handsome face. "Sorry that took so long. Jane and I were firing up this laptop."

She had no clue what that meant. "Just tell me whatever there is to say."

With quick, nimble hands, he opened the top half of the contraption. "Actually, you need to see it for yourself."

Feeling as though she wanted to curse loud and often, she dragged her eyes to the screen. Immediately, she recognized the image of the room she was in. This was from before, however, because as she lay on the bed, she was staring at the bathroom. The frame was frozen like a picture, but then a little white arrow moved when he touched something and the picture became animated.

With a frown, she focused on herself. She was glowing: Any piece of flesh that showed was illuminated from within. Why ever was that—

First she sat up from the pillow, her neck craned so that she could spy on her healer. More leaning to the side. And then maneuvering downward upon the bed . . .

"I sat upright," she breathed. "Onto my knees!"

Indeed, her luminescent form had raised itself up perfectly and hovered with precise balance as she watched him in the shower.

"You most certainly did," he said.

"I am aglow as well. Why is that, though?"

"We were hoping you could tell us. You ever do that before?"

"Not that I was aware of. But I have been imprisoned for so long, I feel as though I know not myself." The file stopped. "Do play it again?"

When her healer didn't reply, and the pictures didn't renew their action, she glanced over at him—only to recoil. His face was showing a thunderous rage, the anger so deep, his eyes were nearly black.

"Imprisoned how?" he demanded. "And by who?"

Strange, she thought dimly. She'd always been told humans were a far milder form of creature than vampires. But her healer's protective response was every bit as deadly as that of her own species.

Unless, of course, it wasn't about protection. It was entirely possible that her having been jailed was not attractive to him.

And who could blame him?

"Payne?"

"Ah . . . Forgive me, healer—perhaps my word choice is incorrect, as English is a second language to me? I have been under my mother's care."

It was nearly impossible to keep the distaste from her voice, but the camouflage must have worked, because the tension left him completely as he released his breath. "Oh, okay. Yeah, that word does not mean what you think it does."

Indeed, humans as well had standards for behavior, did they not: His relief was as great as his tension had been. But then, it was not wrong to look for morality and decency in females—or males.

As he replayed the pictures for her, she shifted her focus to the miracle that had happened . . . and found herself shaking her head at what she saw. "Truly, I was unaware. How is . . . this possible?"

Her healer cleared his throat. "I've talked it over with Jane . . . and she—well, we—have a theory." He stood up and went over to inspect a fixture on the ceiling. "It's crazy, but . . . Marvin Gaye might just have known what he was talking about."

"Marvin?"

With a quick shift, he picked up a chair and placed it under the camera. "He was a singer. Maybe I'll play you a song of his someday." Her healer planted his foot on the seat and rose to the ceiling where he disconnected something with a yank and got back down. "It's good to dance to."

"I do not know how to dance."

He glanced over his shoulder, his lids dropping low. "Something else for me to teach you." As her body warmed, he approached the bed. "And I'm going to like showing you how."

When he leaned down, her eyes latched onto his lips and her breath got tight. He was going to kiss her—dearest fate, he was going to—

"You wanted to know what coming was," he all but growled, their mouths merely inches apart. "Why don't I show you what it is instead of tell you?"

On that note, he flipped a switch and put out the lights, plunging the room into a dimness that was broken only by the light in the bathroom and the line at the base of the door into the hall.

"Do you want me to show you?" he said in a low voice.

At that moment, there was one and only one word in her vocabulary: "Yes . . ."

Except then he backed off.

Just as a protest was about to jump out of her throat, she realized he'd stood in the line of illumination that streamed in from the bathroom.

"Payne . . ."

The sound of her name leaving his mouth had her struggling for air even more. "Yes . . ."

"I want you . . ." Reaching for the bottom of his loose shirt, he pulled it up slowly, exposing the carved muscles of his stomach. ". . . to want me."

Oh, sweet destiny, she did.

And he meant what he said. The more she looked, the more those abdominals of his curled and released as if he were breathing hard as well.

His hand drifted down to his waist. "See what you do to me." He smoothed the baggy fabric over his hips and . . .

"You are *phearsom*," she breathed. "Oh . . . fates, you are."

"Tell me that's a good thing?"

"It is . . ."

She stared at the rigid length that was confined and straining against the front of his no longer billowy slacks. So thick and smooth. So big. The mechanics of sex were not unknown to her, but up until now, she hadn't been able to fathom why they would appeal to a female. Looking at him now? Her heartbeat would cease and her blood would turn to stone if she didn't have him within her.

"Do you want to touch me?" he growled.

"Please . . ." She swallowed through a nearly closed throat. "Oh, yes . . ."

"First, look at yourself, *bambina.* Lift your arm and look at yourself."

She glanced down just to humor him so they could get on with things—

Her skin was aglow from the inside out, as if the heat and the sensations he called forth from her had manifested themselves in illumination. "I know not . . . what this is. . . ."

"I think it's the solution, actually." He sat down next to her feet. "Tell me if you feel this." He gently touched her lower leg, laying his hand upon her calf—

"Warm," she choked out. "Your touch is *warm.*"

"And here?"

"Yes . . . yes!"

When he went to move it upward, onto her thigh, she furiously yanked the coverings off of herself so she would have no impediments. Her heart was thundering and—

He laid his palm upon her other leg.

This time, she felt . . . nothing.

"No, no . . . touch me, touch me again!" The demand was harsh, her focus manic. "Touch me—"

"Hold on—"

"Where did it go—do it again! By all that is holy with your God, do it anew—"

"Payne." He captured her frantic hands. "Payne, look at yourself."

The glow was gone. Her skin, her flesh . . . was normal. "Damn it all—"

"Hey. Beautiful. Hey—look at me." Somehow her eyes found his. "Take a deep breath and just relax. . . . Come on, breathe with me. That's it. That's good. . . . I'll get it back for you. . . ."

When he bent toward her, she felt the gentle stroke of his fingertips on her neck. "You feel this?"

"Yes . . ." Impatience warred with the effect of his deep voice and his slow, meandering touch.

"Close your eyes—"

"But—"

"Close them for me."

When she did as she was told, the pads of his fingers disappeared . . . and were replaced by his mouth. His lips brushed her throat and then sucked at her skin, the subtle pull unleashing a welling heat between her legs.

"Feel this?" he said in a gravelly voice.

"Fates . . . yes . . ."

"Then let me keep going." With subtle pressure, he urged her back against the pillows. "Your skin is so smooth. . . ."

As he nuzzled at her, the sound of his mouth made delicious clicking sounds below her ear, and those fingers of his traveled back and forth on her collarbone . . . then dipped down. In response, a curious, languid warmth boiled in her torso and tightened up her nipples, and she became aware of her whole body . . . every inch of herself. Even her legs.

"See, *bambina*, it's back. . . . Look."

Her lids were heavy as stones as she opened them, but when she glanced down, the glow was a huge relief—and made her hold on to the sensations he was calling out of her.

"Give me your mouth," he said roughly. "Let me in."

His voice was guttural, but his kiss was gentle and teasing, pulling at her lips and stroking, before he licked at her. And then she felt his hand on her outer leg.

"I feel you," she said into his kiss, tears coming to her eyes. "I feel you."

"I'm glad." He eased back a little, his face serious. "I don't know what this is—I'm not going to lie. Jane isn't sure, either."

"I do not care. I just want my legs back."

He had a moment's pause. But then he nodded, as if he were taking a vow to her. "And I'm going to do whatever I can to give them to you."

His eyes drifted to her breasts, and the response was immediate—

with every breath she took, the fabric that covered her nipples seemed to stroke across her and make her even tighter.

"Let me make you feel good, Payne. And we'll see where this takes you."

"Yes." She lifted her hands to his face and pulled him to her mouth once more. "Please."

Verily, as she would take nourishment from a vein, now she drew upon the warmth of his lips and the slick entrance of his tongue and the energy he called out of her.

Moaning into him, she was submersed in sensation, from the weight of her body on the bed, to the blood coursing throughout her, to the pulsing need between her legs and the delicious ache at her breasts.

"Healer." She gasped as she felt her thigh get swept over by his palm.

He shifted back, and she was gratified that he was panting as well. "Payne, I want to do something."

"Anything."

He smiled. "May I unbraid your hair?"

For certain, her tresses were the last thing on her mind, but his expression was so rapt and intense, she could not deny him the request—or any part of herself. "But of course."

His fingers trembled ever so slightly as he reached for the end of her braid. "I've wanted to do this since the moment I first saw you."

Gradually, inch by inch, he freed the heavy weight of the black waves she kept long for no other reason than she was too disinterested to tend to them. Given his profound regard for what he revealed, however, she began to wonder if mayhap she'd far underestimated their significance.

When he was finished, he spread the lengths out o'er the bed and just sat back. "You are . . . indescribably beautiful."

Having never viewed herself as even feminine, much less "beautiful," it was an astonishment to hear the reverence in not just his words, but his voice.

"Indeed . . . you tie my tongue," she said once again to him.

"Let me give you something else to do with it."

As he joined her on the bed and lay beside her, she turned into the cushion of his pectorals and the hard expanse of his stomach. She

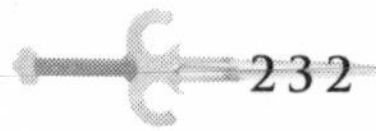

was big compared to other members of her sex, her body retaining the power that had come from her sire's side to the point where she often felt ungainly in comparison to other females: No willowy grace as the Chosen Layla had for her—in truth, she was built for fighting, not spiritual or sensual service.

Here with her healer, however, she felt rather perfectly proportioned. He had not the tremendous heft of her twin brother, but he was bigger and thicker than she was, in all the places a male should be: Lying with him in the dim room with their bodies so close together, and the temperature rising everywhere, she was not something that should not be, a malformation of girth and bulk, but an object of desire and passion.

"You're smiling," he whispered next to her mouth.

"Am I?"

"Yeah. And I love it."

Over at her hip, his hands burrowed into her nightgown and she felt it all, from the light drift of his pinkie finger to the smooth skin of his palm to the hot trail his touch left behind as he slowly went upward. Closing her eyes, she arched into him, very aware that she was asking for something, yet unclear as to what exactly she was in search of—but she knew he would give it to her.

Yes, her healer knew exactly what she needed: That hand of his went up her rib cage and paused beneath her heavy, tender breasts.

"Is this okay?" she heard him ask from a great distance.

"Anything," she gasped. "Anything to feel my legs."

Except even as the words left her, she sensed that what drove her was less her paralysis and more a greed for him and his sex—

"Healer!"

The sensation of her breast being captured in a gentle caress was a wondrous shock, and she jerked up, her thighs spreading, her heels pressing into the mattress beneath them both. And then his thumb passed up and over her nipple, the stroke shooting a blast of fire to her core.

Her legs sawed on the bed, the tight coil in her sex driving them. "I'm moving," she said roughly—and almost as an afterthought. What seemed important now was joining with him and having him . . . come . . . inside of her.

"I know, *bambina*," he avowed. "And I'm going to make sure you keep it up."

TWENTY-SEVEN

Downtown, Butch parked the Escalade in the underground parking garage of the Commodore and took the internal elevator all the way up the spine of the building. He had no fucking clue what he was going to walk into when he got to V's place, but that was where the GPS signal was coming from, so that was where he was going.

In the pocket of his leather coat, he had all the keys to Vishous's private space: the plastic swipe card to get into the parking garage; the silver one you used in the elevator to punch the top button; the copper job that got you past the dead bolts on the doors.

His heart beat hard as a little *ding* sounded and the elevator opened silently. *All-access* was taking on a whole new meaning tonight, and as he stepped out into the hall, he wanted a drink. Badly.

At the door, he took out the copper key, but used his knuckles first. A couple of times.

It was a good minute later when it dawned on him that there was no answer.

Fuck the knuckles. He pounded with his fist.

"Vishous," he barked. "Answer the goddamn door or I'm coming in."

One, Mississippi. Two, Mississippi—

"Fuck this." He shoved the key into the lock and cranked it before throwing his shoulder into the solid metal door and shoving it wide.

Bursting into the place, he heard the alarm beeping quietly. Which meant V couldn't be here. "What the hell . . . ?"

He put the code in, shut the thing off, and locked the dead bolt behind himself. No remnants of lit candlewicks . . . no scent of blood . . . nothing but cool, clean air.

He flipped on the light switch and blinked in the glare.

Yeah, wow . . . Lot of memories in here . . . him coming and crashing after the Omega had gotten into him and he'd left quarantine . . . V losing his ever-loving mind and jumping off the damn terrace . . .

He went over to the wall of "equipment." A fuckload of other things had happened here, too. Some of which he couldn't imagine.

As he went down the display of metal and leather, his shitkickers echoed up to the ceiling, and his mind all but bounced around his skull. Especially as he got to the far end: In the corner, a set of iron cuffs hung from the ceiling by thick chains.

You got someone on them, you could lift them up and dangle 'em like a side of beef.

Reaching out, he fingered one of them. No cushioning on the inside.

Spikes. Dull spikes that would grip the flesh like teeth.

Getting himself back with the program, he marched through the place, checking in all the nooks and crannies . . . and found a little tiny computer chip on the kitchen counter. It was the kind of thing that no one but V would know how to remove from a cell.

"Son of a bitch."

So there was no way of knowing where—

When his phone went off, he checked the screen. Thank *God.* "Where the hell are you?"

V's voice was tight. "I need you down here. Ninth and Broadway. *Stat.*"

"Fuck that—why is your GPS in your kitchen."

"Because that's where I was when I took it out of my phone."

"What the *hell,* V." Butch tightened his grip on his cell and wished there were an app that let you reach through a phone and bitch slap someone. "You can't—"

"Get your ass down here to Ninth and Broadway—we've got problems."

"You're kidding me, right? You go untraceable and—"

"Someone else is killing *lessers*, cop. And if it's who I think it is, we've got problems."

Pause. Big-time. "Excuse me?" he said slowly.

"Ninth and Broadway. Now. And I'm calling in the others."

Butch hung up and rushed for the door.

Leaving the SUV in the parking garage, he took a mere five minutes to run over to the correct coordinates on Caldwell's street grid. And Butch knew when he was getting close because of the sickening scent in the air and the tingling resonance of the enemy deep inside of him.

As he rounded the corner of a short-and-squat, he hit a wall of *mhis* and penetrated the shit, coming out on the other side to a whiff of Turkish tobacco and a tiny orange flare in the way-back of the alley.

He jogged over to V, slowing only when he got to the first of the bodies. Or . . . part of the first. "Hello, halvsies."

As Vishous came up and offed his glove, Butch got a quick impression of dead-meat legs and leaking innards. "Yum."

"Clean cut," V muttered. "Real hot-knife-through-butter time."

The brother was too right. It was practically surgical.

Butch knelt down and shook his head. "Can't be the result of Lessening Society politics. They'd never leave the bodies out in the open like this."

God knew, the slayers regularly went through shifts in leadership, either because the Omega got bored, or because of internal power struggles. But the enemy was incented to keep their biz off the human radar screens as much as vampires were—so no way would they have abandoned this mess for the CPD to find.

As Butch sensed the arrival of the other brothers, he rose to his feet. Phury and Z came out of the ether first. Then it was Rhage and Tohr. And Blay. That was everyone for tonight: Rehvenge often fought with the Brotherhood, but this evening, he was up in the *symphath* colony playing King of the Damned, and it was Qhuinn's, Xhex's, and John Matthew's rotation off.

"Tell me I'm not seeing this," Rhage said grimly.

"Your eyes are working just fine, true." V stabbed his hand-rolled out on the sole of his boot. "I couldn't believe it, either."

"I thought he was dead."

"He?" Butch asked, glancing at the pair. "Who's 'he'?"

"Where to start on that one," Hollywood muttered as he checked out another hunk of *lesser*. "You know, if I had a stake, we could make *lesser*-kebabs."

"Only you could think of food at a time like this," someone drawled.

"I'm just sayin'."

If there was more conversation at that point, Butch didn't hear it because his internal alarm suddenly started to ring-a-ding-ding. "Boys . . . we're about to have company."

Pivoting around, he faced the alley's open end. The enemy was approaching. Fast.

"How many?" V asked as he came forward.

"At least four, maybe more," Butch said, as he thought of the fact that there was no way out behind them. "This may be a trap."

Back at the Brotherhood's training center, Manny was paying special attention to his patient.

As he worked Payne's breast with his hand, she writhed under him, her legs bicycling with impatience on the mattress, her head thrown back, her body glowing like the moon on a cloudless winter night.

"Do not stop, healer," she moaned as he thumbed her nipple in circles. "I feel . . . everything. . . ."

"You don't worry about my stopping."

Yeah, he was so not putting the brakes on this anytime soon—not that they were going to have sex. But still . . .

"Healer . . ." she said against his lips. "More, please."

Licking his way into her mouth, he pinched her nipple ever so slightly. "Let me get this off you," he said as he found the bottom of her johnny with his other hand. "I'm going to take care of you down below."

She worked with him as he stripped her bare and discreetly removed her equipment. When she was utterly and completely naked, he was momentarily dry mouthed and immobile at the sight of her. Her breasts were perfectly formed, with little pink nipples, and her long, flat stomach led down to a bare cleft that had his head pounding.

"Healer . . . ?"

When all he did was swallow hard, she reached for the sheet to pull it across and hide her body.

"No . . ." He stopped her. "Sorry. I just need a minute."

"To what?"

Climax, in a word. Unlike her, he knew precisely what all this naked was heading toward—in about a minute and a half, his mouth was going to be all over her. "You're incredible . . . and you have nothing to be shy about."

Her body was insane, all lean muscle and luscious, smooth skin—as far as he was concerned, she was the perfect female, bar none. Christ, he'd never been even half this desperate for those sticks-and-stones social X-rays, with their hard-as-nails boob jobs and their stringy arms.

Payne was powerful, and that was pure sex as far as he was concerned. But she was absolutely going to leave this experience with her virginity intact. Yeah, she wanted what he was giving her, but it wasn't fair, under these circumstances, to take something she was never getting back: In the quest to return her legs to some sort of functioning, she might well go farther than she would have if it was just sex for the enjoyment of it.

This shit between them was all about purpose.

And the fact that that left him a little hollow was nothing he wanted to look too closely at.

Manny leaned into her. "Give me your mouth, *bambina*. Let me in."

As she did what he asked, he inched his hand back to her perfect breast.

"Shh . . . easy," he told her as she nearly jacked off the bed.

Fucking hell, she was lightning in a bottle, and for a moment he imagined what it would be like to ride those rocking hips and take her hard.

Cut that shit right now, Manello, he told himself.

Disengaging from her mouth, he nuzzled his way down the side of her neck and briefly sank his teeth into her collarbone—just enough so that she felt it, not enough to hurt. And as her hands dug into his hair, he knew by the strength of her grip and the way she panted that she wanted him to go exactly where he was heading.

Palming the outside of her breast, he extended his tongue and dragged a slow trail down to that tight pink top. Circling her nipple, he watched her bite down on her lower lip, her fangs cutting into the flesh and drawing a sliver of bright red blood.

Without conscious thought, he surged up and captured what had been shed, lapping it and swallowing—

His eyes slammed shut at the taste: rich and dark, thick and smooth on the back of his throat. His mouth tingled . . . and then so did his gut.

"No," she said in a guttural voice. "You must not do that."

As he forced his lids open, he watched her own tongue come out and do away with what little was left.

"Yes. I must," he heard himself say. He needed more. So much more—

She put her fingertip on his lips and shook her head. "No. You shall go mad from it."

He was going to go mad if he didn't have a whole mouthful; that's what he was going to do. Her blood was like cocaine and Scotch together on an intravenous drip: From that shallow swallow, his body had become Superman's, his chest pumped up, all the muscles in him swelling with power.

As if she were reading his mind, she grew firm. "No, no . . . not safe."

She was probably right—take out the *probably*. But that didn't mean he wasn't going to try again, assuming he got another chance at it.

He went back to her nipple, sucking it in and flicking. When she arched again, he pushed his arm under her and lifted her up to him. All he could think about was getting in between her legs with his mouth . . . but he wasn't sure how that was going to go over. He needed to keep her in this sweet zone of arousal—not spook her with the kind of shit men liked to do to their women.

He settled for taking his hand where he wanted his lips to be, sweeping his palm slowly down her rib cage and to her stomach. Lower, to her hips. Lower, to her upper thighs.

"Open for me, Payne," he told her, switching to her opposite nipple and working it with a suck. "Open yourself so I can touch you."

She did just as he asked, her graceful legs parting.

"Trust me," he said roughly. And she could. He already felt bad enough that all these firsts were happening with him. He was not going to violate the boundaries he'd set for them.

"I do," she moaned.

God save them both, he thought as his palm slipped into the juncture—

"Fuck . . ." he groaned. Hot and slick, silky smooth. Undeniable.

His arm shot out, the sheets went flying, and his eyes whipped down to lock on the sight of his hand nestled in close to the core of her. As her body arched up, one of her legs fell to the side.

"Healer . . ." she groaned. "Please . . . don't stop."

"You don't know what I want to do to you," he said to himself.

"I am in pain."

Manny gritted his teeth. "Where."

"Where you have touched me and gone no farther. Do not stop this, I beg you."

Manny's mouth opened and he breathed through it.

"Do this thing you want to me, healer," she moaned. "Whatever it is. I know you are holding back."

A growl came out of him and he moved so fast that the only thing that could have stopped him was her saying no. And that word was evidently not in her vocabulary.

In a flash, he was between her thighs, his hands spreading her wider, her sex laid open and weeping in the face of his male urge to dominate and mate.

He gave in. Fuck him, but he let himself go and kissed her core. And there was nothing gradual or gentle about it; he dived in with his mouth, sucking at her and tonguing her as she cried out and scratched at his forearms.

Manny came. Hard. In spite of the number of times he'd orgasmed out there in the office. The tingling buzz in his blood and the sweet taste of her sex and the way she moved against his lips, rubbing herself, seeking even more . . . it was all too much.

"Healer . . . I am . . . on the verge of— I know not what I—"

He licked his way up off the top of her sex and then returned to get serious in a slow, thorough way. "Stay with me," he said against her. "I'm going to make you feel good."

Flicking his tongue lightly, he took one of his hands down and stroked her without entering her, giving her exactly what she wanted, just at a speed that made her struggle with impatience. But she was going to learn that this anticipation before the release was almost as good as the orgasm she was about to have.

God, she was incredible, that hard body of hers flexing, her muscles going tighter, her chin just visible on the far side of her perfect breasts as her head fell back and kicked the pillows off the bed.

He knew just when the snap in her sex happened. She gasped and grabbed the sheet that covered the mattress, ripping it with her nails as she stiffened from head to foot.

His tongue sneaked in.

He simply had to penetrate her a little . . . and those subtle pulses he felt left him dizzy.

When he was sure she had been finished properly, he pushed himself back—and nearly bit his own lip in half. She was oh, so ready for him, glossy and glowing—

Abruptly, he shoved himself from the bed and had to pace it off. His cock felt like it had swollen to Empire State Building dimensions, and his balls were July Fourth blue—so desperate for a release they had their own marching band and fireworks brigade. But that wasn't all. Something in him was roaring at the fact that he wasn't inside of her . . . and the urge was about more than merely sex. He wanted to mark her in some way—which made absolutely no sense.

Strung out, panting, on the edge, he ended up planting his hands on the jambs of the door to the hall and leaning in until his forehead was against the steel. In a way, he almost hoped someone barged in and knocked him the fuck out.

"Healer . . . it persists. . . ."

For a moment, he squeezed his eyes shut. He wasn't sure he could go through it again with her so soon. It was nearly killing him not to—

"Regard me," she said.

He forced his head up, looked over his shoulder . . . and realized that she wasn't talking about sex: She was sitting on the edge of the bed, her legs hanging off the side and inching toward the floor, her glow illuminating her from within. At first, all he could really see were her breasts, and the way they hung so full and rounded, the nipples tight from the cool air in the room. But then he realized she was rotating her ankles, one after the other.

Right, see . . . this was not about the sex, but her mobility.

Got that, asshole? he told himself. This was about her walking: sex as medicine—and he'd better not forget it. This was *not* about him or his cock.

Manny lurched over, hoping that she wouldn't notice the remnants of the release he'd had. But he didn't have to worry. Her eyes were locked on her feet, her concentration fierce.

"Here . . ." He had to clear his throat. "Let me help you stand."

TWENTY-EIGHT

Vishous's fangs elongated as a ring of slayers formed around the opening of the alley. These were old-school numbers, he thought. Half a dozen at least—and they'd clearly been given coordinates by their fellow slayers. Otherwise the *mhis* would have hidden the carnage from them.

Given his mood, all the hi-how're-ya should have been a great thing.

Problem: The alley's construction meant there was only one way out—apart from rushing the enemy's ranks—and that was pulling a disappearing act. Ordinarily, that wouldn't have been an issue, as experienced fighters could, even in the heat of battle, calm themselves enough to focus and dematerialize—but you had to be relatively uninjured, and you couldn't take any fallen-comrade types with you when you went.

So Butch was screwed if shit got out of hand. As a half-breed, that guy was grounded, literally incapable of scattering his molecules to safety.

V muttered under his breath, "Don't be a hero, cop. Let us handle this."

"You're kidding me, right." The glare was immediate and steady. "You worry about yourself."

Not possible. He wasn't losing the only two compass points he had on the same night.

"Hey, boys," Hollywood called out to the enemy. "You just going to stand there or are we gonna do this?"

Annnnnnnnnnd that was the ringside bell. The *lessers* streamed forward and met the Brotherhood face-to-face, fist-to-fist. To ensure they had the privacy they needed, V doubled up on his visual barrier, the buffering creating a mirage of nothing-doing in the event humans trolled on by.

As he started working out one of the enemy, he kept his eye on Butch. The fucker naturally got right in there, taking on a tall, lanky inductee with his bare hands. He loved to brawl, and heads were his favorite punching bags—but Vishous really wished the bastard would take up fencing or, even better, get into rocket launchers. From the rooftop. So he wasn't anywhere near the fighting. He just hated that the cop got so close, because who the fuck knew what would come out of a pocket or how much damage could be done to the guy with a gun or a length of—

The kick came out of nowhere, sailing through the air like an anvil, catching V right in the side of the torso. As he flew back and slammed into the alley's brick flank, he was reminded of what they'd taught their trainees when they'd had them: Rule number one of fighting? Pay the fuck attention to your damn opponent.

After all, you could have the best knife in the world, but if you were clueless? You ended up making like a Ping-Pong ball. Or worse.

V reinflated his lungs with a huge inhale and he used the oxygen rush to leap forward and catch the Rockette's second kick at the ankle with his hands. The *lesser* had spectacular skills, however, and spun a *Matrix* move, using V's hold as an anchor to twist around in midair. The combat boot nailed V right in the ear, his head snapping to the side as all kinds of tendons and muscles were yanked to hell and gone.

Good thing pain always focused him.

Gravity being what it was, the Rockette's hit marked the top of its arc and after that, it went down, throwing its arms out to the asphalt to keep from face-planting it. And clearly the bastard was expecting its opponent to let go of the foot, thanks to the ringing snow globe that was now V's skull.

Nope. Sorry, sweetheart.

Even with the nasty crack-and-sizzle aftermath, V tightened his grip on that ankle and wrenched it in the opposite direction of the pirouette.

Snap!

Something broke or was dislocated, and given that V was holding the foot and lower bones steady, he knew it was probably the knee, the fibula or the tibia.

Mr. High Stepper let out a scream, but V wasn't finished as the bastard flopped on the ground. Popping free one of his black daggers, he sliced through the muscle in the back of the leg and then thought of Butch. Moving higher on the writhing body, he grabbed a hunk of hair, yanked up, and gave the SOB a nice little necklace with his blade.

Partial incapacitation just wasn't enough tonight.

Spinning around, dripping knife in hand, he assessed the fights that were ongoing. Z and Phury were working out a pair of *lessers*. . . . Tohr was holding his own. . . . Rhage was toying with one of the enemy. . . . Where was Butch—

Over in the corner, the cop had asphalted a slayer and was leaning down over its face. The pair had locked eyes and the *lesser's* open, bloodied mouth was working like a guppy's, opening and closing slowly, as if it knew whatever was coming next couldn't possibly be good news for it.

Butch's blessing and curse went to work as he took a deep, even inhale. The transfer started on a wisp of inky smoke that passed from the slayer's mouth into Butch's, but soon grew to a river of the shit, the essence of the Omega funneling from one to another in a sickening rush.

When it was over, the slayer was going to be nothing but an ashy residue. And Butch was going to be sick as a dog and relatively useless.

V jogged over, ducking a throwing star and manhandling a pinwheeling *lesser* back into Hollywood's punching zone.

"What the fuck are you doing," he bitched as he peeled Butch off the pavement and dragged him out of his suck zone. "You wait until afterward, true."

Butch curled over to the side and dry-heaved. He was semipolluted already, the stink of the enemy rising from out of his pores, his body struggling with its load of poison. He needed to be healed here and now, but V wasn't going to take the chance of their—

Later, he would marvel at getting blindsided twice in one fight.

But such introspection was hours off, as it turned out.

The baseball bat caught him in the side of the knee and the fall that came right after the blow was a yard sale in the worse way. He went down hard, his leg pretzeling beneath his considerable weight at an angle that turned his hip into a screaming ball of agony—which suggested that karma might not be about payback so much as it struggled with independent thinking: As he was felled by an injury like the one he'd just given someone, he cursed himself and the bastard with the Louisville Slugger and the Johnny-disloyal-Damon aim.

Time for some quick thinking. He was flat on his back with a leg that hummed like an engine on overdrive. And that bat could do a lot of damage—

Butch came from out of nowhere, lurching with all the grace of a wounded buffalo, the bastard's heavy body careening into the slayer just as that bat went over-the-shoulder with an aim at V's head. The pair of them slammed into the bricks, and after a beat of motionless, fuckin'-hell-that-was-a-stinger, the *lesser* pulled a full-torso jerk and gasped.

It was like watching eggs slide down the side of a kitchen cabinet: The slayer's bones went liquid and the thing slumped onto the pavement, leaving Butch to collapse back with his black-blooded dagger in his hand.

He'd gutted the motherfucker.

"You . . . okay . . ." the cop groaned.

All V could do was look over at his best friend.

As the others continued fighting, the pair of them just stared at each other against the audio backdrop of grunts and metal-to-metal strikes and inventive cursing. There should be something said between them, V thought. There was just so much . . . to be said.

"I want it from you," V bit out. "I need it."

Butch nodded. "I know."

"When."

The cop nodded down at V's fucked-up leg. "Get healed up first." Butch groaned and got to his feet. "On that note, I'll go get the Escalade."

"Be careful. Take one of the brothers with—"

"Fuck off with that. And you stay put."

"I'm not going anywhere with this knee, cop."

Butch walked off, his stride only marginally better than V could have pulled off with the dislocated mess he was rocking. Craning his neck, he looked over at the others. They were prevailing—slowly but surely, the tide was turning in their favor.

Until about five minutes later.

When seven more slayers showed up at the alley.

Clearly the second wave had likewise called for backup, and these were also new recruits who were unsure how to handle the *mhis*: They'd obviously been provided an address by their comrades, but their eyes could see nothing but an empty alley.

They were going to get over the what-the-hell's fast, however, and breach the barrier.

Moving as quickly as he could, V shoved his palms into the ground and dragged his ass into an inset doorway. The pain was so bad, his vision momentarily fritzed out, but that didn't keep him from stripping his glove off and putting it into his jacket.

He hoped like hell Butch didn't double back and come to fight. They were going to need transport as soon as this was over.

As the enemy's next wave surged forward, he let his head flop onto his chest and breathed so shallowly his rib cage barely moved. With his hair falling into his face, his eyes were shielded, and he was able to stare through the black veil at the onslaught of slayers. Given the incredible number of fresh inductees, he knew that the Society had to be drawing psychos and socios from Manhattan—the pool in Caldwell simply wasn't big enough to account for this surge in forces.

Which was going to work in the Brotherhood's favor.

And he was right.

Four of the *lessers* went straight for the thick of the fighting, but one, a bulldog with thick shoulders and arms that hung like a gorilla's, came over to V—probably to check him for weapons.

Vishous waited patiently, not moving, giving off a fuckload of next-stop-coffin.

Even when the bastard went to lean down, V stayed where he was . . . little closer . . . little . . . closer—

"Surprise, motherfucker," he bit out. Then he grabbed the nearest wrist and yanked hard.

The slayer went over like a stack of plates, right across V's bad leg. But it didn't matter—adrenaline was a hell of a painkiller and gave him the strength not just to withstand the agony, but to hold the SOB in place.

Lifting up his glowing hand, Vishous brought his curse down on the face of the *lesser*—no reason to slap or slam; simple contact was enough. And just before it landed, his prey's eyes popped wide, the illumination making the whites fluorescent.

"Yeah, this is gonna hurt," V growled.

The sizzle and the scream were equally loud, but only the former persisted. In the latter's place, a nasty stench like burned cheese wafted up along with a sooty smoke. It took less than a moment for the power in his hand to consume the slayer's puss, the flesh and bone eaten away as the bastard's legs jerked and his arms flailed.

When it was a case of Headless Horseman, V disengaged his palm and sagged. It would have been great to get the weight off his bum knee, but he just didn't have the strength.

His last thought, before he passed out, was that he prayed his boys kicked this one fast. The *mhis* wasn't going to linger if he wasn't there to support it . . . and that meant they would be fighting in public on a big scale—

Lights. Out.

TWENTY-NINE

As Payne's feet hung off the side of her bed, she flexed one and then the other over and over again, marveling at the miracle of thinking something and having her limbs follow the command.

"Here, put this on."

Glancing up, she was momentarily distracted by the sight of her healer's mouth. She couldn't believe that they had . . . that he had . . . until she . . .

Yes, a robe would be good, she thought.

"I won't let you fall," he said as he helped her into the thing. "You can bet your life on it."

She believed him. "Thank you."

"No problem." He jogged his arm. "Come on . . . let's do this."

Except the gratitude she felt was so complex she could not leave it unexpressed. "For all of it, healer. Everything."

He smiled at her briefly. "I'm here to make you better."

"You are."

With that, she carefully pushed herself onto her feet.

The first thing she noticed was that the floor was cold on her soles . . . and then her weight was transferred and things went haywire: Her muscles spasmed under the load and her legs bowed like feathers flexed asunder. Her healer was there when she needed him, however, scooping his arm around her waist and supporting her.

"I stand," she breathed. "I . . . am standing."

"You sure the hell are."

Her lower body was nothing like it had been, her thighs and calves trembling so badly her knees knocked together. But she *stood.*

"We shall walk now," she said, gritting her teeth as shafts of hot and cold rocketed up and down her bones.

"Maybe taking it slow is—"

"To the lavatory," she demanded. "Whereupon I shall relieve myself unattended."

The independence was absolutely vital. To be allowed the simple, profound dignity of taking care of her body's needs seemed like manna from above, proof positive that blessings, like time, were relative.

Except as she tried to step forward, she could not pick her foot up.

"Shift your weight," her healer said as he pivoted her and moved in behind her, "and I'll take care of the rest."

When he clasped her about the waist, she did as he'd told her and felt one of his hands grasp the back of her thigh and lift her leg. Without cueing, she knew to lean forward and place her weight gently as he put her knee in the correct position, restricting the bend in the joint as she straightened her leg.

The miracle was mechanical in its expression, but no less heartwarming for its one-step-two-step: She walked to the loo.

When the goal was obtained, her healer gave her privacy at the toilet, and she used the handlebar bolted into the wall to aid herself.

She was smiling the whole time. Which was utterly ridiculous.

After she had finished, she stood herself up using the bar and opened the door. Her healer was right outside, and she reached for him at the same moment he put his arms out for her.

"Back to the bed," he said, and it was a command. "I'm going to examine you and then get you some crutches."

She nodded and they slowly made their way across to the mattress. She was panting by the time she stretched out, but she was more than satisfied. This she could work with. Numb and cold and going nowhere? That was a death sentence.

Shutting her lids, she swallowed through deep breaths as he checked her vitals with efficiency.

"Your blood pressure's up," he said as he put aside the cufflike object she knew all too well. "But that could be because of what we. . . ah, did." He cleared his throat. Something he seemed to be doing rather a lot. "Let's check your legs. I want you to relax and close your eyes. No looking, please."

After she did as he requested, he said, "Can you feel this?"

Frowning, she sorted through the various sensations in her body, from the softness of the mattress, to the cool breeze on her face, to the sheet her hand was resting upon.

Nothing. She felt—

Sitting up in a panic, she stared at her legs—only to find that his touch was not on her: His hands were down by his sides. "You tricked me."

"No. I'm not assuming anything—that's what I'm doing."

As she resumed her position and shut her eyes once more, she wanted to curse, but she could see his point.

"How about now?"

Down below her knee, there was a subtle weight. She could feel it clear as day.

"Your hand . . . is on my leg. . . ." She cracked one of her eyelids and saw that she was right. "Yes, you are touching me there."

"Any difference from before?"

She frowned. "It's slightly . . . easier to feel."

"Improvement is good."

He palpated the other side. Then went up to nearly her hip. Then down to the bottom of her foot. Then inside her thigh . . . outside her knee.

"And now?" he asked one last time.

Against the darkness, she strained for sensation. "I feel . . . nothing now."

"Good. We're finished."

As she opened her eyes, she looked up at him and felt an odd chill go through her. What was the future for them? she wondered.

Beyond this sequestered period of her convalescence? Her incapacity simplified things in a grand way. But that would end if she were well.

Would he have her then?

Payne reached out and clasped his hand. "You are a blessing unto me."

"Because of this?" He shook his head. "This is you, *bambina*. Your body is healing itself. It's the only explanation." Bending down to her, he smoothed her loose hair back and pressed a chaste kiss to her forehead. "You need to sleep now. You're exhausted."

"You are not leaving, are you?"

"Nope." He glanced at the chair he'd used to get up to the ceiling fixture. "I'll be right over there."

"This bed . . . 'tis large enough for both of us."

When he hesitated, she got the impression something had changed for him. And yet he had just treated her with such erotic perfection—and his scent had flared, so she'd known he'd been aroused. Still . . . there was a subtle distance now.

"Join me?" she asked. "Please?"

He sat down on the bed beside her and stroked her arm slowly, rhythmically—and the kindness he showed her made her nervous.

"I don't think that's a wise idea," he murmured.

"Why ever not?"

"I think it's going to be easier on everyone if the way we're treating you stays between you and me."

"Oh."

"That brother of yours brought me here because he'll do anything to make you better. But there's a difference between theory and practice. He comes in here and finds us in bed together? We're just adding another problem to the pile."

"And if I tell you I do not care what he thinks?"

"I'd ask you to go easy on the guy." Her healer shrugged. "I'll be honest with you. I'm not a fan of his—but on the other hand, your brother's had to watch you here suffering."

Payne took a deep breath, and thought, Oh, if only that were the half of it. "It is my fault."

"You didn't ask to get hurt."

"Not the injury—my brother's consternation. Prior to your arrival, I requested of him something I should not have, and then compounded that with . . ." She slashed her hand through the air. "I am a curse upon him and his mate. For truth, I am a curse."

That she had lacked any faith in the benevolence of destiny was perhaps understandable, but what she had done in asking Jane to help her was unforgivable. The interlude with her healer had been a revelation and a blessing beyond measure, but now all she could think of was her brother and his *shellan* . . . and the repercussions of her selfish cowardice.

On a curse, she shuddered. "I must needs speak to my brother."

"Okay. I'll get him for you."

"Please."

Her healer rose to his feet and went to the exit. With his hand on the knob, he paused. "I need to know something."

"Inquire and I shall tell you anything."

"What happened right before I was brought back to you. Why did your brother come and get me."

Neither was phrased as a question. Which made her suspect he could well guess. "That is between him and me."

Her healer's eyes narrowed. "What did you do."

She sighed and fiddled with the blanket. "Tell me, healer, if you had no hope of getting up out of bed again, and you couldn't get a weapon, what would you do."

His lids squeezed shut for a brief moment. Then he opened the door. "I'll go find your brother right now."

As Payne was left alone with her regrets, she resisted the urge to curse. Throw things. Yell at the walls. On this night of her resurrection, she should have been ecstatic, but her healer was distant, her brother was incensed, and she very much feared for the future.

The state did not last long, however.

Even as her mind churned, her physical exhaustion soon overrode her cognition, and she was sucked down into a dreamless black hole that consumed her, body and soul.

Her last thought, before all went dark and sounds ceased to register, was that she hoped she could make amends.

And somehow stay with her healer forever.

Outside in the corridor, Manny collapsed back against the cinderblock wall and rubbed his face.

He was not an idiot, so deep down, he'd had a feeling what had happened: Only some flavor of true desperation would have gotten that hard-ass vampire to come into the human world and get him. But Christ . . . what if he hadn't been found in time? What if her brother had waited or—

"Fucking hell."

Pushing himself free of the wall, he went into the supply room and grabbed new scrubs, putting his used ones into the laundry bin after he changed. The exam room was the first stop, but Jane wasn't there, so he went down farther, all the way to that office with the glass door.

No one.

Back out in the hall, he heard the same pounding coming from the weight room as before, and he glanced inside, getting an eyeful of a guy with a brush cut who was running his balls off on a treadmill. Sweat was literally pouring out of the SOB, his body so lean it was almost painful to look at.

Manny ducked back out. No reason to ask that motherfucker.

"Are you looking for me?"

Manny turned to Jane. "Nice timing—Payne needs to see her brother. You know where he is?"

"Out fighting, but he'll be back just before dawn. Is there something wrong?"

There was the temptation to reply, *You tell me*, but he resisted. "That's between the two of them. I don't know much more than she wants him."

Jane's eyes drifted away. "Okay. Well, I'll get word to him. How's she doing?"

"She walked."

Jane's head flipped around. "By herself?"

"With only a little assistance. You got any braces? Crutches? That kind of thing?"

"Come with me."

She led him into the professional-size gym and across to an equipment room. No basketballs or volleyballs or ropes in there, though. Hundreds of weapons hung on racks: knives, throwing stars, swords, nunchakus.

"Hell of a gym class you guys got going on here."

"It's for the training program."

"Bringing along the next generation, huh."

"They were—at least until the raids."

Walking past all the Bruce Willis and Ahnold, she pushed through a door marked PT and showed him into a well-appointed rehab suite with everything a pro athlete would need to keep himself loose, limber, and lightning-fast.

"Raids?"

"The Lessening Society slaughtered dozens of families," she said, "and what was left of the population fled Caldwell. They're coming back slowly, but it's been a bad time lately."

Manny frowned. "What the hell is the Lessening Society?"

"Humans are not the real threat." She opened a closet door and swept her hand over every kind of crutch, cane, and cast support. "What are you looking for?"

"Is that what your man is fighting every night?"

"Yes. It is. Now, what do you think you want?"

Manny stared at her profile and added up the math. "She asked you to help her kill herself. Didn't she."

Jane's eyes shut. "Manny . . . no offense, but I don't have the strength for this conversation."

"That's what it was."

"Part of it. A lot of it."

"She's better now," he said roughly. "She's going to be fine."

"So it is working." Jane smiled a little. "Magic touch and all that."

He cleared his throat and resisted footing the floor like a fourteen-year-old who'd been caught necking. "Yeah. Guess so. Ah, I think I'll take a pair of leg braces, as well as a set of arm crutches—I think that should work for her."

As he took out the equipment, Jane's eyes stayed on him. To the point where he had to mutter, "Before you ask, no."

She laughed softly. "I wasn't aware I had a question."

"I'm not staying. I'll get her up and walking, and then I'm going back."

"That wasn't on my mind, actually." She frowned. "But you could hang around, you know. It's happened before. Me. Butch. Beth. And I thought you liked her."

"'Like' doesn't begin to cover it," he said under his breath.

"So don't make any plans until this is over."

He shook his head. "I have a career that's going into the shitter—the cause of which, incidentally, is all the in-and-outing you guys have done to my brain. I have a mother who isn't all that fond of me, but who will nonetheless wonder why she's not hearing from me on major holidays. And I have a horse that is in bad shape. You mean to tell me that your boy and his ilk are going to be down with my having one foot in each world? I don't think so. Besides, what the fuck would I do with myself? Servicing her is a pleasure, I assure you—but I wouldn't want to make a profession out of it or have her end up with the likes of me."

"What's so wrong with you?" Jane crossed her arms over her chest. "Not for nothing, but you're a great guy."

"Nice dodge on the particulars."

"Things could be worked out."

"Okay, say they were. Then answer me this—how long do they live for."

"Excuse me?"

"Life expectancy of vampires. How long."

"It varies."

"By decade or century?" When she didn't reply, he nodded. "Just what I thought—I'm probably good for another, what, forty years? And the shriveling is going to start in about ten. I've already got aches and pains every morning and the beginnings of arthritis in both hips. She needs one of her own to fall in love with, not a human who's going to be a geriatric patient in the blink of an eye." He shook his head again. "Love can conquer everything but reality. Which will win every stinking time."

Now her laugh was hard-edged. "Somehow I can't argue with that one."

He glanced down at the braces. "Thanks for these."

"You're welcome," she said slowly. "And I'll get word to V."

"Good."

Back at Payne's room, he entered silently and stopped just inside the door. She was dead asleep in the dimness, the glow gone from her skin. Would she wake up paralyzed again? Or would the progress stay with her?

He guessed they would have to find out.

Leaning the crutches and braces against the wall, he went over to the hard chair by the bed and sat down, crossing his legs and trying to get comfortable. No way he was going to sleep. He just wanted to watch her—

"Join me," she said into all the quiet. "Please. I need your warmth right now."

As he remained where he was, he realized the stay-sitting routine wasn't really about her brother. It was a coping mechanism to keep him separate from her whenever he could. They were absolutely going to be hooking up again—likely soon. And he would go down on her for hours if that was what it took. But he couldn't afford to lose himself in some fantasy that this was going anywhere permanent for them.

Two different worlds.

He just didn't belong with her.

Manny leaned forward, put his hand on hers and stroked her arm. "Shh . . . I'm right here."

As she turned her head toward him, her eyes were shut, and he had a feeling she was talking in her sleep. "Do not leave me, healer."

"My name is Manny," he whispered. "Manuel Manello . . . M.D."

THIRTY

The whistle was hard and sharp, and as it bulleted around the mansion's foyer, Qhuinn knew the shrill demand had been made by John Matthew.

Fuck knew he'd heard it enough over the last three years.

Stopping with one foot on the grand staircase's bottom step, he mopped up his sweaty face with his balled-up shirt and then caught his balance on the massive carved banister. His head was as light and fluffy as a pillow after his workout—which was in direct contrast to the rest of him: His legs and ass felt like they weighed as much as this goddamned mansion—

When the whistle came again, he thought, Oh, right, someone was talking to him. Pivoting around, he got an eyeful of John Matthew standing in between the ornate jambs of the dining room doorway.

What the hell did you do to yourself, the guy signed before pointing at his own dome.

Well, check his shit out, Qhuinn thought. In the past, a question like that would have covered a fuck of a lot more than a change in hairstyle.

"It's called a trim."

You sure about that? I'm pretty sure it's called a hot mess.

Qhuinn rubbed the fade he'd given himself. "It's no big deal."

At least you know toupees are an option. John's blue eyes narrowed. *And where is all your metal?*

"In my gun closet."

Not your weapons, the shit that was on your face.

Qhuinn just shook his head and turned to go, uninterested in discussing all the piercings he'd taken out. His brain was tangled and his body was exhausted, so stiff and sore from his daily runs—

That whistle came again and nearly had him tossing a fuck-off over his shoulder. He cut the crap, though, because it would save time: John never let up when he was in this kind of mood.

Glancing back, he growled, "What."

You need to eat more. Whether it's at meals or on your own. You're turning into a skeleton—

"I'm fine—"

—so either you start working the chow or I will have that gym locked and not give you the key. Your choice. And I called for Layla. She's in your room waiting for you.

Qhuinn spun completely around. Bad idea; it turned the foyer into a Tilt-A-Whirl. Grabbing for the banister again, he bit out, "I could have done that."

But you weren't going to, so I did it for you—short of slaughtering a dozen lessers, *it's going to be my good deed for the week.*

"You want to be Mother Teresa, you'll have more luck practicing that shit on someone else."

Sorry. I picked you, and you'd better shake a leg—don't want to keep the lady waiting. Oh, and while Xhex and I were in the kitchen, I had Fritz make you a meal and take it up. Later.

As the guy walked off in the direction of the butler's pantry, Qhuinn called out, "I'm not interested in being saved, asshole. I can take care of myself."

John's response was a middle finger flipped up and held over his head.

"Oh, for fuck's sake," Qhuinn muttered.

He so didn't want to deal with Layla right now.

Nothing against the Chosen, but the idea of being in an enclosed space with someone who was interested in sex just shut him right down. Which was ironic as shit. Up until now, fucking had not just been a part of his life; it had all but defined him. For the last week? The idea of being with someone left him nauseous.

Christ, this kept up, and the last person he was going to be with in his whole life was a redhead. Har-har, hardy-har-har: Clearly the Scribe Virgin had a nasty-ass sense of humor.

Forcing his deadweight up the stairs, he was ready to tell Layla as politely as he could that she needed to go on about her business—

The light-headedness that hit on the second landing stopped him in his tracks.

Over the past seven nights, he'd gotten used to the perma-float that came with running as much as he was and eating as little as he did, and he looked forward to the stoned disassociation. For godsakes, it was cheaper than drinking, and it never wore off—at least, not until he ate.

This was something different. He felt like someone had bulldozed him from behind and swept his legs out from under him—except his line of vision told him he was still standing. As did the fact that his hips were against the banister—

Without warning, one of his knees buckled and he went down like a book from the shelf.

Throwing out a hand, he pulled himself up over the damn rail, until he was all but hanging off it. Glaring at his leg, he kicked the thing a couple of times and breathed deeply, willing his body to get with the program.

Didn't happen.

Instead, he slowly slid from the vertical and had to turn around so it looked like he was just copping a squat on the bloodred carpet. He couldn't seem to breathe . . . or rather, he was breathing but it wasn't doing shit. *God . . . damn . . . Pull it together. . . .*

Fucking hell.

"Sire?" came a voice from above.

Make that a double hell.

As he squeezed his eyes shut, he thought Layla's showing up right now was Murphy's frickin' Law alive and in color.

"Sire, may I help you?"

Then again, maybe there was a bright side to this: better her than one of the Brothers. "Yeah. My knee's off. Hurt it running."

He looked up as the Chosen floated down to him, her white robe a shock against the deep color of the carpet and the resonant golden glow of the foyer's artwork.

Feeling like a right moron as she reached down for him, he tried to pull himself to his feet . . . only to get nowhere. "I, ah . . . I warn you, I weigh a lot."

Her lovely hand took his and he was astonished to find that his fingers were shaking as he accepted her help. He was also surprised to get hauled to his feet on a oner.

"You're strong," he said as her arm hitched around his waist and hefted him to the vertical.

"We walk together."

"Sorry I'm sweaty."

"I do not mind."

On that note, they were off. Moving slowly, they inched up the stairs and headed down the second-floor corridor, gimping by all kinds of blissfully closed doors: Wrath's study. Tohrment's room. Blay's—not looking at that. Saxton's—not busting that down and boot-licking his cousin out the window. John Matthew and Xhex's.

"I shall open the way," the Chosen said as they stopped at his own.

They had to turn sideways to get through the jambs because of his size, and he was grateful as shit when she closed them in together and took him to the bed. No one needed to know what was doing, and chances were good the Chosen would buy his just-an-owie excuse.

Sitting upright was the plan. Except the second she let go of him, he flopped back onto the mattress and made like a welcome mat. Looking down his body toward his running shoes, he wondered why he couldn't see the car that was parked on top of him. Definitely wasn't a Prius. More like a Chevy-fucking-Tahoe.

Whatever, try Suburban.

"Ah . . . listen, can you go into my leather coat? I've got a protein bar in there."

Abruptly, there was a shift of metal on porcelain from over by the door. And then a whiff of something dinner-ish. "Perhaps you would like this roast beef, sire?"

His stomach clenched hard as a fist. "God . . . no . . ."

"There is rice."

"Just . . . one of those bars . . ."

A subtle squeaking sound suggested she was rolling a tray over, and a second later, he got so much more than a mere sniff of whatever Fritz had prepared.

"Stop—stop, fuck—" He lurched over and dry-heaved into a wastebasket. "Not . . . the food . . ."

"You need to eat," came the surprisingly strong reply. "And I shall feed you."

"Don't you dare—"

"Here." Instead of the meat or the rice, a small piece of bread was presented to him. "Open. You need food, sire. Your John Matthew said so."

Sinking back against the pillows, he put his arm over his face. His heart was all hopscotch behind his sternum, and on some dim level, he realized he could actually kill himself if he kept going like this.

Funny, the idea struck him as not all that bad. Especially as Blay's face came to mind.

So beautiful. So very, very beautiful. It seemed silly and emasculating to call the guy that, but he was. Those damn lips were the problem . . . nice and cushioned on the bottom. Or maybe the eyes? So fucking blue.

He'd kissed that mouth and loved it. Seen those eyes go wild.

He could have had Blay first—and only. But instead? His cousin . . .

"Oh, God . . ." he groaned.

"Sire. Eat."

Out of energy to fight anything, he did as he was told, opening up, chewing mechanically, swallowing down his dry throat. And then he did it again. And again. Turned out that the carbs quieted the earthquake zone in his stomach, and faster than he would have thought possible, he was actually looking forward to something a little more substantial. Next up on the menu, though, was just some bottled water, which Layla held while he took small sips.

"Maybe we should take a break," he said, holding off on another bread run just in case the tide turned.

As he rolled over onto his side, he felt the bones in his legs knock together and realized his arm was hanging differently across his chest—less pecs to get in the way. His Nike running shorts were likewise baggy at the waistband.

He'd done all this damage in seven days.

At this rate, he wasn't going to look like himself for much longer.

Screw that, he already didn't. As John Matthew had frickin' noticed, not only had he buzzed his head, he'd taken his eyebrow piercing out as well as the one on his lower lip and the dozen or so up his ears. Gone too were his nipple rings. He still had his tongue stud and the shit below, but the visi stuff was gone, gone, gone.

He was through with himself on so many levels. Sick and tired of being the odd man out on purpose. Exhausted with his slut reputation.

And uninterested in rebelling against a bunch of dead stiffs anymore. For fuck's sake, he didn't need some shrink to explain the psychology that had shaped him: His family had been all picture perfect, *glymera*-conservative—and payback had been a bisexual, metal-headed whore with a Goth wardrobe and a needle fetish. But how much of that shit was him and how much was a mismatched-eye-based mutiny?

Who the fuck was he really?

"More now?" Layla asked.

Wasn't that the question.

As the Chosen went front and center again with the baguette, Qhuinn decided to cut the shit. Opening his mouth, he pulled a baby bird and ate the damn stuff. And some more. And then like she read his mind, Layla brought a sterling-silver fork with a piece of roast beef on it to his lips.

"Let us try this, sire. . . . Chew slowly, however."

Fat. Chance. Starvation immediately became the name of the game and he went T. rex on the meat, nearly biting tines off in the rush. But Layla was right on it, feeding him another round as fast as he could take it in.

"Wait . . . stop," he mumbled, afraid he was going to throw up.

He eased over onto his back again and let one hand rest on his chest. Shallow breaths were his savior. Anything deeper and he was going to pull a Technicolor yawn all over himself.

Layla's face appeared above his. "Sire . . . perhaps we should cease."

Qhuinn narrowed his stare on her, and saw her properly for the first time since she'd shown up.

God, she was a looker, all that pale blond hair swept up high on her head, her face stunningly perfect. With strawberry lips and green eyes that were luminous in the lamplight, she was everything the race valued in terms of DNA—not a defect in sight.

He reached up and brushed at her chignon. So soft. No hair spray for her; it was as if the waves knew their job was to frame her features and they were eager to do their best.

"Sire?" she said as she tensed.

He knew what was under that robe of hers: Her breasts were absolutely stunning and her stomach flat as a board . . . and those hips and the silky smooth sex between her thighs were the kinds of things that a naked male would fall on glass shards for.

He knew these particulars because he'd seen all of it, touched a lot of it, and had his mouth in a few choice places.

He hadn't taken her, though. Hadn't gone very far, either. As an *ehros*, she had been trained for sex, but with no Primale to service the Chosen in that way, she was all academic learning, nothing in the "field," as it were. And for a while he'd been happy to show her some of the ropes.

Except it hadn't felt right.

Well, she'd felt a lot that she'd thought was right, but her eyes had had too much in them and his heart way too little for things to keep going.

"Will you take my vein, sire?" she whispered huskily.

He just stared at her.

Those red lips of hers parted. "Sire, will you . . . take me."

Closing his lids, he saw Blay's face again . . . but not how it was now. Not the cold stranger that Qhuinn had created. The old Blay, with those blue eyes that were somehow always pointed in his direction.

"Sire . . . I am yours for the taking. Still. Evermore."

When he finally looked at Layla again, her fingers had gone to the lapels of her robe and she had spread the halves wide, showing him her long, elegant neck and the wings of her collarbones and all that glorious cleavage.

"Sire . . . I want to serve you." Inching the sateen fabric even farther apart, she offered him not just her vein, but her body. "Take me—"

Qhuinn stilled her hands as they went to the tie around her waist. "Stop."

Her eyes dropped to the duvet, and she seemed to turn to stone.

At least until she pulled herself out of his hold and roughly rearranged the robe.

"You shall take my wrist then." Her hand was shaking as she yanked up her sleeve and stuck out her arm. "Take from my wrist what you so obviously require."

She did not look at him. Likely could not.

And yet here she was . . . shut down from a disgrace she had never earned and he had never meant to call out of her . . . still offering herself to him—except not in a pathetic way, but because she had been born and bred to serve a purpose that had nothing to do with what she wanted and everything to do with social expectation . . . and she was determined to live up to the standard. Even if she wasn't wanted for who she was.

Christ, he knew what that was like.

"Layla—"

"Do not apologize, sire. It belittles me."

He took her arm because he got the impression she was about to get to her feet. "Look, this is my fault. I should never have started the sex stuff with you—"

"And I say unto you, 'stop.'" Her back was ramrod straight and her voice strident. "Do let me go, will you."

He frowned. "Shit . . . you're cold."

"Am I."

"Yeah." He ran his hand up and down her arm. "Do you need to feed? Layla? Hello?"

"I have been over on the Other Side in the Sanctuary, so no."

Well, that he could buy. If a Chosen was over there, she existed without existing, her blood needs suspended—and apparently refreshed: For the last couple of years, Layla alone had been servicing the Brothers who couldn't feed from their *shellans*. She was everyone's go-to Chosen.

And then it dawned on him. "Wait, you haven't been up north at all?"

Now that Phury had freed the Chosen from their rigid and confined existence, most of them left the Sanctuary they'd been stuck in for aeons and went to the Adirondack great camp to learn about the freedoms of life over on this side.

"Layla?"

"No, I do not go there anymore."

"Why?"

"I cannot." She waved the conversation away and pulled up her sleeve again. "Sire? Are you taking my vein?"

"Why don't you go there?"

Her eyes finally met his and they were flat-out pissed. Which was a strange relief. Her meek acceptance of everything made him question how smart she was. But going by her expression now? There was a whole lot of something underneath the mantle she wore—and he wasn't just talking about her perfect body.

"Layla. Answer me. Why not?"

"I cannot."

"Says who?" Qhuinn wasn't totally tight with Phury, but he knew the Brother well enough to bring a problem to the guy. "Who."

"'Tis not a who, and worry not." She pointed to her wrist. "Partake so that you are as strong as you need to be, and then I shall leave you in peace."

"Fine, if you want to joust about words—*what* is it, then."

Frustration flared in her face. "That is not your concern."

"I'll decide what's my concern." He wasn't into bullying females, but apparently his dormant gentlemale had gotten off its powder-puff bed and found its knickers in a bunch. "Talk to me."

He was the last person to put the share/care card on the table, yet here he was, slapping it down. The thing was, though, he wouldn't stand for anything hurting this female.

"Fine." She threw up her hands. "If I tarry up north, I cannot supply all of you with what you need for blood. Therefore I go unto the Sanctuary for my recovery and I wait to be summoned. Then I come unto this side and service you and after that I must needs return. So no, I cannot go to the mountains."

"Jesus . . ." What a bunch of users they were. They should have anticipated this problem—or Phury should have. Unless . . . "Have you talked to the Primale?"

"About what, precisely," she snapped. "Tell me, sire, would you be in a hurry to present your failures on the field to your king?"

"How the hell are you failing? You're keeping, like, four of us going."

"Exactly. And I am serving you all in a very limited capacity."

Layla burst up and walked over to the window. As she stared out, he wanted to want her: In that moment, he would have given anything to feel for her what she did for him—she was, after all, everything his family valued, the social pinnacle for a female. And she wanted him.

But when he looked inside, there was another in his heart. And nothing was going to change that. Ever . . . he feared.

"I do not know who or what I am, exactly," Layla said, as if she were speaking to herself.

Well, looked like both of them were on the same train to nowhere with that question. "You won't find out unless you leave that Sanctuary."

"Impossible if I am to service—"

"We'll use someone else. It's just that simple."

There was a sharp inhale, and then, "But of course. You shall do as you wish."

Qhuinn stared at the hard line of her chin. "That's supposed to help you."

She glared over her shoulder. "It does not—for then you would leave me with nothing. Your choice, my repercussion."

"It's your life. You can choose."

"We shall not speak of this anymore." She threw up her hands. "Dearest Scribe Virgin, you have *no* idea what it is like to desire things you are not fated to have."

Qhuinn let out a hard laugh. "The fuck I don't." As her brows popped, he rolled his eyes. "You and I have more in common than you think."

"You have all the freedom in the world. What could you possibly want for?"

"Trust me."

"Well, I want you and I cannot have you. That is not of my choosing. At least by servicing you and the others, I have a purpose other than mourning the loss of something I dreamed of."

As Qhuinn took a deep breath, he had to respect the female. There was no pity party going on over there at the window. She was stating the facts as she knew them.

Shit, she really was precisely the kind of *shellan* he'd always wanted. Even as he'd been fucking anything that walked, in the back of his mind, he had always seen himself with a female, long-term. One with impeccable bloodlines and a lot of class—the kind his parents would have not only approved of, but might have respected him a little for getting.

That had been his dream. Now that it had shown up, however . . . now that it was standing across his bedroom and looking him in the face . . . he wanted something else entirely.

"I wish I did feel something deep for you," he said roughly, meeting truth for truth. "I would do almost anything to feel what I should for you. You are . . . my fantasy female. Everything I always wanted, but thought I could never have."

Her eyes got so wide they were like two moons, beautiful and shining. "Then why . . ."

He rubbed his face and wondered what in the fuck he was saying. What the fuck he was doing.

When he took his palms away, there was a slickness left behind, one that he refused to think too much about.

"I'm in love," he said hoarsely. "With someone else. That's why."

THIRTY-ONE

Commotion out in the hall. Scrambling footsteps . . . low cursing . . . the occasional dull thud.

All the noise woke Manny up, and he went from out like a light to fully conscious in a split second as the parade of sound passed by in the corridor. The disturbance continued onward before it got cut off sharply, as if a door had been shut on the show. Whatever it might be.

Straightening from where he'd put his head down on Payne's bed, he looked at his patient. Beautiful. Simply beautiful. And sleeping steadily—

The shaft of light smacked him right in the face.

Jane's voice was strained as she stood in the lee of the doorway, a black cutout of herself. "I need another set of hands in here. Stat."

No asking twice. Manny shot for the door, the surgeon in him ready to go to work, no questions asked.

"What we got?"

As they rushed along, Jane brushed at her red-stained scrubs. "Multiple traumas. Mostly knives, one gunshot. And there's another being driven in."

They broke into the exam room together, and God . . . damn . . . there were wounded men everywhere—standing in the corners, propped on the table, leaning down on the counter, cursing while they paced. Elena or Elaina, the nurse, was busy getting out scalpels and thread by the dozen and the yard, and there was a little old man bringing water to everyone on a silver tray.

"I haven't triaged yet," Jane said. "There're too many of them."

"Where's an extra stethoscope and BP cuff?"

She went over to a cabinet, popped a drawer, and tossed both over. "BP is much lower than you're going to be used to. So is the heart rate."

Which meant that, as a medical professional, he had no true way of judging whether they were in trouble or not.

He put the equipment aside. "You and the nurse had better make the assessments. I'll do prep."

"Probably better," Jane agreed.

Manny stepped up to the blond nurse who was working efficiently with the supplies. "I'm going to take over from here. You help Jane with the readings."

She nodded briefly and got right to work taking vitals.

Manny threw open drawers and took out surgical kits, lining them up on the counters. Pain meds were in an upright cupboard; syringes were down below. As he rifled through everything, he was impressed by the professional quality: He didn't know how Jane had done it, but everything was hospital-grade.

Ten minutes later, Jane, he, and the nurse met in the middle of the room. "We've got two in bad shape," Jane said. "Rhage and Phury are both losing a lot of blood—I'm worried that arteries have been nicked because those cuts are so damned deep. Z and Tohr need X-rays, and I think Blaylock's got a concussion along with that nasty gash on his stomach."

Manny headed for the sink and started scrubbing up. "Let's do this." He glanced around and pointed to the mammoth blond son of a bitch with the puddle of blood under his left boot. "I'll take him."

"Okay, I'll deal with Phury. Ehlena, you start getting pictures of those broken bones."

Given that this was a field situation, Manny took his supplies over to his patient—who was stretched out on the floor, right where he'd collapsed earlier. The big bastard was dressed in black leather from head to foot, and he was in a lot of pain, his head kicked back and his teeth gritted.

"I'm going to work on you," Manny said. "You got a problem with that?"

"Not if you can keep me from bleeding out."

"Consider it done." Manny grabbed a pair of scissors. "I'm going to cut off your pant leg first and ditch the boot."

"Shitkicker," the guy groaned.

"Fine. Whatever you call it, it's coming off."

No unlacing—he cut through the latticework at the front of the damn thing and slipped it off a foot the size of a suitcase. And then the leathers sliced easily up the outside all the way to the hip, falling open like a set of chaps.

"What we got, Doc?"

"A Christmas turkey, my friend."

"That deep?"

"Yup." No need to mention that the bone was showing through and blood was pumping out in a steady stream. "I've got to rescrub. I'll be right back."

After he hit the sink, Manny snapped on a pair of gloves, sat back down, and went for a glass bottle of lidocaine.

Big, Blond, and Bleeding stopped him. "Don't worry about the pain, Doc. Stitch me up and treat my brothers—they need it more than I do. I'd take care of it myself, but Jane won't let me."

Manny paused. "You'd sew yourself up."

"Done it for more decades than you've been alive, Doc."

Manny shook his head and muttered under his breath. "Sorry, tough guy. I'm not running the risk of you jerking right when I'm working on your leak."

"Doc—"

Manny pointed his syringe right into the stunningly handsome face of his patient. "Shut it and lie back. You should be put out cold for this, so don't worry—there's going to be plenty to suck up and be a hero about."

Another pause. "Okay, okay, Doc. Don't get your thong in a wad. Just get through me . . . and help them."

Hard not to respect the guy's loyalty.

Working fast, Manny numbed the area as best he could, pushing the needle into the flesh in a controlled circle. Christ, this took him back to medical school and, in a strange way, brought him alive in a manner that the operations he'd been doing lately didn't.

This was . . . reality with the volume turned way up. And damn him if he didn't like the sound of it.

Grabbing a stack of clean towels, he shoved them under the leg and rinsed the wound out. As his patient hissed and stiffened, he said, "Easy, big guy. We're just getting it cleaned."

"No . . . problem . . ."

The hell it wasn't, and Manny wished he could have done more in the pain-control realm, but there was no time. There were compound fractures to deal with: Stabilize. Move on.

As someone moaned and yet another string of curses rang out over on the left, Manny took care of a minute tear in the artery; then he closed the muscle and moved on to the fascia and the skin. "You're doing great," he murmured as he noticed those white-knuckled fists.

"Don't worry about me."

"Right, right . . . your brothers." Manny paused for a split second. "You're all right, you know that."

"Fuck . . . that . . ." The fighter smiled, flashing fangs. "I'm . . . perfect."

Then the guy closed his eyes and lay back, his jaw so tight it was a wonder he could swallow.

Manny worked as quickly as he could without sacrificing quality. And just as he was swiping down his line of sixty sutures with a gauze cloth, he heard Jane cry out.

Jacking his head around, he muttered, "Fucking hell."

In the doorway to the exam room, Jane's husband was draped in the arms of Red Sox, looking like he'd been run over by a car: His skin was pasty, his eyes had rolled back in his head, and . . . holy hell, his boot—shitkicker—was facing the wrong way.

Manny called out for the nurse. "Could you bandage this?" Glancing at his current patient, he said, "I've got to go look at—"

"Go." The guy slapped his shoulder. "And thanks, Doc. I won't forget this."

As he headed for the newest arrival, Manny had to wonder whether that goateed big-mouth was going to let him operate. Because that leg? It looked utterly destroyed even from across the damn room.

Vishous was lapsing in and out of consciousness by the time Butch got him to the exam room. That knee and hip combo of his was beyond agony and into some other kind of territory, and the overwhelming sensations were sapping his strength and his thought processes.

He wasn't the only one in bad shape, however. As Butch lurched weakly through the doorway, he knocked V's head against the jamb.

"Fuck!"

"Shit—sorry."

"Drop . . . in the bucket," V gasped as his temple started screaming, the fucker harmonizing an a cappella version of "Welcome to the Jungle."

To shut out the concert from hell, he opened his eyes and hoped for a distraction.

Jane was right in front of him, a suturing needle in one bloody, gloved hand, her hair pulled back by a headband.

"Not her," he groaned. "Not . . . her . . ."

Medical professionals should never treat their mates; it was a recipe for disaster. If his knee or hip was permanently fucked-up, he didn't want that on her conscience. God knew they had enough problems between them already.

Manny stepped in front of his *shellan*. "Then I'm your only option. You're welcome."

Vishous rolled his eyes. Great. What a choice.

"Do you consent?" the human demanded. "Or maybe you'd like to think about it for a while so that your joints heal up like a flamingo's. Or the leg goes gangrenous and falls the fuck off."

"Well, if that . . . isn't a . . . sales pitch."

"And the answer is . . . ?"

"Fine. Yes."

"Get him on the table."

Butch was careful with the layout routine, but even so, V nearly threw up over both of them as his weight was redistributed.

"Motherfucker—" Just as the curse was leaving his lips, the surgeon's face appeared over his own. "Word up, Manello—you don't want . . . to be that close to me . . ."

"You want to punch me? Okay, but wait until after I've worked on your leg."

"No, sick . . . to stomach."

Manello shook his head. "I need some pain control over here. Let's get some Demer—"

"Not Demerol," V and Jane said together.

V's eyes shot over in her direction. She'd gone across the way and was down on the floor, leaning over Blaylock's stomach, stitching up a mean-looking slice. Her hands were rock-steady and her work was absolutely perfect, everything about her the very picture of professional competence. Except for the tears running down her face.

With a moan, he looked up to the chandelier above him.

"Morphine okay?" Manello asked as he cut through the sleeve of V's biker jacket. "And don't bother being tough. The last thing I need is you woofing all over yourself while I'm poking around down there."

Jane didn't answer this time, so V did. "Yeah. That's cool."

As a syringe was filled, Butch stepped up into the surgeon's grille. Even as incapacitated as the cop was from the inhaling, he was straight-up deadly as he spoke. "I don't need to tell you not to fuck my buddy. Right."

The surgeon looked around his little-glass-bottle-and-needle routine. "I'm not thinking about sex at the moment, thank you very much. But if I was, it sure as shit wouldn't be with him. So instead of worrying about who I'm tapping, how'd you like to do us all a favor and have a shower. You stink."

Butch blinked. Then smiled a little. "You have balls."

"And they're made of brass. Big as church bells, too."

Next thing V knew, something cold was rubbing on the juncture of his arm; then there was a prick, and shortly thereafter, he went on a little ride, his body turning into a cotton ball, all light and airy. From time to time, pain broke through, rocking up from his gut and nailing him in the heart. But it wasn't connected to whatever Manello was doing to his injury: V couldn't take his eyes off his mate as she treated his brothers.

Through the wavy pane of his vision, he watched as she dealt with Blay and then worked on Tohrment. He couldn't hear what she was saying because his ears weren't really working all that well, but Blay was clearly grateful and Tohr seemed eased just by her presence. From time to time, Manello asked her something, or Ehlena stopped her with a question, or Tohr winced and she paused to calm him.

This was her life, wasn't it. This healing, this pursuit of excellence, this abiding devotion to her patients.

Her duty to them defined her, didn't it.

And seeing her like this made him rethink what had happened between her and Payne. If Payne had been hell-bent on taking her own life, Jane would undoubtedly have tried to stop her. And then when it became apparent she couldn't . . .

Abruptly, as if she knew he was staring at her, Jane's eyes flipped to his. They were so shadowed he could barely tell their color, and she momentarily lost her corporeal form, as if he'd sucked the will to live right out of her.

That surgeon's face got in the way. "You need more pain relief?"

"What?" V asked around his thick, dry tongue.

"You groaned."

"Not . . . about . . . the knee."

"It's not just your knee."

". . . what . . . ?"

"I think your hip's dislocated. I'm going to take the pants all the way off."

"Whatever . . ."

As V went back to staring at Jane, he was only vaguely aware of scissors going up both sides of his leathers, but he knew exactly when the surgeon got all the cowhide off of him. The guy let out a sharp hiss . . . that was quickly covered up.

Sure as shit the reaction was not about the tattooed warnings in the Old Language.

"Sorry, Doc," V mumbled, not sure why in the hell he was apologizing for the mess down below his waist.

"I'll, ah . . . I'll cover you up." The human shot off and returned with a blanket that he put on V's lower abdomen. "I just need to look your joints over."

"You . . . do that."

Vishous's eyes returned to Jane and he found himself wondering . . . if she hadn't died and been brought back as she had, would they have tried to have young? It was doubtful he could sire anything other than an orgasm with the damage his father had done to him. And he'd never wanted kids—still didn't.

She would have been a stellar mother, though. She was good at everything she did.

Did she miss being alive?

Why had he never asked her that?

The return of the surgeon's face cut off his thinking. "Your hip's dislocated. I'm going to have to set it before I work on the knee because I'm worried about your circulation. Okay?"

"Just fix me," V moaned. "Whatever it takes."

"Good. I've put the knee in a temporary brace for this." The human looked over to Butch, who, shower-request notwithstanding, had propped himself up against the wall no less than two feet away. "I need your help. There's no one else around with free hands."

The cop was right on it, shoring up his strength and coming over. "What do you want me to do?"

"Hold his pelvis in place." The human hopped up onto the stainless-steel table at V's legs, crouching down to avoid banging his head on the chandelier. "This is going to be a muscle job—there's no other way to do it. I want you facing me, and I'll show you where to put your hands."

Butch got right with the program, sidling in close and reaching down. "Where?"

"Here." V had some vague sensation of warm weight on both sides of his hips. "Little more to the outside—right. Good."

Butch looked around his own shoulder at V. "You ready for this?"

Silly question. Like asking someone if they were prepared for a head-on collision.

"Stoked," V muttered.

"Just focus on me."

And V did . . . seeing the flecks of green in the cop's hazel eyes and the contours of that busted nose and the five-o'clock shadow.

When the human grabbed V's lower thigh and started lifting, V jacked up against the table, his head kicking back, his jaw straining.

"Easy, there," the cop said. "Focus on me."

Uh-huh, right. There was pain, and then there was PAIN. This was **PAIN**.

Vishous labored for breath, his neural pathways crammed with signals, his body exploding even as his outer skin stayed intact.

"Tell him to breathe," someone said. Probably the human.

Yeah, that was going to happen. Not.

"Okay, on three I'm going to force the joint back into place—you ready?"

V had no clue who the guy was talking to, but if it was him, there was no way to answer. His heart was jumping and his lungs were stone and his brain was Las Vegas at night and—

"Three!"

Vishous screamed.

The only thing that was louder was the pop as the hip was relocated, as it were. And the last thing he saw before he checked out of the Conscious Inn & Suites was Jane's head whipping around in a panic. In her eyes was stark terror, as if the single worst thing that she could imagine was him in agony. . . .

And that was when he knew that he still loved her.

THIRTY-TWO

Up at the mansion, in Qhuinn's bedroom, there was nothing but a whole lot of silence—which was typical when you dropped a bomb, be it real or metaphorical.

Jesus Christ, he couldn't believe he'd said the words: Even though only he and Layla were in here, he felt like he'd gone to the top of a building in downtown Caldwell and bullhorned the announcement.

"Your friend," Layla whispered. "Blaylock."

Qhuinn's heart froze. But after a moment, he forced himself to nod. "Yeah. It's him."

He waited for some kind of disgust or grimace or . . . even shock. Coming from where he did, he was all too versed in homophobia—and Layla was a Chosen, for godsakes, which made that old-school-*glymera* bull crap look positively enlightened.

Her beautiful stare lingered on his face. "I think I knew. I saw the way he looked at you."

Well, that was no more. And . . . "It doesn't bother you? That he's another male?"

There was a slight pause. And then the answer she gave him transformed him in a curious way: "Not in the slightest. Why would it?"

Qhuinn had to look away. Because he worried about what was shining in his eyes. "Thank you."

"Whatever for?"

All he could do was shrug.

Who'd have thought acceptance would be as curiously painful as all that rejection had always been.

"I think you'd better go," he said roughly.

"Why?"

'Cause he was strongly considering a job as a lawn sprinkler, and he didn't want to go all weeping-willow in front of anyone. Even her.

"Sire, it is all right." Her voice was rock-solid serious. "I judge you not by the sex of whom you love . . . but by how you love them."

"Then you should hate me." Christ, why the hell was his mouth still going? "Because I broke his fucking heart."

"So . . . he knows not how you feel?"

"Nope." Qhuinn narrowed his eyes at her. "And he's not going to, clear? No one knows."

She inclined her head. "Your secret is safe with me. But I know well the way he regarded you. Mayhap you should tell him—"

"Let me save you from a lesson I learned the hard way. There are times when it is too late. He's happy now—and he deserves that. Fuck it, I *want* him to have love, even if I'm just watching it from on the sidelines."

"But what about you?"

"What about me." He went to drag his fingers through his hair and realized he'd cut it all off. "Listen, enough with this . . . I only told you because I need you to know that this shit between you and me isn't about you not being good enough or attractive enough. Honestly? I'm done with being with other people sexually. I'm not doing that anymore. It gets me nowhere and . . . yeah. I'm finished with all that."

How ironic. Now that he wasn't with Blay, he was being faithful to the fucker.

Layla came across to him and sat down on the bed, arranging her legs and smoothing her robe with her elegant, pale hands. "I am glad you told me."

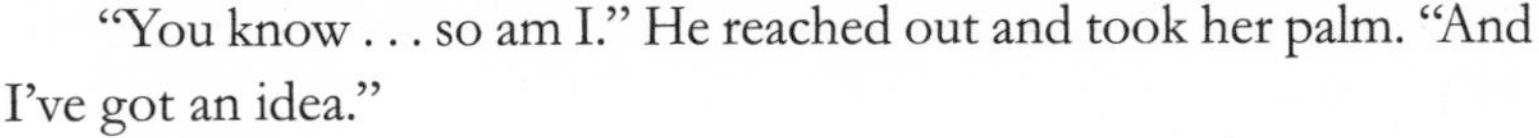

"You know . . . so am I." He reached out and took her palm. "And I've got an idea."

"Indeed?"

"Friends. You and me. You come here, I'll feed you, and we'll hang together. As friends."

Her smile was incredibly sad. "I must say . . . I always knew you cared not for me in that special way. You touched me with great restraint and showed me things that enraptured me—but beneath the flush of passion that I felt, I knew. . . ."

"You're not in love with me, either, Layla. You just aren't. You felt a lot of physical shit, and that made you think it was emotional. The trouble is, body needs a hell of a lot less than the soul does to connect."

She placed her free hand over her heart. "The sting is there."

"Because you've had a crush on me. That'll fade. Especially when you meet the right guy."

God, check his shit out. From slut to camp counselor in a week. Next up: a guest stint on *The*-fucking-*View*.

He extended his forearm. "Take my vein so you can stay longer on this side and figure out what it is that you want from life—not what you're supposed to be or do, but what *you* want. I'll even help you if I can. God knows I'm well-versed in being lost."

There was a long moment. And then her green eyes shifted to his. "Blaylock . . . knows not what he is missing."

Qhuinn shook his head grimly. "Oh, he's very aware of it. Trust me."

Cleanup was not a cinch.

As Jane rolled a bucket and mop out from the housekeeping closet, she ran through the reordering that was going to be necessary to get her supplies back where they needed to be: They'd used up a hundred packages of gauze; her needle-to-thread ratio was a joke; they were straight out of wrap bandages. . . .

Opening the door to the exam room with her butt, she swung the pail around using the mop head and then took a breather. There was blood everywhere on the floor, and also down the walls. Wads of red-stained white gauze were the Freddy Krueger equiv of dust bunnies.

Three biohazard bags were full to the point of needing an antacid for the bloating.

And a paaaartridge in a pear treeeeeeeeeeee . . .

Confronting the aftermath, she realized that if Manny hadn't been with her, they might have lost one of the Brothers. Rhage, for instance, could have bled out. Or Tohr—because what had looked like a simple shoulder injury had turned out to be oh, so much more.

Manny had ended up having to operate on him. After he'd finished doing surgery on Vishous.

Closing her eyes, she propped her heavy head against the pointy top of the mop. As a ghost, she didn't become exhausted the way she'd used to: no aches or pains, no dragging sense like someone had tied barbells to both her ankles. Now it was her psyche that grew weary, to the point where she had to shut her lids and see and do absolutely nothing—like her brain's circuit board needed to be turned off and cooled down.

And she did sleep then. And dreamed.

Or . . . as probably would be the case today . . . not. Insomnia was still an issue from time to time—

"You're going to need to broom it first."

Snapping her head up, she tried to smile for Manny. "I think you're right."

"How about you let me take care of this."

No. Way. She was not in a hurry to go lock herself in the other recovery room and stare at the ceiling. Besides, Manny had to feel as tired as she did.

"How long has it been since you ate last?" she asked him.

"What time is it?"

She glanced at her watch. "One o'clock."

"In the afternoon?"

"Yes."

"About twelve hours or so." He seemed surprised at that.

She reached for the phone on the desk. "I'll call Fritz."

"Listen, you don't have to—"

"You must be about to fall over."

"Actually, I feel great."

Wasn't that just like a man. Unless . . . Well, hell, he did look energized instead of drained.

Whatever. She was still feeding him.

The ordering didn't take longer than a minute, and Fritz was thrilled by the request. Usually after Last Meal, the butler and his staff retired for a brief rest before the daily cleaning started, but they would much rather have been working.

"Where's the housekeeping closet?" Manny asked.

"Out in the hall. To your left."

While she filled the bucket with Lysol and water, he found a broom, came back and took care of business.

While they worked side by side, all she could think about was Vishous. During the rush of treating the Brothers, there had been so much to concentrate on, but now, sweeping the mop's sloppy dreads back and forth over the tiled floor, it was as if all the angst that had been behind the scenes in her brain broke free and rushed her mental guardrails.

Anyone but her.

She heard him say that over and over again, saw his ashen face and his icy eyes and the way he had closed her out.

Funny . . . the eternity she'd been granted had always seemed like the grandest blessing. Until she pictured going aeons without the man she loved.

Now it was a curse.

Where would she go? She couldn't very well continue at the compound. Not if they were estranged like this. It was too hard on everyone—

"Here."

Jane jumped as a tissue fluttered in front of her face. The little white square was hanging from Manny's blunt fingertips, and he wagged it again as she just stared at the thing.

"You're crying," she heard him say.

Moving the mop handle into the crook of an elbow, she took what he offered and was surprised to find that he was right: When she blotted at her eyes and took a peek, the Kleenex was damp.

"You know," Manny drawled, "seeing you like this makes me wish I'd amputated that damn leg of his."

"This is only partially his fault."

"So say you. I'm allowed to look at it any way I like."

She glanced over. "You have another one of those?"

He held a box forward and she snapped out a couple more. Dab. Dab. Delicate nose blow. Dab. She rounded out the crying jag with a quick one . . . two . . . three . . . tosses into the trash bin.

"Thank you for helping me." As she glanced up, his glower was front and center on his face and she had to smile. "I've missed that."

"Missed what."

"That pissed-off expression you wear so often. Reminds me of the good old days." She regarded him steadily. "Is V going to be okay?"

"If I don't kick his ass for fucking with you—yes."

"So gallant." And she meant that. "You were amazing tonight."

She meant that, too.

He put the Kleenex aside on a counter. "So were you. That happen a lot?"

"Not really. But I have a feeling that may be changing."

Getting back to work, she made some perfunctory passes with the mop, not really improving the condition of the floor, but just moving the blood around. At this point, she probably would have more luck hosing the place down.

A few minutes later, there was a knock on the door and Fritz put his head in. "Your repast is ready. Where would you wish to dine?"

"He'll take it in the office," Jane answered. "At the desk." She glanced over at her former colleague. "Better go before it gets cold."

The look in Manny's eye was the ocular equivalent of a middle finger, but she just waved bon voyage. "Go. And then get some rest."

Except no one told Manny Manello what to do. "I'll be right there," he said to the butler.

As Fritz ducked out, her old boss put his hands on his hips. And although she braced herself for an argument, all he said was, "Where's my briefcase."

When Jane blinked, he shrugged. "I'm not going to berate you into talking to me."

"So you've turned over a new leaf."

"Go, me." He nodded over at the phone that was mounted on the wall. "I'm going to have to check my messages, and I want my damn cell phone back."

"Ah . . . okay, your car has to be in the parking garage. Just go down the corridor. Maybe it's in your Porsche?"

"Thanks—"

"Are you thinking of leaving?"

"All the time." He turned and went for the door. "It's all I can think about."

Well . . . didn't that make two of them. But then, Jane had never imagined that she'd not be here.

Proof positive that it wasn't helpful to have a lot of bright ideas about your future.

THIRTY-THREE

Traditionally, in and among the *glymera*, when one entered the house of another, a calling card was to be placed upon a silver tray that was held out by the butler *doggen* of the host. The card was to have one's unique name and lineage listed, and the purpose was to announce the visitor, whilst at the same time pay homage to the social mores that shaped and defined the upper classes.

However, when one could not write or read . . . or more to the point, when one preferred methods of communication that were more visceral and less viceroy?

Well, then one left the bodies of the dead he'd rendered in an alley for his "host" to find.

Xcor got up from the table he had been sitting afore and took his mug of coffee with him. The others were asleep below, and he knew he should join them, but there would be no rest. Not this day. Mayhap not the next.

Leaving those split yet writhing *lessers* behind had been a calculated risk. If humans found them? Trouble. And yet it was worth it. Wrath and the Brotherhood had too long ruled this continent, and to what end? The Lessening Society persisted. The vampire population had scattered. And those arrogant, flabby, feckless humans were everywhere.

Xcor paused in the downstairs hallway and looked around his permanent accommodations. The house that Throe had secured was indeed appropriate. Made of stone, it was old and on the outskirts, two measures of value that were highly appropriate for their purposes. At some point in its life, it had been quite a showplace, but that time had faded and so had its gentility. Now, it was a shell of what it had been, and all of what he required: stout of wall, sturdy of roof, and more than big enough to house his males.

Not that anyone would be up in these aboveground rooms or the seven bedrooms on the second floor very often. Even though heavy drapery was pulled o'er every window, the countless panes of glass needed to be bricked in before things were really safe enough during the daylight hours.

Indeed, all stayed underground, in the cellar.

It was the good old days returned, he thought, for only in modern times had the conception of separate accommodations taken root. Afore they had eaten together, fucked together, and taken their repose as a group.

As soldiers should.

Mayhap he would require them to remain beneath the earth. Together.

And yet he was not down there with them and had not been. Antsy and unsettled, ready to pursue but lacking prey at the moment, he'd been going from empty room to empty room, stirring dust along with his desire to conquer this new world.

"I have them. All of them."

Xcor stopped. Took a grab off the lip of his mug. Turned around. "How clever of you."

Throe entered what had once been a rather grand parlor room, but was now naught but cold and empty. The fighter was still dressed in leather, except somehow he gave off an elegant appearance. Not a surprise. Unlike the others, his pedigree was as perfect as his golden hair and his sky blue eyes. So too were his body and visage: No defects dwelled upon him or within him.

He was, however, very much one of the bastards.

As the male cleared his throat, Xcor smiled. Even after all these years together, Throe was uncomfortable in his presence. How quaint.

"And . . ." Xcor prompted.

"There are remnants of two families in Caldwell at present. What is left of the other four main bloodlines is scattered around what is classed as New England. So some are mayhap up to five hundred to seven hundred miles away."

"How many are you related to?"

More with the throat clearing. "Five."

"Five? That would fill your social calendar rather quickly—planning on dropping by for any visits?"

"You know that I cannot."

"Oh . . . indeed." Xcor finished off his coffee. "I had forgotten you'd been denounced. Guess you shall have to tarry with us heathens herein."

"Yes. I shall."

"Mmm." Xcor took a moment to enjoy the awkward silence.

Except then the other male had to ruin it: "You have no grounds to proceed," Throe said. "We are not of the *glymera*."

Xcor flashed his fangs in a smile. "You worry o'ermuch about rules, my friend."

"You cannot call a meeting of the Council. You do not have standing."

"True enough. It is, however, another story to present them with a reason to convene. Was it not you yourself who said there were grumbles about the king following the raids."

"Aye. But I am well aware of what you seek, and the end goal is treason at best, suicide, at worst."

"Such a narrow thinker you are, Throe. For all of your practical education, you have a gross lack of vision."

"You cannot depose the king—and surely you are not thinking of trying to kill him."

"Kill?" Xcor cocked a brow. "I do not wish him a coffin for a bed. Not a'tall. I bid him a long life . . . such that he may stew in the juices of his failure."

Throe shook his head. "I know not why you hate him so."

"Please." Xcor rolled his eyes. "I have nothing against him personally. It is his status that I covet, pure and simple. For him to be alive whilst I sit upon his throne is just an added spice for my meal."

"Sometimes . . . I fear you are mad."

Xcor narrowed his eyes. "I assure you . . . I am neither enraged nor insane. And you should walk carefully the line you stand upon with comments like that."

He was fully capable of killing his old friend. Today. Tonight. Tomorrow. His father had taught him that soldiers were no different from any other weapon—and when they were in danger of misfiring? They had to go.

"Forgive me." Throe bowed slightly. "My debt to you remains. As does my loyalty."

Such a sap. Although in truth, Xcor murdering the male who had defiled Throe's sister had been a very worthwhile investment of time and blade, for it had tied this steadfast and true fighter to him. E'ermore.

Throe had sold himself to Xcor to get the deed done. Back then, the male had been too much of a dandy to commit the murder with his own hand, and so he had forced himself into the shadows to seek what he would never have invited in through even the service entrance of his mansion. He had been shocked when the money offered had been turned down, and had started to walk off when Xcor had made his demand.

A quick jogging of the memory as to the condition his sister had been found in had been enough to get a pledge out of him.

And subsequent training had done wonders. Under Xcor's tutelage Throe had hardened o'er time, like steel forged in heat. Now he was a killer. Now he was useful for something other than playing social statue at dinner parties and balls.

Such a shame his bloodline hadn't seen the transformation as an improvement—in spite of the fact that his father had been a Brother, for godsakes. You'd think the family would have been grateful. Alas, they had disowned the poor fucker.

It made Xcor positively weep every time he thought about it.

"You will write to them." Xcor smiled again, his fangs tingling, his cock doing likewise. "You will write to all of them and you will announce our arrival. You will point out their losses, reminding them of the young and the females that were cut down that summer night.

You will recall to their minds all the audiences they have not had with their king. You will express the proper outrage on their behalf and you will do it in a way they will understand—because you were once one of them. And then we shall wait . . . to be summoned."

Throe bowed. "Aye, my *leahdyre*."

"In the meantime, we shall hunt for *lessers* and keep a tally of our killings. So that when they ask after our health and well-being, which the aristocracy is wont to do, we can inform them that although prime-bred horses are pretty in the stables . . . a pack of wolves is what you want guarding your back door."

The *glymera* were worthless on so many levels, but they were as predictable as a pocket watch; self-preservation was what made their hands, big and small, go 'round and 'round . . . and 'round once more.

"Best go get your rest," Xcor drawled. "Or are you already on the hunt for one of your diversions." When there was no answer, he frowned at the reply hidden within the lack of response. "You have a purpose above and beyond what passed our fighting hours previously. The human dead are of far less concern than the living enemy of ours."

"Aye."

Read: *Nay*.

"Do not tarry in other pursuits to the disadvantage of our goals."

"Have I ever let you down?"

"There is still time, old friend." Xcor stared at the male from beneath half-masted lids. "There is always time for your bleeding-heart nature to get you into trouble. And lest you disagree, may I remind you of the circumstances you have found yourself in for the last two centuries."

Throe stiffened. "No. You need not. I am perfectly aware of where I am."

"Good." Xcor nodded. "That is rather important in this life. Carry on."

Throe bowed. "I bid you good sleep, my *leahdyre*."

Xcor watched the male depart, and as he found himself alone once again, the burning in his body annoyed him. Sexual need was such a waste of time, for it neither killed nor nourished, but on a regular basis, his cock and balls needed something other than a rough tugging session.

When darkness fell this coming night, Throe was going to have one other thing to procure for the band of bastards, and this time, Xcor was going to be forced to have his fill of it.

And they were going to need blood, as well. Preferably not human, but if they had to make do for now?

Well, they'd just have to get rid of the bodies, wouldn't they.

THIRTY-FOUR

Back in the training center, Manny woke up on the hospital bed, not in the chair. After a momentary confusion, hazy memories brought it all back: After the butler had shown up with the food, Manny had eaten in the office, as Jane had told him to do—and that, as opposed to inside his car, was where he'd found his cell phone, wallet, keys, and briefcase. The little collection of Manello-mentos had been right out in full view, just sitting on a chair, and the lack of security surprised him, given how locked-down everything else was.

Except then he'd turned his cell phone on and found that the SIM card was gone.

And he'd been willing to bet that he'd need an atomic bomb to get into or out of the garage without their permission. So his keys were immaterial.

Briefcase? Nothing but a PowerBar and some paperwork that had absolutely nothing to do with underground facilities, vampires, or Payne.

Guess all the why-bother explained the out-in-the-open.

He'd been ready to throw in the proverbial towel when it came to checking his voice mail, but then he'd taken a flyer and reached for the AT&T office phone at his elbow. Picking up the receiver, he'd hit 9 . . . and the dial tone had been a total shocker. Although, really, what were the chances that anyone would be left unattended down here? Slim to none.

Except on a day when ninety percent of them had been injured fighting, and the other ten percent were worried about their brothers.

In short order, Manny had run through three voice mail systems: home, cell, and office. The first had had two messages from his mother. Nothing specific—house repairs were needed and she'd bogeyed the dreaded ninth hole. The cell had had one from the vet that he'd had to listen to twice. And the office . . . had been just as depressing as the Glory shit: There had been seven messages from colleagues around the country and it was all so shatteringly normal. They wanted him to fly out and do consults or give papers at conferences or make spaces in his residency program for their kids or family friends.

The sad truth was, those run-of-the-mill requests lagged behind where his life was really at, kind of like he'd hung a tight louie and faked out the poor bastards who were calling him. And he had no idea, once these vampires worked on his brain again, whether there would be anything left to count to ten with, much less use to operate on a patient or run a surgical department. There was no way of knowing what condition he was going to be in when he came out of all this—

The sound of a toilet flushing had him bolting upright.

As the bathroom door opened, he saw Payne's silhouette spotlit from behind, her johnny disappearing into nothing more than a filmy sheet.

Sweet . . . baby . . . Jesus . . .

His morning hard-on started to pound, and didn't that make him wish he'd slept in the damn chair. Trouble was, when he'd finally come back to her, he hadn't had the strength to say no when she'd asked him to join her.

"You wake," she said in a husky voice.

"And you are up." He smiled a little. "How're the legs feeling?"

"Weak. But they work." She glanced over her shoulder. "I should like a shower. . . ."

Shit, with the way that trailed off, she was looking for some help—and his mind went straight to the pair of them separated by nothing but soap.

"I think there's a bench to sit on." He got up on the far side of the bed so that he could tuck his erection into the waistband of the scrubs.

Going over to her, he tried to give her as much room as possible as he ducked into the bath. "Yeah, right here."

He reached in and turned on the water, then angled the bench around. "I'll set this up—"

Glancing over his shoulder, he froze solid. Payne had loosened the ties of her hospital gown and was slowly, inexorably . . . letting the front . . . fall from her shoulders.

As the spray hit his arm and started soaking the top of his scrubs, he swallowed hard—and found himself wanting to scream when her hands caught the very top and held it to her breasts.

She stayed like that, as if she were waiting to see what he was going to say, and as their eyes locked, his cock strained so hard, it was a wonder it didn't bust open the front of his frickin' pants.

"Let it go, *bambina*," he heard himself say.

And she did.

Fucking hell, he'd never wanted to worship the law of gravity before, but he did now: He wanted to prostrate himself at Newton's altar and weep with gratitude for the blessing that made all things fall to the goddamn ground.

"Look at you," he growled, watching those pink tips get tight.

Without conscious thought or any warning, his wet arm reached out and grabbed her, pulling her to his mouth, holding her hard as he sucked her nipple in and tongued her. But he didn't need to worry he'd offended her. Payne's hands dove into his hair and she cradled him against her as he suckled on her, bending her back until he was holding her upright and she was all naked female ready to be devoured.

Maneuvering her around, he canned the light and took them both under the warm spray of the shower. As her body illuminated from within, he sank onto his knees, catching with his tongue the hot water that sluiced between her breasts and ran down her stomach.

As she threw her hand out to catch her balance, he was on it, guiding her down so that she was safely sitting on the bench. Arching up, he palmed her nape and kissed her deep as he went for the soap and got ready to make sure she was very, very clean. As her tongue met his own, he was so into the feel of her nipples brushing against his chest and her lips against his own that he didn't notice or care that his hair was plastering onto his skull or that the scrubs had Saran Wrapped on him, clinging to his body.

"Healer . . ." she gasped as he started soaping her skin.

Her upper body grew slick and hot as his palms went all over her, from her neck to the tops of her hip bones. And then he started in on her legs, working her delicate feet and ankles and moving ever upward, over her calves and the backs of her knees.

Water was all around them, falling between them, washing her off as soon as he sudsed her up, and the sound of it falling on the tile was drowned out only by her moans.

Shit was only going to get louder, too.

Sucking on her neck, he spread her knees wider and wider, pushing himself between them. "I told you"—he bit her a little—"you would like bathtime."

In response, her hands speared into his shoulders, her nails digging in and making him wonder if it wasn't time to start thinking about baseball stats, zip codes . . . car prices.

Eleanor Roosevelt.

"You were correct, healer," she said, panting. "I love it—but you are too well clothed."

Manny closed his eyes as he shuddered. And then he got enough control over himself so he could speak. "Nah . . . I'm good the way I am. You just lean back and let me take care of this."

Before she could respond, he sealed his mouth on hers and pushed her against the wall with his chest. To get her to stay away from the subject of his getting naked, he slid both hands up the insides of her thighs and ran his fingertips across her sex.

As he felt how wet she was—and it was the kind of wet that had nothing to do with water and everything to do with what he wanted all over his tongue—he pulled back a little and looked down.

Fucking . . . hell . . . she was so ready for him. And, man, what she looked like, all bent back, the water making her breasts glisten, her lips parted and a little bruised from him kissing her, her legs spread apart.

"Will you take me now?" she moaned, her eyes flashing, her fangs elongating.

"Yes . . ."

He gripped her knees and went down, putting his mouth where his eyes had locked. As she cried out, he went for it hard and fast, engulfing her sex, driving her hard, making no excuses for how much he wanted her. When she blew apart, his tongue went into her and he felt it all, the pulses, the way she jerked against his chin and nose, the hard grip of her hands on his head.

No reason to stop there.

With her, he had endless stamina, and he knew, as long as his scrubs stayed on him, he could keep going like this with her . . . forever.

Vishous woke up in a bed that was not his own, but it didn't take him more than a nanosecond to know where he was: the clinic. In one of the recovery rooms.

After giving his eyes a good rub, he glanced around. The light was on in the bathroom and its door was cracked, so there was plenty to see by . . . and the first thing that stood out was the duffel bag across the way on the floor.

It was one of his. Specifically, the one he'd given Jane.

She wasn't here, however. Not in this room, at least.

As he sat up, he felt as if he'd been in a car accident, aches and pains blooming all over his body like he was an antenna and every single radio signal in the world was channeling into his nervous system. With a groan, he shifted around so that his legs dangled off the bed—and then he had to take a little breather.

Couple of minutes later, it was a case of push and pray: He shoved his weight off the mattress and hoped—

Bingo. Legs held.

The side that had been worked on by Manello was not exactly ready to run a marathon, but as V ripped off the bandages and did some flexing, he had to be impressed. The scars from the knee surgery were almost completely healed already, nothing except a pale pink line left behind. But more importantly, what was underneath was straight-up magic: The joint felt fantastic. Even with the stiffness that remained, he could tell it was functioning perfectly.

Hip felt good as new, too.

Goddamn human surgeon was a miracle worker.

On his way to the loo, his eyes passed over that duffel bag. Memories from his morphine trip filtered back and were far clearer than the actual experience had been. God, Jane was a spectacular doctor. In the night-to-night running of life, he hadn't so much forgotten that as not experienced it in a while. She always went the extra mile with her patients. Always. And she didn't treat his brothers so well because they were tied to him. It had nothing to do with his ass—those people were hers in those moments. She would have treated civilians, members of the *glymera* . . . even humans in exactly the same way.

Inside the bathroom, he got into the shower, and man, it was crowded in the stall. As he thought about Jane and his sister, he had a terrible feeling he'd oversimplified what he'd walked in on the night before yesterday. He hadn't stopped to consider that there was some other relationship at work between the two females. It had been all about him and his sister . . . nothing about the doctor/patient bond.

Scratch that. It had been all about him; nothing about Payne and what she wanted out of her life. Or what Jane had done or not done for her patient.

Standing with his head down and the water hitting the back of his neck, he stared at the drain between his feet.

He wasn't good with apologies. Or talking.

But he was not a pussy, either.

Ten minutes later, he threw on a hospital johnny and limped out into the corridor for the office. If his Jane was down here, he figured she'd be asleep at the desk, given how many of the recovery beds were no doubt filled with Brothers she'd treated.

He still had no clue what to say to her about The Leathers, but he could at least give it a shot about Payne.

Except the office was empty.

Sitting down at the computer, it took him less than fifteen seconds to find his *shellan*. When he'd hardwired the security system for the mansion, the Pit, and this facility, he'd put cameras in every single room there was—except for the First Family's suite. Naturally, the equipment could be disconnected easily with an unplug, and what do you know, the bedrooms of his brothers all showed black on the computer screen.

Which was a good thing. He didn't need to see all that banging.

The blue toile guest room up at the big house, however, was

still being monitored, and in the light of the bedside lamp that had been left on, he saw the curled figure of his mate. Jane was dead to the world, but it was damn clear she wasn't resting comfortably: Her brows were clenched as if her brain were desperately trying to hold on to the sleep she was getting. Or maybe she was dreaming of things that prickled instead of pleasured her.

His first instinct was to march right over there, but the more he thought about it, the more he realized that the kindest thing he could do was leave her where she lay and let her rest. She and Manello had gone for hours straight, all morning long. Besides, he was staying in tonight: Wrath had taken everyone off rotation in light of all the injuries.

Christ . . . that Lessening Society. He hadn't seen so many slayers in years—and he wasn't thinking about just the dozen that had shown up last night. Over the previous two weeks, he was willing to bet the Omega had turned a hundred of those fuckers—and he had a feeling they were like cockroaches. For every one you saw, there were another ten that you didn't.

Good thing the Brothers were lethal as fuck. And Butch healed relatively easily after doing his *Dhestroyer* business—hell, Vishous had even been able to take care of the cop after the operation. Not that he remembered much about doing it, but still.

Stifled by so much, he patted his pockets for his rolling paper and tobacco . . . and realized he was wearing a johnny: no merch for a smoke.

Out of the chair. Back in the hall. Heading down to where he'd crashed.

The door to Payne's room was closed, and he didn't hesitate before he opened the way in. Chances were good that the human surgeon was in there with her, but there was no way the guy wasn't out like a light. He'd worked his ass off.

As Vishous stepped inside, the scent in the air probably should have registered more clearly. And he maybe should have paid a little more attention to the fact that the shower was running. But he was just so shocked to see the bed was empty . . . and that there were braces and crutches over in the corner.

Patient was paralyzed? You needed a wheelchair, not equipment that aided mobility. So . . . was she *walking*?

"Payne?"

He raised his voice. "Payne?"

The response he got back was a moan. A very deep, satisfied moan . . .

Which was not the kind of thing evoked even by the best shower anyone ever had.

V shot across and nearly broke the door down as he burst into the hot, humid bathroom. And holy shit, the scene before him was so much worse than he'd thought.

The irony, however, was that what they were—oh, God, he couldn't even put into words what was doing—saved the surgeon's life: V was so horrified, he had to look away, and the ostrich routine kept him from tearing a hole the size of a sewer pipe in Manello's neck.

As Vishous stumbled back out, he heard all kinds of scrambling from the bath. And then it was a case of him going asswipe-AWOL: He slammed into the bed, rebounded, knocked over a chair, bounced into a wall.

At this rate, he'd find his way out in a week. Or so.

"Vishous . . ."

As Payne came up to him, he kept his eyes on the floor, and ended up with a clear shot of his twin's bare feet. So she'd regained feeling in her legs.

Yay.

"Please spare me an explanation," he bit out before glaring over at Manello. The bastard was soaking wet, hair slicked to his head, scrubs sucked into his body. "And do *not* get used to her. You're here only until I don't need you anymore—and given how well she's doing? It ain't for much longer—"

"How *dare* you—it is for me to choose with whom I mate."

He shook his head at his sister. "Then pick something other than a human half your size and a quarter your strength. Life down here is not what it's like in the clouds, sweetheart—and the Lessening Society's slapped a bull's-eye on your chest just like the rest of us wear. He's weak, he's a security risk, and he needs to go back where he belongs—and stay there."

Well, didn't that make his twin furious: Her icy eyes went nuclear, her black brows slamming down. "Get. Out."

"Ask him what he did all morning long," V demanded. "Wait—I'll tell you. He sewed me and the Brotherhood up because we were trying to defend our females and our race. That human? He's a *lesser* waiting to happen, in my opinion—nothing less, nothing more."

"How dare you! You know naught of him."

V leaned in to her. "And neither do you. Which is my fucking point."

Before shit got really out of control, he spun around to leave, only to catch sight of them all in the mirror on the wall. What a fucking tableau they were: his sister, naked and unashamed; the human, wet and grim; himself, wild eyed and ready to kill something.

Rage built up so fast and so high, it broke free before he even recognized the emotion.

Vishous took two steps over, reared back his head, and slammed his face into the glass, shattering the reflection to fuck and gone.

As his sister screamed and the surgeon shouted, he left them to their own devices and stalked off.

Out in the hall, he knew precisely where he was going.

Out in the tunnel, he was oh, so very aware of what he was about to do.

As he went, the blood dripped down his cheeks and off his chin, the red tears falling onto his chest and his abs.

He didn't feel any pain at all.

But with any luck, he would. Very soon.

THIRTY-FIVE

By the time Payne got herself dressed and went out into the hall, her twin was gone.

The blood on the floor told her in which direction he had headed, however, and she followed the trail down the corridor and into the glass-enclosed space marked OFFICE. Inside, the little specks of red cut a path around the desk and disappeared through a door, so she went over and opened up—

Just a closet. Nothing but supplies of papers and writing instruments.

There was more to it, however. There had to be. The track of droplets terminated at a wall of shelving.

Patting around, she searched for a lever or release to shift the casing over, all the while replaying the scene of the mirror smashing. She had such fear, not for herself, but for Vishous—and what she had driven him to. Again.

She had wanted a relationship with her brother. Not like this, though.

Never this toxic interplay.

"You getting anywhere?"

She looked over her shoulder at her healer. Standing in the doorway to the office, he was still wet, but no longer dripping, and had a white towel wrapped around his neck. His short, dark hair was askew, as if he had rubbed it dry and left it as it stood.

"I cannot find the way through." And wasn't that apt on so many levels.

Payne wasted some time just staring at the neatly lined-up stacks of yellow pads and boxes of pens and orderly rows of things the purposes of which she could only guess at. When she finally gave up and stepped out, her healer was still in the doorway to the office, still staring at her. His eyes were black with emotion, his lips thin . . . and for some reason, his expression made her realize how fully clothed he was.

How fully clothed he had always been whenever he had lain with her.

He hadn't let her touch him, had he.

"You agree with my brother," she said darkly. "Do you not."

It was not a question. And she was not surprised when he nodded. "This isn't a long-term thing," he said with horrible gentleness. "Not for you."

"So that is why I have not had the pleasure of your sex."

His brows flared briefly, as if her candor discomforted him. "Payne . . . this can't work between us."

"Says who. It is our choice whom we—"

"I've got a life to go back to."

As her breath grew tight, she thought . . . how incredibly arrogant of her. It had never occurred to her that he had somewhere else to go. Then again, just as her brother had pointed out, how much did she know of him?

"I've got family," he continued. "A job. A horse I have to go see."

Payne walked over to him, approaching him with her head high. "Why do you assume it is an either/or? And before you try, do not waste words telling me you do not want me. I know it is true—your scent does not lie."

He cleared his throat. "Sex isn't everything, Payne. And when it comes to you and me, even that's just about getting you to where you are now."

At that, another chill ran through her, sure as if there were a draft in the room. But then she shook her head. "You wanted me, healer. When you came back here and saw me in that bed—your scent was nothing about the condition I was in, and you are a coward if you pretend otherwise. Hide if you will, healer—"

"My name is Manny," he snapped. "Manuel Manello. I was brought here to help you—and in case you haven't noticed, you're on your feet. So I have. Right now? I'm just waiting until you people rip into my brain again and leave me strapped to separate night from day and dreams from reality. This is your world, not mine, and there is *only* either/or."

Their eyes locked together, and in that moment, if the facility had been on fire, she would not have been able to look away . . . and neither, she realized, would he.

"If it could work," she said roughly, "if you were allowed to come and go as you pleased, would you stay with me."

"Payne—"

"My question is clear. Answer it. Now." As his brows rose, she could not tell whether he was excited or repulsed by her brashness, and she did not care in that moment. "The truth is what it is, spoken or not. So we might as well have it all out."

He slowly shook his head. "Your brother doesn't think—"

"Fuck my brother," she countered. "Tell me what *you* think."

In the strained silence that followed, she realized what she had just said, and wanted to curse anew. Dropping her head, she stared at the floor, not in meekness, but out of frustration. Females of worth did not use words like that, and they did not pressure people for a tea towel, much less something like this.

Indeed, a proper female would stand by as the eldest male of her family handled the big decisions in her life, shaping the course of everything from where she lived to unto whom she was betrothed.

Outbursts. Sex. Swearing. Any more of this and she was going to make Vishous's wishes come true, because her healer—Manuel, that was—would find her so unattractive he would beg to be taken away from her with no memories of their time together.

Would she never fit the Layla standard of feminine perfection?

Rubbing her temples, she muttered, "You are both right—just for the wrong reasons. You and I could never last, because I am not a good match for any male."

"What?"

Tired of everything . . . of him and her brother, of herself, of females and males in general . . . she waved him off and turned away. "You say this is my world? You have that so very wrong. I do not belong here any more than you do."

"What the hell are you talking about?"

Verily, he might as well get the true picture of things on his way out. What the hell.

She stared over her shoulder. "I am the daughter of a god, Manuel. A deity. That glow you call forth from me? It is her very essence as an entity. That is what she is. As for my father? He was nothing but a sadistic bastard who imparted unto me the urge to kill—that was his 'gift.' And do you want to know what I did with it? Do you?" She was aware that her voice was rising but was singularly disinclined to quiet herself. "I killed him, Manuel. And for that crime against mine bloodline, for that offense against the standards of behavior for females, I was imprisoned and held for centuries. So you are too right. Go—and do it now. It is for the best. But do *not* think that I fit in here any better than you do."

With another curse, she pushed past him and strode out into the corridor, figuring Manuel would find himself freed very shortly—

"It was your brother. Wasn't it."

The calm, low words echoed down the barren hallway, stopping not just her feet, but her heart.

"I saw the condition he's in," Manuel said in a deep voice. "Any chance your father did that to the guy?"

Payne slowly turned back around. Standing in the middle of the corridor, her healer was showing neither shock nor horror, just an intelligence she was coming to expect from him.

"Why would you think that," she said in a dead tone.

"When I operated on him, I saw the scars, and it's pretty clear someone tried to castrate him. Extrapolating? From my limited interaction with him, I'd say he's way too touchy and aggressive for anyone to get the better of him. So it was either a gang of people or somebody who got him when he was really, profoundly vulnerable. I'm thinking the latter is more likely because . . . well, let's just say I'd be surprised if abusive parents didn't happen for your kind, too."

Payne swallowed hard, and it was a long, long while before she could find her voice. "Our father . . . had him held down. A blacksmith was ordered to tattoo him . . . and then get a pair of pliers."

Manuel squeezed his eyes shut briefly. "I'm sorry. I'm really . . . damned sorry."

"Our father was chosen as a sire for his aggression and ruthlessness, and my brother was given over to him when he was very young—whereas I stayed up at the Sanctuary with our *mahmen*. With naught to pass my time, I watched what transpired down here on Earth in the seeing bowls and . . . over the course of years in the war camp, my brother was abused. I brought this to my mother time and time again, but she insisted upon adhering to the deal she had made with the Bloodletter." She curled her hands into tight fists. "That male, that forsaken, sadistic male . . . he was not capable of siring sons, but she guaranteed him one so he would agree to mate with her. Three years after we were born, she relinquished Vishous unto our father's cruelty whilst she did her best to force me into a mold I would ne'er fit into. And then that last episode where Vishous was . . ." Tears speared into her eyes. "No more—not any longer could I do nothing. I came down here and . . . and I hunted the Bloodletter down. I held him to the ground whilst I burned him into ash. And I do not regret it."

"Who put you in jail?"

"My mother. But the imprisonment was only partially because he was dead. Sometimes I believe it was more her colossal disappointment in me." She wiped her face quickly and rubbed the wetness away. "But enough of this. Enough of . . . all of it. Go now . . . I shall speak to the king and send you off. Good-bye, Manuel."

Rather than waiting for him to respond, she headed off once more—

"Yes, I want you."

Payne stopped, and then looked over her shoulder again. After a moment, she said, "You are a fine healer and you have done your job, as you so aptly pointed out. We have no further cause to speak."

When she resumed walking, his footsteps approached fast and he caught her, wheeling her around. "If I didn't keep my pants on, I couldn't have kept myself out of you."

"Really."

"Give me your hand."

Without looking, she held one unto him. "Why ever for—"

He moved fast, putting her palm between his legs, and pressing her into the hot, hard length at his hips. "You're right." He moved against her, his pelvis undulating, the arousal pushing against her palm as he started to breathe deeply. "Even as I tried to tell myself otherwise, I knew that if I got naked, you were going to stay a virgin only long enough for me to get you on your back. Not romantic, but really, totally fucking true."

As her lips parted, his eyes dropped to her mouth and he growled, "You can feel the truth, can't you. It's in your goddamn hand."

"Do you not care about what I did . . ."

"You mean with your father?" He stopped the rubbing and frowned. "No. To be clear, I'm a *lex talionis* kind of guy. Your brother could easily have died from those wounds—I don't care how fast you people heal. But more to the point, I'm willing to bet that father/son bonding moment fucked his head up for the rest of his life—so yeah, I don't have a problem with what you did."

Retaliatory justice, she thought as his words sank in.

Tightening her hold on him, she resumed what he had stopped, tracing up and down his sex, stroking. "I am glad you feel this way."

And wasn't that true on a lot of levels: His erection was delicious, so hard and blunt at the tip. She wanted to explore him as he had her . . . with her fingers . . . her mouth . . . her tongue. . . .

Manuel's eyes briefly rolled back into his head as he gritted his teeth. "But . . . your brother's still right."

"Is he . . ." She leaned in and licked at his lips. "Are you sure?"

When she drew back, there was a sizzling moment as their eyes met . . . and then, with a growl, he spun her around and pushed her into the wall.

"Be careful," he growled.

"Why." She dipped her lips to his neck and slowly, inexorably dragged one fang up over his jugular.

"Oh . . . fuck . . ." With a desperate curse, he locked his hand on hers, holding her palm in place at his hips, obviously trying to refocus. "Listen to me. As good as this is between us . . ." He swallowed hard. "As good . . . Shit, look, your brother knows what's doing—I can't take care of you properly and—"

"I can take care of myself." She pressed her mouth to his, and she knew she had him when his pelvis began to push forward and ease back again: He may have halted her hand, but his body was more than making up the slack on the friction front.

"Fucking hell," he groaned, "do you want me to come right here?"

"Yes, I do. I want to know what it is like."

More kissing. And even though he was the one gripping her and pinning her against the wall, she was the aggressor.

Manuel pulled back, but only, it seemed, upon a great struggle within himself. After taking a number of deep breaths, he said, "You asked me whether I would stay if I could? In a heartbeat. You are beautiful and sexy and I don't know what the hell your mother or anyone else is doing comparing you to anything or anybody. Nothing comes close to you . . . on any level."

As he spoke, he was lethally serious and abidingly sincere . . . and the acceptance he offered was as generous as it was unique: She had never gotten it from anyone. Even her own brother wanted to deny her her choice of mate.

"Thank you," she whispered.

"It's not a compliment. That's just the way it is." Manuel kissed her mouth softly, and lingered with the contact. "But the Goateed Hater is still right, Payne."

"Goateed . . . Hater?"

"Sorry. Little nickname I dreamed up for your twin." He shrugged. "But even still, I really think he does have your best interests at heart, and you do need someone other than me long-term—whether I can stay here or not is just part of the problem."

"Not in my eyes."

"Then you need to see more clearly. I'm going to be dead in another four decades. If I'm lucky. Do you really want to watch me age? Die?"

She had to close her eyes and turn her head away at the thought of him passing away. "Fates . . . no."

In the quiet that followed, the energy between them changed, shifting from everything sexual . . . to a different kind of yearning. And as if he felt as she did, he tucked her in against his body, holding her tightly within his strong arms.

"If there's one thing that I've learned as a doctor," he said, "it's that biology prevails. You and I can do all the deciding we want, but the biological differences are nothing that we can change. My life expectancy is a fraction of yours—at most, we'd get a ten-year window before I'm in Cialis land."

"What's that?"

"A very, very flat, gelded place," he said drily.

"Well . . . I would go there with you, Manuel." She pulled back so she could look into his beautiful brown eyes. "Wherever it is."

There was a beat of silence. And then he smiled sadly. "I love the way you say my name."

Sighing, she put her head on his shoulder. "And I love saying it."

As they stood there, one against the other, she wondered whether it was for the very last time. And that made her think of her brother. She was worried about Vishous and needed to talk with him, but he had chosen to leave her with no way of finding him.

So be it. Difficult as it was, she would let Vishous go temporarily for now . . . and focus on the male who was with her.

"I have something to ask of you," she said to her healer—Manuel, she corrected herself.

"Name it."

"Take me into your world. Show me . . . if not everything, then something."

Manuel stiffened. "I don't know if that's such a hot idea. You've been on your feet for just over twelve hours at this point."

"But I feel strong, and I have ways of dealing with travel." Worse came to worst, she could just dematerialize back here to the compound: She knew from the seeing bowls that her brother had surrounded this facility with *mhis*, and that was a beacon she could readily find. "Trust me, I shall be in no danger."

"How would we get out together, though?"

Payne stepped from his hold. "You re-dress your body whilst I take care of everything." When it looked like he was going to argue, she shook her head. "You say biology always wins? Fine. But I say to you, we have this night—why should we waste it."

"More time together . . . is only going to make it harder to leave."

Oh, how that hurt. "You said you would grant me a favor. I have put it upon you. Is your word not your bond?"

His lips thinned out. But then he inclined his head. "Fair enough. I'll go change."

As he headed back to their room, she returned to the office and picked up the phone, as Jane and Ehlena had shown her how to do. The dialing went well enough—and the butler *doggen* answered in a cheery voice.

This had to work, she told herself. This absolutely had to work.

In the Old Language, she said, *"This is Payne, blooded sister of the Black Dagger Brother Vishous, son of the Bloodletter. I should wish to speak with the king, if he would grant me the courtesy."*

THIRTY-SIX

As Vishous burst into the Pit from the underground tunnel, he had to wipe his bloody face with his palm so he could keep going down to the bedrooms. He supposed it was a good thing that the mirror had mostly bull's-eyed, because it meant there were few shards in him—but in truth, he didn't really give a shit.

When he came up to Butch and Marissa's door, he knocked. Hard.

"Gimme a minute."

Butch didn't take that long to open up, and he was still pulling his robe on when he did. "What is—" That was as far as he got. "Jesus Christ . . . *V*."

Over the guy's shoulder, Marissa sat up in their bed, her cheeks flushed, her long blond hair tangled, the covers pulled up to her breasts and held there. Drowsy satisfaction was quickly replaced with shock.

"I should have just called." V was impressed at the calm tone of his voice, and he tasted copper as he spoke. "But I don't know where my phone is."

As his stare locked onto his best friend's, he felt like a diabetic desperate for insulin. Or maybe it was more like a heroin addict pining for a needle. Whatever the metaphor, he had to get out of himself or he was going to lose his mind and do something criminally stupid.

Like get his blades on and turn that surgeon into so much hamburger meat.

"I caught them together," he heard himself say. "But don't worry. The human is still breathing."

And then he just stood there, the question that he'd come to ask as plain as the blood on his face.

Butch glanced back at his *shellan*. Without hesitation, she nodded, her eyes sad and kind and so understanding that V was momentarily touched—even in his numbed-out state.

"Go," she said. "Take care of him. I love you."

Butch nodded at her. Probably mouthed an "I love you" back.

Then he looked at V and muttered gruffly, "You go wait in the courtyard. I'll bring the Escalade around—and get a towel from the bathroom, would ya? You look like Freddy-frickin'-Krueger."

As the cop peeled off for the closet and ditched his robe to get dressed, V looked at the male's *shellan*.

"It's all right, Vishous," she said. "It's going to be all right."

"I do not crave this." But he needed it before he became a danger to himself and others.

"I know. And I love you, too."

"*You are a blessing beyond measure*," he pronounced in the Old Language.

And then he bowed to her and turned away.

When the world came back into focus sometime later, V found himself sitting on the passenger side of the Escalade. Butch was behind the wheel, and the pedal-metal routine the cop was pulling meant some serious mileage had been covered: The lights of downtown Caldwell were not just in the distance; they were all around, glimmering through the front and side windows.

The silence in the SUV was as tense as a dagger hand and as dense as a brick. And even as they closed in on their destination, V had trouble comprehending this trip they were taking. There was no going back, however. Not for either of them.

Down into the Commodore's parking garage.

Engine off.

Two doors opening . . . two doors closing.

And then the ride up in the elevator. Which was like the trip from the compound to the Commodore: nothing that stuck in V's mind.

Next thing he knew, Butch was using the copper key to open the way into the penthouse.

V walked in first and he willed the black candles on their stanchions to light up. The instant the black walls and flooring were illuminated, he went from zombie to live wire, his senses coming alive to the point where his own footfalls sounded like bombs dropping, and the sound of the door shutting them both in was like the building falling in on itself.

Every breath he took was a gust of wind. Every beat of his heart was a boxer's punch. Every swallow he took was a guzzle down his throat.

Was this how his subs had felt? This too-alive tingle?

He stopped by his table. No jacket to take off. Nothing but the now-bloody hospital johnny on his back.

Behind him, Butch's presence loomed big as a mountain.

"Can I use your phone," V asked roughly.

"Here."

V spun around and caught the tossed BlackBerry with his gloved hand. Calling up a blank text, he chose *Doc Jane* out of the address book.

His fingers stilled at that point. His brain was clogged with emotion, the screams he needed to let out getting in the way and turning his normal reserve into a solid-steel set of bars that bolted him inside of himself.

But then, this was why they were here.

With a soft curse, he canceled the empty text.

When he went to pass the phone back, Butch was over by the bed, taking off one of his many fancy-dancy leather jackets. No biker's spiky bullshit for the cop's downtime—the coat was hip-length and had been fitted perfectly to his barrel chest, the material beyond butter and into cloud-soft. Which V knew because he'd handed the thing over a number of times.

This was not something the guy fought in.

And he was taking it off for the right reasons.

No reason to get blood on the likes of that.

As V put the phone down on the bed and backed away, Butch folded the jacket with careful, precise hands, and when he laid the leather down, it was as if he were settling a young on the black duvet. Then those strong, blunt fingers of his pulled up his belted black slacks and smoothed his black silk shirt.

Silence.

And not the comfy kind.

Vishous looked to the banks of plate glass that ran around the penthouse, and stared at his best friend's reflection.

After a moment, the cop's head turned.

Their eyes met in the glass.

"Are you going to leave that on?" Butch asked darkly.

Vishous reached up to the tie at the back of his neck and popped the bow that held the two halves of the johnny together. And then he did the same at his waist. As the shift fell from his body, the cop watched from across the room as it hit the floor.

"I need a fucking drink," Butch said.

Over at the bar, the guy poured himself a shot of Lagavulin. And another. And then he pushed the squat glass away, picked up the bottle, and sucked hard.

Vishous stayed where he was, his mouth open, his breath shooting in and out of him as he remained focused on the image of his best friend.

Butch put the bottle down, but held on to it, his head falling forward as if he'd closed his eyes.

"You don't have to do this," V said hoarsely.

"Yeah . . . I do."

The cop's dark head lifted and then he pivoted.

When he finally came forward, he left the booze at the bar, and he stopped when he was behind Vishous. He was close . . . close enough so that the heat from his body easily registered.

Or maybe that was V's own blood beginning to boil.

"What are the rules," the cop said.

"There are none." Vishous spread his stance and braced himself. "Do whatever you want . . . but you have to break me. You've got to tear me apart."

Back at the compound, Manny changed into yet another set of scrubs. Things kept going like this and he should buy stock in the goddamned garment company. Or in laundry machines.

Out in the hall, he took up res against the concrete wall and stared at his Nikes. He so did not think the soles should get excited—he had a feeling that he and Payne were not going anywhere. At least, not together.

Daughter of a deity.

Annnnnd . . . it didn't matter to him. She could have been the offspring of an ostrich, for all he cared.

Rubbing his face, he couldn't decide whether he was impressed with himself or terrified that he was so accepting of that news flash. Probably healthier to be shocked and disbelieving and all about the hell-no. His brain just rolled with it, though—which meant he was either getting really flexible with what he considered reality or his gray matter had fallen into a state of learned helplessness.

Probably the former. Because all in all, he felt with-it. . . . Shit, he felt better than he had in ages: In spite of the fact that he'd operated for ten hours straight, and he'd slept in a chair for part of the night—or day, or whatever time it was—the body/mind combo of his was strong and healthy and sharp as a tack. Even as he stretched, there was no stiffness . . . or creaks or pops. It was as if he'd been on vacation for a month, getting massages and doing yoga in front of the ocean.

Not that he'd ever done the Downward Dog.

Annnnnnnnnnnd on that note, a truly fabulous, utterly filthy image of Payne came to mind. As his cock raised its hand to be called on, he thought it would no doubt be a good idea not to take her on a guided tour of, say, his bedroom. Actually, given recent events, which had involved him on his knees . . . his bathroom was probably off-limits, too. Maybe he should avoid rooms with tile? So his kitchen was a no-go. His front hall, too—

Payne all but jumped out from the office, and she had his briefcase and other things with her. "We're free!"

With all the grace of an athlete, she ran to him, her hair flowing out behind her, her stride just as fluid as those dark waves on her head.

"We're free! We're free!"

As she leaped into his arms, he caught her and spun her around. "They're letting us go?" he said.

"Indeed! We have clearance to take your automobile out from here." As she handed him his things, she smiled so widely her fangs flashed. "I thought you might need these. And the phone works now."

"How did you know they're mine?"

"They carried your scent. And Wrath told me about the card thingy that my twin removed."

Phone-schmone. The fact she recognized him by smell turned him on, reminding him of exactly how close they had gotten—

Okay, time to stop that film reel.

She put her hand up to his face. "You know what?"

"What?"

"I like the way you look at me, Manuel."

"Oh, yeah?"

"It makes me think of when your mouth was upon me."

Manny groaned and nearly lost it. So to keep things from getting out of hand, he put his arm around her waist. "Come on. Let's take off before we lose the chance."

Her laugh was so carefree that for some reason it split his chest wide and exposed the beating heart behind his ribs. And that was before she leaned in and kissed his cheek.

"You are aroused."

He glanced over at her. "And you are playing with fire."

"I like being hot."

Manny barked out a laugh. "Well, don't you worry—you are just that."

When they came up to the fire door, he put his palm on the push bar. "This really going to open?"

"Try it and find out."

He tilted in . . . and what do you know, the latch sprang free and the heavy metal panel went wide.

As vampires with guns and machetes didn't come streaming down on them from every direction, he shook his head. "How in the hell did you manage this."

"The king was not happy. But I am not a prisoner here, I am of age, and there is no reason I should not be able to leave the compound."

"And at the end of the evening . . . what then?" As her joy diminished, he thought, Uh-huh, that was how she'd pulled it off. Technically, she was escorting him home. . . . This was their good-bye.

He smoothed her hair back. "It's okay. It's . . . all right, *bambina*."

She seemed to swallow hard. "I shall not think of the future, and neither should you. There are hours and hours to be had."

Hours. Not days or weeks or months . . . or years. Hours.

God, he didn't feel free at all.

"Come on," he said, stepping out and taking her hand. "Let's make this count."

His car was parked in the shadows on the right, and when he got over to it, he found the thing unlocked. But come on, like anyone was going to get at it?

He opened the passenger-side door. "Let me help you in."

Taking her arm like a gentleman, he settled her and then stretched the seat belt across her breasts, clicking it into place.

As her eyes bounced around the interior and her hands stroked the sides of the bucket seat, he figured this could be her first car ride. And how cool was that?

"You ever been in one of these before?" he asked.

"Verily, I have not."

"Well, I'll take it slow."

She caught his hand as he straightened. "Does this go fast?"

He laughed a little. "It's a Porsche. Fast is what it does."

"Then you shall take us upon the wind! It shall be as my days astride were!"

Manny took a mental snapshot of the wild happiness on her face: She was glowing—and not in the ethereal sense, but in the simple joy-of-life way.

He leaned in and kissed her. "You are so beautiful."

She captured his face. "And I thank you for it."

Oh, but it so wasn't him. What was lighting her up was freedom and health and optimism—and she deserved nothing less out of life.

"I have someone I want you to meet," he blurted.

Payne smiled at him. "Then drive on, Manuel. Take us into the night."

After a moment more of staring at her . . . he did just that.

THIRTY-SEVEN

Standing naked in his penthouse, Vishous waited for something . . . anything.

Instead, Butch backed off and disappeared into the kitchen. As he was left to his lonesome, V closed his eyes and cursed. This was a bad idea. You didn't ask a good Catholic boy to play with the kind of toys V—

The hit came from behind, fast and sure.

It was a modified body slam, and executed beautifully: Two huge arms wrapped him at the chest and the hips and he was slung around and spun out into the far wall by the worktable. Which was when the "slam" part came in: Every square inch of him made impact. No bounce-back, though. No ricocheting.

He was pinned in place by the nape and the ass.

"Arms over your head."

That growl was like a gun to the back of his skull and V struggled to comply, fighting against the pressure that trapped both his arms in front of his chest. The right side came free first—and the instant his wrist was out from under, it was grabbed and forced into a cuff. Left side happened just as fast.

Then again, cops were good with the steel.

There was a brief release where he was able to catch some air. And then the sound of metal chain links being churned through a gear announced where things were headed: up.

Gradually, his weight shifted off his feet and onto the sockets and lengths of his arms. The ascent stopped right before his toes left the floor completely . . . and then he just hung there, facing toward the windows, breath squeezing in and out of his lungs as he heard Butch moving behind him.

"Open your mouth."

At the command, V cranked his jaw wide, the joint at his cheekbone cracking, his eyes pulling down at the corners, his facial cuts coming alive with a chorus of howls.

The gag was pulled down over his head and it fit right where it should, the ball squeezing between his fangs and forcing shit open even farther. With a quick jerk, the leather strapping tightened across the back of his skull and the buckle was fastened until it dug into his scalp.

It was a perfect setup: The suspension and the choking confinement did their job, spurring on his adrenaline, making his body strain in so many different ways.

A barbed corset was next, the contraption not going over his shoulders, but around his torso, the metal points on the inside of the leather bindings sinking into his skin. Butch started with the strap right across the sternum, and then it was a case of sequential squeeze, down, down, down . . . until from V's rib cage to his stomach to the tops of his hips, concentric circles of bright white pain tingled into his spine, shooting north to the receptors in his brain and south into his rock-hard cock.

Oxygen whistled through his nostrils as there was a brief calm of no-touch, and then Butch was back with four lengths of rubber strapping. For an amateur, he had great instincts: Both the ball gag and the chest harness had stainless-steel rings that hung inch by every inch, and clearly the cop was going to put them to good use.

Working steadily, Butch slipped hooks through the gag's fixtures and stretched the tubing down, attaching it on the front and the back of the corset.

Which effectively locked Vishous's head into the forward position.

Then Butch gave him a swing and sent him on a little merry-go-round. In his frozen state, it was a mind fuck and a half, and it didn't take long before he wasn't sure whether he was moving or the room was on the ride: Things passed by one after the other, the bar, the door out, the worktable . . . Butch . . . the bed, the glass . . . then it was back to the bar, the door, the table . . . and Butch—

Who had walked over to the hanging whips and chains.

The cop just stood there, his eyes locked on Vishous.

Like a train pulling into a station, the rotation grew slower and slower until it stopped altogether . . . with the pair of them facing each other.

"You said no rules," Butch gritted out. "Do you still mean that."

With no way to nod or shake his head, V did what he could with his feet, moving them up and back on the floor.

"Are you sure."

When he repeated the motion, Butch's eyes glittered in the candlelight—as if there were tears in them. "Okay, then," he said hoarsely. "If that's the way it's going to be."

Butch wiped his face, turned to the wall, and then walked down the lineup of toys. As he approached the whips, V imagined the spiked fringe cutting into his back and his thighs . . . but the cop kept going. Next were the cat-o'-nines, and V could just feel them lashing his flesh . . . but Butch didn't stop. Then it was the nipple clips and the barbed, stainless-steel cuffs that could be applied to ankles, forearms, the throat. . . .

When each section was passed, Vishous frowned, wondering if the cop was just being a tease, and how unimpressive was that—

Butch did stop, however. And his hand reached out—

V moaned and began to thrash against the binds that held him aloft. Eyes peeling wide, he did what he could to beg, but there was no moving his head and no way to speak.

"You said no limits," Butch choked out. "So this is how we're going to do it."

V's legs spasmed and his chest started to scream for lack of oxygen.

The mask the cop had chosen had no holes in it, not for the eyes or ears or mouth. Made of leather and stitched together with thin stainless-steel thread, the only way oxygen got in was via two mesh side panels that were far enough back so that there was no leaching of light—and the air would be circulated across hot, panicked skin before it went through the mouth and down into the lungs. The contraption was something V had bought but had never used: He'd kept it only because it had terrified him, and that was reason enough to own the thing.

To be robbed of sight and hearing was the one thing guaranteed to make him lose his fucking shit—which was precisely why Butch picked the mask. He knew too well the buttons to push—physical pain was one thing . . . but the psychological stuff was so much worse.

And therefore more effectual.

Butch walked slowly around and out of sight. With furious paddling, V tried to get himself repositioned to face the guy, but his toes couldn't quite manage good purchase on the floor—which was another success of the cop's strategy. To fight and squirm and get nowhere just heightened the terror.

On a oner, it was lights-out.

Jerking uncontrollably, Vishous tried to fight, but it was a battle he was going to lose: With a quick yank, the mask went tight around his neck, secure and going nowhere.

Mental hypoxia set in immediately. There was no oxygen to be had, none coming through, nothing—

He felt something on his leg. Something long and thin. And cold.

Like a blade.

He went utterly still. To the point where his previous exertions swung him back and forth on the chains above him, his body a statue suspended by twin strings of metal.

V's inhales and exhales inside the hood were a roar in his ears as he zeroed in on the sensation below his waist: The knife traveled slowly, inexorably upward, and as it went, it moved to the inside of his thigh. . . .

In its wake, a liquid trail welled and eased down over his knee.

He didn't even feel the pain of the cutting as that blade headed for his sex: The implications were that much of a sucker punch to his destruct button.

In a flash, past and present mixed, the alchemy ignited by the adrenaline pumping through every vein he had; he was instantly ripped back through the many years to the night when his father's males had held him down in the dirt at the Bloodletter's command. The tattoos had not been the worst of it.

And here it was, happening again. Just not with the pliers.

Vishous screamed around the ball gag . . . and kept at it.

He screamed for all he had lost . . . screamed for the half male he was . . . screamed for Jane . . . screamed for who his parents were and what he wished for his sister . . . screamed for what he had forced his best friend to do. . . . He screamed and screamed until there was no breath, no consciousness, no nothing.

No past or present.

Not even himself anymore.

And in the midst of the chaos, in the strangest way, he became free.

Butch knew the moment his best friend fainted. It wasn't just that those dangling feet went still; it was the sudden relaxation of all that musculature. No more straining in those huge arms and massive thighs. No more pumping of that big chest. No more ripped cords in the shoulders or down the back.

Butch immediately took the spoon he'd gotten from the kitchen off V's leg, and likewise stopped pouring the lukewarm water out of the glass he'd grabbed from the bar.

The tears in his eyes didn't help him loosen the hood and pull it free. Nor did they make removing the immobilizer setup simple. And he struggled with the ball gag especially.

The corset was a bitch and a half to get loose, but however desperate he was to get V down, it was vastly easier to take everything off when he had a three-sixty to work with. And soon enough, the brother was bloody, but unencumbered.

Over at the wall, Butch released the winch and slowly lowered Vishous's tremendous, inanimate body down. There were no signs that the change in altitude registered, and the floor made an impact only so far as it collapsed V's loose legs, those knees bending up as the marble rose to greet his butt and torso.

There was more blood when Butch released the cuffs.

God, his friend was a mess: The gag's straps had left red welts on his cheeks; the corset's damage was even more pervasive; and then there were the wrists that were torn ragged.

And that was in addition to the condition the guy's face was in, courtesy of whatever he'd slammed the thing into.

For a moment, all he could do was brush V's jet-black hair back with hands that shook like he had palsy. Then he looked down his friend's body, to the ink below the waist, and the flaccid sex . . . and the scars.

The Bloodletter was a shit beyond measure for torturing his son as he'd done. And the Scribe Virgin was a useless planker to have let it happen.

And it had killed Butch to use that horrible past to crack his friend wide.

Except he hadn't wanted to beat V physically—he wasn't a pussy, but he did not have the stomach for that. Besides, the mind was the most powerful weapon anyone had against themselves.

Still, tears had been rolling as he'd taken the spoon and put it against the inside of that leg—because he'd known instantly the extrapolation that would be made. And he'd been well aware that the lukewarm water would really cement the dislocation from the present.

The screaming had been muffled by the gag and the hood . . . and yet the no-sound had pierced Butch's ears as nothing else could.

It was going to be a long, long while before he got over this: Every time he closed his eyes, all he could see was his best friend's body jerking and spasming.

Scrubbing his face, Butch got up and went to the bathroom. From off the shelf in the closet, he grabbed a stack of black towels. Some he left dry; others he wet with warm water at the sink.

Back beside Vishous on the floor, he wiped off the blood and fear-sweat from his best friend's body, rolling him from side to side so there was nothing missed.

The cleanup took a good half an hour. And several trips back and forth to the sink.

The session had lasted a fraction of that.

When he was finished, he gathered V's tremendous weight in his arms and carried the guy to the bed, laying him out with his head against the black satin pillows. The sponge bath, such as it had been, had left V's skin with a rash of goose bumps, so Butch taco'd the brother, untucking the sheets and rolling them up and over him.

The healing was already happening, the flesh that had been scraped or cut reknitting and erasing the marks that had been made.

This was good.

As he stepped back, part of Butch wanted to get on the bed and hold on to his friend. But he hadn't done this for himself—and besides, if he didn't get out of here and get drunk fast, he was going to lose his motherfucking mind.

When he was sure V was settled, he grabbed his jacket, which he'd had to shove off onto the floor—

Wait, the bloody towels and the mess under the hanging unit.

Moving quickly, he swiped over the floor and then grabbed the load of damp-and-weighty and took it in to the hamper in the bathroom—which made him wonder who the hell did the housekeeping here? Maybe it was Fritz . . . or maybe V did the Merry Maids routine himself.

Back in the main room, he took a second to double-check that all the evidence was gone except for the glass and the spoon . . . and then he went over to see if V was still asleep . . . or in that semicoma.

Stone. Cold. Out.

"I'm getting you what you really need," Butch said softly, wondering if he was ever going to breathe right again—his chest seemed as constricted as V's had just been in reality. "Hold tight, my man."

On his way to the door, he got out his cell phone to dial—and dropped the damn thing.

Huh. Looked like his hands were still shaking. Go fig.

When he eventually hit *send*, he prayed that the call would be—

"It's done," he said roughly. "Come over here. No, trust me—he's going to need you. This was for the two of you. No . . . yeah. No, I'm leaving now. Good. Okay."

After he hung up, he locked V in and called for the elevator. As he waited, he tried to put his coat on and fumbled with the suede so badly, he gave up and slung it over his shoulder. When the doors dinged and opened, he stepped inside, hit the button that had a P on it . . . and went down, down, down, falling in a controlled, seamless way thanks to the little metal box of the elevator.

He texted his *shellan* instead of calling her for two reasons: He didn't trust his voice, and in truth, he wasn't ready to answer the questions she would inevitably and fairly have.

All ok. Am going home 2 rest. I love you xxx B

Marissa's response was so fast, it was pretty clear she'd had her phone in her hand, and been waiting to hear from him: *I love you too. Am at Safe Place but can come home?*

The elevator opened and the sweet smell of gasoline told him he'd reached his destination. As he went over to the Escalade, he texted back: *No, really am fine. You stay and work—I'll be there when you're done.*

He was taking out his keys as his phone went off. *Okay, but if you need me, you are the most important thing.*

God, she was such a female of worth.

Right back at you xxx, he typed out.

Canning the SUV's alarm and unlocking the driver's side, he got in, shut the door, and relocked.

He was supposed to get driving. Instead, he put his forehead down on the steering wheel and took a deep breath.

Having a good memory was an overrated skill set. And as much as he didn't envy Manello and all the erasing, he would have given almost anything to get rid of the pictures in his head.

Not V, though. Not that . . . relationship.

He would never give the male up. Ever.

THIRTY-EIGHT

"Here, thought you might like some coffee."

As José de la Cruz put the Starbucks venti latte on the desk of his partner, he parked his ass in the seat across the way from the guy.

Veck should have looked like roadkill, considering he was in the same clothes he'd had on when he'd *Mission Impossible*d that car hood the night before. Instead, the SOB somehow managed to seem rugged instead of ratty.

So José was willing to bet the six other cups of half-drunk java around the computer had been brought by various ladies in the department.

"Thanks, man." As Veck palmed up the newest offering of hot-and-steamy, his eyes didn't budge from the Dell monitor—fair guess that he was searching the missing persons files and pulling out women aged seventeen to thirty.

"Whatchu doin'?" José asked anyway.

"Missing persons." Veck stretched in his chair. "Have you noticed how many eighteen-to-twenty-fours have been listed recently? Men, not women."

"Yup. The mayor's pulling together a task force."

"There are plenty of girls as well, but Christ, there's an epidemic going on."

Out in the hall, a pair of unis walked by and both he and Veck nodded to the officers. After the footsteps faded, Veck cleared his throat.

"What did Internal Affairs say." Not a question. And those dark blues stayed locked on the database. "That's why you've come, right."

"Well, and also to deliver the coffee. Looks like you were taken care of, though."

"Reception downstairs."

Ah, yes. The two Kathys, Brittany spelled Britnae, and Theresa. They probably all thought the guy was a hero.

José cleared his throat. "Turns out the photographer already has some harassment charges pending against him because he's got a habit of showing up in places he's not welcome. He and his lawyer just want to make it all go away, because another trespassing-into-a-crime-scene thing is so not going to go well for him. IA has taken statements from everyone, and bottom line, it's a simple assault on your part—nothing aggravated. Plus the photog says he'll refuse to cooperate with the DA against you if it comes to that. Likely because he thinks that it'll help him."

Now those peepers shifted over. "Thank God."

"Don't get too excited."

Veck's eyes narrowed—but not in confusion. He knew exactly what the hitch was.

And yet he didn't ask; he just waited.

José glanced around. At ten o'clock in the evening, the homicide department's office was empty, although the phones were still ringing, little chirping noises springing up here and there until voice mail ate the callers. Out in the hall, the housekeeping staff was all about the rug-suck, the whirring of multiple vacuums coming from far down the way, by the CSI lab.

So there was no reason not to talk straight.

José shut the main door anyway. Back with Veck, he sat down again and picked up a stray paper clip, drawing a little invisible picture with it on the desk's fake wood top.

"They asked me what I thought about you." He tapped his temple with the clip. "Mentally. As in how tight you are."

"And you said . . ."

José just shrugged and stayed quiet.

"That motherfucker was taking pictures of a *corpse*. For *profit*—"

José held up his palm to cut the protest off. "You'll get no argument there. Fuck it, we all wanted to beat him. The question is, though—if I hadn't stopped you . . . how far would it have gone, Veck."

That got another frown from the guy.

And then shit got real quiet. Dead quiet. Well, except for the phones.

"I know you've read my file," Veck said.

"Yup."

"Yeah, well, I am *not* my father." The words were spoken on a low-and-slow. "I didn't even grow up with the guy. I barely knew him and I'm nothing like him."

File that one under: Sometimes You Luck Out.

Thomas DelVecchio had a lot of things going for him: He'd gotten straight As in his criminal justice major . . . top of his class at the policy academy. . . . His three years on patrol were spotless. And he was so good-looking he never bought his own coffee.

But he was the son of a monster.

And this was the root of the problem they had. By all that was right and proper, it was not fair to lay the sins of the father around the neck of the son. And Veck was right: On his own psych assessments, he'd come up as normal as anyone else.

So José had taken him on as a partner without a second thought about that pops of his.

That had changed since last night, and the issue was the expression that had been on Veck's face when he'd gone for that photog.

So cold. So calm. With no more affect than if he'd been popping the top off a soda can.

Having worked in Homicide almost all of his adult life, José had seen a lot of murderers. You had your crime-of-passion types who lost it over a guy or a woman; you had the stupid-ass department, which in his mind covered drug- and alcohol-related as well as gang violence; and then you had the sadistic sickos who needed to be put down like rabid dogs.

All of these variations on the theme caused unimaginable tragedy for their victims' families and the community. But they weren't the ones who kept José up at night.

Veck's dad had murdered twenty-eight people in seventeen years—and those were only the bodies that had been found. The bastard was on death row right now, a mere hundred and twenty-five miles away in Somers, Connecticut, and he was about to get the injection, in spite of the number of appeals his lawyer had filed. But what was really fucked-up? Thomas DelVecchio, Sr., had a fan club—that was worldwide. With one hundred thousand friends on Facebook, merchandise on CafePress, and songs that had been written about him by death-metal bands, he was an infamous celebrity.

Fucking hell, as God was his witness, all that shit made José mental. Those idiots who idolized the fucker should come work his job for a week. See how cool they thought killers were in RL.

As things went, he'd never met DelVecchio, the elder, in person, but he'd seen plenty of video from various DA and police department interviews. On the surface, the guy was straight-up lucid and as calm as a yoga instructor. Pleasant, too. No matter who was in front of him or what was said to inflame him, he never wavered, never broke, never gave an indication that any of it mattered.

Except José had seen the tell in his face—and so had a few of the other professionals: Every once in a while, he'd get a twinkle in his eye that made José reach for his cross. It was the kind of thing a sixteen-year-old boy might have when he saw a cherry ride drive by or an apple-bottomed girl with a belly shirt. It was like sunlight glinting off of a sharp blade—a brief flash of light and delight.

That was all he'd ever given away, however. The evidence had convicted him; never his testimony.

And *that* was the kind of murderer who left José staring at the ceiling while his wife slept beside him. DelVecchio Senior was smart enough to stay in control and cover his tracks. He was self-reliant and resourceful. And he was as relentless as the change of seasons. . . . He was Halloween in a parallel universe: Instead of a normal Joe with a mask on, he was a fiend behind a friendly, handsome face.

Veck looked just like his dad.

"Did you hear what I said."

At the sound of the kid's voice, José refocused. "Yeah, I did."

"So is this it for you and me," Veck said sharply. "You saying you don't want to work with me anymore? Assuming I still have a job?"

José went back to his paper-clip sketching. "Internal Affairs is going to give you a warning."

"Really?"

"I told them your head was where it needed to be," José said after a moment.

Veck cleared his throat. "Thanks, man."

José kept moving the clip around, the little scratching noise so very loud. "The pressure in this job is a killer." At this, he looked Veck right in the eye. "It is not going to get easier."

There was a pause. Then his partner murmured, "You don't believe what you told them, do you."

José shrugged. "Time will tell."

"Why the hell did you save my job, then?"

"I guess I feel that you should have a chance to right your wrongs—even if they're not really yours."

What José kept to himself was that it wasn't the first time he'd taken on a partner who had things to work out on the job, so to speak.

Yeah, and look at how Butch O'Neal had turned out: Missing. Presumed dead. In spite of whatever José had thought he'd heard on that 911 tape.

"I am not my father, Detective. I swear to you. Just because I was being professional when I hit the guy—"

José leaned forward, his eyes boring into the kid's. "How did you know that was what bothered me about the attack. How did you know the calm was the thing."

As Veck blanched, José eased back again. After a bit, he shook his head. "It doesn't mean you're a killer, son. And just because you fear something doesn't mean it's true. But I think you and I need to be real clear with each other. Like I said, I don't think it's fair for you to be held to a different standard because of your pops—but if you have another outburst like that over anything—and I mean parking tickets"—he nodded toward the Starbucks mug—"bad coffee, too much starch in your shirt . . . the goddamn photocopier . . . it's game over. Do we understand each other? I'm not going to let someone dangerous wear a badge—or a gun."

Abruptly, Veck went back to staring at his monitor. On it was the face of a pretty blond nineteen-year-old who had disappeared about two weeks prior. No body yet, but José was willing to bet she was dead by now.

After nodding, Veck picked up the coffee and sat back into his chair. "Deal."

José exhaled and put the paper clip where it belonged, in the little clear box with the magnetic rim. "Good. Because we've got to find this guy before he takes anyone else."

THIRTY-NINE

Traveling south on "the Northway," as Manuel called it, Payne's eyes were starved for the world around her. Everything was a source of fascination, from the streaming lines of traffic on either side of the road, to the vast black heavens above, to the bracing night chill that rushed into the car's cockpit every time she opened her window.

Which was about every five minutes. She just loved the change in temperature—warm to cool, warm to cool. . . . It was so totally unlike the Sanctuary, where everything was monoclimatic. Plus there was the great blast of air that blew into her face and tangled her hair and made her laugh.

And then, of course, every time she did it, she looked over at Manuel and found that he was smiling.

"You haven't asked where we're going," he said, after her most recent shutting.

In truth, it did not matter. She was with him and they were free and alone and that was more than enough—

You scrub him. At the end of the night, you scrub him and come back here. Alone.

Payne kept her wince to herself: Wrath, son of Wrath, had the kind of voice that went with the likes of thrones and crowns and black daggers hung about the chest. And the royal tone 'twas not window dressing. He expected to be obeyed, and Payne was under no misapprehension that just because she was the Scribe Virgin's daughter, somehow she was not subject to his rule. As long as she was down here, this was his world and she was in it.

Whilst the king had uttered those awful words, she had squeezed her eyes shut, and upon the silence that had reigned thereafter, promptly realized that she and Manuel would be going nowhere unless she avowed.

And so . . . she had.

"Would you like to know? Hello? Payne?"

With a start, she forced a smile to her face. "I would prefer to be surprised."

Now he grinned deeply. "Even more fun—well, as I said, I want to introduce you to someone." His smile faded a little. "I think you might like her."

Her? As in a female?

Like?

Verily, that would happen only if the "she" in question had a horse face and a big butt, Payne thought.

"How lovely," she said.

"Here's our exit." There was a soft *click-click-click* and then Manuel turned the wheel and drew them off the larger road onto a declining ramp.

As they stopped in a line of other vehicles, she saw off on the far, far horizon a huge city, the likes of which her eyes struggled to comprehend: Great buildings marked with an incalculable number of pinhole lights rose up from a ground cover of smaller structures, and it was not a static place. Red and white lights snaked in and around its edges . . . no doubt hundreds of cars on roads similar to the one they had just traveled upon.

"You're looking at New York City," Manny said.

"It's . . . beautiful."

He laughed a little. "Parts of it certainly are. And darkness and distance are great makeup artists."

Payne reached out and touched the clear glass window in front of her. "Where I tarried in the above, there were no long vistas. No grandeur. Nothing but the oppressive milky sky and the choking boundary of forest. This is all so wondrous—"

A harsh sound rang out behind them, and then another.

Manny glared into the small mirror o'erhead. "Relax, buddy. I'm going . . ."

As he accelerated, quickly closing the distance to the next car ahead, she felt badly that she had distracted him.

"I am sorry," she murmured. "I do not mean to go on."

"You can talk forever and I'll listen quite happily."

Well, wasn't that good to know. "I am not unfamiliar with some of the things I witness here, but for the most part this is all a revelation. The seeing bowls we have on the Other Side offer but snapshots of what transpires upon the Earth, focusing on people, not objects—unless such an inanimate is part of someone's fate. Indeed, we are provided only destiny, not progress . . . life, not landscape. This is . . . everything I wanted to become free for."

"How did you get out?"

Which time? she thought. "Well, in the first instance . . . I realized that when my mother granted audiences to people from down below, there was a small window whereby the barrier between the two worlds was . . . a kind of mesh. I discovered that I could move my molecules through the tiny spaces that were created—and that was how I did it." The past drew her in, memories flaring to life and burning not just in her mind, but her soul. "My mother was furious and came forth unto me, demanding that I return to the Sanctuary—and I told her no. I was on a mission and not even she could derail me." Payne shook her head. "After I . . . did what I had to . . . I thought I would just live my life, but there were things I did not anticipate. Down here, I need to feed and . . . there are other concerns."

Her needing, specifically—although she wasn't going to explain the way her fertile time had hit and crippled her. It had been such a shock. Up above, the Scribe Virgin's females were ready to conceive nearly all of the time, and thus the great swings of hormones did not o'ertake their bodies. Once they came down below, however, and spent more than a day or so thus, the cycle came upon them. Thank fate it was only once a decade—although Payne had wrongly assumed she'd have ten years until she had to worry about it.

Unfortunately, it had turned out that that was ten years *after* the cycle first initiated itself: Her needing had started up no more than a month after she'd been out of the Sanctuary.

As she remembered the great pains to mate that had left her defenseless and desperate, she focused on Manuel's face. Would he service her in her time of needing? Take care of her violent cravings and ease her with the release of his sex? Could a human even do that?

"But you ended up back there again?" he said.

She cleared her throat. "Yes, I did. I had some . . . difficulty and my mother came unto me anew." Verily, the Scribe Virgin had been terrified that rutting males would set upon her only daughter—who had already "ruined" so much of the life that she had been given. "She told me that she would aid me, although only on the Other Side. I agreed to go with her, thinking that it would be as before—and I could once again find the way out. That was not what transpired, however."

Manny's hand covered her own. "You're out of all that now, though."

Was she? The Blind King was seeking to rule her destiny just as her mother had. His reasons were less selfish, granted—after all, he had the Brotherhood and their *shellans* and a young living under his roof and that was a lot worthy of protecting. Except she feared her brother's view of humans was shared by Wrath: namely that they were but *lessers* waiting to be called into service.

"You know what?" she said.

"What."

"I think I could stay in this automobile with you forever."

"Funny . . . I feel the exact same way."

More *click-click-click*ing and then they took a right.

As they went along, there were fewer cars and more buildings, and she saw what he meant about night improving a city's visage; there was no grandeur to be had in this neighborhood. Broken windows were blackened out like missing teeth, and the grime that faded down the flanks of the warehouses and stores were age lines. Pockmarks made by rot or accident or vandalism marred what once had no doubt been smooth facades and bright, fresh paint jobs had faded, the bloom of youth long lost to the elements and to time's passage.

And indeed, the humans who were propped up in the shadows were in no better condition. Wearing wrinkled clothes in the colors of pavement and asphalt, they appeared to be weighted down from above, as if an invisible bar had forced them all to their knees—and was going to keep them there.

"Don't worry," Manuel said. "The doors are locked."

"I am not afraid. I am . . . saddened, for some reason."

"Urban poverty will do that to you."

They went by yet another rotting, barely roofed box attended by two humans sharing a single coat. She never thought she would find any value in the Sanctuary's oppressive perfection. But mayhap her mother had created the haven to protect the Chosen against sights like this. Lives . . . like those.

The environs soon improved slightly, however. And shortly thereafter, Manuel pulled off the road into a lot that ran parallel to a sprawling, new facility that appeared to cover a great plot of land. All around, lights on towering, craned arms cast peachy illumination upon the low-slung building and the shiny tops of the two vehicles that were parked and the clipped shrubs that bordered the walkways.

"Here we are," he said, stopping their ride and turning to her. "I'm going to introduce you as a colleague, okay? Just roll with it."

She grinned. "I shall endeavor to do that."

They got out together and . . . oh, the air. Such a complex bouquet of good and bad, of metallic and sweet, of dirty and divine.

"I love this," she said. "I love this!"

She put her arms out and swung herself in a circle, pivoting on a foot that had been booted just prior to their leaving the compound. As she halted her spin and her arms came to rest at her sides, she found him staring at her and had to laugh in embarrassment.

"I am sorry. I—"

"Come here," he growled, his eyelids dropping low, his stare hot and possessive.

Instantly, her sex was aroused, her body flushing. And somehow, she knew to take her time as she approached him, knew to draw it out and make him wait, even if it wasn't for long.

"You want me," she drawled when they were face-to-face.

"Yeah. Hell, yeah." His hands grabbed her waist and pulled her in tight. "Gimme your mouth."

As she did just that, she wrapped her arms around his neck and melded into his solid body. The kiss had ownership all over it, on both sides, and when it ended, she could not stop smiling.

"I like it when you demand of me," she said. "It takes me back to the shower, when you were—"

He let out a groan and cut her off, putting his hand gently over her mouth. "Yeah, I remember. *Trust me*—I remember."

Payne gave his palm a lick. "You will do that to me again. Tonight."

"I should be so lucky."

"You shall be. And so shall I."

He laughed a little. "You know what? I'm going to need to put one of my coats on."

Manuel reopened his door and leaned into the car. When he reemerged, he drew on a pressed white jacket that had his name in cursive by the lapel. And she knew by the way he closed the two halves that he was trying to cover up his body's response to her.

Pity. She liked to see him in that condition, all proud and hard.

"Come on—let's go inside," he said, taking her hand. And then under his breath, he seemed to add, "Before I come inside . . ."

As he didn't finish the sentence, Payne left her smile right where it was, front and center on her face.

Upon closer examination, the facility seemed to be fortified for a siege, with discreet bars on its windows and a tall fencing stretching far down into the distance. The doors they approached were also barred, and Manuel didn't test their handles.

Logical to secure the building, she thought. Given what the greater part of town had looked like.

Manuel pushed a button and immediately a tinny little voice said, "Tricounty Equine Hospital."

"Dr. Manuel Manello." He turned his head toward a camera. "I'm here to see—"

"Hey, Doc. Come right in."

There was a buzz and then Manuel held the door open for her. "After you, *bambina*."

The interior they walked into was sparse and very clean, with a smooth stone floor and rows of seating, as if people spent much time tarrying in this front room. On the walls, pictures of horses and cattle were framed, many of the animals with ribbons of red and blue hanging from their halters. Over across the way, there was a glass panel with the word RECEPTION embossed upon it in formal gold letters, and there were doors . . . so many doors. Those with a male symbol and a female symbol . . . those with signs such as VETERINARY DIRECTOR . . . and FINANCE . . . and STAFF MANAGER.

"Whatever is this place?" she asked.

"A lifesaver. Come on—we go this way."

He pushed their way through a pair of double doors and went over to a uniformed human male who was seated behind a desk.

"Hey, Dr. Manello." The man put down a newspaper that had *New York Post* in big letters across the top. "We haven't seen you for a little bit."

"This is a colleague of mine, Pa—Pamela. We're just going to see my girl."

The human man focused on Payne's face. And then seemed to shake himself. "Ah . . . she's where you left her. Doc spent a lot of time with her today."

"Yeah. He called." Manuel knocked the desktop with his knuckles. "See you in a few."

"Sure thing, Doc. Nice to meet you . . . Pamela."

Payne inclined her head. "It is lovely to meet with you as well."

There was an awkward silence as she straightened. The human man was absolutely struck by her, his mouth slightly parted, his eyes wide . . . and very appreciative.

"Easy there, big guy," Manuel said darkly. "You can resume blinking at any time . . . like, as in, now. Really. Truly."

Manuel put himself in between the two of them, and took her hand at the same time, both blocking the view and establishing dominion over her. And that wasn't all: Dark spices wafted up from him, the scent a warning to the other man that the female being admired was available only over Manuel's cold, dead body.

And didn't that make her feel like there was a blazing sun in the center of her chest.

"Come on, Pay—Pamela." As Manuel tugged at her and the pair of them started walking, he added in a mutter, "Before John-boy's jaw drops off his face and lands on the sports section."

Payne skipped once. And then did it again.

Manuel looked over. "That poor guard back there almost has a near-death experience with his badge being shoved down his throat and you're happy?"

Payne kissed Manuel's cheek quickly, seeing behind the faux grim on his handsome face. "You like me."

Manuel rolled his eyes and pulled her over by the neck, returning the kiss. "Duh."

"Duh," she mimicked—

Someone tripped over someone's foot, hard to say who it was, and Manuel was the one who caught them from falling.

"We'd better pay attention," her male said. "Before we're the ones who need resuscitating."

She elbowed him. "A wise extrapolation."

"Are you smacking my ass."

Payne glanced over his shoulder. And then slapped his butt—hard. As he yelped, she winked at him. "Indeed. Verily. I am." Dropping her lids and her voice, she hammed, "Would you like me to do it again, Manuel. Perhaps . . . on the other side?"

As she joggled her eyebrows at him, the sound of his laughter broke out and filled the empty hallway, ringing far and wide. And when they bumped into each other again, he pulled her to a stop.

"Wait, we need to do this better." He tucked her under his arm, kissed her forehead, and lined himself up with her. "On three, lead with the right. Ready? One . . . two . . . three."

On cue, they both stretched out their long right legs, and then it was left . . . and right . . . and left . . .

Perfectly in step.

Side by side.

They went down the corridor. Together.

It had never dawned on Manny that his sexy vampire might have a sense of humor. And didn't that round out her package perfectly.

Ah, hell, it wasn't just that. It was her wonder and her joy and the sense that she was up for anything. She was absolutely nothing like those fragile, brittle socialites or the pretzel-thin models he'd dated.

"Payne?"

"Yes?"

"If I told you I wanted to climb a mountain tonight—"

"Oh! I would love to! I should love to see a long view from . . ."

Bingo. Although, God, he had to wonder at the cruelty of finally finding his perfect match . . . in someone so fundamentally incompatible.

When they came up to the second set of double doors that led into the clinical part of the horse-pital, he pushed one half wide, and without missing a beat, they turned sideways and shuffled through . . . and that was when it happened.

That was when he fell completely in love with her.

It was her happy chatter, and the bounce in her step, and the icy eyes that shone like crystal. It was the backstory she'd shared and the dignity she showed and the fact that she'd been judged against a standard he'd used to date—and now wouldn't be able to bear sitting across a dinner table from. It was the power in her body and the sharpness of her mind and—

Christ . . . he hadn't even thought about the sex.

Ironic. She'd given him the orgasms of his life and they hadn't even made the top of his I Love You Because list.

He guessed she was just that kind of spectacular.

"Whatever are you smiling for, Manuel," Payne said. "Perhaps anticipating some future instance of my hand upon your derriere?"

"Yup. That's exactly it."

He pulled her in for another kiss—and tried to ignore the pain in his chest: No need to spoil the time they had with the good-bye that was waiting for them. That was going to come soon enough.

Besides, they'd nearly reached their destination.

"She's over here," he said, hanging a left and pushing into the recovery-stall area.

The instant the door opened, Payne hesitated, a frown appearing as whinnies and the occasional hoof stamping broke through the hay-scented air.

"Farther down." Manny tugged at her hand. "Her name's Glory."

Glory was the last one on the left, but the instant he said her name, her long, elegant neck stretched out and her perfectly proportioned head emerged from the top of her stall.

"Hey, girl," he said. In response, she let out a proper greeting, her pointed ears pricking, her muzzle pumping the air.

"Merciful fate," Payne breathed, dropping his hand and going forward ahead of him.

As she approached the stall, Glory tossed her head, her black mane flaring, and he had a sudden vision of Payne getting bitten. "Be careful," he said as he broke into a jog. "She doesn't like—"

The instant Payne put her hand on that silken muzzle, Glory went right in for more, bumping against the palm, seeking a proper cuddle.

"—new people," Manny finished lamely.

"Hello, darling one," Payne murmured, her eyes going over the horse as she leaned into the stall. "You are so beautiful . . . so big and strong. . . ." Pale hands found a black neck and stroked in a slow rhythm. "Why are her forelegs bandaged?"

"She broke the right one. Badly. About a week ago."

"May I go inside?"

"Ah . . ." God, he couldn't believe it, but Glory appeared to be in love, her eyes all but rolling back into her head as she got a good scratching behind the ears. "Yeah, I think it'll be okay."

He sprang the latch on the door and they both slipped in. And when Glory went to move back, she hobbled . . . on what had been her good side.

She'd lost so much weight that her ribs were showing like picket-fence rails under her coat.

And he was willing to bet when the newness of her visitors dimmed, her burst of energy would fade fast.

The voice mail message from the doctor had been all too apt: She was failing. That broken bone was healing, but not nearly fast enough, and the redistribution of mass had caused the layers of the opposite hoof to weaken and separate.

Glory extended her muzzle into his chest and gave him a quick shove. "Hey, girlie."

"She is extraordinary." Payne patted her way around the filly. "Just extraordinary."

And now he had another thing on his conscience: Maybe bringing Payne here was not a gift, but a cruelty. Why introduce her to an animal who was likely going to be . . .

God, he couldn't even think it.

"You are not the only one who is territorial," Payne said softly.

Manny glanced around Glory's head. "I'm sorry?"

"When you told me I was to meet a female, I . . . I had hoped she was one with a horse face."

He laughed and smoothed Glory's forehead. "Well, she has that, all right."

"What are you going to do with her?"

As he tried to form the words, he gathered the mane that fell just above the filly's nearly black eyes.

"Your lack of reply is answer enough," Payne said sadly.

"I don't know why I brought you here. I mean . . ." He cleared his throat. "Actually, I know why—and it's pretty fucking pathetic. All I have is my job. . . . Glory is the only thing that is not my job. This is personal for me."

"You must be brokenhearted."

"I am." Abruptly, Manny looked over the back of his failing horse to the dark-headed vampire who had laid her cheek against Glory's flank. "I am . . . absolutely destroyed at the loss."

FORTY

Mere moments after Butch called her, Jane became solid on the terrace of V's penthouse. As her form took weight within its shape, the night air cold-fingered her hair and made her eyes water.

Or . . . maybe that was just her tears.

Looking in through the glass, she saw everything much too clearly: the table, the lashes, the whips, the . . . other things.

When she'd come here with Vishous before, those trappings of his hard-core predilections had seemed nothing more than a tantalizing and slightly frightening backdrop to the incredible sex they themselves had. But her version of "play" was poodle to his werewolf.

And how clearly did she know that now.

What had Butch used? What kind of shape was her mate in? Was there going to be a lot of blood—

Wait a minute. Where was V?

Passing through the sliding glass door, she . . .

No blood on the floor. Or dripping from instruments. No suspension hooks hanging from the ceiling. Everything was exactly as it had been the last time she'd been here, as if nothing had happened—

A groan came from outside the circle of candlelight, and the sound ripped her head around. Of course. The bed.

As she pierced the veil of darkness, her eyes adjusted and there he was: under a wrap of satin sheets, stretched out flat, writhing in pain . . . or was it sleep?

"Vishous?" she said softly.

With a shout, he came instantly awake, his torso shooting upright, his lids popping wide. Immediately, she noticed that his face was marked by fading scars . . . and there were others across his pecs and abdomen as well. But the expression he wore was what really got to her: He was terrified.

Abruptly, there was a furious flapping as he shoved the covers off his body. As he looked down at himself, sweat broke out across his chest and shoulders, his skin taking on a sudden gleam even in the shadows as he cupped his sex . . . like he was protecting what was left.

Hanging his head, he drew great breaths. Inhale. Exhale. Inhale. Exhale—

The pattern transformed into sobs.

Curling into himself, his hands sheltering the butcher job that had been done long, long ago, he wept in great heaves of emotion, his reserve gone, his control gone, his intelligence no longer ruler of his realm, but a subject.

He didn't even realize she was standing next to him.

And she should leave, Jane thought. He wouldn't want her to see him this way—not even before everything had fallen apart between them. The male she knew and loved and had mated wouldn't want any witness to this—

It was hard to say what got his attention . . . and later she would wonder how he had picked that moment just as she was going to dematerialize to look up at her.

She was instantly incapacitated: If he had been pissed off about what had happened with Payne, he was going to hate her now—there was absolutely no going back from this invasion of privacy.

"Butch called me," she blurted. "He thought you'd—"

"He hurt me. . . . My father hurt me."

The words were so thin and soft that they nearly didn't register. But when they did, her heart just stopped.

"Why," Vishous asked. "Why did he do it to me. Why did my mother? I never asked to be born to the pair of them . . . and I wouldn't have chosen to be if either had asked me. . . . Why?"

His cheeks were slick with tears that spilled over his diamond eyes, a ceaseless flow he neither noticed nor appeared to care about. And she had a feeling it was going to be a while before the leaking stopped—an inner artery had been nicked and this was the blood of his heart, spilling out of him, covering him.

"I'm so sorry," she croaked. "I don't know any of the whys . . . but I know that you didn't deserve it. And . . . and it's not your fault."

His hands uncupped himself and he stared downward. It was a long while before he spoke, and when he did, his words were slow and considered . . . and as ceaseless as his quiet tears. "I wish I were whole. I wish I could have given you young if you'd wanted them and could conceive them. I wish I could have told you that it killed me when you thought I had been with anyone else. I wish I had spent the last year waking up every night and telling you I loved you. I wish I had mated you properly the evening you came back to me from the dead. I wish . . ." Now his shimmering stare flipped up to hers. "I wish I were half as strong as you are and I wish I deserved you. And . . . that's about it."

Right. Okay. Now they were both tearing up.

"I'm so sorry about Payne," she said hoarsely. "I wanted to talk to you, but she'd made up her mind. I tried to work with her, I really did, but in the end, I just . . . I didn't . . . I didn't want you to be the one to do it. I would have rather lived with the horrible truth on my conscience for an eternity than have you kill your sister. Or have her hurt herself even more than she was."

"I know . . . I know that now."

"And to be honest, the fact that she is healed? It gives me the cold sweats because of the near miss we had."

"It's all right, though. She's okay."

Jane wiped her eyes. "And I think when it comes to . . ." She glanced over at the wall that was draped in a buttery yellow candlelight that did nothing at all to soften the sharp spikes and even sharper implications of what hung there. "When it comes to. . . things . . . about you and sex, I've always worried that I might not be quite enough for you."

"Fuck . . . no . . . you're *everything* to me."

Jane put her hand over her mouth so she didn't lose it completely. Because it was exactly what she needed to hear.

"I never even got your name in my back," V said. "I thought it was stupid and a waste of time . . . but how can you feel like we're mated without it—especially when every single male at the compound has been marked for his *shellan*?"

God, she hadn't thought of that.

V shook his head. "You've given me space . . . to hang with Butch and fight with my brothers and do my shit on the Internet. What have I given you?"

"My clinic, for one thing. I couldn't have built it without you."

"Not exactly a bouquet of roses."

"Don't underestimate your carpentry skills."

He smiled a little at that. And then grew serious once again. "Can I tell you something that I've thought every time I've woken up next to you."

"Please."

Vishous, the one who always had an answer for everything, seemed to get tongue-tied. But then he said, "You're the reason I get out of bed every night. And you're the reason I can't wait to come home every dawn. Not the war. Not the Brothers. Not even Butch. It's . . . you."

Oh, such simple words . . . but the meaning. Good lord, the meaning.

"Will you let me hug you now?" she said roughly.

Her mate stretched out his massive arms. "How about I hold you instead?"

As Jane leaped forward and dived into him, she countered, "It doesn't have to be one or the other."

Instantly, she became fully corporeal without any effort at all, that magical internal chemistry between them calling her into being and holding her there. And as Vishous buried his face in her hair and shuddered like he had run a vast distance and was finally home . . . she knew exactly how he felt.

With his *shellan* flush against him, V felt like he'd been blown wide-open . . . and then stitched back together.

God, what Butch had done for him. For them all.

The route the cop had gone had been the right one. Horrific and terrible . . . but the absolute right one. And as V held his female now, his eyes searched the space where it had all gone down. Everything had been cleaned up . . . except for a pair of things that were out of place on the floor: a spoon and a glass that was mostly empty of what had to be water.

It had all been an illusion: Nothing had in fact cut him open. And how'd you like to bet Butch had left those two things front and center so that when V woke up and looked over, he'd know the means that had taken him to his end.

In retrospect, it seemed so fucking dumb . . . not the session with the cop, but the fact that V never really thought about the Bloodletter and those years in the war camp. The last time that piece of the past had come up at all had been when Jane had first been with him—and then it had only been because she'd seen him naked and he'd had to explain.

My father didn't want me to reproduce.

That was pretty much all he'd had to say. And afterward, like a dead body that had rolled over faceup in still water, that shit had sunk down again, resettling on the sandy riverbed of the very core of him.

BJ, or Before Jane, he'd only ever had sex with his pants on. Not from shame—or at least that was what he'd told himself—but because he simply hadn't been interested in going there with the anonymous males and females he'd fucked.

AJ? It had been different. Naked was more than cool, likely because Jane had kept a tight head at his revelation. And yet as he thought about it now, he'd always held her at arm's length, even if she'd been in his arms. If anything, he'd been closer to Butch—but that was male-to-male, which was somehow less threatening than male-to-female.

Shades of Mommy issues, no doubt: After everything his *mahmen* had pulled, he simply couldn't trust females like he could his brothers or his best friend.

Except Jane had never betrayed him. In fact, she'd been willing to battle her own conscience just to save him from the unspeakable act his twin had been demanding.

"You are not my mother," he said into his *shellan*'s hair.

"Damn right." Jane pulled back and looked him right in the eye—as was her way. "I never would have abandoned my son. Or treated my daughter that way."

V took a long inhale, and when he let the oxygen out of his lungs, he felt like he was expelling the myths by which he'd defined himself . . . and Jane . . . and their mating.

He needed to change the paradigm.

For them. For himself. For Butch.

Christ, the expression on the cop's face when things had been going down here had been beyond tragic.

So, yeah, it was time to stop using outside shit to self-medicate his emotions. The extreme sex and the pain had seemed like excellent solutions for a long time, but in reality, they had been concealer over a pimple: The ugliness had stayed within him.

What he had to do was deal with the inside crap so he didn't need Butch or anyone else to break him down just so he could let things out. That way, the kink could truly be only for pleasure with Jane.

Check his shit out—looked like he was finally prepared to try a psychiatric version of Proactiv.

Next thing he knew he was going to be on TV, staring into a camera and saying, "All it takes is a little dab of Self-awareness . . . and then I rinse with the patented Defining Yourself Wash, and my mind and emotions are clean and glowing—"

Okay, now he was really losing his damn marbles, true.

Stroking Jane's soft hair, he murmured, "About . . . the things I have here. If you're game, I'm still going to want to play . . . if you know what I mean. But from now on, it's just for fun, and only for you and me."

Hell, they'd had a shitload of good, leathered-up, freaky sex in this place, and he was always going to want that with her. Hopefully, she'd feel the same—

"I like what we do here." She smiled. "It turns me on."

Well . . . didn't that get his cock pumping. "Me, too."

As he smiled back at her, he recognized the one spanner in the mix: This turn-a-new-leaf resolution was all well and good—but how did he keep it going? Tomorrow evening he simply couldn't afford to wake up and be that guy who went off the rails anymore.

Shit, he guessed he was going to find out how. Wasn't he.

With a gentle hand, he brushed his *shellan*'s cheek. "I've never been in a relationship before you. I should have known that we'd hit a wall at some point."

"That's the way it works."

He thought of his brothers and the number of times there had been fallouts and fights and arguments among that bunch of meat-headed fighters. Somehow, they'd always worked it out—usually by popping each other from time to time. Which was a guy thing.

Clearly, he and Jane were going to be the same. Not with the popping, of course, but with the bumpy roads and the eventual resolutions. After all, this was life . . . not a fairy tale.

"But you know what the best thing is?" his Jane asked, as she put her arms around his neck.

"I don't feel like I died anymore because you're not in my life?"

"Well, yeah, that, too." She craned up and kissed him. "Two words: makeup sex."

Ohhhhhh, yeaaaaaaaaah. Except—"Wait, is that three words? Or did you hyphenate it?"

"I had a hyphen in my head. But I think it goes both ways?"

"Or is it 'makeup,' one word."

"That's also a possibility." Pause. "Have I mentioned you are the hottest geek I've ever known?"

"I resemble that remark." He dipped his head and brushed his mouth against hers. "Just keep it to yourself. I have a reputation as a hard-ass to protect."

"Your secret is safe with me."

V grew serious. "*I'm* safe with you."

Jane touched his face. "I can't promise you we're not going to hit rough patches again, and I know we're not always going to agree. But on this I'm very sure—you will always be safe with me. Always."

Vishous drew her close and tucked his head into her throat. He'd assumed there were no more levels to go after she'd died and then come back to him in her lovely, ghostly form. But he was wrong. Love, he realized, was like the daggers he made in his forge: When you first got one, it was shiny and new and the blade glinted bright in the light. Holding it against your palm, you were full of optimism for what it would be like in the field, and you couldn't wait to try it out. Except those first couple of nights out were usually awkward as you got used to it and it got used to you.

Over time, the steel lost its brand-new gleam, and the hilt became stained, and maybe you nicked the shit out of the thing a couple of times. What you got in return, however, saved your life: Once the pair of you were well acquainted, it became such a part of you that it was an extension of your own arm. It protected you and gave you a means to protect your brothers; it provided you with the confidence and the power to face whatever came out of the night; and wherever you went, it stayed with you, right over your heart, always there when you needed it.

You had to keep the blade up, however. And rewrap the hilt from time to time. And double-check the weight.

Funny . . . all of that was *well, duh* when it came to weapons. Why hadn't it dawned on him that matings were the same?

Rolling his eyes at himself, he thought, Christ, maybe Hallmark would be open to establishing a line of medieval-inspired Valentine's Day cards, some kind of a Holly-Goth-Lightly kind of thing. He'd be frickin' perfect for supplying content.

Closing his eyes, and holding his Jane, he was almost glad he'd lost his shit, just so they could get to this place.

Well, he would have picked an easier route if there had been one. Except he wasn't sure it worked that way. You had to earn where they were now.

"I have a question to ask you," he said softly.

"Anything."

Pulling back a little, he stroked her hair with his gloved hand, and it was a while before he asked what was on the tip of his tongue.

"Will you . . . let me make love to you?"

As Jane stared at Vishous and felt his body against hers, she knew she was never letting him go. Ever. And she also knew that if they could make it through the past week, they had the staying power that good marriages—or matings—required.

"Yes," she said. "Please . . ."

Her *hellren* had come to her so many times since they'd been together: in the night and in the day; in the shower and in the bed; clothed, unclothed, half-clothed; fast and hard . . . hard and fast. The edge in him had always been part of the excitement—that and the unpredictability. She never knew what to expect—whether he was going to demand things of her, or take control of her body, or restrain himself so that she could do whatever she wanted to him.

The constant, though, was that he was never one for going slow.

Now, he just stroked her hair, running his fingers through the waves and tucking them behind her ears. And then he kept his eyes locked with hers as he brought their mouths together softly. Stroking and caressing, he licked at her lips—but when she opened, he didn't dive in as he always did. It was only more with the kissing . . . until she felt drugged by the sucks and drags of flesh on flesh.

Her body usually roared for his. Now, though, a delicious unfurling washed through her, relaxing and easing her, bringing a peaceful arousal that was somehow just as profound and shattering as the desperate passion she typically felt.

As he shifted position, she followed his lead, going fully onto her back as he reared up and covered her upper body with his. The kissing just kept going, and she was so into it that she didn't notice that he had slipped a hand under the bottom of her shirt. His warm palm lazied upward, honing in on her breasts . . . finding and capturing. No teasing, no pinching, no tweaks. Just a passing of his thumb back and forth across her nipple, until she arched up and moaned into his mouth.

Her hands went to his sides and—oh, God, there was that pattern of marks she'd seen. And they went all the way around his torso—

Vishous took her wrists and moved her arms back down to the bed. "Don't think about it."

"What did he do to you—"

"Shh."

The kissing resumed, and she was tempted to fight it, but the pulling strokes gently submerged her brain in sensation.

It was over and done with, she told herself. And whatever had happened had helped them get here.

That was all she needed to know.

Vishous's voice drifted into her ear, deep, low. "I want to take your clothes off. May I?"

"Please—yes . . . God, yes."

Him undressing her was a part of the pleasure, the means as glorious as the end that brought them together skin-to-skin. And somehow, the gradual reveal of what he had seen so many times made it feel like it was new and special.

Her breasts tightened even more as the cooler air hit them, and she watched his face as he looked at her. The need was there, except there was so much more . . . reverence, gratitude . . . a vulnerability that she had sensed but never seen clearly before.

"You are everything I need," he said as he dipped his head.

His hands were everywhere, on her stomach, her hips, between her thighs.

On her slick sex.

The orgasm he gave her was a warm wave coursing through her body, radiating outward, taking her over in a blissful cloud of pleasure. And in the midst of it, he mounted her and slipped inside. No pounding, just more of the wave, inside her and outside, as his body moved and his erection pulled up and back.

Nothing fast, only more of the slow love.

No urgency, only all the time in the world.

When he finally came, it was on a last curl of his spine and a pulsing in her core, and she went along with him, the two of them wrapped up tight, fusing, body . . . and soul.

With a roll, he brought her on top of him, and she lay draped across his hard, muscled chest, languid as a summer breeze and just about as weighty. She was floating and warm and . . .

"Are you okay," Vishous said as he looked up at her.

"More than okay." She searched his face. "I feel like I've made love to you for the very first time."

"Good." He kissed her. "That was the plan."

Laying her head down on his beating heart, she looked across at the wall behind his table. She'd never thought she'd be grateful for such a terrifying bunch of "toys," but she was. Through the storm . . . they'd found the calm.

Once apart . . . now they were one again.

FORTY-ONE

Back at the mansion, Qhuinn was pacing around his bedroom like a rat looking for a way out of its cage. Of all the fucking nights for Wrath to hold them penned in.

Fuckin' A.

As he made yet another trip past the open door into the bath, he thought the fact that the quarantine made sense somehow pissed him off even more: Only he and John and Xhex were not hurt at this point. Everyone else had been in that melee and gotten sliced, diced, or shaved in some way.

It was Casa del Heal-the-fuck-up around here.

But come on, the three of them could have been out and about doing payback.

Stopping in front of the terrace doors, he looked over the manicured gardens that were on the verge of getting their spring on. With the lights turned off in his room, he could clearly see the swimming pool with its winter cover stretched over its belly—like the biggest set of Spanx the world had ever seen. And the trees that were still mostly bare. And the flower beds that were—

Blay had been injured.

—still nothing but orderly boxes of dark brown earth.

"Shit."

Rubbing his now-short hair, he tried to negotiate with the pressure at the center of his chest. According to John, Blay had been hit on the head and striped on the stomach. The former was being monitored; the latter had been stitched up by Doc Jane. Neither was life-threatening.

S'all good.

Too bad his sternum wasn't buying the hunky-dory. Ever since John Matthew had told him the news, this goddamn ache had set up shop, mole-ing into him and going Barcalounger on his bronchial tubes.

He literally couldn't take a deep breath.

Goddamn it, if he were a mature male—and given the way he handled things sometimes, that was seriously debatable, if not downright wrong—he would go out into the hallway, march over to Blay's room, and knock on the door. He'd put his head inside, see for himself that the redhead had a heartbeat and was making sense . . . and then he'd go about his night.

Instead, here he was, trying to pretend he was not thinking about the guy while he wore a path into his carpet.

On that note, more with the walking. He would have rather gone to the weight room and had a run, but the fact that Blaylock was up here in this wing was like a tether that kept him stuck in the vicinity. Without a larger purpose to pull him away, like going out to fight or . . . say . . . the house being on fire, he was evidently incapable of breaking free.

And when he found himself in front of the French doors again, he had an inkling why he kept stopping there.

He tried to talk his palm out of hitting the handle.

Didn't work.

Pop went the latch, and slap went the cool air on his face. Stepping out in his bare feet and his bathrobe, he barely noticed the ice-cube-cold slate or the draft that shot up his legs and nailed him in the balls.

Up ahead, light streamed out from the double doors of Blay's room. Which was good news—surely they'd close the curtains before they had sex.

So it was probably safe to look in. Right . . . ?

Besides, Blay was just coming off an injury, so they couldn't be going Tilt-A-Whirl in there.

Resolving himself to the role of Peeping Qhuinn, he stuck to the shadows, and tried not to feel like a stalker as he tiptoed over. When he got next to the door, he braced himself, leaned in and—

Took a deep, relieved breath.

Blay was alone on the bed, lying all propped up against the headboard, his black robe tied at the waist, his ankles crossed, his feet covered in black socks. His eyes were closed and his hand rested just above his belly, as if he were carefully looking after what was probably still bandaged.

Movement across the way brought Blay's lids up and took his eyes in the opposite direction of the windows. It was Layla emerging from the bathroom, and she was walking slowly. The two exchanged some words—no doubt he was thanking her for the feeding he'd just had and she was telling him that it was her pleasure: not a surprise that she was here. She'd been making the rounds of the house, and Qhuinn had already run into her shortly before First Meal—or what would have been First Meal if anyone had shown.

And as she left Blay's room, Qhuinn waited for Saxton to come in. Naked. With a red rose between his teeth. And a motherfucking box of chocolates.

And a hard-on that made the Washington Monument look stumpy.

Nothing.

Just Blay letting his head fall back and his lids drift down. He looked utterly exhausted and, for the first time, older. That was no recently out-of-transition boy over there. That was a full-blooded male.

A stunningly beautiful . . . full-blooded . . . male.

In his mind, Qhuinn saw himself opening the door and stepping inside. Blay would look over and try to sit up . . . but Qhuinn would wave him down as he walked over.

He would ask about the injury. And Blay would open the robe to show him.

Qhuinn would reach out and touch the bandage . . . and then he would let his fingers wander off the gauze and the surgical tape onto the warm, smooth skin of Blay's stomach. Blay would be shocked, but in this fantasy, he wouldn't push the hand away. . . . He would take it lower, down past the injury, down onto his hips and his—

"Fuck!"

Qhuinn leaped back, but it was too late: Saxton had somehow come into the room, walked over to the windows, and started to pull the drapery shut. And in the process, he'd seen the ass-wipe outside on the terrace who was making like a security camera.

As Qhuinn wheeled around and hotfooted it back for his room, he thought, Don't open the door . . . don't open the door—

"Qhuinn?"

Busted.

Freezing like a burglar caught with a plasma-screen under his armpit, he made sure his robe was closed before he turned around. Shit. Saxton was stepping out, and the bastard was also in a robe.

Well, he guessed they were all sporting them. Even Layla had been in one.

As Qhuinn faced off at his cousin, he realized he hadn't said more than two words to the guy since Saxton had moved in.

"I just wondered how he was." No reason to use a proper noun—pretty damn obvi who he'd been staring at.

"Blaylock's asleep at the moment."

"He feed?" Even though Qhuinn already knew that.

"Yes." Saxton shut the door behind himself, no doubt to keep the cold out, and Qhuinn tried to ignore the fact that the guy's feet and ankles were bare. Because it meant that chances were good the rest of him was also.

"Ah, sorry to have disturbed you," Qhuinn muttered. "Have a good n—"

"You could have just knocked. From the hall inside." The words were spoken with an aristocratic inflection that made Qhuinn's skin tighten up all over. Not because he hated Saxton. It just reminded him too much of the family he'd lost.

"I didn't want to bother you. Him. Either one of you."

As a gust curled up against the house, Saxton's impossibly thick and wavy blond hair didn't even ruffle—as if every part of him, down to his follicles, was simply too composed and well-bred to be affected by . . . anything.

"Qhuinn, you wouldn't be interrupting a thing."

Liar, Qhuinn thought.

"You were here first, cousin," Saxton murmured. "If you wished to see him, or be with him, I would leave you two alone."

Qhuinn blinked. So . . . the pair of them had an open relationship? What the hell?

Or wait . . . maybe he'd just done a masterful job in convincing not only Blay, but Saxton, that he didn't want his best friend for anything sexual.

"Cousin, may I speak candidly?"

Qhuinn cleared his throat. "Depends on what you have to say."

"I'm his lover, cousin—"

"Whoa . . ." He put his hand up. "That's so none of my business—"

"—not the love of his life."

Qhuinn pulled another double blink. And then for a split second, he got sucked into someplace where his cousin bowed out gracefully and Qhuinn more than filled the SOB's chic shoes. Except whatever . . . there was a big-ass glitch in that fantasy: Blay was through with him.

He'd engineered that result over too many years.

"Do you understand what I'm saying to you, cousin?" Saxton kept his voice down, even though the wind was rolling and the door was closed. "Do you hear me."

Okay, this was not a corner Qhuinn had expected to come to tonight . . . or any other evening. Fucking hell, his body was suddenly tingling all over, and he had half a mind to tell his cousin to beat it and go wax his eyebrows or some shit—or better yet move the hell out.

Except then he thought about how old Blay looked. The guy had finally found a stride in his life, and it was criminally unfair for that to be negotiated away out here in the dark.

Qhuinn shook his head. "It's not right."

Not for Blay.

"You are a fool."

"No. I used to be one."

"I would beg to differ." Saxton's elegant hand pulled the lapels of his robe closer together. "If you'll excuse me, I'd best return to the interior. It's cold here on the outside."

Well, wasn't that an ass-smacker of a metaphor.

"Don't tell him about this," Qhuinn said roughly. "Please."

Saxton's eyes narrowed. "Your secret is all too well protected. Trust me."

With that, he turned and went back into Blaylock's room, the door shutting with a click and then the light getting cut off as those heavy drapes were tugged into place.

Qhuinn rubbed his hair again.

Part of him wanted to bust in and say, *I changed my mind, cuz—now get the fuck out of here so I can . . .*

Tell Blay what he'd told Layla.

But Blay might well be in love with Saxton, and God knew Qhuinn had fucked his best friend too many times.

Or not, as the case was.

When he eventually headed back to his room—only because it was just too damn pathetic to be out here staring at the ass sides of drapery—he realized his life had always been about him. What he wanted. Needed. Had to have.

The old Qhuinn would have driven a bus through that opening—

On a wince, he tried not to take that turn of phrase quiiiiiiiite so literally.

The thing was, though, the ridiculous, pansy-ass saying was right: If you loved someone, you set them free.

In his room, he went over and sat on the bed. Looking around, he saw furniture he hadn't bought . . . and decorations that were gorgeous, but anonymous and not to his style. The only things that were his were the clothes in the closet, the razor in the bathroom, and the running shoes he'd kicked off when he'd come back earlier.

It was just like his parents' house.

Well, here, people actually valued him. But as lives went, he didn't have one of his own, really. He was John's protector. The Brotherhood's soldier. And . . .

Shit, now that he wasn't indulging in his sex addiction anymore, that was the end of the list.

Pushing himself back against the headboard, he crossed his feet at the ankles and arranged his robe. The night stretched out ahead of him with a horrible flatness—like he'd been driving and driving and driving through the desert . . . and he had only nights more of the same up ahead.

Months of the same.

Years.

He thought of Layla and the advice he'd given her. Man, the two of them were in the exact same place, weren't they.

Closing his eyes, he was relieved when he started to drift. But he had a feeling any peacefulness he found wasn't going to last long.

And he was right.

FORTY-TWO

At Tricounty Equine Hospital, Manny stood still while Glory snuffled around his scrubs, and knew he should probably leave her. But he found that he was unable to separate himself or Payne from the horse.

Time was running out for his Glory and it killed him. But he couldn't very well leave her to waste away, growing thinner and more crippled with each passing day. She deserved so much better than that.

"You love her," Payne said softly, her pale hand skimming across the Thoroughbred's back and going down onto the hip.

"Yeah. I do."

"She is very lucky."

No, she was dying, and that was a curse.

He cleared his throat. "I guess we need to—"

"Dr. Manello?"

Manny leaned back and looked over the stall door. "Oh, hey, Doc. How're you?"

As the head vet strode down to them, his tuxedo was as out of place as a pitchfork in an opera box. "I'm okay—and you're clearly looking well." The guy repositioned his bow tie. "The monkey suit is because I'm on my way home from the Met. I just had to stop and see your girl, though."

Manny ducked out and offered his hand. "Me, too."

As they shook, the vet glanced into the stall—and his eyes popped when he saw Payne. "Ah . . . hello."

When Payne offered the man a small smile, the good doctor blinked like the sun had broken through a cloud bank and shone down upon him.

Okaaaaaaaaaay, Manny was so through with bastards staring at her like that.

Putting himself in the way, he said, "Is there any kind of suspension we could get her into? To relieve some pressure?"

"We've had her strapped for a couple of hours each day." As the vet replied, he inched to the side until Manny had to follow with his torso to keep blocking the view. "I don't want to run the risk of gastrointestinal or breathing problems."

Bored with the tilting thing, and wanting to spare Payne where the conversation was heading, Manny took the guy's arm and moved them off to the side. "What's our next step?"

The vet rubbed his eyes as if to give his mind a second to unscramble. "To be honest, Dr. Manello, I don't have a good feeling about where we are. That other hoof is foundering, and although I've been doing everything I can to treat it, it's not responding."

"There has to be something else."

"I'm so damned sorry."

"How long until we're sure—"

"I'm sure now." The man's stare was positively grim. "That's why I came in tonight—I was hoping for a miracle."

Well, didn't that make two of them.

"Why don't I give you some time with her," the vet said. "Take all you need."

Which was doctor talk for *Say your good-byes.*

The vet put his hand on Manny's shoulder briefly, and then he turned and walked away. As he went, he looked in every single stall, checking his patients, patting a muzzle now and then.

Good guy. Thorough guy.

The kind who would exhaust every single avenue before laying down a stop-loss scenario.

Manny took a deep breath and tried to tell himself that Glory was not a pet. People didn't have racehorses as pets. And she deserved better than suffering in a little stall while he worked up the courage to do right by her.

Putting his hand to his chest, he rubbed his cross through his scrubs and had a sudden urge to go to church—

At first, all he noticed was the shadows getting stronger on the wall across the way. And then he thought maybe someone had turned the overhead lights up.

Finally, he realized that the illumination was coming out of Glory's stall.

What . . . the . . .

Skidding around, he recoiled . . . and then had to catch his balance.

Payne was on her knees in the fluffy sawdust, her hands on his horse's forelegs, her eyes closed, her brows tight.

And her body glowing with a fierce and beautiful light.

Above her, Glory was stock-still, but her coat was twitching and her eyes were rolling back in her head. Little chuffing whinnies rolled up her long neck and came out her flaring nostrils . . . as if she were overcome by a feeling of relief, an easing of pain.

Those injured front legs of hers were softly aglow.

Manny didn't move, didn't breathe, didn't blink. He just held his cross even harder . . . and prayed that no one would interrupt this.

He wasn't sure how long the three of them stayed as they were, but eventually, it became obvious Payne was straining from the effort: Her body began to vibrate and she started to breathe unevenly.

Manny broke into the stall and pulled her free from Glory, holding her lax body against his, and moving her out of the way in case the horse spooked or did something unpredictable.

"Payne?" Oh, God—

Her eyes fluttered. "Did I . . . aid her?"

Manny stroked her hair back as he looked at his filly. Glory was standing in place, lifting one front hoof and then the other and then going back to the first as if she were trying to figure out what had caused the abrupt comfort. Then she shook herself . . . and went over to nip at the hay that she hadn't touched.

As that wonderful sound of a muzzle tip working at dry grass filled the silence, he looked back down at Payne. "You did," he said hoarsely. "I think you did."

Her eyes seemed to struggle to focus. "I wished not for you to lose her."

Overcome by a gratitude he didn't have enough words for, Manny curled her up closer to his heart and held her for a moment. He wanted to stay like that for so much longer, but she wasn't looking well, and Christ knew who else may have noticed the light show. He had to get them out of here.

"Let's go to my place," he said. "So you can have a lie-down."

When she nodded, he swung her into his arms, and damn if she didn't feel perfect. As he shut the stall behind them, he glanced over at Glory. The horse was woofing back the hay like the stuff was going out of style.

Holy shit . . . had it really worked?

"I'll be back tomorrow," he said to her, before he strode away, buoyed by an incandescent hope.

Down at the security guard's station, he smiled as he shrugged at the guy. "Someone's been pulling double shifts at the hospital. She's wiped."

The man rose from his seat as if Payne's mere presence, even if she were out cold, was enough to get his attention. "Better get her home. You have to take care of a woman like that."

Too right. "That's just where I'm headed."

Moving quickly, he went out to reception and then waited for the buzz to sound so that he could push the final doors open. With any luck, the head vet hadn't seen a thing—

"Thank you, Jesus," Manny muttered, as he got his cue and shoved with his hip.

He wasted no time going over to the car, although getting out his keys while keeping Payne off the ground was a scramble. So was opening her door. But then he put her in the passenger seat, all the while wondering if she was ill. Shit, he had no way of getting into contact with anyone from her world.

Going around and sitting behind the wheel, he thought, Fuck it, he was just going to drive her back to the vampires—

"May I ask something of you?" she said in a slurred way.

"Anything—what do you—"

"May I take your vein for a moment? I find myself . . . curiously depleted."

Okay, right. Talk about your Johnny-on-the-spots: He locked them in and all but tore off his arm and threw it at her.

Her soft lips found the inside of his wrist, but her bite was not swift, as if she were having trouble summoning the energy. Still, she got the job done and he jumped, the sharp pain nailing him in the heart and making him a little light-headed. Or . . . maybe that was a function of the sudden, overwhelming arousal that shot not just through his balls and into his cock, but raced around his entire body.

On a groan, his hips rolled in the Porsche's seat and he let his head fall back. God, this felt good . . . the sucking rhythm she fell into might as well have been on his erection—and even though it should have hurt, the pull and swallow registered only as pleasure, a stinging, sweet pleasure that he was damned certain he would die for.

He fell into a blissful state; it felt like centuries that they were linked with her fangs in his flesh. Time had no meaning, and neither did the reality that they were in a parking lot in a car with clear windows.

Fuck the world.

It was only him and her together.

And that was before her diamond eyes opened and looked up at him, locking not on his face but his neck.

Vampire . . . he thought. Beautiful vampire.

Mine.

As that thought coalesced in his mind, he acted on autopilot, shifting his head to the side, offering his jugular to her—

He didn't have to ask twice. In a great surge, Payne sprang up, all but launching her whole body onto him, her hand shoving into his hair and tightening on his nape. As she held him in her grip, he was utterly immobilized, hers for the taking . . . prey for her predator. And now that she had him, she moved slowly, her fangs dropping to his skin and dragging up the column of his throat, making him stiffen in anticipation of the puncturing and the sucking. . . .

"Fuck!" he barked when she bit him. "Oh . . . *yeah* . . ."

His hands grabbed onto her shoulders, pulling her even closer. "Take it all . . . take— Oh God . . .oh, *shit*—"

Something stroked his cock. And given that he knew exactly

where his palms were, it had to be her. Shifting around, going straight-up greedy, he gave her as much space to move as he could . . . and move she did, up and down against his straining erection, his hips helping her, countering the strokes.

His breath was loud in the inside of the car as he panted, and so were his moans: It didn't take long at all until his balls went numb and the tip of his cock tightened up against the mounting pressure.

"I'm going to come," he groaned. "You'd better stop if you don't want me to—"

At that, she popped the bow on the scrubs and burrowed inside—

Manny saw motherfucking stars. The instant her skin was against his, he orgasmed like he'd never had one before, his head jacking back hard, his hands digging into her shoulders, his hips bucking like crazy. And she didn't stop the drinking or the pumping—so just as it had been before, he kept it up with the releasing, the pleasure ramping higher with every spasm through his erection.

It ended way too soon.

Then again, they could have kept at it for a decade and he would have remained starved for more.

When Payne pulled out of him, she eased back and licked her way around the sharp points of her fangs, her tongue pink against the white. Man . . . that gorgeous glow was back underneath her skin, making her seem like a dream.

Oh, wait, she was one, wasn't she.

"Your blood is strong," she said in a husky way as she bent to him again and licked her way up his throat. "So very strong."

"Is it?" he mumbled. And then he wasn't sure whether he'd even spoken. Maybe he'd just thought the words.

"I can feel the power coursing through me."

Man, he'd never been into the SUVs before—the damn things were too clunky and drove like boulders falling down a mountainside—but what he wouldn't have given for a backseat that you could fit more than a set of golf clubs in. He wanted to lay her out and—

"I want more of you," Payne murmured as she nuzzled him.

Well, he was still hard as stone even though he'd—

"I want you in my mouth."

Manny's head kicked back and he groaned as his cock twitched like it was taking a jog down there. But as much as he wanted her, he wasn't sure she knew what she was in for. Even the thought of her lips on his—

Payne's head went down into his lap before he could find the breath to speak, and there was no preamble; she sucked him right down, pulling him in and holding him in her wet, warm mouth.

"Fuck! Payne!"

His hands went to her shoulders, ostensibly to pull her back . . . but she was having none of that. Without coaching, she knew just how to rock him, pulling up and sucking down before licking under his shaft. And then she explored him with a thoroughness that told him she was enjoying it as much as he was, and wasn't that a turn-on.

Except then he felt her fangs teasing around his head.

He jacked her up fast on that one, capturing her mouth in a hard kiss while he held on to her face and started to lose it all over her hands. But that didn't last. She jerked out of his palms and went back to where she'd been, catching him in midorgasm, lapping up what his body seemed to have in spades for her.

When the kicking spasms stopped, she pulled back, looked at him . . . and slowly licked her lips.

Manny had to close his lids at that, his erection pulsing to the point of pain.

"You are taking me to your home now," she growled.

Not a request from her. And the tone suggested that she was thinking exactly as he was.

So that was going to lead to one and only one thing.

Manny gathered himself from the inside out and then opened his eyes. Reaching up, he touched her face and then rubbed her lower lip with his thumb.

"I'm not sure we should, *bambina*," he said roughly.

Her hand tightened on his cock and he moaned. "Manuel . . . I think that is very much where we need to be."

"Not . . . a good idea."

She pulled back farther, and retracted her hand, her glow fading. "But you are aroused. Even now."

You think? "And that's my point." His eyes raked over her face and went to her breasts. He was so desperate for her, he was tempted to rip her scrubs in half and take her virginity in his car. "I'm not going to be able to hold back, Payne. I'm barely doing that now. . . ."

She purred in satisfaction and licked those red lips again. "I like when you lose control."

Oh, God, that was soooo not helping.

"I . . ." He shook his head, thinking this was pure fucking hell—denying them both hurt that badly. "I think you need to do what you have to and leave me now. While I can still let you go—"

The knocking sound on the window made no sense at first. It was just the two of them in the empty parking lot. But then the mystery was solved:

"Get out the car. And give me your grip."

The male voice snapped Manny's head around to the window . . . where he stared into the barrel of a gun.

"You heard me, man. Out the car or I'll shoot you."

As Manny moved Payne back into her seat and away from point-blank range, he said softly to her, "When I get out, lock the doors. It's right here."

He moved his hand over to the dash and tapped the button.

"Just let me handle this." He had about four hundred dollars in cash in his wallet and plenty of credit cards. "Stay inside."

"Manuel—"

He didn't give her a chance to respond—as far as he was concerned, that gun held all the answers and made all the rules.

Snagging his wallet, he was slow in opening the door, but quick about his up and out—and when he shut Payne in, he waited to hear the locks go down.

And waited.

Desperate to hear the punching sound of Payne getting as safe as she could, he only half heard the guy in the ski mask bark, "Your wallet. And tell the bitch to get out the car."

"There's four hundred—"

The wallet disappeared. "Tell her to get out or she comes with me. And the watch. I want the watch."

Manny glanced over to the building. There were windows everywhere, and surely that guard had to take a wander to check shit out from time to time.

Maybe if he went slow with the handover—

That gun muzzle pushed right up into his face. "Watch. Now."

It wasn't his good one—he didn't operate with his Piaget on, for chrissakes. But whatever—asshole could have the fucking thing. Plus, as he feigned hands that shook, he figured it would eat up—

Hard to say what happened in what order.

In retrospect, he knew that Payne had to have opened her door first. But it seemed like the instant he heard the horrific sound of the passenger side getting cracked, she was behind the robber.

And another bizarre thing was that it wasn't until Manny cursed that the bastard seemed to realize a third party had entered the scenario. Except that couldn't be true—he would have seen her coming around the car, right?

Whatever—however it all went down, Ski Mask ended up leaping to the left and going back and forth with the weapon between Payne and Manny.

That tennis match thing wasn't going to last. With god-awful logic, Manny knew the guy was going to zero in on Payne because she was the weaker of the—

Next time the gun muzzle swung back in her direction, Payne . . . disappeared. And not as in ducked or dodged or took off at a dead run. She was there, taking up space one moment—and gone the next.

She reappeared a split second later, and caught the man's wrist as he went to put the gun back in Manny's face. The disarming was just as fast: One, she twisted the weapon away; two, she snapped it out of the SOB's hold; three, she tossed it at Manny, who caught the thing.

And then it was beat-down time.

Payne spun the guy around, grabbed the back of his head, and pounded him face-first into the Porsche's hood. After she polished the paint job a little with his piehole, she repositioned him and got a grip on the SOB's baggy-ass jeans. Hefting him up by the hair and what was either his waistband or his rectum, she hauled him back and threw him . . . about ten yards.

Superman didn't fly half as well—and the robber ended up knocking on the side of the horse-pital with his forehead. The building didn't have much to say in response, and what do you know, neither did he. He landed facedown in a flower bed, and stayed there, his limbs going dead meat and then some.

No twitching. No moaning. No attempt to get up.

"Are you all right, Manuel?"

Manny slowly turned his head to Payne. She wasn't even breathing hard.

"Jesus . . . Christ . . ." he whispered.

As Manuel's words drifted away on a breeze, Payne fussed with her baggy top and her loose pants. Then she smoothed her hair. It seemed like the only thing she could do to make herself more presentable in the wake of the violence.

Such a wasted effort at trying to feminize herself. And meanwhile, Manuel was still just staring at her.

"Will you say nothing further?" she asked in a low tone.

"Ah . . ." Manuel put his free hand on his head. "Yeah. Ah . . . let me go see if he's alive."

Payne wrapped her arms around herself as he walked over to the human man. In truth, she did not really care in what condition she had left the robber. Her priority had been to get that lethal weapon out of Manuel's face, and she had accomplished her task. Whatever happened to the thief was immaterial . . . but she clearly didn't know the rules of this world. Or the implications of what she had done.

Manuel was halfway across the grass when the "victim" rolled over with a groan. Hands that had been on the gun went to the mask that covered his face and shoved the knit weave up to his forehead.

Manuel knelt down. "I'm a doctor. How many fingers am I holding up."

"What . . . ?"

"How many fingers?"

". . . three . . ."

Manuel put his palm on the guy's shoulder. "Don't get up. That was a hell of a belt to the head. Do you have any tingling or numbness in your legs?"

"No." The guy stared at Manuel. "Why . . . are you doing this?"

Manuel waved the question off. "It's called medical school—creates a compulsive need to treat the ill or injured regardless of circumstance. I think we need to call an ambulance—"

"No fucking way!"

Payne dematerialized over to them. She appreciated Manuel's

good intentions, but she was concerned that the robber had another weapon on him—

The instant she appeared behind Manuel, the guy on the ground shrank away in horror, raising his arms and cringing back.

Manuel looked up over his shoulder—and that was when she saw that he wasn't naive. He had the gun pointed at the man. "It's okay, *bambina*. I got him—"

In a sloppy scramble, the robber got to his feet and Manuel let the muzzle follow him as the human stumbled and caught his balance against the building. Obviously, he was getting ready to run.

"We're keeping the gun," Manuel said. "You understand. And I don't need to tell you, you're lucky to be alive—you don't aggress on my girlfriend."

As the human tore off into the shadows, Manuel rose to his full height. "I need to turn this weapon in to the police."

Then he just looked over at her.

"It is all right, Manuel. I can take care of my presence with the guard so naught will be known. Do what you must."

On a nod, he took out a small phoning device, opened it, and hit a few buttons. Putting it up to his ear, he said, "Yeah, my name is Manuel Manello and I was held up at gunpoint in my vehicle? I'm at the Tricounty . . ."

As he spoke, she looked around, and thought she didn't want it to end like this. Except . . .

"I have to go," she said as Manuel hung up. "I cannot . . . be here if there are going to be more humans. It will just complicate things."

His phone slowly lowered to his side. "Okay . . . yeah." He frowned. "Ah, listen . . . if the police are coming, I need to remember what just happened or—shit, I've got a gun in my hand for no reason I can give them."

Indeed, it would appear that they were trapped. And for once, she was grateful for an imprisonment.

"I want you to remember me," she said softly.

"That wasn't the plan."

"I know."

He shook his head. "You are the most important piece in all this. So you have to take care of yourself and that means wiping me—"

"Dr. Manello! Dr. Manello—you okay?"

Payne glanced over her shoulder. The first human male they had seen at the desk inside was running across the lawn in a panic.

"Do it," Manuel said. "And I'll figure something out—"

As the scampering guard came up to them, Payne faced the new arrival.

"I was on my rounds," the man said, "and when I was checking the offices at the other end of the building, I saw you through the window—I ran as fast as I could!"

"We are fine," she said to the guard. "But would you look at something for me?"

"Of course! Have the police been called?"

"Yes." She touched below her right eye. "Look at me, please."

He was already locked on her face, and the extra focus just made her work easier; all she had to do was open the way into his brain and put a mental patch over everything that pertained to her.

As far as the human knew, her surgeon had come and gone alone.

She kept the man in a trance, and turned to Manuel. "You need not worry. His memories are so short-term, he will be fine."

From far off, a howling sound rang out, high-pitched and urgent.

"That's the police," Manuel said.

"Then I shall go."

"How will you get home?"

"In the same manner as I got out of your car."

She waited for him to reach for her . . . or say something . . . or . . . But he just stood there with the cold, silent night air between them.

"Are you going to lie to them?" he asked. "And tell them that you scrubbed me?"

"I do not know."

"Well, in case you need to come back to do that, I'm at—"

"Good night, Manuel. Please be safe."

With that, she raised her hand and quietly, inexorably disappeared.

FORTY-THREE

As tricks went, this one was fucking weird. "So where's your friend at?"

Karrie Ravisc, a.k.a. Kandy on the streets, had been doing the whore thing proper for about nine months so she'd seen a lot of shit. But this . . .

The huge man by the motel room's door spoke softly. "He's coming."

Karrie took another toke and thought, Well, at least the one in front of her was hot. And he'd also paid her five hundred and set her up in this room. Still . . . there was something off here.

Weird accent. Weird eyes. Weird ideas.

But very hot.

As they waited, she lay buck-ass naked on the bed with all the lights off. It wasn't totally dark, though. This john with the heavy wallet had set up a big boxy flashlight across the room, over on the cheapie dresser. The beam was pointed so that it shone on her body. Kind of like she was onstage. Or maybe a piece of art.

Which actually was less weird than some of the things she'd done.

Shit, if prostitution didn't make you think men were nasty, sick bastards, nothing else would: Aside from your run-of-the-mill cheaters and the types who were on power trips, you had fuckers with foot fetishes, and those who liked to get spanked, and others who wanted to get pissed on.

Finishing up her White Owl, she stabbed out the stub and thought maybe this spotlight thing wasn't so bad. Some jackass had wanted to eat hamburgers off her two weeks ago and that had just been gross—

The click of the lock turning into place made her jump, and she realized with a start that someone had somehow arrived without her knowing it; that was the door *being* locked. From the inside.

And now there was a second man over by the first.

Good thing her pimp was right next door.

"Evenin'," she said, as she stretched mechanically for both of them. Her breasts were fake, but they were good fake, and her stomach was flat even though she'd had one kid, and she was not just shaved, but electrolyzed.

All of which was how she got to charge what she did.

Man . . . another big one, she thought as the second guy came forward and stood at the foot of the bed. Actually, this fucker was huge. Absolutely mammoth. And not as in fat and sloppy—his shoulders were so square they looked drawn on with a ruler, and his chest formed a perfect triangle into his tight hips. She couldn't see his face, given the light that streamed from behind him, but it didn't matter as the first john stretched out on the bed next to her.

Shit . . . she suddenly found herself turned on. It was the size of them and the danger of the darkness and the scents. Jesus . . . they smelled amazing.

"Roll onto your stomach," the second one demanded.

God, that voice. The same foreign accent as the guy who had set this up, but so much deeper—and there was an edge to it.

"You really want to see my ass?" she drawled, as she sat up. Cupping her DDs, she hefted them and then squeezed them together. "Because the front of me is even better."

With that, she stretched one breast up and extended her tongue downward, licking her own nipple while her eyes went back and forth between the men.

"On your stomach."

Okay, clearly, there was a pecking order here: The guy lying next to her was sporting a tremendous erection, but he made no moves toward her. And Mr. Do-It-Now was the only one talking.

"If that's the way you want it."

Pushing the pillows off the bed, she made a show of the roll, twisting her torso around so that one of her breasts was still showing. With her black fingernail, she ran circles around the tip as she arched her lower back and stuck out her ass—

A subtle growling weaved its way through the stale, still air of the room, and that was her cue. Spreading her legs, she curled the lower halves up, pointing her toes and arching her spine again.

She knew exactly what she was showing the one at the end of the bed—and his growl told her he liked what she had. So it was time to take it further. Looking back at him, she put her middle finger in her mouth and sucked on it; then she shifted her weight up and took it down to her sex, rubbing herself.

Whether it was the weed or . . . shit, something about the men . . . she was really frickin' horny all of a sudden. To the point where she wanted what was about to happen.

As he loomed over her, the one in charge put his hand to the front of his hips.

"Kiss her," he ordered.

She was so ready for that, even though she didn't normally allow it. Turning her face to the other one, she felt her mouth get owned by a set of soft, demanding lips . . . and then a tongue entered her—

Just as big hands latched onto her upper thighs and spread her farther apart.

And another set of hands went for her breasts.

Even though she was a professional, her mind went on a little road trip, all the shit she usually preoccupied herself with while she was doing what she did fleeing—and taking with it things like, where were the condoms? What were the ground rules?

Buckle. Zipper. And then the sliding sounds of pants going down and the bucking of the mattress as something heavy got up on it.

Dimly, she wondered whether the cock that had been sprung was as big as the rest of the man behind her—and if it was, she thought, hell, she might be willing to give them a second round for free. Assuming they could go that long—

A blunt head pushed into her as hands lifted her hips off the mattress and got her on all fours. God, he was *huge*—and she braced herself for a hammering as a palm rode up her spine and fingers threaded through her short hair. He was going to yank her head back, but she didn't care. She just wanted even more of him inside—

Except he didn't get rough and he didn't move right away. Instead, he stroked her as if he liked the feel of her flesh, running his hand down onto her shoulders and again around to her waist . . . and then down further to her wet sex. And when he entered her fully, it was on a smooth slide, and he even gave her a second to get used to his girth and length.

Then he locked onto her hips with his palms and got with the fucking. Just as his friend pushed himself under her to suck on her hanging breasts.

With the pace intensifying, her nipples whipped back and forth across the mouth of the one underneath her to the beat of the slapping hips that hit her ass over and over again. Faster. Harder. Faster—

"Fuck me," she barked. "Oh, fuck, yeah—"

Abruptly, the one lying on the mattress pivoted himself, repositioned her and filled her mouth with the largest cock she'd ever swallowed.

She actually had an orgasm.

They kept going like this and *she* was going to tip *them*.

A split second later, the man behind her pulled out and she felt something hot spray across her back. But he wasn't finished. He was at it again a moment later, as fat and stiff as he'd been on the first stroke.

The one she was sucking off was moaning, and then she was separated from him by his lifting her head. He came on her breasts, hot jets draping her chest with more of that incredible scent as the other one popped out and ejaculated again on her back.

And then the world spun and she found herself on her back, the guy with the wallet taking the place of the one in charge at her sex and filling her just as thickly.

She was the one who reached for his silent, commanding friend, bringing his cock to her mouth, pulling him out of his role of spectator and into her once again.

He was so big that she had to stretch her jaw to fit him in, and he tasted fantastic—nothing like she'd had before. Sucking on him as his buddy fucked her good, she was all about the sensations of being filled, of being invaded by hard, blunt cocks that rocked her body.

In her delirium, she tried to see the man she was blowing, but he somehow always kept his back to the flashlight—and that made everything more erotic. Like she was sucking off a living shadow. Shit, unlike the other one, he made no sounds now, and he didn't even breathe hard. But he was into it, for real, pushing into her mouth and withdrawing and pushing back in. At least until he popped himself out and palmed up that erection. Holding her breasts together, she gave him one hell of a landing pad to come on, and holy crap, even though it was number three, he covered her.

Until her chest was glossy and slippery and dripping.

Next thing she knew, her knees were up at her ears and the one with the cash was going for broke in the best possible way. And then his boss was at her lips again, pressing in, wanting more. Which she was perfectly happy to give him.

Staring up at them as they moved in sync, she felt a passing fear. Curled beneath them, she had the sense that they could snap her in half if they were so inclined.

But they didn't hurt her.

And it went on and on, the two of them trading places again and again. They'd obviously done this a lot, and God, she was so giving them her number.

Finally, it was over.

Neither of them said a thing. Not to her or to each other—which was odd because most of the threesomes she'd been in had ended with the pair of idiots high-fiving each other. Not these two. They zipped up their cocks and . . . well, what do you know, wallets were coming out again.

As they stood over her, she brought her hands to her mouth and neck and her breasts. She was covered in so many places she couldn't count, and she loved it, smoothing what they'd left on her skin, playing with it because she wanted to—not for their benefit.

"We want to give you another five," the first one said in a low voice.

"For what?" Was that satisfied drawl really her?

"It'll feel good. I promise."

"Is it kinky?"

"Very."

She laughed and rolled her hips. "Then I say yes."

As the man peeled off the benjamins, there appeared to be plenty of others in that billfold—and maybe if he were someone else, she might have hit up her pimp and told Mack to hold him up out in the parking lot. She wasn't going to do that, though. Part of it was the incredible sex. More was the fact that these guys would likely beat the ever-living shit out of her boss.

"What do you want me to do?" she asked as she took the money and crushed it in her fist.

"Spread your legs."

She didn't hesitate, her knees flopping wide.

And they didn't hesitate, both of them bending over her weeping core.

Holy shit, they were going to suck her off? Just the thought of it made her eyes roll back in her head and she groaned—

"Ouch!"

She jacked up, but hands forced her back down onto the mattress.

The subtle sucking that came next made her light-headed. It wasn't on her sex, though. It was right off center on both sides, in the juncture where her legs met her torso.

Rhythmic sucking . . . like nursing.

Karrie sighed and gave herself up to it. She had the shocking sense that they were feeding from her in some way, but it felt amazing—especially as something entered her. Maybe it was fingers—probably.

Yeah, definitely.

Four of them filled her and two separate hands fell into an alternating push and pull as two mouths suckled on her flesh.

She came again.

And again.

And again.

After God only knew how long, they nuzzled her a couple of times—the places where they'd been sucking, not where their hands were.

And then everything was disengaged, mouths, fingers, bodies.

Both of them straightened up. "Look at me," the leader said.

Her lids were so heavy that she had to struggle to obey. And the moment she did, she felt a searing pain at her temples. That didn't last long, though, and afterward . . . she was just floating.

Which was why she didn't pay much attention to the distant, muffled scream that came from next door a little later—not the room that Mack was in, but the one on the other side of her.

Boom! Thump. Bump . . .

Karrie started to fall asleep at that point, dead to the world, the cash glueing to her palm as what had been wet turned to dry.

She wasn't worried about anything. In fact, she felt amazing.

Fuck . . . who had she been with . . . ?

As Xcor stepped outside the whore's motel room with Throe directly behind him, he shut the door and looked left and right. The facility that his soldier had chosen for this carnal diversion was on the outskirts of town. Run-down and rotting in places, the single-story building had been cut up into some fifty little cupboard-like boxes, with the office all the way down on the left. He had wanted the terminal room on the other end for privacy, but the best Throe had been able to do was the next in from that.

Though, truly, what were the chances of occupancy? There was hardly anyone here.

Scanning the parking spaces in front of them, he saw a black Mercedes that was desperately trying to look newer than it actually was . . . and a truck with a cap over its bed. The other two cars were way down at the far end, by the office.

This was perfect for the kind of purpose they'd fulfilled. Secluded. Populated with people who wanted no one in their business and were prepared to extend a similar courtesy to others. And the exterior lighting was poor: Only one out of every six bulbs by the doors worked—hell, the lighting fixture next to his head had been smashed. So everything was dim and dark.

He and his band of bastards were going to have to find females of their race to service their blood needs long-term, but that would come. Until then? They would partake from the likes of what he and Throe had just fucked, and they would do it here in this deserted place.

Throe spoke quietly. "Satisfied?"

"Aye. She was well and good."

"I'm glad—"

A scent upon the air drew both of their heads toward the door to the terminating room. As Xcor inhaled deeply to confirm what he had caught a mere whiff of, the smell of fresh human blood was an unwelcome surprise.

Unlike the expression on Throe's face. Which was an unwelcome nonsurprise.

"Do not even consider it," Xcor bit out. "Throe— *Fuck*."

The fighter was turning to the door with a thunderous expression—his aggression no doubt inflamed because that was female blood being spilled: The fertility was obvious in the air.

"We have no time for this," Xcor spat.

In a manner of reply, Throe kicked the fucking door in.

As Xcor cursed, he only briefly considered dematerializing out of the scene; all it took to cure the impulse was a look inside. Throe's ridiculous heroic streak had opened the way to a mess. Literally.

A human female was tied down onto the bed, with something crammed into her mouth. She was almost dead—and too close to the edge of her grave to save. Her blood was everywhere, on the wall beside her, dripping onto the floor, soaking into the mattress. The tools of whoever had done this were on the bedside table: two knives, duct tape, scissors . . . and half a dozen small clear jars with colorless fluid in them and tops that were set aside.

There were things floating in the—

A slam echoed out of the bathroom. As if a transom or window had been opened and shut.

As Throe ran in, Xcor lunged forward and caught the other male by the arm. In a quick one/two, Xcor unclipped the steel cuff he kept on his weapons belt and clamped it on the thick wrist of his soldier. Hauling back with all his weight, he hauled the male around, swinging him like the ball on the end of a chain. There was a thump on the far wall as the cheap plaster stopped the vampire pendulum.

"Let me go."

Xcor yanked the guy right in close. "This is not your concern."

Throe pulled back his arm and threw out a punch into the wall, smashing the flat plane. "It is! Release me!"

Xcor slapped his palm on the back of the male's neck. "Not. Your. World!"

They struggled at that point, the two of them wrestling and

knocking into things, creating more noise than they should. And they were just about to fall on the bloodied carpet when a human man with no neck and sunglasses the size of windowpanes slid into the doorway. He took one look at the bed, another at Xcor and Throe, and then he muttered under his breath, covering his eyes with his forearms as he ducked out.

A split second later, the door to the room they had fucked in opened and shut . . . then opened and shut again. High heels clip-clopped fast and uncoordinated, and there was a *clomp*, *clomp* of people getting into a car.

An engine roared and the Mercedes peeled out of the parking lot, no doubt with the whore and the cash in it.

And didn't the fast departure prove Xcor's assumption about the clientele here.

"Listen to me," he said to Throe. "Listen to me, you stupid bastard—this is not our problem. But if you stay here, you make it so—"

"The killer got away!"

"And so are we."

Throe's pale eyes shot over to the bed, and the mask of anger slipped for a brief moment. What was underneath arrested even Xcor's aggression. Such pain. God, such pain.

"She is not your sister," Xcor whispered. "Now come with me."

"I can't . . . leave her. . . ." Wide glassy eyes hit his. "You cannot ask me to."

Xcor spun around while keeping hold of his soldier. There had to be something of the murderer's in here, something they could—

Xcor dragged his fighter into the bathroom, and there was a grim satisfaction to be found upon the window above the toilet. The single, thick pane of frosted glass was unbroken, but there was a bright red streak on the edge of the sharp metal casing.

Just the remnant that they needed.

Xcor reached up to the window and ran his two fingers around what had caught and torn the flesh of that human.

The blood cleaved unto his flesh, pooling.

"Open," he commanded.

Throe parted his mouth and sucked those fingers down, closing his eyes to concentrate as distant sirens began to peal through the night.

"We must needs depart," Xcor said. "Come with me now and I shall grant you leave to find the man. Agree? Nod." When Throe did, he decided he needed more. "Swear to me."

Throe bowed at the waist. "I so swear."

The cuff came off . . . and then the pair of them disappeared into thin air just as flashing blue lights announced the arrival of the human police.

Xcor was not one for mercy on any occasion. But if he had been, he would have offered no pity unto that human defiler—who was now Throe's target . . . and soon to be prey.

FORTY-FOUR

"Dr. Manello?"

At the sound of his name, Manny snapped back into reality and found that, yes, in fact he was still at Tricounty, out on the lawn. Damn ironic that the security guard had had a mind job done on him, and yet he was the guy who had the focus.

"Ah . . . yeah. Sorry. What did you say?"

"You okay?"

"No, I'm not."

"Well, you got jumped—I can't believe how you handled him. One minute he was all up in your face . . . the next you had the gun and he was . . . flying. 'Course you'd be out of it."

"Yeah. That's it. Exactly."

The cops showed up two seconds later and then it was a flurry of questions and answers. And it was amazing. The security guard never mentioned Payne. It was as if she had never been there.

Shouldn't have been a news flash, considering what Manny had been through not only with her but with Jane. Still was, though.

He just didn't understand so much of it all: how Payne had disappeared into thin air in front of him; how there had been nothing of her, at least as far as the security guard knew, but the guy remembered Manny just fine; how she had been so calm and in control in a deadly situation.

Actually, that last bit had been erotic as hell. Watching her pummel the fuck out of that guy had been an incredible turn-on—Manny wasn't sure what that said about him, but there you go.

And she was so going to lie, he thought. Tell her people that he was scrubbed. Say that she'd taken care of things.

Payne had found the solution that worked: He had his mind, she had her legs, and no one was the wiser among her brother and his ilk.

Yup, everything was taken care of. All he had to do now was spend the rest of his life pining after a female he should never have met. Piece of fucking cake.

An hour later, he got into his Porsche and headed back for Caldwell. Driving by himself, the car seemed not just empty but a wasteland, and he found himself putting the windows up and down. Wasn't the same.

She didn't know where he lived, he thought. But that didn't matter, did it. She wasn't coming back.

God, it was tough to decide what would have been harder: A long protracted good-bye where he looked into her eyes and bit his tongue to keep from talking too much? Or that short, rip-the-Band-Aid shit?

Sucked either way.

At the Commodore, he went underground, parked in his spot, and got out. Hit the elevator. Went up to his apartment. Walked in. Let the door close.

As his cell phone went off, he fumbled to take it out of his pocket, and when he saw the number, he cursed. Goldberg from the medical center.

He answered without any enthusiasm. "Hey."

"You picked up," the guy said with relief. "How are you?"

Right. So not going there. "I'm okay." When there was a pause, he said, "And you?"

"I'm good. Things have been . . ." *Hospital. Hospital. Hospital hospital, hospitalh ospit alhosp. Ital hospit alhospital . . .*

In one ear, out the other. Manny did get busy, however. He went to the bar in the kitchen, took out the Lag, and felt like he'd been punched in the head when he saw how little was in the bottle. Leaning into the cabinet, he took out some Jack from the back that had in there so long there was dust on the cap.

Sometime later, he hung up the phone and got serious about the drinking. Lag first. Jack next. And then it was a case of the two bottles of wine that were in the fridge. And what was left of a six-pack of Coronas—that had been left in the pantry and weren't cooled.

His synapses, however, didn't recognize any difference between alcohol that was lukewarm and the shit that was chilly-chilly.

All told, the festival of consumption took him a good hour. Maybe longer. And it was highly effective. When he grabbed the last beer and started for the bedroom, he walked like he was on the bridge of the *Enterprise*, shuffling left and right . . . and then listing back again. And even though he could see well enough with the city's ambient light, he ran into a lot of stuff: By some inconvenient miracle, his furniture had become animated and the shit was determined to get in his way—everything from the stuffed leather chairs to the—

"Fuck!"

—coffee table.

Annnnnnnnd the fact that he now was rubbing his shin as he went along was like adding a set of roller skates to the party.

When he got to his room, he took a slug from the Corona to celebrate and stumbled into the bath. Water on. Clothes off. Stepped right in. No reason to wait for the hot stuff; he couldn't feel anything anyway, and that was the point.

He didn't bother to dry off. Just walked over to the bed with the water dripping off his body, and he finished off the beer as he sat down. Then . . . whole lot of nothing. His alkie meter was spiking really frickin' high, but it had yet to reach critical mass and knock him the fuck out.

Consciousness was a relative term, however. Although he was arguably awake, he was utterly unplugged—and not just because of the alcohol/blood count he was sporting. He was out of gas on the inside in the most curious way.

Falling back on the mattress, he supposed now that the Payne situation had resolved itself it was time to start pulling his life back together—or at least give it a shot tomorrow morning, when his hangover woke him up. His mind was fine, so there was no reason he couldn't go back to work and make it his business to put distance between this fucked-up interlude and the rest of his normal life.

As he stared at the ceiling, he was relieved when his vision got fuzzy.

Until he realized he was tearing up.

"Fucking pussy."

Wiping his eyes, he was absolutely, positively not going there. Except he did—and he stayed. God, he missed her to the point of agony already.

"Fucking . . . hell—"

Abruptly, his head shot up and his cock swelled. Looking out through the sliding glass door onto his terrace, he searched the night with a desperation that made him feel like the mental crazies were back.

Payne . . .

Payne . . . ?

He struggled to get up off the bed, but his body refused to budge—like his brain was talking one language and his arms and legs couldn't translate. And then the hooch won, pulling a Ctrl-Alt-Del and shutting his program down.

No rebooting his ass, however.

After his lids crashed shut, it was lights-out, no matter how hard he fought the tide.

Outside on the terrace, Payne stood in the cold wind, her hair whipping around, her skin tingling from the chill.

She had disappeared from Manuel's sight. But she hadn't left him.

Even though he had proved capable of taking care of himself, she wasn't trusting his life to anyone or anything. Accordingly, she'd coated herself in *mhis* and stood on the lawn at the equine hospital, watching him speak with the police and the security guard. And then when he'd gotten in the car, she had followed, dematerializing from spot to spot, tracking him thanks to the small amount of blood he'd tasted of her.

His trip home had culminated in the depths of a city that was smaller than the one that she had seen from his car, but was still impressive, with its tall buildings and paved streets and beautiful, soaring bridges that spanned a broad river. Caldwell was indeed lovely at night.

Would that she had come for aught but an invisible good-bye.

When Manuel had pulled into some kind of underground facility for vehicles, she had let him go on his own. Her purpose had been served when he had safely reached this destination so she'd known she had to depart.

Alas, however, she had tarried down at street level, standing in her *mhis*, watching the cars go by and seeing pedestrians cross corner to corner. An hour had passed. And then some more time. And still she couldn't leave.

Giving in to her heart, she had gone up, up, up . . . honing in on where Manuel was, taking form on this terrace outside his home . . . and finding him in the midst of leaving the kitchen to walk through his living room. Clearly unsteady on his feet, he kept running into pieces of furniture—although likely not because the lights were off. 'Twas the drink in his hand, no doubt.

Or more accurately, all the drink he'd taken in addition to it.

In his bedroom, he didn't disrobe so much as dishevel himself out of his clothes, and then he was into the shower. When he emerged dripping wet, she wanted to cry. It seemed so very hard to comprehend that merely a day separated her and him from the time she had first witnessed him thus—although, indeed, she felt as if she could almost reach through time and touch those electric moments when they had been on the verge of . . . not just a present, but a future.

No longer.

Over at the bed, he sat down . . . then fell over onto the mattress.

When he went to wipe his eyes, her devastation was complete. And so was her need to go to him—

"Payne."

With a yelp, she spun about. Across the terrace, standing in the breeze . . . was her twin. And the instant she laid eyes upon Vishous, she knew something had changed within him. Yes, his face was already healing up from the damage he'd inflicted upon it with the mirror—but that was not what had altered. The inside of him was different: Gone were the tension and the anger and the frightening coldness.

As the wind whipped her hair around, she quickly tried to compose herself, swiping clear the tears that had glossed over her eyes. "How did you know . . . I was . . ."

With his gloved hand, he pointed upward. "I have a place here. On the top of the building. Jane and I were just leaving when I sensed you were down here."

She should have known. Just as she could sense his *mhis* . . . he could feel and find hers.

And how she wished he had just kept going. The last thing she needed was another round of a male figure of "authority" telling her what she had to do. Besides, the king had already laid down the law. It wasn't as if Wrath's decree needed buttressing from the likes of her brother.

She put her hand up to stop him before he said one word about Manuel. "I am not interested in your telling me what our king already has. And I was just leaving."

"Is he scrubbed."

She kicked up her chin. "No, he is not. He took me out and there was an . . . incident—"

The snarl her brother released was louder than the wind. "What did he do to—"

"Not him. Fates, will you just . . . stop hating him." As she rubbed her temples, she wondered if anyone's head had actually ever exploded—or whether everybody on earth just felt that way from time to time. "We were attacked by a human and in the process of disarming him—"

"The human?"

"Yes—in the process of that, I hurt the man and the police were called—"

"You *disarmed* a human?"

Payne glared at her twin. "When you remove a gun from someone, that is what it is called, is it not."

Vishous's eyes narrowed. "Yeah. It is."

"I could not scrub Manuel's memories because he would not have been able to field the questions put to him from the police. And I am here . . . because I wanted to see him home safely."

In the silence that followed, she realized she had just backed herself into a corner. By having to protect Manuel, she had just proven her twin's point that the male she wanted could not take care of her. Oh, but what did it matter. Given that she was prepared to obey the king, there was no future for her and Manuel anyway.

When Vishous went to open his mouth, she moaned and put her hands to her ears. "If you have any compassion at all, you will leave me to mourn here alone. I cannot listen to all the reasons I must needs separate myself from him—I know them all. *Please.* Just *go.*"

Closing her eyes, she turned away and prayed to their mother above that he would do as she asked—

The hand on her shoulder was weighty and warm. "Payne. Payne, look at me."

With no energy left to fight, she dropped her arms and met his grim eyes.

"Answer me one thing," her twin said.

"What."

"Do you love the bas—him. Do you love him?"

Payne looked back through the glass at the human on the bed. "Yes. I am in love with him. And if you try to dissuade me by the fact that I have not lived yet enough to judge, I say unto you . . . fuck off. I need not know the world to realize my heart's desire."

There was a long silence. "What did Wrath say?"

"The same thing you would. That I must erase myself from his memory and never, ever see him again."

When her brother did not say anything further, she shook her head. "Why are you still here, Vishous. Are you trying to think of what to say to get me to go home? Let me save you the effort—when dawn comes, I shall go—and I shall abide by the rules, but not because it is good for you or the king or myself. It is because it's safest for him—he does not need enemies such as yourself and the Brotherhood to torture him just because I feel as I do. So it will be done just as you wish. Except"—at this, she glared at him—"I will not scrub him. His mind is too valuable to waste—and it cannot withstand another episode. I shall keep him safe by ne'er coming here again, but I will not condemn him to a life of dementia. That is not going to happen—he has done nothing but help me. He deserves better than to be used and discarded."

Payne returned her eyes to the glass.

And after a long while of silence, she assumed that her twin had left. So she nearly screamed when he stepped in front of her and blocked the view of Manuel.

"Are you *still* here," she snapped.

"I'll take care of it for you."

Payne recoiled and then growled, "Do not you dare think of killing him—"

"With Wrath. I'll take care of it. I'll . . ." Vishous scrubbed his hair. "I'll work something out so you can keep him."

Payne blinked. And then felt her mouth drop open. "What . . . what did you say?"

"I've known Wrath for a lot of years. And technically, according to the Old Laws, I'm the head of our little happy family down here. I'll go to him and tell him that I approve of this . . . match and that I think you should be able to see the bas—guy. Man. Manello." He cleared his throat. "Wrath is very security-conscious, but with the *mhis* around the compound . . . Manello couldn't find us if he wanted to. Besides, it's hypocritical to deny you what other Brothers have done from time to time. Fuck it, Darius had a kid with a human woman—and Wrath's now married to that young. Matter of fact—if you had tried to separate our king from his Beth when he'd met her? He'd have killed anyone who even made the suggestion. Rhage's Mary? Same diff. And it should . . . be likewise for you. I'll even talk to *Mahmen*, if I have to."

Payne put her palm up to her pounding heart. "I . . . don't understand why you would . . . do this?"

He glanced over his shoulder, staring at the human she loved. "You're my sister. And he's what you want." He shrugged. "And . . . well, I fell in love with a human. I fell in love with my Jane within an hour of meeting her—and . . . yeah. I've got nothing without her. If what you feel for Manello is even half what I have for my *shellan*, your life is never going to be complete without him—"

Payne tackled her brother in an embrace. Nearly knocked him right off his feet. "Oh . . . brother mine . . . !"

His arms came around her and held her. "I'm sorry I was such an asshole."

"You were . . ." She searched for another word. "Yes, you were such an asshole."

He laughed, the sound rumbling up through his chest. "See? We can agree on something."

As she held on to him, she said, "Thank you . . . thank you . . ."

After a moment, he pulled back. "Let me talk to Wrath first before you go to Manello, okay? I want to work it all out beforehand—and yes, I'm going home right now. Jane's doing rounds and the Brotherhood is off tonight, so I should get right in with the king." There was a pause. "I only want one thing from you in return."

"What. Anything. Name it."

"If you're going to hang around until dawn, go inside. It's fucking freezing as shit out here, true." He stepped back. "Go on . . . go hang with your . . . male. . . ." He rubbed his eyes and she had a feeling he was remembering what he'd walked in on when she'd been in the shower with her healer. "I'll come back . . . ah, call. . . . Do you have a phone? Here, take my— Fuck, I don't have it."

"It is okay, brother mine. I shall return at dawn."

"Good, yeah—I should know by then."

She stared at him. "I love you."

Now he smiled. Broadly, and without reserve. Reaching out, he brushed her face. "I love you, too, sis. Now get in there and get warm."

"I shall." She jumped up and kissed him on the cheek. "I shall!"

With a wave, she dematerialized through the glass.

Oh, how the interior felt hot in comparison to the terrace . . . or perhaps it was the rush of joy that had spread throughout her. Whatever it was, she did a spin on one foot and then went over to the bed.

Manuel was not just aslumber, but passed out—she did not care, though. Climbing onto the bed, she put an arm around him—and instantly, he groaned and turned to her, pulling her close, holding her. As their bodies melded together, and his erection pushed into her hip, her eyes shot to the terrace.

No reason to force their luck with Vishous—but alas, he was gone.

Grinning in the dark, she got comfortable and stroked her male's shoulder. This was all going to work out, and the key was the overwhelming logic that Vishous had detailed. In fact, the argument was so dispositive, she couldn't believe she hadn't thought of it herself.

Wrath might not like it; however, he was going to agree because facts were facts—and he was a fair ruler who had proven time and again that he was not a slave to the old ways.

As she settled in, she knew there was no chance she was going to fall asleep and thereby run the risk of getting burned by the sun: She was incandescent herself as she lay on the bed beside Manuel, glowing so bright she cast shadows in the room.

No sleeping for her.

She just wanted to enjoy this feeling.

Forever.

FORTY-FIVE

Vishous got home in the blink of an eye, and after he checked in with Jane in the clinic, he headed for the big house through the underground tunnel. As he came out in the foyer, all he heard was a resounding nothing-much-at-all and he was uncomfortable with the silence.

So frickin' quiet.

Of course, typically, this would be because it was two a.m. and the Brothers would be out in the field. Tonight, though, everyone was hunkered down, probably having sex, recovering from sex, or in the midst of doing it again.

I feel like I've made love to you for the very first time.

As Jane's voice came back at him, he didn't know whether to smile or kick his own ass. But whatever, it was a brave new world for him, starting tonight—not that he was entirely sure what that meant, but he was on it. He was so on it.

Hitting the grand staircase, he beelined for Wrath's study, while patting every pocket he didn't have. He was still in the damn johnny. With the bloodstains. And no damn cigs.

"Son of a bitch."

"Sire? Do you require aught?"

As he stopped at the head of the stairs, he looked over at Fritz, who was cleaning the banister, and nearly kissed the butler on the piehole. "I'm out of my tobacco. Rolling papers—"

The old *doggen* smiled so widely, the wrinkles in his face made him look like a Shar-Pei. "I have more of it all down in the pantry. I shall be right back—are you going in to meet with the king?"

"Yeah."

"I shall bring them to you there—as well as a robe, perhaps?"

The second half was said delicately.

"Shit, thank you, Fritz. You're a lifesaver."

"No, you are, sire." He bowed. "You and the Brotherhood save us all each night."

Fritz scurried along his way, going down the staircase with more spring in his step than you'd expect. Then again, he loved nothing more than to be of service. Which was very cool.

Right. Time to go to work.

Feeling like a total reject in the johnny, V marched over to the closed doors of Wrath's study, curled up a fist and knocked.

The king's voice came through the heavy wood panels: "Come in."

V pushed inside. "It's me."

"S'up, brother."

At the far end of the pansy-ass colored room, Wrath was behind his massive desk, sitting on his father's throne. Down on the floor beside him, lying on a personalized Orvis dog bed in royal red, George lifted his blond head and pricked his perfect triangle ears. The golden retriever thumped his tail in greeting, but did not leave his master's side.

The king and his Seeing Eye dog were never apart. And not just because Wrath needed the help.

"So, V." Wrath eased back in the carved chair, his hand falling down to stroke his dog's head. "Your scent is interesting."

"Is it." V took the seat across from the king, putting his palms on his thighs and squeezing in an attempt to distract himself from his nicotine craving.

"You left the door open."

"Fritz is bringing me some smokes."

"You're not lighting up around my dog."

Fuck. "Ah . . ." He'd forgotten the new rule . . . and asking George to take a breather was a no-go—after all, Wrath may have lost his sight, but the fucker was still deadly, and V had gotten enough of the S and M tonight, thank you very much.

Fritz came in just as the king's black brows dropped behind his wraparounds.

"Sire, your tobacco," the butler said happily.

"Thanks, my man." V accepted the rolling papers and the pouch . . . and the lighter that the *doggen* had thoughtfully provided. As well as the robe.

The door shut.

V looked over at the dog. George's big boxy head was down on his paws, his kind brown eyes seeming to apologize for the shutdown on the whole light-up routine. He even gave a tentative tip-of-the-tail wag.

Vishous stroked the bag of Turkish delicious like a pathetic loser. "Mind if I just rolled up a couple?'

"One flick of the flint and I'll pound you into the carpet."

"Roger that." V lined things up on the desk. "I've come to talk about Payne."

"How is your sis?"

"She's . . . amazing." He cracked open his pouch, took an inhale and had to suck back his *mmmm.* "It worked—I'm not sure how, but she's up and around, true. On her feet, good as new."

The king eased forward. "No . . . shit? For real?"

"One hundred."

"It's a miracle."

Named Manuel Manello, evidently. "You could say that."

"Well, this is great fucking news. You want to get her a room in here? Fritz can—"

"It's a little more complicated than that."

As those brows disappeared under the wraparounds again, V thought, man, even though the king was fully blind, he still appeared to focus like he always did. Which kind of made you feel like you had a gunsight trained on your frontal lobe.

V started laying out little white squares. "It's that human surgeon."

"Oh . . . for shit's sake." Wrath popped his sunglasses onto his forehead and rubbed his eyes. "Do not crank my crap out and tell me they've hooked up."

V remained silent, grabbing the pouch and busying himself with the pinching stage of things.

"I'm waiting for you to tell me I got it wrong." Wrath let his glasses fall back into place. "*Still* waiting."

"She's in love with him."

"And you're okay with this?"

"Of course not. But she could date a Brother and the motherfucker wouldn't be good enough for her." He picked up one of the loaded papers and began rolling. "So . . . if she wants him, I say live and let live."

"V . . . I know what angle you're going to take and I can't allow it."

Vishous stopped in mid-lick and considered bringing Beth into the happy convo. But the king already looked like he was getting a headache. "The hell you can't allow it. Rhage and Mary—"

"Rhage got beaten, remember? For a reason. Besides, times are changing, V. The war is heating up, the Lessening Society is recruiting like a motherfucker—and on top of that, there's the sliced-not-diced, halvsie shit you found downtown last night."

Goddamn it, V thought. Those slaughtered slayers . . .

"Plus I just got this." Without looking, Wrath patted to the left and held up a page of Braille. "It's a copy of a letter that was e-mailed to what's left of the Founding Families. Xcor has relocated with his boys—which was why you found those *lessers* in the condition you did."

"Fucking . . . *hell.* I knew it was him."

"He's setting us up."

V stiffened. "For what?"

Wrath sent a *get real* over the desk. "People have lost entire branches of their families. They've fled their homes, but they want to come back here. Meanwhile, things are getting more dangerous, instead of safer in Caldwell. Nothing should be taken for granted right now."

Read: He wasn't assuming his throne was secure. No matter what he happened to be sitting on.

"So it's not that I don't understand where Payne's at," Wrath said.

"But we've got to circle the wagons and hunker down. Now is not the time to layer on the complication of a human in here."

Things grew quiet for a moment.

As V considered his counterpoints, he picked up another square, rolled it tight, licked the flap, twisted. "He helped my Jane last night. When the Brothers and I came back here after the melee in that alley, Manello was hands-on and then some. He's a spectacular surgeon—and I should know. He operated on me. He's far from useless." V looked across the desk. "If the war intensifies further, we could use an extra set of surgical hands down in the clinic."

Wrath cursed in English. And then in the Old Language. "Vishous—"

"Jane is awesome, but there's only one of her. And Manello has technical skills she doesn't."

Wrath popped up his glasses again and rubbed. Hard. "You telling me that guy is going to want to live here in this house day and night for the rest of his life? Lot to ask."

"So I'll ask him."

"I don't like this."

Loooong silence. Which told V he was making headway. He knew better than to push, however.

"I thought you wanted to kill the bastard," Wrath groused. As if that would be preferable as a goal.

Abruptly, the image of Manello on his knees in front of Payne blazed into V's mind, until he wanted to snag a pen and poke his own eyes out. "I still do," he said darkly. "But . . . he's who she wants, true. What am I gonna do."

Another loooong silence, during which he made a satisfyingly tall pile of light-ables.

Finally, Wrath dragged a hand through his mile-long black hair. "If she wants to see him outside of here, that's none of my business."

Vishous opened his mouth to argue, and then shut his trap. This was better than a flat-out no, and who knew what the future held: If V could evolve to a place where, even after The Shower Nightmare, Manello remained aboveground and breathing, anything could fucking happen.

"Fair enough." He resealed the pouch. "What are we going to do about Xcor?"

"Wait until the Council calls a meeting about him—which will be in the next couple of nights, no doubt. The *glymera* is going to eat this shit up, and then we've got real problems." In a dry voice, the king tacked on, "As opposed to all our half-assed ones."

"You want the Brotherhood up here for a meeting?"

"Nah. Give 'em the rest of the night off. This is not going away."

V stood, pulled on the robe and gathered up his smoking para. "Thanks for this. You know, about Payne."

"It's not a favor."

"It's a better message to carry back to her."

Vishous was halfway to the door when Wrath said, "She's going to want to fight."

V pivoted around. "Excuse me."

"Your sister." Wrath put his elbows on all the paperwork and leaned in, his cruel face grave. "You need to prepare yourself for when she asks to go out and fight."

Oh, hell, no. "I'm not hearing that."

"You will be. I've sparred against her. She's as lethal as you and I are, and if you think she's going to be content prowling around this house for the next six hundred years, you're fucked in the head. Sooner or later, that's what she's going to want."

Vishous opened his mouth. Then shut it.

Well, he'd had a rockin' good time enjoying life for about . . . twenty-nine minutes. "Don't tell me you'd allow it."

"Xhex fights."

"She's Rehvenge's subject. Not yours." Wrath's brows made a third disappearance. "Different standard."

"Number one, everyone under this roof is my subject. And two, it's not any different just because she's your sister."

"Of course"—*It. Is.*—"not."

"Uh-huh. Right."

Vishous cleared his throat. "You're seriously thinking about letting her—"

"You've seen what I looked like after we worked out, right? I was giving her no leeway at all, Vishous. That female knows what she's doing."

"But she's . . ." *My sister.* "You can't let her go out there."

"Right now, I need as many fighters as I've got."

Vishous put a hand-rolled between his lips. "I think I'd better go."

"Good idea."

The second he was out and had shut the door, he flicked the gold lighter Fritz had given him and inhaled like a Dyson.

As he thought about his next move, he supposed he could flash back to the Commodore and deliver the happy news to his sister—but he was more than a little afraid of what he'd materialize into. Besides, he had until dawn to convince himself that Payne out in the field was not an Edsel-like idea.

Also, he had someone else he had to see.

Taking the staircase down, he crossed the foyer, and hit the vestibule. Outside, he walked fast through the pebbled courtyard and entered the Pit through its stout front door.

The familiarity of the couches and the plasma screen and the Foosball table eased him.

The sight of the empty bottle of Lag on the coffee table? Not so much.

"Butch?"

No answer. So he went down the hall to the cop's room. The door was open and inside . . . there was nothing but Butch's huge wardrobe and a messy, empty bed.

"I'm in here."

Frowning, V doubled back and leaned into his own room. The lights were off, but the sconces in the hall gave him enough to go by.

Butch was sitting on the far side of the bed, his back to the door, his head hanging, his heavy shoulders curled in.

Vishous stepped inside and closed them in together. Neither Jane nor Marissa was going to show up—both were busy with their jobs. But Fritz and his crew were probably going to sweep through here some time, and that butler, God love him, never even knocked on closed doors. He'd lived here too long.

"Hey," V said into the darkness.

"Hey."

V went forward, rounding the foot of the bed, using the wall to navigate. Lowering his ass onto the mattress, he sat beside his best friend.

"You and Jane okay?" the cop asked.

"Yeah. S'all good." Such an understatement. "She arrived right around the time I woke up."

"I called her."

"I figured." Vishous turned his head and looked over, even though that hardly mattered in the pitch black. "Thank you for that—"

"I'm sorry," Butch croaked. "Oh, God, I'm so sorry. . . ."

The hoarse exhale that came out was a sob barely covered up.

In spite of being blind, V put his arm out and curled it around the cop. Pulling the male close to his chest, he laid his head down on his buddy's.

"It's okay," he said roughly. "It's all right. It's okay. . . . You did the right thing. . . ."

Somehow he ended up moving the guy around so that they were stretched out together and he had his arms around the cop.

For some reason, he thought of the first night they'd spent together. It had been one million and a half years ago, back at Darius's in-town mansion. Two twin beds side by side upstairs. Butch had asked about the tats. V had told him to mind his own biz.

And here they were in the dark again. Given all that had happened since then, it was almost unfathomable that they'd ever been those two males who had bonded over the Sox.

"Don't ask me to do that again anytime soon," the cop said.

"Deal."

"Still. If you need it . . . come to me."

It was on the tip of V's tongue to say something like *Never again*, but that was bullshit. He and the cop had done rounds on this psychiatric floor of V's too many times, and although he was turning over a new leaf . . . you never knew.

So he just repeated the vow he'd made to himself back with Jane. From now on, he was letting shit out. Even if it made him uncomfortable to the point of screaming, it was better than the bottle-up strategy. Healthier, too.

"I'm hoping it won't be necessary," he murmured. "But thanks, my man."

"One other thing."

"What."

"I think we're dating now." As V barked out a laugh, the cop shrugged. "Come on . . . I got you naked. You wore a damn corset. And don't get me started about the sponge bath afterward."

"Fucker."

"To the end."

As their laughter faded, V closed his eyes and briefly shut his brain down. With his best friend's big barrel chest up against his own, and the knowledge that he and Jane were tight again, his world was complete.

Now, if he could just keep his sister off the streets and out of the alleys at night . . . life would be frickin' perfect.

FORTY-SIX

When José pulled up to the Monroe Motel & Suites, it was pretty clear that the only thing new around the place was the crime scene tape that had just been wrapped around the far end. Everything else was wilted and sagging, including the cars that were parked by the office.

Heading past the lineup of beaters, he went all the way down to the last room on the row and pulled his unmarked in diagonally to the other CPD units.

As he put the sedan in park, he looked across the seat. "You good to go?"

Veck was already reaching for the door handle. "You'd better believe it."

When the two of them got out, the other officers came over, and Veck got surrounded by a whole lot of backslapping. In the department, people thought the guy was a hero for The Paparazzi Incident—and that approval roll wasn't slowed in the slightest by the fact that the guy always brushed off any attaboys.

Staying tight and cool, he just jacked up his slacks and took out a cigarette. After lighting it and inhaling, he talked through the exhale. "How we doing here."

José left the kid to get up to speed and ducked under the tape. The broken door to the crime scene had been shut loosely, and he nudged it open with his shoulder.

"Shit," he said under his breath.

The air was choked with the smell of fresh blood . . . and formaldehyde.

At that moment, the photographer's flash went off and the body of the victim was spotlighted on the bed—as were the specimen jars on the bedside table. And the knives.

He closed his eyes briefly.

"Detective?"

José glanced over his shoulder at Veck. "Yeah?"

"We have the registration on the truck. Illinois. Owned by a David Kroner. It has not been reported stolen, and guess what—Kroner is a white male, thirty-three years old . . . unmarried . . . on disabili—fucking hell." Veck's convo stopped altogether as he came to stand by the bed. "Jesus."

The flashbulb went off again, and there was an electronic wheeze as the camera recovered from the effort.

José looked at the coroner. "How long's she been dead?"

"Not long. She's still warm. I'll give you a better idea when I'm done here."

"Thanks." José walked over to the crappy bureau and used a pen to push around a thin gold ring, a pair of sparkly earrings, and a bracelet that was pink and black.

The tattoo that had been cut out of the victim's skin and relocated to the specimen jar next to her was pink and black, too. Probably favorite colors of hers.

Or had been.

He continued to wander around, looking for things that were out of place, checking the wastepaper baskets, peeking into the bathroom.

Someone had clearly disturbed the killer's fun. Somebody had heard or seen something and busted the door open, causing a fast departure out this back window above the toilet.

The 911 call that had come in had been made by a male who refused to identify himself. He'd said only that there was a dead body in the room at the end and that was it. Wasn't their killer. Bastards like him didn't stop unless they had to, and they didn't willingly leave behind the kinds of trophies that were on the nightstand and the bureau.

"Where did you go after this?" José said to himself. "Where did you run to . . ."

There were K-9 units searching the woods out back, but José had a hunch that was going to come to nothing. A mere tenth of a mile from the motel was a river shallow enough to wade through—he and Veck had gone over the little bridge that spanned the damn thing on the way here.

"He's changing his MO," Veck said. When José turned, the guy planted his hands on his hips and shook his head. "This is the first time he's done it in this public a place. His work is really messy—and potentially noisy. We'd have found more scenes like this after he was done."

"Agreed."

"David Kroner is the answer."

José shrugged. "Maybe. Or he could be another body we're about to find."

"No one's reported him missing."

"Like you said, unmarried, right? Maybe he lives alone. Who'd know he was gone?"

Except even as José poked holes in the theory, he did the math and came up with a similar conclusion. It was rare that a person could disappear without somebody missing them—family, friends, coworkers, apartment manager. . . . It wasn't impossible, but very unlikely.

The question was, where was the killer going to go next? If the bastard followed conventional wisdom, he was probably entering a gorging stage with his pathology. In the past, victims had shown up months apart, but now they'd found two in a week?

So if he worked off that assumption, he knew the careful actions that had masked the killer previously were going out the window, whatever patterns he'd fallen into dissipating in the face of a frenetic drive. The good news was that sloppy was going to make him easier to catch. The bad news was that this might well get worse before it got better.

Veck came up to him. "I'm going to get into that truck. You want to be there?"

"Yeah."

Outside, the air didn't smell like copper and chemicals, and José took some deep breaths as Veck snapped on gloves and went to work. Naturally the vehicle was locked, but that didn't stop the guy. He got a slider and popped open the driver's-side door like he was an old hand with the B&E.

"Whoa," he muttered as he reared back.

It didn't take long for the stench to hit José, and he coughed into his hand. More formaldehyde, but also the sweet stench of dead things.

"It's not in the cab." Veck swung his flashlight around the seats. "In the back."

There was a padlock on the square double doors of the cap, but Veck just went to the trunk of the unmarked and returned with a battery-powered Sawzall.

There was a high-pitched whine . . . a *ping!* . . . and then Veck was in.

"Oh . . . fuck . . ."

José shook his head as he came around to see what his partner had cursed at.

Veck's flashlight beam was illuminating an entire collection of little jars with things floating in or sunken down at the bottom of clear liquid. The containers were held safe in a custom-made rack system mounted on the left side. The right side was reserved for tools: knives and ropes, duct tape, hammers, chisels, razor blades, scalpels, retractors.

Hello, David Kroner: highly improbable that the killer had installed this setup in someone else's truck—and what do you bet that the trophies in all those jars filled the holes in the dermis of the victims.

Their best hope was that the K-9 units tracked him in the woods.

Otherwise, they were going to lose another woman. José was willing to bet his house on it.

"I'll sync with the FBI," he said. "They need to come down here and see this."

Veck scanned the interior. "I'll give the CSI boys a hand. I'd like to get this vehicle moved back to HQ ASAP so everything can be logged properly."

José nodded, cocked his cell phone, and hit speed dial. As the ringing started, he knew that after he got off with the feds' regional field office he was going to have to call his wife. No chance he was coming home in time for breakfast.

None at all.

FORTY-SEVEN

"The sun! Oh, my God! Quick, you'd better—"

Manny came fully awake in midair: Evidently, he'd leaped out of bed, taking the duvet and several pillows with him, and they all landed at once, his feet, the comforter, and the quartet of puffies.

Bright sunlight was streaming in the glass windows, flooding his bedroom with brilliant illumination.

Payne was here, his brain told him. She was *here.*

Looking around frantically, he rushed into the bathroom. Empty. Ran through the rest of the condo. Empty.

Rubbing his hair, he went back to the bed . . . and then realized, holy shit, he still had all his memories. Of her. Of Jane. Of the Goateed Hater. Of the operation and the . . . that incredible shower hookup. And of Glory.

What the hell . . .

Bending down, he picked up a pillow and put it to his nose. Yeah, she'd definitely been lying beside him. But why had she come? And if she had, why hadn't she scrubbed him?

Marching out into the front hall, he grabbed his cell phone and . . . Except it wasn't as if he could call her. He didn't have her number.

He stood there for a moment like a planker. And then remembered he'd agreed to meet Goldberg in less than an hour.

Pent-up and strangely panicked over nothing he could really point a finger at, he changed into his running gear and hit the elevator. Down in the gym, he nodded at the three other guys who were pumping iron or doing sit-ups, and got on the treadmill he usually used.

He'd forgotten his damn iPod, but his mind was churning, so it wasn't like there was silence between his ears. As he fell into his pace, he tried to recall what had happened after he'd taken his shower the night before . . . but he just came up with nothing. No headache, however. Which seemed to suggest his black hole was a natural one, courtesy of the alcohol.

Through the course of the workout, he had to juice the machine a couple of times—some jackass had obviously tuned the damn thing up and the belt was sluggish. And when he reached the five-mile mark, it dawned on him that he didn't have a hangover. Then again, maybe he had so much buzzing through his head, he was too distracted to care about any ow-ow-ow.

When he stepped off the treadmill about fifteen minutes later, he needed a towel and headed for the stack by the exit. One of the lifters got there at the same time, but the guy backed off in deference.

"You first, man," he said, holding his hands out in offering.

"Thanks."

As Manny mopped up and headed for the door, he had a moment's pause as he realized no one was moving: Everybody in the place had stopped whatever he was doing and was staring at him. Quick check downward and he knew he wasn't suffering from a wardrobe malfunction. What the hell?

In the elevator, he stretched his legs and his arms and thought, Hell, he could go another ten . . . fifteen miles easy. And in spite of the hooch, he'd had a cracking night's sleep apparently, because he felt wide-awake and full of energy—but that was endorphins for you. Even when you were falling apart, a running buzz was better than caffeine . . . or sobriety.

Undoubtedly he was going to crash at some point, but he'd worry about that when the exhaustion hit.

Half an hour later, he walked into the Starbucks on Everett that he and Goldberg had first met in years ago—only, of course, back then the little café hadn't been taken over by the chain yet. The guy had been an alum of Columbia and applying for an internship at St. Francis and Manny had been on the recruiting team that had been convened to snag the bastard—Goldberg had been a star, even back then, and Manny had wanted to build the strongest department in the country.

As he got in line to order a venti latte, he looked around. The place was packed, but Goldberg had already gotten them a table at the window. No surprise there. That surgeon was always early for meetings—he'd likely been here for a good fifteen, twenty minutes. He wasn't scanning for Manny, though. He was staring into his paper mug as if he were trying to psychically stir his cappuccino.

Ah . . . he had a message.

"Manuel?" the guy behind the counter called out.

Manny accepted what he'd ordered and threaded in and around the caffeine addicts, the displays of mugs and CDs, and the triangled whiteboard that announced specials.

"Hey," he said as he took the seat across from Goldberg.

The other surgeon glanced up. And did a double take. "Ah . . . hey."

Manny took a sip of java and eased back in the chair, the curved back rail biting into his spine. "How you been?"

"I'm . . . good. God, you look fantastic."

Manny rubbed his stubbled jaw. What a lie that was. He hadn't bothered to shave, and he was in a fleece sweatshirt and blue jeans. Hardly pinup material.

"Let's cut through the pleasantries." Manny took another pull on his latte. "What do you have to tell me."

Goldberg's eyes shot off in all kinds of different directions. Until Manny took pity on him.

"They want me to go on a leave of absence, don't they."

Goldberg cleared his throat. "The hospital board feels that it would be best for . . . everyone."

"They asked you to be acting chief, yes?"

Another throat clearing. "Ah . . ."

Manny put his mug down. "It's okay. It's cool. I'm glad—you're going to be great."

"I'm sorry . . ." Goldberg shook his head. "I . . . This just feels so wrong. But . . . you can always come back, you know, later. Besides, the rest has done you good. I mean, you look—"

"Fantastic," Manny said drily. "Uh-huh."

That was what people told folks they felt sorry for.

The pair of them drank their coffees for a while in silence, and Manny wondered if the guy was thinking the same thing he was: Christ, how shit had changed. When they'd first been in this place, Goldberg had been as nervous as he was now, just for such a very different reason. And who'd have predicted that Manny would be getting benched. Back then, he'd been gunning for the top and nothing was going to stop him—or did.

Which made his reaction to this request from the board a surprise. He actually wasn't all that upset. He felt . . . unplugged somehow, as if it were happening to someone he'd once known, but had long since lost touch with: Yeah, it was a big deal, but . . . whatever.

"Well—" The sound of his phone ringing cut him off. And the clue as to what really mattered to him was in the way he scrambled like his fleece had caught fire to get the thing out.

It wasn't Payne, however. It was the vet.

"I have to take this," he said to Goldberg. "Two secs. Yeah, Doc, how is—" Manny frowned. "Really. Uh-huh. Yeah . . . yeah . . . uh-huh . . ." A slow grin grabbed traction on his face and took over, until he was probably beaming like a headlight. "Yeah. I know, right? It's a fuckin' miracle."

When he hung up the phone, he looked across the table. Goldberg's eyebrows were scaling the heights of his forehead.

"Good news. About my horse."

And that pair of brows went even higher. "I didn't know you had one."

"Her name's Glory. She's a Thoroughbred."

"Oh. Wow."

"I'm into racing."

"I didn't know that."

"Yeah."

And that was about it for the personal convo. Which gave Manny a sense of how much they talked about work. At the hospital, he and Goldberg had gone for hours talking about patients and staff issues and the running of the department. Now? They didn't have much to say to each other.

Still, he was sitting across from a very good man . . . one who was probably going to be the next chief of surgery at St. Francis. The board of directors was going to do a nationwide search, of course, but Goldberg would be chosen, because the other surgeons, who spooked easily and thrived on stability, knew and trusted him. And they should. Goldberg was technically brilliant in the OR, administratively proficient and way more even-tempered than Manny had ever been.

"You're going to do a great job," Manny said.

"What—oh. It's just temporary until you . . . you know, come back."

The guy seemed to believe it, which was testament to his kind nature. "Yeah."

Manny shifted in his chair, and as he recrossed his legs, he glanced around . . . and saw three girls across the way. They were probably eighteen or so, and the instant he made eye contact, they giggled and put their heads together like they were pretending that they hadn't been staring at him.

Feeling like he was back in the gym again, he double-checked himself. Nope. Still very much not naked. What the hell—

When he looked up, one of them had gotten to her feet and come over. "Hi. My friend thinks you're hot."

Um . . . "Ah, thanks."

"Here's her number—"

"Oh, no—nope." He took the piece of paper she put on the table and forced it back in her hand. "I'm flattered, but—"

"She's eighteen—"

"And I'm forty-five."

At this, the girl's jaw dropped. "No. Way."

"Yes. Way." He pulled a hand through his hair, wondering when he'd decided to channel *Gossip Girl* or some shit. "And I have a girlfriend."

"Oh." The chippie smiled. "That's cool—but ya coulda just said. You don't have to lie about being an old fart."

With that she sauntered off, and as she sat back down, there was a collective groan. And then he got a couple of winks.

Manny looked over at Goldberg. "Kids. I mean, honestly."

"Um. Yeah."

Okay, it was time to end this awkwardness. Looking out the window, Manny started to plan his exit—

In the glass, he saw the reflection of his face. Same high cheekbones. Same square jaw. Same lip-and-nose combo. Same black hair. But there was something different.

Leaning in, he thought . . . his eyes were . . .

"Hey," he said calmly. "I'm going to hit the loo. Will you watch my coffee before we leave?"

"Of course." Goldberg smiled in relief, as if he were glad to have both a departure strategy and a job. "Take your time."

Manny got up and went over to the single unisex bathroom. After knocking and getting no response, he opened the door, and turned on the light. As he locked himself in and the overhead fan came on, he stepped up to the mirror with its little EMPLOYEES MUST WASH THEIR HANDS sign.

The light was directly over the sink he was in front of. So by all that was right and proper, he should have looked like shit, all hollow-eyed from exhaustion, with bags you could pack for a week away, and skin the color of hummus.

That was not what the mirror was showing. Even with the piss-poor fluorescent light shining down on him, he looked ten years younger than he remembered. He was positively glowing with health, like someone had Photoshopped an earlier version of his head onto his current body.

Stepping back, he stretched his arms out in front of his chest and sank down into a squat, giving his hip an opportunity to stand up and holler. Or his thighs, which he'd run hard less than an hour ago. Or his back.

No pain. No stiffness. No aches.

His body was raring to go.

He thought about what the head vet had said to him just now over the phone, the man's voice confused and thrilled at the same time: *She's regenerated the bone and the hoof has spontaneously healed itself. It's as if the injury never occurred at all.*

Holy . . . *Christ.* What if Payne had worked her magic on him? While they'd been together? Without either of them being aware of it, what if she'd healed his body in terms of time . . . turning the clock back not just months, but a decade or more?

Manny grabbed the cross that hung from his neck.

When someone knocked on the door, he flushed the empty toilet and then ran some water to make it sound like he wasn't doing something skeevy. As he stepped out in a daze, he nodded to the round woman who wanted to get in, and headed back to Goldberg.

Sitting down, he had to wipe his sweating palms on the knees of his jeans.

"I have a favor," he said to his former colleague. "It's something I wouldn't ask of anyone else—"

"Name it. Anything. After all you've done for me—"

"I want you to give me a physical. And take some scans of me."

Goldberg immediately nodded. "I wasn't going to say it, but I think that's a good idea. The headaches . . . the forgetfulness. You need to find out if there's an . . . impairment." The guy stopped there, as if he didn't want to tee up an argument or get morbid. "Although God, I'm serious . . . I've never seen you look so good."

Manny snagged his coffee and rose to his feet, his sense of buzzing urgency having nothing to do with caffeine. "Let's go. If you have the time now?"

Goldberg was right with him. "For you, I'll always have time."

FORTY-EIGHT

Every once in a while, Qhuinn's death came back to him. It happened in dreams. In rare moments when he was still and quiet. And sometimes just to fuck his head for kicks and giggles.

He always tried to avoid the collage of sights and smells and sounds like the plague, but though he'd filed for a restraining order with his inner court, opposing counsel was being a little bitch and putting up objections . . . so the shit kept popping up.

As he lay in his bed now, the foggy stretch of mental landscape that was neither sleep nor waking was like an open line for that horrible night to phone in, and what do you know, it did some dialing, the memories ringing his bells and somehow forcing him to answer.

His own brother had been part of the honor guard who had come to beat him and the bunch of black-robed bastards had tracked him down at the side of the road as he'd walked away from his family's mansion for the last time. He'd had the few things he'd owned on his back, and he'd had no idea where he was headed. His father had thrown him out and he'd been struck from the family tree, so . . . there you go. Rootless. Directionless.

All because of his mismatched eyes.

The honor guard was just supposed to have beaten him for his offense to the bloodline. They were not supposed to kill him. But shit had gotten out of hand, and in a surprising shift, his brother had tried to stop it.

Qhuinn really remembered that part. His brother's voice telling the others to stop.

It had been too late, however, and Qhuinn had floated away not just from the pain but also from the earth itself . . . only to find himself in a sea of white fog that had parted to reveal a door. Without being told, he'd known it was the entrance to the Fade, and he'd also known that once he opened it he was donzo.

Which had seemed like a great idea at the time. Nothing to lose and all that . . .

And yet, he'd balked at the last moment. For a reason he couldn't remember.

It was the strangest thing. . . . For all that night was etched in his brain, that was the one piece he couldn't recall no matter how hard he tried.

But he remembered slamming back into his own body: As he'd regained consciousness, Blay had been doing CPR on him, and wasn't that a lip lock worth living for—

The knock that sounded on his door woke him up fully and he jacked off the pillows, willing the lights on so he was sure he knew where he was.

Yup. His bedroom. Alone.

But not for much longer.

As his adjusting eyes slowly slid over to the door, he knew who was on the other side. He could catch the delicate scent drifting in, and he knew why Layla had come. Hell, maybe that was why he hadn't been able to truly sleep—he'd expected to be woken up by her at any moment.

"Come in," he said softly.

The Chosen slipped inside silently, and as she turned to him, she looked like hell. Worn-out. A wasteland.

"Sire . . ."

"You can call me Qhuinn, you know. Please do, I mean."

"Thank you." She bowed at the waist and seemed to struggle getting herself upright. "I was wondering if I may avail myself once again of your kind offer to . . . take your vein. Verily, I am . . . depleted and unable to render myself back to the Sanctuary."

As he met her green stare, something percolated deep in his mind, some kind of . . . realization that took root and put out sprouts of I-almost-got-it, it's-just-about-to-come.

Green eyes. Green as grapes and jade and spring buds.

"Why ever are you looking at me thus?" she said, drawing the lapels of her robe more closely together.

Green eyes . . . in a face that was . . .

The Chosen glanced back at the door. "Perhaps . . . I shall just go—"

"I'm sorry." Shaking himself, he made sure the covers were at his waist and motioned her over. "Just woke up—don't mind me."

"Are you certain?"

"Abso, come here. Friends, remember?" He held out his hand, and when she got within range, he took her palm and urged her down into a sit.

"Sire? You're still staring at me."

Qhuinn searched her face and then trolled down her body. Green eyes . . .

So what about the damn eyes? It wasn't like he'd never seen them before—

Green eyes . . .

He swallowed a curse. Christ, this was like having a song in your head that you could remember everything but the words to.

"Sire?"

"Qhuinn. Say it, please."

"Qhuinn."

He smiled a little. "Here, take what you need."

As he lifted his wrist, he thought, Man, she was so damned thin, as she bent down and opened her mouth. Her fangs were long and very white, but delicate. Not like his. And her strike was as gentle and ladylike as the rest of her.

Which the traditionalist in him thought was only proper.

While she fed, he looked at her blond hair that was twisted into a complex weave, and her spare shoulders, and her pretty hands.

Green eyes.

"Christ." When she made as if to pull out, he put his hand on the back of her neck and kept her at his wrist. "It's okay. Foot cramp."

More like brain cramp.

In frustration, he lifted his head and, in lieu of hitting the wall with it, rubbed his eyes. When he refocused, he was staring at the door . . .

. . . Layla had just come through.

Instantly, he was sucked back into the dream. But not about the beating or his brother. He saw himself standing at the entrance unto the Fade . . . standing in front of the white panels . . . standing with his hand out, about to reach for the knob.

Reality warped and pulled and went taffy-twisted until he didn't know whether he was awake or asleep . . . or dead.

The swirl started to form in the center of the door, as if whatever it had been made of had liquefied to the consistency of milk. And from out of the tornadic center an image coalesced and came forward, more as a sound would carry than as if something visual would take shape.

It was the face of a young female.

A young female with blond hair and refined features . . . and pale green eyes.

She was staring out at him, holding his eyes sure as if she had captured his face in her small, pretty hands.

Then she blinked. And her irises changed color.

One became green and the other blue. Just like his.

"Sire!"

At first he was utterly confused—wondering why in the hell the young female had called him that. How did she know who he was?

"Qhuinn! Let me seal you up!"

He blinked. And discovered that he had thrown himself against the headboard, and in the process, he'd torn Layla's fangs from his flesh and he was hemorrhaging all over the sheets.

"Let me—"

He strong-armed the Chosen back and sealed his own mouth on the wound. As he took care of himself, he couldn't take his eyes off Layla.

It was waaaaay too easy to overlay that young female's features on Layla's face and find something so much deeper than similarity.

As his heart started pounding, he took a little time out to remind himself that he'd never done the prescient thing. Unlike V, he couldn't see into the future.

Layla moved slowly as she got off the bed, like she didn't want to spook him. "Shall I go get Jane? Or perhaps it would be best if I just left."

Qhuinn opened his mouth . . . and found that nothing came out.

Wow. He'd never been in a car accident, but he imagined the curling dread he felt now was probably the way things went when you saw someone blow a stop sign and come gunning for your side door: You triangulated their direction and their speed against your own and came to the conclusion that impact was imminent.

Although he couldn't imagine a world in which he got Layla pregnant.

"I have seen the future," he said from a distance.

Layla's hands lifted to her throat as if she were choking. "Is it bad?"

"It's . . . not possible. At all."

As he put his head in his palms, all he could see in the darkness was that face . . . the one that was part Layla's and part his.

Oh, God . . . save them both. Save . . . all of them.

"Sire? You're scaring me."

Well, that made two of them . . .

Except it couldn't be. Could it?

"I'm going to go," she said roughly. "I thank you for your gift."

He nodded and couldn't look at her. "You're welcome."

As the door shut shortly thereafter, he shuddered, a cold, bracing fear settling into his bones . . . and going right into his soul.

Ironic, really, he thought. His parents had never wanted him to reproduce, and go fig—the idea of shafting Layla with a defective daughter, or even worse, laying his fucked-up eyes upon an innocent young female, made him embrace his vow of celibacy like nothing else could.

And actually, he should be glad. Of all the destinies he could have seen, this was one hundred percent avoidable, wasn't it.

He just was never going to have sex with Layla.

Ever.

So it was all an impossibility. End of.

FORTY-NINE

Manny got back to his condo around six p.m. All told he had spent eight hours at the hospital getting poked and prodded by various people he knew better than members of his extended family.

The results were in his e-mail in-box—because he'd forwarded copies of everything from his hospital account to his personal one. Not that there was any reason to open all those attachments. He knew the notes by heart. The results by heart. The X-rays and CAT scans by heart.

Tossing his keys down on the counter in the kitchen, he cracked the Sub-Zero and wished there were fresh orange juice in there. Instead . . . soy sauce packets from the Chinese takeout down the street . . . a bottle of ketchup . . . and a round tin of some kind of leftovers from a business dinner he'd had two weeks ago.

Whatever. He wasn't all that hungry.

Restless and twitchy, he measured the light in the sky: Still some lingering to the west.

He wasn't going to have to wait long, though.

Payne was going to come back to him after the sun had set. He could feel it in his bones. He was still not sure why she'd spent the night with him or why his memories remained, but he had to wonder if she was finally going to fix that when she got here.

Heading down to the bedroom, his first move was to snag the pillows from the floor and put them back where they belonged. Then he smoothed out the duvet . . . and was ready to get packing. Over at his bureau, he started taking out clothes and stacking them on the neatened bed.

Nothing to go back to at St. Francis. He'd resigned in the midst of all the tests.

No reason to stay in Caldwell—if anything, it was probably better that he get out of town.

No clue where he was headed, but you didn't need a destination to leave somewhere.

Socks. Boxers. Polo shirts. Jeans. Khakis.

One advantage to having a wardrobe that consisted mainly of scrubs provided by a hospital was that he didn't have a lot to pack. And God knew he had enough gym bags.

In the bottommost drawer of the bureau, he took out the only two sweaters he owned—

The picture frame underneath them was facing down, the little cardboard kickstand lying nice and flat against the back.

Manny reached out and picked the thing up. He didn't have to turn it over to see who it was. He'd memorized the man's face years and years ago.

And yet it was still a shock to pivot the picture in his hands and look at his father's image.

Handsome SOB. Very, very handsome. Dark hair—just like Manny's. Deep-set eyes—just like Manny's.

Annnd that was as far as he was going to go with the retrospective. As always, when it came to shit about his dad, he just pushed it all into a mental corner and got on with his life.

Which tonight meant that the frame went into the nearest duffel and that was that—

The knock on the glass came too soon to be her, he thought.

Except then he glanced at the clock and realized that this packing routine had lasted a good hour.

Looking over his shoulder, his heart went triple-time as he saw Payne standing on the far side of the glass. God . . . damn . . . she knocked him out. She'd braided her hair and she was in a long white robe that was tied at the waist and she was . . . breathtaking.

Going over to the slider, he opened the door, and the cold blast of the night hit him in the face, snapping him into focus.

Smiling broadly, Payne didn't so much come in as leap into his arms, her body so very solid against his own, her arms so very strong around his neck.

He gave himself a split second of holding her . . . for the last time. And then, as much as it killed him, he set her down and used the excuse of closing the gusting wind out to move away even farther.

When he glanced back at her, the joy that had been in her face was gone and she was wrapping her arms around herself.

"I figured you would come back," he said hoarsely.

"I . . . I had good news." Payne glanced at the lineup of gym bags on the bed. "Whatever are you doing?"

"I have to leave here."

As her eyes shut briefly, it nearly destroyed him not to go over and comfort her. But this was hard enough already. Touching her again was going to break him in half.

"I went to the doctor today," he said. "I spent all afternoon at the hospital."

She blanched. "Are you ill?"

"Not exactly." He paced around and ended up at the bureau, where he pushed the empty bottom drawer back into place. "Far from it, actually . . . It appears that my body has regenerated parts of itself." His hand went down to his lower body. "For years, I've had an arthritic hip from too much sports—I've always known that eventually it was going to need replacing. As of the X-rays taken today? It's in perfect condition. No arthritis to be found, no inflammation. Good as it was when I was eighteen."

As her mouth fell open, he figured he might as well hit her with all of it. Pulling up his shirtsleeve, he ran his hand over his forearm. "I've had freckles from sun damage for the last two decades—they're gone now." He bent over and lifted his pant leg. "The shin splints I have from time to time? Disappeared. And this is in spite of the fact that I ran eight miles this morning without even thinking about it—in under

Someone caught his hand and froze his arm. "Not here."

The fact that it was not the bleeding-heart Throe was the only thing that stopped him. It was Zypher.

"We take her and bring her home." The warrior laughed darkly, the erotic tone in his voice deepening. "You have been relieved, but there are others among us who require what you had last night. After that? Then you can teach her the repercussions of vengeful acts."

Zypher was the one among them mostly likely to think up a plan like that. And though the idea of slaughtering her outright held vast appeal, Xcor had waited too long not to savor her demise.

So many years.

Too many years—until he had given up hope of finding her, only his dreams keeping alive the memory of what had defined him and given him his position in life.

Yes, he thought. It would be fitting to have this done the Bloodletter's way. No easy out for the female.

Xcor resettled his scythe, just as the murderess went to work properly on the slayers. Without warning, she leapt forward and took one of them at the waist, ducking under its flailing arms and driving it back against the building. It happened so fast that the second *lesser* was too surprised—and obviously untrained—to save its friend.

Although even if number two had been more of a match for her, it wouldn't have stood a chance. In virtually the same moment as she attacked, the female spun out a hubcap from behind her and it hit the slayer right in the neck, slicing deep and distracting it immediately from the quest to get her. As black oil sprang forth and its knees wobbled, she dispatched the slayer she had pinned against the brick by punching it twice in the face and once in the Adam's apple. Then she picked it up bodily and slammed it down upon her upraised knee.

The crack of the spine was loud.

And as it faded, she spun around to confront those who had been watching her work. Which was not a surprise. Someone as good as she was would have been immediately aware that others were upon her.

Tilting her head to one side, she was not alarmed—but then, why would she be? They were in the shadows and very clearly of her species: Until Xcor revealed himself, she would have no idea the danger she was in.

"Good evening, female," he said in a low tone from the darkness.

"Who is there?" she called out.

Now is the time, he thought, stepping forward into a shaft of light—

"We are not alone," Throe whispered abruptly.

Xcor stopped his advance, his eyes narrowing on the seven slayers that had stepped into view at the far end of the alley.

Indeed. They were very much not alone.

And later, Xcor would come to believe that the only reason he successfully took the female into his custody was the arrival of those fresh *lessers*. The advancing front of the enemy demanded her eyes—and her attention. But before she could dematerialize into another position, Xcor was upon her.

In spite of the way his heart was pounding, vengeance gave him the focus to scatter his molecules just as she turned to confront the squadron which approached. His steel cuff went upon her wrist in the blink of an eye, and as she wheeled around with bald fury in her face, he was reminded of the incineration she had cast upon his sire.

What saved him was a *lesser's* gunshot.

The pop was of little note, but its consequence was of spectacular benefit: Just as she was lifting her free hand to lay upon him, her leg went loose and she tumbled toward the ground, the bullet clearly having hit something vital. And in her moment of weakness, Xcor dominated her—he had one chance to get her under his control. If he didn't take it, he was not sure he would walk away from this.

Slapping the other cuff on her free wrist, he then grabbed her braid and wound it around her throat. Pulling the hair tight, he cut off her air supply just as his fighters surged forward with weapons drawn.

Oh, how she struggled. So valiant. So powerful.

She was but a female . . . except so much more than that. She was nearly as strong as he was, and that was not her only advantage. Even captured and on the verge of asphyxiation, her pale eyes remained locked on his own, until he felt as though she could reach into his mind and take over his very thoughts.

But he would not be daunted. Whilst the sounds of fighting broke out in the alley, he held the diamond stare of his sire's killer as his huge arms cranked the noose tighter and tighter about her neck.

Struggling to breathe, she gasped and writhed, her lips moving.

Dipping down his ear, he wanted to hear what she had to—

". . . why . . . ?"

Xcor recoiled, just as the fight went out of her and those stunning eyes rolled back into her head.

Dearest Scribe Virgin, she didn't even know who he was.

FIFTY-ONE

As man caves went, V had always thought that the billiards room at the Brotherhood's mansion had it all. Giant-screen TV with surround sound. Couches with enough padding to qualify as beds. Fireplace for heat and that attractive smoldering-ember shit. Bar with every conceivable drink, soda, cocktail, tea, coffee, beer, whatever in it.

And a billiards table. Duh.

The only "bad" thing was a bene, anyway: The popcorn machine was a recent addition—and an odd sort of battlefield. Rhage loved to play with the damn thing, but every time he did, Fritz got nervous and wanted in on the action. Either way, it was cool. The little wicker baskets would get filled and then whichever of the pair hadn't done the loading and dispensing got a shot at it.

As Vishous waited to take his next pool shot, he snagged a square of blue chalk and polished the tip of his cue. Across the green felt, Butch bent over and lined up his angles while Rick Ross's "Aston Martin Music" pumped.

"Seven in the corner," the cop said.

"You're going to make that, aren't you." V put the chalk back down and shook his head as there was a smack, a roll, and a clunk. "Bastard."

Butch glanced over, a whole lot of "gotcha" glowing on his puss. "I'm just that good. Sorry, sucker."

The cop took a drink from his Lag and repositioned himself on the other side of the table. As he sized up the balls, his smart-ass smile was right where it should be: front and center, revealing that slightly off porcelain cap.

V had been keeping his eye on the guy. After they'd spent hours alone together, they'd parted awkwardly and taken separate showers. Fortunately, though, the hot water had been a reset for them both, and when they'd met up again in the Pit's kitchen, it had been business as usual.

And shit had remained that way.

Not that there wasn't the temptation to ask the guy whether all was still cool. Like, every five minutes. It felt like they had fought a battle together, and were sporting the stress fractures and the fading black-and-blues to prove it. But V was going with what was in front of him: his best friend whipping his ass at pool.

"And that's game over," the cop announced as the eight ball circled and got good and sunk.

"You beat me."

"Yup." Butch grinned and raised his glass. "You want another round."

"You bet your balls."

The scent of melted butter and the buckshot sound of kernels going apeshit announced Rhage's arrival—or maybe Fritz's? Nope, it was Hollywood over by the machine with his Mary.

V leaned back so he could look through the archway, across the foyer and into the dining room, where the butler and his staff were setting up Last Meal.

"Man, Rhage is playin' with fire," Butch said as he started to rack up the balls.

"I give Fritz thirty seconds before he's— Here he comes."

"I'm going to pretend I'm not here."

V took a swig of his Goose. "Me too."

While they got busy grabbing balls, Fritz came steaming across the foyer like a missile seeking a heat source.

"Watch your ass, Hollywood, true?" V muttered as Rhage came over with a basket of popped-and-fluffy.

"It's good for him. He needs the exercise—Fritz! How are you, buddy?"

While Butch and V rolled their eyes, Rehv came in with Ehlena under his mink-clad arm. The Mohawked motherfucker was bundled up, as usual, and he was as always relying on his cane, but his mated-male perma-grin was in place, and his *shellan* was glowing at his side.

"Boys," he said.

Various grunts greeted him as Z and Bella came in with Nalla, and Phury and Cormia arrived because they were spending the day. Wrath and Beth were likely still up in the study—maybe looking at paperwork; maybe putting George briefly at the head of the stairs so they could have some "private time."

When John and Xhex came down with Blay and Saxton, the only people not in attendance were Qhuinn and Tohrment, who were likely in the gym, and Marissa, who was at Safe Place.

Well, those three and his Jane, who was down in the clinic re-stocking the supplies that had been drained from the other night.

Oh, and of course his twin, who was no doubt . . . "um, yeah-ing" . . . with that surgeon of hers.

With all the new arrivals in the room, the sound of deep voices multiplied and exploded as people poured drinks and passed the baby around and copped handfuls of popcorn. Meanwhile, Rhage and Fritz were opening a fresh load of kernels. And someone was changing the channels on the TV—likely Rehv, who was never satisfied with whatever was on. And another person was poking at the roaring fire.

"Hey. You still all right?" Butch said softly.

V camouflaged his startle routine by taking a hand-rolled out of the pocket of his leathers. The cop had spoken so quietly there was no way anyone else had heard it, and this was a good thing. Yeah, he was trying to ditch the ultrareserved shit, but he didn't want anyone to know how far he and Butch had gone. That was private.

Flicking up a light, he inhaled. "Yeah. I really fucking am, true." Then he glanced into the hazels of his best friend. "And . . . you?"

"Yeah. Me, too."

"Cool."

"Cool."

Heeeeeeeeeeey, check his shit out with the relating. Any more of this and he was going to get a gold star on his chart.

A knuckle tap later and Butch was back to the game, lining up his first shot as V basked in the glow of interrelating like a pro.

He was taking another hit from his short-and-squat of Goose when his eyes skipped to the arched doorway of the room.

Jane hesitated as she glanced inside, her white coat opening as she leaned to the side, as if she were looking for him.

When their eyes met, she smiled a little. And then a lot.

His first impulse was to hide his own grin behind his Goose. But then he stopped himself. New world order.

Come on, *smile*, motherfucker, he thought.

Jane gave a short wave and played it cool, which was what they usually did when they were together in public. Turning away, she headed over to the bar to make herself something.

"Hold up, cop," V murmured, putting his drink down and bracing his cue against the table.

Feeling like he was fifteen, he put his hand-rolled between his teeth and tucked his wife-beater tightly into the waistband of his leathers. A quick smooth of the hair and he was . . . well, as ready as he could be.

He approached Jane from behind just as she struck up a convo with Mary—and when his *shellan* pivoted around to greet him, she seemed a little surprised that he'd come up to her. "Hi, V . . . How are—"

Vishous stepped in close, putting them body to body, and then he wrapped his arms around her waist. Holding her with possession, he slowly bent her backward until she gripped his shoulders and her hair fell from her face.

As she gasped, he said exactly what he thought: "I missed you."

And on that note, he put his mouth on hers and kissed the ever-living hell out of her, sweeping one hand down to her hip as he slipped his tongue in her mouth, and kept going and going and going . . .

He was vaguely aware that the room had fallen stone silent and that everything with a heartbeat was staring at him and his mate. But whatever. This was what he wanted to do, and he was going to do it in front of everyone—and the king's dog, as it turned out.

Because Wrath and Beth came in from the foyer.

As Vishous slowly righted his *shellan*, the catcalls and whistling started up, and someone threw a handful of popcorn like it was confetti.

"Now that's what I'm talkin' 'bout," Hollywood said. And threw more popcorn.

Vishous cleared his throat. "I have an announcement to make."

Right. Okay, there were a lot of eyes on the pair of them. But he was so going to suck up his inclination to bow out.

Tucking his flustered and blushing Jane into his side, he said loud and clear: "We're getting mated. Properly. And I expect you all to be there and . . . Yeah, that's it."

Dead. Quiet.

Then Wrath released the handle on George's harness and started to clap. Loud and slow. "About. Fucking. Time."

His brothers and their *shellans* and all the guests of the house followed suit, and then the fighters broke out into a chant that raised the roof and then some—their voices vibrating through the air.

As he glanced over at Jane, she was glowing. Utterly glowing.

"Maybe I should have asked first," he murmured.

"Nope." She kissed him. "This is *perfect*."

Vishous started to laugh. Man, if this was living out loud, he'd ditch the tight-ass routine any night: His brothers were behind him, his *shellan* was happy, and . . . okay, he could do without the popcorn in his hair, but whatever.

Minutes later, Fritz brought in champagne flutes, and now there was a different kind of popping, corks going flying as people talked even louder than before.

As someone shoved a glass into his mitt, he whispered in Jane's ear, "Champagne makes me horny."

"Really . . ."

Slipping his hand down her hip . . . and lower . . . he tugged her in against his sudden arousal. "You ever meet the hall bathroom?"

"I do believe we've been formally introd— Vishous!"

He stopped nipping at her neck, but kept up with rolling his hips against hers. Which was a little indecent, but nothing that any of the other couples hadn't done from time to time.

"Yes?" he drawled. When she seemed speechless, he sucked on her lip and growled, "If you recall, we were discussing the bathroom? I was thinking maybe I could reacquaint the pair of you. Not sure if you're aware of it, but that sink counter has been crying out for you."

"And you do some of your best work at sinks."

V dragged one fang up her throat. "True that."

As his erection started thumping, he took his female's hand—

The grandfather clock in the corner started to chime, and then he heard four deep bongs. Which made him pull back a little and check his watch even though he didn't need to—because that clock had kept time correctly for two hundred years.

Four a.m.? Where the hell was Payne?

As the urge to go to the Commodore and bring his sister home struck hard, he reminded himself that although dawn was coming fast, she still had maybe an hour left. And given what he and Jane were about to do behind a closed door, he couldn't really blame her for eking out every moment she had with her male—even if he was absolutely, positively not going there.

"Everything okay?" Jane asked.

Getting back with the program, he dropped his head. "It will be as soon as I get you up on that counter."

He and Jane were in the loo for forty-five minutes.

When they came out, everyone was still in the billiards room. The music had been cranked and Lil Wayne's "I'm Not a Human Being" was echoing up to the foyer's ceiling. The *doggen* were buzzing around with little fancy crap on silver trays, and Rhage had a circle of laughing people around him as he cracked jokes.

For a moment, it felt like the good old days.

But then he didn't see his sister in the crowd. And no one came over to tell him she'd gone up to the guest room she'd been using.

"I'll be right back," he said to Jane. A quick kiss and he ducked out of the party, skated across the foyer, and went into the empty dining room. Rounding the fully set but very empty table, he got his cell from his pocket and dialed the phone he'd given her.

No answer.

He tried again. No answer. Third time? No . . . goddamn answer.

With a curse, he punched in Manello's number, and shuddered at what he might be interrupting—but they'd probably pulled the drapes and lost track of time. And phones could defo get lost in sheets, he thought with a wince.

Ring . . . ring . . . ring . . .

"Fucking pick up—"

"Hello?"

Manello sounded bad. Gunshot bad. Mortal-injury bad.

"Where is my sister." Because there was no way the surgeon was like that if she were in his bed.

The pause was not good news, either. "I don't know. She left here hours ago."

"Hours?"

"What's going on?"

"Jesus Christ—" V hung up on the guy, and called her phone again. And again.

Cranking his head around, he looked out to the foyer and the door to the vestibule.

With a subtle whirring sound, the steel shutters that protected the house from the sun started to ease down into place.

Come on, Payne . . . come home. Right now.

Right . . .

Now . . .

Jane's gentle touch snapped him back to reality. "Is everything okay?" she asked.

His first instinct was to cover it all up with a crack about Rhage's impression of Steve-O in a projectile Porta-Potty. Instead, he forced himself to be real with his mate.

"Payne is . . . maybe MIA." As she gasped and reached out with her other hand, he kind of wanted to bolt. But he held his feet to the Oriental rug. "She left Manello's"—*hours ago*—"ah, hours ago. And now I'm just praying to a mother I despise that she comes through that door."

Jane didn't say anything further. Instead, she angled herself so she could also see the way in from the vestibule and waited with him.

Taking her hand, he realized that it was a relief not to be alone as the party raged on across the way . . . and his sister still did not come home.

That vision he'd had of her on the black horse, going at a screaming tilt, came back to him in the silence of the dining room. Her dark hair was flying out behind her as the stallion's mane streaked as well, the pair on a tear . . . to God only knew where.

Allegorical? he wondered. Or just the yearnings of her brother that she finally be free . . . ?

Jane and he were still standing there together, staring at a door that did not open, when the sun officially rose twenty-two minutes later.

As Manny paced around his condo, he was going balls. Absolute balls. He'd meant to leave his condo shortly after Payne had, but he'd run out of gas and had ended up spending the whole night staring out . . . into the night.

Too fucking empty.

He'd been just too fucking empty to move.

When the phone had rung beside him, he'd checked the number and come briefly alive. Private caller. It had to be her.

And considering his mind had been going over what he'd said to her again and again, he'd needed a second to pull things together after all that useless spinning. That speech he'd rolled out had, at the time, seemed so rational and reasonable and smart . . . until he'd stared down the barrel at a future that was beyond vacant and deep into black hole.

He'd accepted the call not expecting anything male on the connection. Much less her brother.

Much less the bastard going all surprise-surprise when Payne wasn't at the condo.

While Manny marched around in circles, he stared at his phone, willing it to ring again . . . willing the fucking piece of shit to go off and have it be Payne telling him she was okay. Or her brother. Anyone.

Any-cocksucking-one.

For chrissakes, Al Roker could call him with the goddamn news she was all right.

Except the dawn arrived way too soon and his phone stayed way too quiet. And like a loser, he went into his recent-calls list and tried to hit back "private caller." When all he got was a dial tone again, he wanted to throw the cell across the room, but then where would that leave him.

The impotence was a crusher. A total crusher.

He wanted to go out and . . . shit, find Payne if she was lost. Or bring her the fuck back home if she was out by herself. Or—

The phone went off. Private caller.

"Thank fuck," he said as he accepted it. "Payne—"

"No."

Manny closed his eyes: Her brother sounded like hell. "Where is she."

"We don't know. And there's nothing that we can do from here—we're trapped inside." The guy exhaled like he was smoking something. "What the fuck happened before she left? I thought she'd be spending all night with you. It's cool if you two . . . you know . . . but why did she leave so early?"

"I told her it wasn't going to work out."

Long silence. "What the *fuck* are you thinking?"

Clearly if it hadn't been all bright and sunny outside, motherfucker would have been knocking on Manny's door, looking to kick some Italian ass.

"I thought that would make you happy."

"Oh, yeah. Abso—break my sister's fucking heart. I'm all for that." Another sharp exhale, like he was blowing smoke. "She's in *love* with you, asshole."

Didn't that stop him in his tracks. But he got back with the program. "Listen, she and I . . ."

At that point, he was supposed to explain the stuff about the results of his physical and how he was all freaked out and didn't know what the repercussions were. But the trouble was, in the hours since Payne had taken off, he'd come to realize that however true that shit was, there was a more fundamental thing going on at the core of him: He was being a little bitch. What the go-away had really been about was the fact that he was shitting in his pants because he'd actually fallen in love with a woman . . . female . . . whatever. Yeah, there was a tremendous overlay of metaphysical stuff he didn't understand and couldn't explain, blah, blah, blah. But at the center of it all, he felt so much for Payne that he didn't know himself anymore, and *that* was the terrifying part.

He'd pussied out when he'd had the chance.

But that was done now. "She and I are in love," he said clearly.

And damn him to hell, he should have had the balls to tell her. And hold her. And keep her.

"So like I said, what the *fuck* are you thinking."

"Excellent question."

"Jesus . . . Christ."

"Listen, how can I help—I can be out in daylight, and there is nothing I won't do to get her back. *Nothing.*" Energized by obsession, he headed for his keys. "If she isn't with you, where would she go. What about that place . . . the Sanctuary?"

"Cormia and Phury went there. *Nada.*"

"So . . ." He hated thinking like this. "What about your enemies. Where are they during the day—I'll go there."

Cursing. More exhaling. Pause. Then a flicking sound and an inhale, as if the guy were lighting up another cigarette.

"You know, you shouldn't smoke," Manny heard himself say.

"Vampires don't get cancer."

"Really?"

"Yup. Okay, here's the deal. We don't have a specific locale for the Lessening Society. The slayers tend to imbed themselves in the human population in small groups so it's nearly impossible to find them without serious disturbance. The only thing . . . Go to the alleys by the riverfront downtown. She might have met up with some *lessers*—you're going to look for evidence of a fight. There'd be black oil everywhere. Like engine oil. And it would smell sweet—like roadkill and baby powder. It's pretty fucking distinctive. Let's start with that."

"I need to be able to reach you. You need to give me your number."

"I'll text you with it. Do you have a gun? Any weapon?"

"Yeah. I do." Manny was already taking the licensed forty out of his closet. He'd been living in the city all his adult life and shit happened—so he'd learned his way around a gun about twenty years ago.

"Tell me it's bigger than a nine."

"Yup."

"Get a knife. You're going to need a stainless-steel blade."

"Roger that." He headed for the kitchen and took out the biggest, sharpest Henckels he had. "Anything else?"

"A flamethrower. Nunchakus. Throwing stars. Uzi. You want me to go on."

If only he had that kind of arsenal.

"I'm going to get her back, vampire. Mark my fucking words—I'm getting her back." He grabbed his wallet and was heading for the door when dread stopped him. "How many of them are there. Your enemies."

"An endless supply."

"Are they . . . male?"

Pause. "Used to be. Before they got turned, they were human men."

A sound came out of Manny's mouth . . . one that he was very sure he had never uttered before.

"Nah, she can handle herself with the hand-to-hand," her brother said in a dead tone. "She's tough like that."

"Not what I was thinking." He had to scrub his eyes. "She's a virgin."

"Still . . . ?" the guy asked after a moment.

"Yeah. It wasn't right for me to . . . take that from her."

Oh, God, the idea she could be hurt . . .

He couldn't even finish the sentence to himself.

Snapping into action, he stepped out of his place and went over to call the elevator. As he waited, he realized that there had only been silence on the other end of the phone for a while. "Hello? You there."

"Yeah." Her twin's voice cracked. "Yeah. I'm here."

The connection between them remained open as Manny got into the elevator and hit P. And the entire trip down to his car was passed with the two of them saying absolutely nothing at all.

"They're impotent," her twin finally muttered just as Manny was getting into the Porsche. "They can't have sex."

Well, didn't that do nothing to make him feel better. And going by the tone of her brother's voice, the other guy was thinking the same way.

"I'll call you," Manny said.

"You do that, my man. You frickin' do that."

FIFTY-TWO

When Payne came back to consciousness, she did not open her eyes. No reason to give away the fact that she was aware of her surroundings.

Bodily sensation informed her of her situation: She was on her feet, with her wrists shackled and pulled out to the sides and her back against a stone wall that was damp. Her ankles were likewise tethered and stretched apart and her head had lolled forward into a very uncomfortable position.

When she drew breaths in, she smelled musky dirt, and the voices of males percolated up from the left of where she was.

Very deep voices. Cast with drumming excitement, as if a benefit had fallen into their clutches.

She was it.

As she gathered her strength, she was under no illusions of what they were going to do to her. Soon. And as she drew herself together, she shied away from thoughts of her Manuel . . . of how, if these males had their way, they would spoil her many times over before they murdered her, taking what rightly should have been her healer's—

Except she could not and would not think of him. That cognition was a black pit that would suck her in and trap her and render her defenseless.

Instead, she pulled at the threads of memory, melding the images of the faces of her kidnappers with what she knew from the bowls in the Sanctuary.

Why? she wondered. She had not a clue why the one with the ruined lip had set upon her with such hatred—

"I know you wake." The voice was impossibly low and heavily accented and right next to her ear. "Your breathing pattern has changed."

Lifting her lids along with her head, she shifted her eyes unto the soldier. He was in the shadows beside her so she could not see him properly.

Abruptly, the other voices silenced, and she sensed many stares were upon her.

So this was what prey felt like.

"I'm hurt that you remember nothing of me, female." At that, he brought a candle close to his face. "I have thought of you every night since we first met. A hundred and a hundred years afore."

She narrowed her eyes. Black hair. Cruel eyes of dark blue. And a harelip that he had obviously been born with.

"Remember me." It was not a question, but a demand. "*Remember* me."

And then it came back. The small village on the edge of a wooded glen. Where she had killed her father. This was one of the Bloodletter's soldiers. No doubt they all were.

Oh, she was definitely prey, she thought. And they were looking forward to hurting her before they killed her in retaliation for taking their leader from them.

"*Remember me.*"

"You are a soldier of the Bloodletter's."

"*No*," he barked, putting his face in hers. "I am *more* than that."

As she frowned, he just backed off and paced around in a tight circle, his fists cranked tight, the candle dripping wax onto his curled hand.

When he returned front and center afore her, he was in control. Barely. "I am his son. His *son*. You stole from me my father—"

"Impossible."

"—unjustly— *What?*"

Into his stuttered silence, she said loudly and clearly, "It is impossible that you are his son."

When her words registered, the blind fury in his face was the very definition of hatred, and his hand shook as he lifted it up over his shoulder.

He slapped her so hard she saw stars.

As Payne righted her head and met him in the eye, she was not going to have any of this. Not his mistaken belief. Not this group of males sizing her up. Not the criminal ignorance.

Payne held the stare of her captor. "The Bloodletter sired one and only one male offspring—"

"The Black Dagger Brother Vishous." Hard laughter echoed. "I have heard well the stories of his perversions—"

"My brother is not a pervert!"

At this point, Payne lost all control, the anger that had carried her through that night she had killed her father coming back and taking over: Vishous was her blood and her savior for all he had done for her. And she was not going to have him disrespected—even if defending him cost her her life.

Between one heartbeat and the next she was consumed by an inner energy that illuminated the cellar they were all in with a brilliant white light.

The cuffs burned away, falling down to the packed dirt floor with a clanking.

And the male before her leaped back and braced into a fighting stance while the others grabbed for weapons. But she was not going to attack—at least, not physically.

"Listen to me now," she proclaimed. "I am birthed of the Scribe Virgin. I am of the Chosen Sanctuary. So when I say unto you the Bloodletter, my father, bore no other male issue, that is *fact*."

"Untrue," the male breathed. "And you—you cannot have been born unto the Mother of the race. There is none born unto her—"

Payne lifted her glowing arms. "I am what I am. Deny it at your peril."

The male's complexion drained of what color had been in it, and there was a long, tense standoff, as conventional weapons pointed in her direction and she glowed with holy fury.

And then the head soldier's fighting stance relaxed, his hands falling to his sides, his thighs straightening. "It cannae be," he choked out. "None of it . . ."

Fool male, she thought.

Kicking up her chin, she declared, "I am the begotten issue of the Bloodletter and the Scribe Virgin. And I say to you now"—she stepped forward to him—"that I killed *my* father, *not* yours."

Lifting her palm, she peeled back and slapped him across the face. "And do *not* insult my blood."

As the female struck him, Xcor's head whipped so far and so fast to the side that he pulled his shoulder in the attempt to keep the damn thing stuck to his spine. Blood immediately flooded into his mouth, and he spit some of it out before righting himself.

Verily, the female before him was majestic in her fury and her resolve. Nearly as tall as he was, she stared him straight in the eye, her feet planted, her hands in fists she was prepared to use against him and his band of bastards.

No ordinary female, this. And not just because of the way she had dissolved those cuffs.

In fact, as she met his gaze full-on, she reminded him of his father. She had the Bloodletter's iron will not just in her face or her eyes or her body. It was in her soul.

Indeed, he had the very clear sense that they could all fall upon her and she would fight them each and every until the last breath and beat of her heart.

God knew she slapped like a warrior. Not some limp-wristed female.

But . . .

"He was my father. He told me that."

"He was a liar." At that, she did not blink. Nor did she duck her eyes or her chin. "I have witnessed within the seeing bowls countless bastard daughters. But there was one and only one son, and that is my twin."

Xcor was not prepared to hear this in front of his males.

He glanced over at them. Even Throe had armed himself, and on each of their faces was impatient rage. One nod from him and they would set upon her, even if she incinerated them all.

"Leave us," he commanded.

Not surprisingly, Zypher was the one who started to argue. "Let us hold her whilst you—"

"Leave us."

There was a beat of immobility. Then Xcor screamed, *"Leave us!"*

In a flash, they peeled off and disappeared up the stairwell to the darkened house above. Then the door was shut, and footsteps rang out from up above as they paced around like caged animals.

Xcor refocused on the female.

And for the longest time, he just stared at her. "I have searched for you for centuries."

"I was not upon the Earth. Until now."

She remained unbowed as he confronted her in private. Totally unbowed. And as he searched her face, he could feel a glacial shift in the ice fields of his heart.

"Why," he said roughly. "Why did you . . . kill him."

The female blinked slowly as if she didn't want to show vulnerability and needed a moment to make sure she put none out. "Because he hurt my twin. He . . . tortured my brother, and for that he needed to die."

So perhaps the lore had a veracity after all, Xcor thought.

Indeed, like most soldiers, he had long known the gossiped story of the Bloodletter having demanded for his begotten son to be pinned upon the ground and tattooed . . . and then castrated. The tale had it that the wounding had been but partial—it was rumored that Vishous had magically burned through the binds that had held him and then escaped into the night before the cutting had been complete.

Xcor looked over to the cuffs that had fallen from the female's wrists—burned off.

Lifting his own hands, he stared down at the flesh. That had never glowed. "He told me I was born unto a female he had visited for blood. He told me . . . she didn't want me because of my . . ." He touched his malformed upper lip, leaving the sentence unfinished. "He took me and . . . he taught me to fight. At his side."

Xcor was vaguely aware that his voice was rough, but he didn't care. He felt as though he was looking into a mirror and seeing a reflection of himself he did not recognize.

"He told me I was his son—and he owned me like his son. After his death, I stepped into his boots, as sons do."

The female measured him, and then shook her head. "And I say unto you that he lied. Look into my eyes. Know that I speak the truth you should have heard long, long ago." Her voice dropped to a mere whisper. "I know well the betrayal of blood. I know that pain which you feel now. It is not right, this burden you carry. But base not a vengeance on fiction, I beg of you. For I shall be forced to kill you—and if I do not, my twin will hunt you down with the Brotherhood and make you pray for your own demise."

Xcor searched into himself and saw something he despised, but could not ignore: He had no memory of the bitch who had born him, but he knew too well the story of how she had cast him out from the birthing room because of his ugliness.

He had wanted to be claimed. And the Bloodletter had done that—the physical disfigurement had never mattered to that male. He had cared only about the things Xcor had had in abundance: speed, endurance, agility, power . . . and deadly focus.

Xcor had always assumed he'd gotten that from his father's side.

"He named me," he heard himself say. "My mother refused to. But the Bloodletter . . . named me."

"I am so very sorry."

And the strangest thing? He believed her. Once ready to fight to the death, she now appeared to be saddened.

Xcor paced off from her and walked around.

If he was not the son of the Bloodletter, who was he? And would he still lead his males? Would they follow him into battle e'er again?

"I look into the future and see . . . nothing," he muttered.

"I know how that feels as well."

He stopped and faced the female. She had linked her arms loosely over her breasts and was not looking at him, but at the wall across the way from her. In her features he saw the same voided emptiness he had within his own chest.

Pulling his shoulders up, he addressed her. "I have no issue to settle against you. Your actions directed unto my"—pause—"the Bloodletter . . . were taken for your own valid reasons."

In fact, they had been driven by the same blood loyalty and vengeance that had animated his search for her.

As a warrior would, she bowed at the waist, accepting his reversal and the clearing of the air between them. "I am free to go?"

"Yes—but 'tis daylight." When she looked around at the bunks and cots as if imagining the males who had wanted her, he interjected, "No ill shall befall you herein. I am the leader and I . . ." Well, he had been the leader. "We shall pass the day upstairs for your privacy. Food and drink are upon the table o'er there."

Xcor made the concessions for modesty and provision not because of the bullshit propriety issues that revolved around a Chosen. But this female was . . . something he respected: If anyone was likely to understand the importance of revenge against an insult upon your family, it was him. And the Bloodletter had done permanent damage to her brother.

"Upon nightfall," he said, "we shall take you out from here blindfolded, as you cannot know where we tarry thus. But you shall be released unharmed."

Turning his back on her, he went over to the only bunk that did not have an upper layer. Feeling like a fool, he nonetheless straightened the rough blanket. There was no pillow, so he bent down and picked up a stack of his laundered shirts.

"This is where I sleep—you may use this for your rest. And lest you feel worried for your safety or virtue, there is a gun under each side upon the floor. But worry not. You shall find yourself arriving unto the sunset in safety."

He did not take a formal vow upon his honor, for verily, he had none. And he did not look back as he took to the stairs.

"What is your name?" she said.

"You do not know that already, Chosen?"

"I know not everything."

"Aye." He put his hand on the rough banister. "Neither do I. Good day, Chosen."

As he mounted the stairs, he felt as though he had aged centuries since he had carried the unanimated, warm body of that female underground.

Opening the stout wooden door, he had no idea what he would

be walking into. Following his announcement of his status, his males could well caucus and decide to shun him—

There they all were, in a semicircle, Throe and Zypher bookending the group. Their weapons were in their hands, and their faces were death-knell grim . . . and they were waiting for him to say something.

He closed the door and leaned back against it. He was no coward to run from them or what had happened down below, and he saw no benefit to padding what had been revealed with careful words or pauses.

"The female spoke the truth. I am not a blooded relation of the one who I thought was my sire. So what say you all."

They didn't utter a word. Didn't look at each other. And there was no hesitation.

As one, they fell down upon their knees, sinking to the floorboards, and bowing their heads. Throe spoke up.

"We are e'er yours to command."

Upon the response, Xcor cleared his throat. And did it again. And one more time. In the Old Language, he pronounced, *"No leader has o'erseen stronger backs with greater loyalty than those gathered afore me."*

Throe's eyes lifted. "It has not been the memory of your father that we have served all these years."

There was a great whoop of agreement—which was better than any vow that could have been spoken in flowery language. And then daggers were buried in the wooden floorboards at his feet, the hilts clasped in the fists of soldiers who were, and remained, his to send forth.

And he would have left things there, but his long-term plans demanded a revelation and a further confirmation.

"I have a larger purpose than fighting parallel to the Brotherhood," he said in a quiet tone, so that the female on the lower level could hear naught. "My ambitions are a death sentence if discovered by others. Do you understand what I'm saying."

"The king," someone whispered.

"Aye." Xcor looked into each of their eyes. "The king."

None of them glanced away or got up. They were a solid unit of muscle and strength and lethal determination.

"If that changes anything for any of you," he demanded, "you shall tell me now and you shall leave at nightfall, ne'er to return without penalty of death."

Throe broke ranks by dropping his head. But that was as far as it went. He did not get up and walk away, and no one else did either.

"Good," Xcor said.

"What of the female," Zypher said with a dark smile.

Xcor shook his head. "Absolutely not. She deserves no punishment."

The male's brows popped. "Fine. I can make it good for her, instead."

Oh, for chrissakes, he was just too much like the damned *Lhenihan*. "No. You shall not touch her. She is a Chosen." This got their attention, but he was going to go no further with the revelations. He'd had quite enough of them. "And we are sleeping up here."

"What the hell?" Zypher got to his feet and the rest followed. "If you say she is off-limits, I shall leave her alone, as will the others. Why—"

"Because that is what I decree."

To buttress the point, Xcor sat down at the foot of the door, putting his back in place against the panels. He trusted his soldiers with his life in the field, but that was a beautiful, powerful female down there, and they were rutting, horny sonsabitches, the lot of them.

They would have to get through him to get to her.

After all, he was a bastard, but he was not completely codeless, and she deserved protection she likely did not need for the good deed she had done him.

Killing the Bloodletter?

Now, that had been a favor to Xcor, as it turned out.

Because it meant he did not have to render the liar's demise upon the fucker's ugly head himself.

FIFTY-THREE

Manny was behind the wheel of his car, hands cranked down hard, eyes sharp on the road in front of him, when he took a tight turn . . . and drove right into exactly the kind of scene Vishous had described.

About. Fucking. Time. It had taken him only a good three hours of making boxes and boxes around block after block after cocksucking block to run across the damn thing.

But yeah, this was what he was looking for: In the ten a.m. sunlight that bled in between the buildings, a slick, oily mess gleamed all over the pavement and the brick walls and the Dumpster and those chicken-wired windows.

Popping the clutch, he flipped the gearshift into neutral and hit the brakes.

The instant he opened the door, he recoiled. "Fucking *hell* . . ."

The stench was indescribable. Likely because it shot directly into his nose and shut down his brain, it was so frickin' awful.

But he did recognize it. The guy with the Sox hat had reeked of it that night Manny had operated on the vampires.

Cocking his phone, he called up Vishous's supersecret number and hit *send.* The line barely rang once before Payne's twin answered.

"I got it," Manny said. "It's everything you told me about—man, the *smell.* Right. Yeah. Got it. Talk to you in two."

As he hung up, part of him was losing it, thinking of Payne's possibly have been involved in what was clearly a bloodbath. But he kept it together as he searched around for something, anything, that could tell them what had happened—

"Manny?"

"Motherfucker!" As he spun on his heel, he grabbed his cross—or maybe it was his heart, so the damn thing didn't break out from behind his sternum. "Jane?"

The ghostly form of his former head of trauma solidified before his eyes. "Hi."

His first thought was, Oh, God, the sun—which showed just how much his life had changed. "Wait! Are you okay with daylight—"

"I'm fine." She reached out and calmed him. "I've come to help—V told me where you were."

He gripped her shoulder briefly. "I am . . . really fucking glad to see you."

Jane gave him a quick, hard hug. "We're going to find her. I promise."

Yeah, but what kind of condition was she going to be in?

Working together, the pair of them scoured the alleyway, weaving in and out of both the shadows and the lit parts. Thank God it was still early and this was a deserted part of the city, because he was not in a mind-set where he could deal with the complication of people—especially the police—showing up.

Over the next half hour, he and Jane went through every square inch of the alley, but all they found were the remnants of drug use, some litter and a number of condoms he had no intention of looking very closely at.

"Nothing," he muttered. "Goddamn nothing."

Fine. Whatever. He was just going to keep moving, keep combing, keep hoping—

A rattling sound snapped his head around and then took him over to the Dumpster.

"Something's making a noise over here," he called out as he knelt down. Except knowing their luck, it was nothing more than a rat having breakfast.

Jane came over just as he reached under the bin. "I think . . . I think it's a phone," he grunted as he stretched and paddled with his fingertips, hoping to get purchase— "Got it."

Easing back, he found that, yup, it was a busted-up cell phone and the thing was ringing on vibrate, which explained the noise. Unfortunately, whoever was calling dumped into voice mail just as he tried to hit *answer* and got locked out.

"Man, there's inky shit all over it." He wiped his hand clean on the edge of the Dumpster—which was saying something. "And the thing's password-protected."

"We need to take it back to V—he can hack into anything."

Manny got to his feet and looked over at her. "I don't know if I'm allowed there." He tried to hand the phone over. "Here. You take it, and I'll see if I can find any other sites like this."

Although honestly, it seemed like he'd been through all of downtown.

"Wouldn't you rather know what's going on firsthand?"

"Fuck, yeah, but—"

"And if V finds something, wouldn't you rather go out to deal with it with the right equipment?"

"Well, yeah, but—"

"So haven't you ever heard of doing something and apologizing after the fact?" As he popped a brow, she shrugged. "It's how I dealt with you at the hospital for years."

Manny tightened his hand on the cell phone. "Are you serious?"

"I'll drive us back to the compound, and if anyone has a problem, I'll take care of it. And may I suggest we stop by your house first and get anything you might need to stay a while?"

He slowly shook his head. "If she doesn't come—"

"*No.* We don't say 'doesn't.'" Jane's eyes were dead on his. "When she *comes* home, no matter how long it takes, you will be there. V said you've left your job—because Payne told him. And we can talk about that later—"

"There's nothing to discuss. The St. Francis board all but asked me to resign."

Jane swallowed hard. "Oh, God . . . Manny . . ."

Christ, he couldn't believe what came out of his mouth: "It doesn't matter, Jane. As long as she comes back okay—that's all I care about."

She nodded over at the car. "So why are we still talking?"

Good fucking point.

They both ran for the Porsche, strapped in, and took off with Jane behind the wheel.

As she sped over to the Commodore, he was transformed by purpose: He'd blown his shot with his woman once. It was not happening again.

Jane live-parked in front of the high-rise while he jogged into the foyer, shot up the elevator, and hit his place. Moving lightning-fast, he grabbed his laptop, his cell phone charger—

The safe.

Gunning for the closet in his room, he cracked the combo and unlatched the little door. With quick hands and a rock-solid mind, he took out his birth certificate, seven thousand dollars in cash, two gold Piaget watches, and his passport. Dragging over a random bag, he crammed all of that into the thing, along with his computer and charger. Then he picked up two more duffels that were all but throwing up clothes and blasted out of his condo.

As he waited for the elevator, he realized he was checking out of his life. For good. Whether he ended up with Payne or not, he was not returning here—and that wasn't just about the physical address.

The moment he'd given his keys to Jane, for the second time, he'd turned a corner in a metaphorical snowstorm: He had no idea what was in front of him, but there was no going back, and he was fine with that.

Back down on the street, he tossed his shit into the trunk and the rear seat. "Let's do this."

About thirty-five minutes later, Manny was once again in the foggy terrain of the vampires' mountain.

Glancing down at the near-ruined cell phone in his palm, he prayed to God that this possible link between him and Payne brought them back together again—and gave him a shot at what he'd thrown away—

"Holy . . . shit . . ." Up ahead, emerging from out of the strange haze, a tremendous pile of rock loomed, big as Rushmore. "That's a . . . fucking house."

Mausoleum was another word for it.

"The Brothers take security very seriously." Jane pulled the car up in front of a set of stairs that was worthy of a cathedral.

"Either that," he muttered, "or someone's in-laws have a quarry."

They got out together, and before he snagged his bags, he surveyed the landscape. The retaining wall that led off in both directions rose to a good twenty feet off the ground, and there were cameras all over its exterior, as well as twists of barbwire across the top. The mansion itself was enormous, sprawling in all directions, looking to be four stories high. And talk about a fortress: All the windows were covered with sheets of metal, and those double doors? Looked like you'd need a tank to get through them.

There were a number of cars in the courtyard, some of which, under other circumstances, he'd have had a serious jones for, and also another, far smaller house made from the same stone as the castle. The fountain in the center was dry, but he could imagine the peaceful sounds it would make as the water fell.

"This way," Jane said as she popped the trunk and took out one of his duffels.

"I'll get that." He took what she'd grabbed, as well as the other two. "Ladies first."

She'd called her man on the way in, so Manny had a pretty good idea that Payne's people weren't going to kill him outright. But who could tell for sure?

Good thing he didn't give a shit about himself right now.

At the grand entrance, she rang the bell and a lock switched open. Stepping inside with her, he found himself in a windowless vestibule that made him think of a jail . . . a very classy, expensive jail with hand-carved wood panels and the scent of lemon in the air.

No way they were coming out of this space unless someone let them.

Jane spoke into a camera. "It's us. We're—"

The second set of doors was cracked immediately, and Manny had to blink a couple of times as the way in was opened. The brilliant, colorful foyer on the far side was nothing he'd expected: Majestic and with all the hues of the rainbow, it was everything the fortified exterior was not. And dear Lord, it seemed like every conceivable type of decorative marble and stone had been used . . . and holy shit from all the crystal and the gold leafing.

Then he stepped inside and saw the frescoed ceiling three stories up . . . and a staircase that made the one from *Gone With the Wind* look like a stepladder.

Just as the door shut behind him, Payne's brother came out of what looked like a poolroom, with Red Sox by his side. As the vampire strode forward, he was all business as he put a hand-rolled between his fangs and jacked up his black leathers.

Stopping in front of Manny, the two of them locked eyes . . . until you had to wonder if it was all going to be over before it started—with Manny being made a meal of.

Except then the vampire held out his palm.

Of course—the cell phone.

Manny dropped his bags and took the BlackBerry out of his coat pocket. "Here—this is—"

The guy accepted what was offered but didn't look at the thing. He just shifted it over to his free hand and put his palm out again.

The gesture was so very simple; its meaning very, very deep.

Manny grabbed for that palm with his own, and neither of them said anything. No reason to have to because the communication was clear: Respect was paid and accepted on both sides.

When they dropped palms, Manny said, "The phone?"

For the vampire, getting into the thing was the work of a moment.

"Jesus . . . you're fast," Manny murmured.

"No. This is the one I gave her. I was calling it every hour on the hour. The GPS is busted—otherwise I would have given you the addy you found it in."

"Fuck." Manny rubbed his face. "There was nothing else there. Jane and I combed the alley—and I've driven around downtown for hours. What now?"

"We wait. It's all we can do while the sunlight is out. But the instant we go dark, the Brotherhood is tearing out of here with a vengeance. We'll find her, don't you worry—"

"I'm coming too," he said. "Just so we're clear."

As Payne's twin started shaking his head, Manny cut any protesting, be-reasonable shit off. "Sorry. That might be your sister out there . . . but she's my woman. And that means I'm going to be a part of this."

At that, the one with the baseball cap took off his hat and smoothed his hair. "Shit on a shingle—"

Manny froze in place, the rest of what the guy said not registering at all.

That face . . . that fucking face.

That—*holy shit*—face.

Manny had been wrong about where he'd seen the guy.

"What?" the guy said, glancing down at himself.

Manny was vaguely aware of Payne's brother frowning and Jane looking worried. But his focus was on the other man. He searched those hazel eyes, that mouth, and that chin, trying to find something that didn't fit, something out of place . . . something that disproved the two-plus-two-is-four he was rocking.

The only thing that was even slightly off was the nose—but that was just because it had been broken at least once.

The truth was in the bones.

And the connection was not the hospital or even St. Patrick's Cathedral—because come to think of it, he had definitely seen this man, male . . . vampire, whatever . . . at church before.

"What the hell?" Butch muttered, looking at Vishous.

By way of explanation, Manny bent down and rifled through his bags. As he searched for what he hadn't intentionally brought with him, he knew without a doubt he was going to find it. Fate had lined these dominos up too perfectly for this moment not to happen.

And yup, there it was.

As Manny straightened, his hands were shaking so badly that the picture frame's bracer flapped against the back of the matting.

Given that his voice was gone, all he could do was turn the glass around and give the three of them a chance to look at the black-and-white photograph.

Which was the spitting image of the male named Butch.

"This is my father," Manny said roughly.

The guy's expression went from *yeah, whatever* to bald, blanching shock, and his hands started trembling as well as he reached out and carefully took the old picture.

He didn't bother denying anything. He couldn't.

Payne's brother exhaled a cloud of wonderful-smelling smoke. "Fucking. A."

Well, didn't that just sum it all up nicely.

Manny glanced at Jane and then eyed the man who might well be a half brother. "Do you recognize him?"

When the guy slowly shook his head, Manny looked over at Payne's twin. "Can humans and vampires . . ."

"Yup."

As he went back to staring at a face that shouldn't have been so familiar, he thought, Shit, how did he put this. "So are you . . ."

"A half-breed?" the guy said. "Yeah. My mother was human."

"Son of a bitch," Manny breathed.

FIFTY-FOUR

As Butch held the picture of a man who was undeniably identical to himself, he thought, rather bizarrely, about the yellow signs on highways.

The ones that said things like BRIDGE MAY BE ICY . . . or, WATCH FOR FALLING ROCK . . . or the temporary GIVE 'EM A BRAKE before you got to a work zone. Hell, even the ones with the silhouette of a deer leaping or a big black arrow pointing to the left or the right.

At this moment, standing here in the foyer, he would really have appreciated some advance warning that his life was about to go pig-slick, off-the-rails.

Then again, collisions were collisions and couldn't be planned.

Raising his stare from the photograph, he looked into the human surgeon's eyes. They were a deep brown, a good old-fashioned port color. But the shape of them . . . God, why hadn't he seen the similarity to his own before?

"You're sure," he heard himself say. "This is your father."

Except he knew the answer before the guy nodded.

"Who . . . how . . ." Yeah, great journalist he would make, huh. "What . . ."

There you go. Add *when* and *where* and he was Anderson-fucking-Cooper.

The thing was, though, after having mated Marissa and gone through his transition, he'd finally found peace with who he was and what was doing in his life. Over in the human world, on the other hand, he'd been estranged from everyone, running parallel but never truly intersecting with his mother and his sisters and his brothers.

And his father, of course.

Or at least the guy he'd been told was his pops.

He'd assumed that with his true home and mate here, he was done with assimilating, having reached a peaceful reconciliation with so much that had been painful.

But didn't this just kick all that shit up again.

The human spoke gravely. "His name was Robert Bluff. He was a surgeon at Columbia Pres in New York City when my mom was working there as a nurse—"

"My mother was a nurse." Butch's mouth felt dry. "But not at that hospital."

"He practiced a number of places—even . . . over in Boston."

There was a long silence, during which Butch tested the cold, confusing waters of a possible unfaithfulness on his mother's part.

"Anyone need a drink, true?" V said.

"Lag—"

"Lagavulin—"

Butch and surgeon both fell silent as Vishous rolled his eyes. "Why is this not a surprise."

As the brother hit the bar in the billiards room, Manello said, "I never really knew him. Met him, like . . . once? I can't really remember, to be honest."

V made like a flight attendant and returned front-and-centered the liquor.

As Butch took a haul from a glass, Manello did the same and then shook his head. "You know, I never liked this shit until after . . ."

"What."

"You boys started fucking with my head. Used to like Jack. Last year, though . . . everything changed."

Butch nodded even though he wasn't tracking. Man, he just couldn't stop looking at the picture, and after a while, he found that in the strangest way, this was all a relief. Ancestor regression had proven that he was related to Wrath, but he'd never known, or particularly cared to know, exactly how. And yet here it was. In front of him.

Shit, it was kind of like he'd had a disease all this time, and someone had finally put a name to it.

You have Other-father-itis. Or was it a Bastard-oma?

It all made sense. He'd always thought his father had hated him and maybe this was the why behind that. Although it was nearly impossible to imagine his pious, straitlaced mother ever straying, this picture told the story of at least one night with someone else.

His first thought was that he had to get to his mom and ask her for specifics—well, *some* specifics.

But how was that going to work? Dementia had taken her away from reality, and she was now so far gone she barely recognized him when he dropped by—which was the only reason he could visit her at all. And it wasn't as if he could ask his sisters or brothers. They'd written him off when he'd disappeared from their orbits, but more to the point, it was unlikely they knew any more than he did.

"Is he still alive?" Butch asked.

"I'm not sure. I used to think he was buried in Pine Grove Cemetery. Now? Who the hell knows."

"I can find out." As V spoke up, Butch and Manny both looked over at the brother. "Say the word and I will find him—whether he's in the vampire world or the human one."

"Find who?"

The deep voice came from the head of the stairs, and everyone looked up as the words reverberated throughout the foyer. Wrath was standing on the second-floor landing with George at his side, and the king's mood was easy to guess at even though his eyes were hidden behind those wraparounds: He was in a deadly frame of mind.

Hard to know, however, whether it was the human in the foyer or not because God knew there were a thousand things riding the guy's ass right about now.

Vishous spoke up—which was a good call. Butch had lost his voice and so had Manello, evidently. "Looks like this fine surgeon may be a relative of yours, my lord."

As Manello recoiled, Butch thought, *Holy crap.*

Didn't that throw another iron into the fire.

Manny rubbed his temples as that tremendous vampire with the waist-long black hair came down the stairs, a blond dog seeming to lead the way. The bastard looked like he owned the place, and given the "my lord" shit, he probably did.

"Did I hear you right, V?" the male asked.

"Yeah. You did."

Annnnnnnnnnd that settled another question—because Manny was wondering if he'd been having trouble with his ears, too.

"This is our king," Vishous announced. "Wrath, son of Wrath. This is Manello. Manny Manello, M.D. Don't think you two have met formally."

"You're the one who's Payne's."

No hesitation on that. No hesitation on his reply either: "Yeah. I am."

The low rumble that came out of a cruel mouth was part laugh, part curse. "And you think that we're related how?"

V cleared his throat and jumped in. "There is a striking physical resemblance between Manny's dad and Butch. I mean . . . shit, it's like looking at a picture of my boy."

Dark brows disappeared behind those wraparounds. Then the expression eased. "Needless to say, I can't make that call."

Ah, so he was blind. Explained the dog.

"We could ancestor-regress him," Vishous suggested.

"Yeah," Butch said. "Let's do—"

"Wait a minute, can't that kill him?" Jane interjected.

"Hold up." Manny pulled an out-and-safe with his hands. "Just wait a fucking minute. Ancestor what?"

Vishous exhaled smoke. "It's a process by which I get into you and see how much of our blood is in your veins."

"But it could kill me?" Shit, the fact that Jane was shaking her head so did not inspire confidence.

"It's the only way to be sure. If you're a half-breed, it's not like we can go into the lab and look at your blood. Half-breeds are different."

Manny glanced around at all of them: the king, Vishous, Jane . . .

and the guy who might be a half brother. Christ, maybe this was why he felt so differently about Payne—from the second he saw her, it was like . . . a part of him woke up.

Maybe it explained his hot-blooded temper, too.

And after a lifetime of wondering about his father and his roots, he thought . . . he could find out the truth now.

Except as they stared back at him, he remembered heading into the hospital the week before and thinking it was morning only to find out it was night. And then the shit with Payne and his body changing came to mind.

"You know what?" he said. "I think I'm good."

When Jane nodded as if she agreed with him, he was sure he was on the right train.

Besides, they were getting distracted from the real issue.

"Payne is going to come back, someway, somehow," he said. "And I'm not sucking on a loaded gun right before I see her again—even if it means the difference between belonging in this world or not. I know who my father is—and I'm fucking looking at his reflection right now standing across from me. That's as far as I need to go—unless Payne feels differently."

God . . . his mother, he thought abruptly. Had she known?

As Vishous crossed his arms over his chest, Manny braced himself for an arguement.

"I like your white ass," the guy said instead. "I really do."

Considering what the bastard had walked in on not so long ago, this was a surprise. But he'd take it. "Okay, we agree. My woman wants it—I'll do it. But otherwise, I'm good with who I am."

"Fair enough," Wrath pronounced.

At that point, there was nothing but silence. Although what was there to say? The reality of where Payne was—and was not—hung around everyone's neck.

Manny had never felt so powerless in his life.

"'Scuse me," his semi-brother said, "I need another drink."

As Butch peeled off and went into the other room, Manny watched him disappear through an elaborate archway. "You know, I'll second that on the hooch."

"My house is yours," the king said darkly. "Bar's that way."

Fighting back an odd urge to bow, Manny nodded instead.

"Thanks, man." When knuckles were presented, he tapped them and then gave Jane and her husband a nod.

The room he walked into was like the best horse racing hospitality suite anyone had ever seen. Hell, they even had a popcorn machine.

"More Lag?" the guy muttered from across the way.

Manny pivoted and found himself measuring one fuck of a bar. "Yeah. Please."

He brought his glass over, and gave it to the man. And when the sound of Scotch splashing seemed loud as a scream, he wandered up to a sound system that could probably be used to play Madison Square Garden.

Pushing the buttons, he called up a mix of . . . gangsta rap.

Quick shift and he was into the high-def radio, on a search for the metal station. As Slipknot's "Dead Memories" started banging, he took a deep breath.

Nightfall. He was just waiting for nightfall.

"Here," the cop said, delivering the liquor. With a grimace, he nodded to one of the speakers. "You like that shit?"

"Yeah."

"Well, that's one way we ain't related."

Payne's twin put his head into the room. "What the hell is that *noise*?" Like someone had decided to speak in tongues. Or maybe bust out some Justin Bieber.

Manny just shook his head. "It's music."

"Only if you say so."

Manny rolled his eyes and retreated into a very dark, dangerous place in his mind. The reality that there was nothing he could do for his woman at the moment made him want to hurt something. And the fact that it appeared he had some vampire in him was exactly the kind of revelation he did not need on a day like today.

God, he felt like death.

"Pool, anyone?" he said numbly.

"Fuck, yeah."

"Absolutely."

Jane stepped in and gave him a quick hug. "Count me in."

Guess he wasn't the only one desperate for a distraction.

FIFTY-FIVE

As Payne sat on something padded with her hands in her lap, she surmised that she was in a car because the subtle vibrating sensation was similar to what she had felt when she had traveled beside Manuel in his Porsche. She could not visually confirm such, however, because just as the Bloodletter's soldier had promised, she was blindfolded. The scent of the male in charge was beside her, however; although he was frozen in place, so someone else had to be piloting the vehicle.

Naught had happened to her in the intervening hours betwixt their confrontation and this ride now: She had passed the daylight time sitting on the leader's bed, knees tucked in against her chest, both of the guns next to her on the rough blanket. No one had bothered her, however, so after a while she'd stopped prickling at each noise from above and relaxed some.

Thoughts of Manuel had soon commanded the majority of her attention, and she had played and replayed scenes from their too-short time together until her heart ached from the agony. Before she'd known it, though, the leader came back down to her and asked her if she required a repast before they left.

No, she hadn't wanted to eat.

Thereafter, he had blindfolded her with a pristine white cloth—one so clean and lovely that it made her wonder where he had come up with it. And then he took her elbow in a firm grip and led her slowly up the stairs he had carried her down previously.

It was hard to know exactly how long they had been in the car. Twenty minutes? Maybe a half hour?

"Here," the leader said eventually.

Upon his command, whatever they were in slowed, then stopped, and a door was unlatched. As fresh, cool air wafted in, her elbow was taken once again and she was steadied as she stepped out. The door shut and there was a bang—as if a fist had been knocked on a part of the vehicle.

Spinning tires kicked up dirt onto her robe.

And then she was alone with the leader.

Although he was silent, she sensed him moving behind her, and the fabric about her head was loosened. As it fell free, her breath caught.

"I thought if you were to be released, it should be upon a view worthy of your pale eyes."

The entire city of Caldwell was revealed down below them, its twinkling lights and streaming traffic a glorious feast for her vision. Indeed, they were upon the shoulders of a small mountain rise, with the city sprawling out at their veritable feet by the banks of the river.

"This is lovely," she whispered, glancing over at the soldier.

As he stood a ways away, he was remote to the point of being removed, his disfigurement hidden in the shadows he had stepped back into. "Fare thee well, Chosen."

"And you . . . I still know not your name."

"True enough." He gave her a half bow. "Good evening."

With that he was gone, dematerializing away from her.

After a moment, she turned back to the view, and wondered where in the city Manuel was. It would be in the thicket of tall buildings, so going by the bridge's location, it would be . . . there.

Yes, there.

Lifting her hand, she drew an invisible circle around the tall, thin construction of glass and steel that she was certain was where he lived.

As her chest pained her and she became breathless, she tarried a moment longer and then scattered north and east, toward the Brotherhood's compound. There was no enthusiasm to the trip, just an abiding obligation to inform her twin that she was in fact alive and unharmed.

When she took form on the stone steps of the vast mansion, she approached the double doors with a strange dread. She was grateful to be back to a home of sorts, but the absence of her male hollowed out any of the joy she should have felt at the reconnections that were to come.

After she rang the bell, the door into the vestibule immediately unlatched and she was able to step out of the night—

The second, inner door was opened even quicker by the smiling butler.

"Madam!" he cried out.

As she entered a foyer that had charmed her from the moment she'd first seen it days ago, she had a brief impression of her shocked twin leaping into the archway of the billiards room.

Brief was all she got of him, however.

Some great force knocked Vishous out of the way so hard he went flying, the glass in his hand popping out of his hold, whatever drink was in it spraying into the air.

Manuel ripped into the foyer, his body surging forth, the expression on his face one of disbelief and terror and relief all at once.

Except it made no sense that he was running toward her, no sense that he was here in the—

He had her in his arms before she could finish the thought, and oh, fate, he smelled the same, that dark spice that was unique to him and him alone flooding her senses. And his shoulders were just as wide as she remembered. And his waist just as lean. And his embrace just as wonderful about her.

His strong body shook as he held her tightly for a moment and then he backed off as if he were afraid he was injuring her.

His eyes were frantic. "Are you all right? What can I do for you? Do you need a doctor? Are you hurt— I'm asking too many questions—I'm sorry. God . . . what happened? Where did you go? Shit, I have to stop . . ."

As romantic reunions went, perhaps those were not the flowery words some females would want to hear, but to her, they meant everything in the world.

"Why ever are you here?" she whispered, putting her hands to his face.

"Because I love you."

In so many ways, that explained nothing . . . and told her everything she needed to know.

Abruptly, she jerked her hands back. "But what about what I've done to your body—"

"I don't care. We'll work with it—figure it out—but I was wrong about you and me. I was a pussy—a coward, and I was wrong and I'm so fuck—damned sorry. Shit." He shook his head. "I have to stop cursing. Oh, God, your robe . . ."

She glanced down and saw the black blood of the slayers she'd killed, as well as the red stain that was of her own.

"I am whole and I am well," she said clearly. "And I love you—"

Cutting her off, he kissed her on the mouth solemnly. "Say that again. Please."

"I love you."

As he groaned and wrapped his arms back around her, Payne felt within her heart a great welling of warmth and gratitude, and she let the emotion carry her against him. And whilst they embraced, she looked over the shoulder of her male. Her brother was standing with his own *shellan* at his side.

Meeting the eyes of her twin, she read all of the questions and fears in his stare.

"I am uninjured," she told both her male and her twin.

"What happened?" Manuel asked against her hair. "I found your phone smashed up."

"You were looking for me?"

"Of course I was." He inched back. "Your brother called me at dawn."

All at once she was surrounded by people, as if some gong had gone off and called into the foyer all the males and females of the house. No doubt the commotion of her arrival had summoned them, and they had stayed in the periphery out of respect.

It was clear there were more than just two minds to put at rest.

And that made her feel as if she were a part of this family.

"I was down at the river," she said loudly enough so that all could hear, "when I caught the scent of the enemy. Drawn to them, I traversed the alleyways and set upon two *lessers*." She felt Manuel stiffen and saw her brother do likewise. "It felt good to fight—"

At this, she hesitated. Except the king nodded. And so did a powerful female with short hair—as if she, too, fought in the war and knew both the drive and the satisfaction. The Brothers, however, clearly felt uncomfortable.

She continued. "Upon me there arrived a group of males—strong backed, well-weaponed, indeed, a squadron of soldiers. The leader was very tall, with dark eyes and dark hair and a"—she put her hand to her mouth—"defect of his upper lip."

Now the cursing started—and as it did, she wished she'd been able to use the seeing bowls on the Other Side more before she'd left. Clearly, the male she described was not unknown to them, and not welcomed in her narrative.

"He apprehended me—" There were not one, but two growls at that—from her twin and from Manuel. And as she soothed the male who stood so close to her, she looked at her brother. "He was under the misunderstanding that I had wrought a calamity upon his bloodline. He believed he was the Bloodletter's son—and he'd been a witness to the night I brought death upon our sire. Verily, he had searched for me with vengeance for centuries."

At this point, she stopped herself, realizing she had just admitted to patricide. No one seemed fazed, however—which spoke volumes about not only the kind of males and females these were, but also the bastard who had been her father.

"I disabused the soldier of the mis-notion he was operating under." She left out the fact that he had struck her, and was glad the bruising on her face had faded. Somehow, she did not believe anyone needed to know about that. "And he believed me. He did not hurt me—in fact, he protected me against his males, giving me his bed—"

Manuel bared his teeth as if he had fangs . . . and did not that just turn her on.

"Alone, I slept alone. He kept all of his subordinates upstairs with him." More soothing of Manuel—at least until she realized he was fully aroused, as a male driven to mark his female would be. And how erotic was that. "Ah . . . he blindfolded me and had me driven out to a scenic ledge with a view of the city. And then he let me go. That was all."

Wrath spoke up. "He abducted you against your will."

"He believed he had cause. He thought I had killed his father. And as soon as he was set correct on that, he was prepared to release me, but it was daylight, so I could go nowhere. I would have called but my phone was lost and it did not appear that they had any to hand as I did not see such. In fact, they were living in the old way, communally and modestly, in an underground room that was alit with candles."

"Any idea where they stay?" her twin asked.

"I haven't a clue. I was unconscious when they—" As a loud shout of alarm rose up from so many throats, she shook her head. "I was shot by a *lesser*—"

"What the fuck—"

"You were what?!"

"A gun—"

"Shot with a—"

"—injured?!"

Hmm. Mayhap that was not of help.

As the Brothers all talked over each other, Manuel scooped her up and held her aloft, his face a mask of bald fury. "That's it. We're done here. I'm going to do an exam on you." He looked over at her brother. "Where can I take her."

"Upstairs. Hang a right. Three doors down there's a guest room. I'll have food sent up, and let me know if you need medical supplies."

"Roger that."

And with that, her male hit the stairs with her in his arms.

Good thing she was essentially finished with her story: Given the angle of Manuel's chin, she was not going to do any more talking about her ordeal for some time.

Unless she wanted him in an utter rage.

Indeed, as he was now, it would appear that that soldier had something to worry about if the two of them ever crossed pathways.

"I am so glad to see you," she said roughly. "You were all I thought of when I was . . ."

He closed his eyes briefly, as if he were in pain. "They didn't hurt you?"

"No." And that was when she realized what he was worried about.

Placing her palm on his face, she said, "He didn't touch me. None of them did."

The shudder that went through the strong body that carried her was so great, he nearly tripped. But her male recovered fast . . . and kept going.

As Vishous watched the human take his sister up the grand staircase, he realized he was witnessing a future unfold right before his very eyes. The pair of them were going to work it out, and that surgeon with the highly questionable musical taste was going to be a part of her life . . . and V's . . . forevermore.

Abruptly, his mind shifted back twelve months, the *rewind* button stopping when he got to the place in the narrative when he'd gone to the surgeon's office to scrub the guy's memories of V's own time at St. Francis.

Brother.

He had heard the word *brother* in his head.

At the time, he hadn't had a fucking clue what it meant—because, come on, like that would ever happen?

And yet here it was, reality once again living up to one of his visions.

Although, for true accuracy, that word should probably have been *brother-in-law.*

Except then he glanced over at Butch. His best friend was likewise staring upward at the guy.

Shit, he guessed *brother* might just fit. Which was good. Manello was the kind of guy you wouldn't mind being related to.

As if the king read his mind, Wrath announced, "The surgeon can stay. Long as he wants. And he can have contact with any human family he has—if he wants. As a relation of mine, he is welcome in my home without restriction."

There was a grumble of agreement at that: As always, when it came to the Brotherhood, secrets never stayed secrets for very long, so everyone already knew about the Manello/Butch/Wrath connection. Hell, they'd all looked at that photograph. Especially V.

Although V had done a little more than that. The name "Robert Bluff" had turned out to be a shell—duh. And the male had to be a half-breed; otherwise there was no way he could have worked at any hospital in the daylight hours. The question was whether and how much he knew about his vampire side—and if he was still alive.

As Jane put her head on his heart, he wrapped his arms around her even further. And then he looked over at Wrath. "Xcor, true."

"Yup," the king said. "Verified sighting. And this is not the last time we're going to hear from him. It's only the beginning."

Too right, V thought. The arrival of that band of bastards was not good news for anyone—but most especially Wrath.

"Gentlemen," the king called out, "and ladies, First Meal is getting cold."

Which was the cue for everyone to head back to the dining room and actually eat what had been only studiously ignored up until now.

With Payne safe and at home, appetites were free to roam once more . . . although as God was his witness he was *not* going to think about what the hell that surgeon and his sister were no doubt about to get into.

As he groaned, Jane tightened her arm around his waist. "Are you all right?"

He glanced down at his *shellan*. "I don't think my sister is old enough to have sex."

"V, she's the same age you are."

He frowned for a moment. Was she? Or had he been born first?

Yeah, only one place to go for the answer to that.

Shit, he hadn't even thought of his mother in all this. And now that he was . . . he had absolutely no desire or interest to pop up there and announce that Payne was doing *great*, fuck you very much.

Nope. If the Scribe Virgin wanted to keep tabs on what her "children" were up to? She could look into those *fakakta* seeing bowls she liked so much.

He kissed his *shellan*. "I don't care what the calendar says or about the birth order. That's my baby sister, and she's never going to be old enough to . . . 'um, yeah.'"

Jane laughed and retucked herself under his arm. "You are a very sweet male."

"Nah."

"Yeah."

Leading her into the dining room and over to the table, he gallantly pulled her chair out for her, and then he sat to her left so that she was at his dagger hand.

As talk took root in the air, and people set to their plates, and his Jane laughed at something Rhage had said, Vishous looked across to see Butch and Marissa smiling at each other, and holding hands.

You know what, he thought . . . life was pretty fucking good right now.

It truly was.

FIFTY-SIX

Upstairs, Manny kicked the door shut behind him and his woman, and then he walked her over to a bed the size of a football field.

No reason to lock them in. Only an idiot would disturb them.

The glow from the now unshuttered windows gave him enough light to see by, and damn if he didn't like what was before his eyes: his woman, safe and sound, laid out on . . . Well, okay, this wasn't their bed, but he was damn well going to turn it into that before morning came.

As he sat down beside her, he discreetly tried to hide the raging hard-on he'd had ever since he'd seen her walk through that door. And though there was a lot they had to talk about, all he could do was stare at her.

Except then the physician in him came out. "You were injured?"

Her lovely hands went down to her robe, and the higher her hem came up, the lower her lids drifted. "I think you'll find I'm healed. It was but a grazing wound way . . . up here."

He swallowed hard. Fuck . . . yeah, she was fine. The skin of her upper thigh was as smooth as porcelain.

"Mayhap you should examine me closely, however," she drawled.

His lips parted as his lungs got tight. "Are you sure you're okay—and they didn't . . . hurt you."

He would never get over that.

Payne sat up and met him straight in the eye. "What has always been meant for you remains yours for the taking."

He closed his eyes briefly. Then he didn't want her to get the wrong impression. "It's not like it would matter to me if you weren't . . . I mean, it's not a propriety thing—" Hell's bells, he couldn't seem to talk tonight. "I just can't bear for you to be hurt."

Her smile made him grateful for the mattress under his ass. Because if he'd been standing, she'd have knocked him out.

"I'm sorry about last night," he said. "I made a mistake—"

She put her hand to his mouth. "We are where we are now. That is all I care about."

"And I have something I need to tell you."

"Are you leaving me?"

"Never."

"Good. Then let us be together first and then we shall talk." Easing upright even farther, she replaced her fingers with her mouth, kissing him deep and long. "Mmmm . . . yes, much better than speech, I should think."

"Are you sure you want—" That was as far as he got before her tongue robbed him of thought.

Groaning, he got up on the bed, holding himself above her. And then meeting her eyes, he slowly lowered his body on top of hers . . . with the last contact being his erection between her legs.

"No going back if I kiss you now." Shit, his voice was so guttural, he was practically growling at her. But he meant the words. There was some other force driving him—this was not about sex, although the mechanics of the act were involved. In taking her virginity, he was marking her in a way he didn't understand, but didn't question.

"I want you thus," she said. "I've been waiting for centuries for what only you can give to me."

Mine, he thought.

Before he kissed her again, he turned to the side and released her hair from its braid. Spreading the dark waves out over the satin bedspread, he ran his fingers through the length.

Then he curled his hips into her core, pushing and retreating, and repeating the move . . . as his hand swept up to below her breast and gripped the fragile fabric of the robing.

Frankly, he was shocked at what he wanted to do.

"I wish to be naked before you," she commanded. "Make it so, Manuel."

That frickin' robe didn't stand a chance. Jacking up, he grabbed onto both the lapels and split it right down the front, ripping the material clean apart, baring her breasts to his hot eyes and the cool air. In response, she arched and moaned—and that was it: He was on her tightening nipples with his mouth and down to her core with his hands. He was all over her, driving her to an orgasm by sucking on her and rubbing her carefully, and when her fast, desperate release came, he swallowed her cry.

He wanted to give her more—and he had every intention of doing so—but his body wasn't going to wait. His hands fumbled with his pants, cracking his belt and downing his zipper to spring his cock.

She was ready for him, slick and open—and aching, given the way her legs sawed against him.

"I'll go slow," he said against her mouth.

"I am not afraid of pain. Not with you."

Shit, so maybe in this they worked physically as human women did. Which meant the first time was not going to be easy on his woman.

"Shhh," she whispered. "Do not worry. Take me."

Reaching down, he positioned himself, and—oh, fuck . . . he nearly came. She was hot and wet and—

She moved so fast, he couldn't have stopped her if he'd wanted to. Her hands reached down and clamped on his ass, her nails digging into him and then—

Payne thrust up with her hips and at the same time pulled him down and he went in all the way to the hilt, the penetration utterly and irrevocably complete. As he cursed, she went rigid and hissed from the strike—which was just too damn unfair, because, fucking hell, she felt good. But he wasn't moving—not until she recovered from the invasion.

And then it dawned on him.

Snaking a hand around the back of her neck, he drew her lips close to his throat. "Take me."

The sound she made had him orgasming inside of her—it was too fucking hot for him to hold back. And as his cock spasmed, her fangs struck deep into his vein.

The sex went wild. She moved against him, her tight core fisting him up and milking him as he came again . . . and then he started to pump his hips hard. The drinking and the crazy rhythm swept them both away into a heady pounding of bodies that he knew they were each going to feel in the morning: There was nothing civilized to this; it was male and female distilled down to the most primal core.

And it was the very best of anything he had ever had.

FIFTY-SEVEN

Thomas DelVecchio knew exactly where his killer was going next.

There was no question in his mind. Even as Detective de la Cruz was back at HQ, working with the other boys on theories and leads—all of which were smart enough—Veck knew where to go.

And as he approached the parking lot of the Monroe Motel & Suites with his lights off and his motorcycle in an idle, he thought it was probably a good idea to call de la Cruz and let the guy know where he was.

Ultimately, however, he left his phone where it was in his pocket.

Halting the BMW in the trees to the right of the parking lot, he kicked out the stand, dismounted, and hung his helmet on the handlebars. His gun was in its holster under his armpit, and he told himself it was going to stay there if anyone showed.

Mostly believed the lie, too.

The terrible truth, however, was that he was animated by something that had been dormant for a long, long time. De la Cruz was right to be wary about him as a partner—and correct to question where the father's sins ended and the son's began.

Because Veck was a sinner. And he'd joined the police force to try to drain that out of himself.

It was probably better to get that shit exorcised, however. Because sometimes he felt like there was a demon inside of him, he really did.

Still, he wasn't here to kill anyone. He was here to take a killer into custody before the bastard got back to work.

Honest.

As Veck approached the motel, he stuck to the darkness of the trees and focused on the room where that latest girl had been found. Everything was as the CPD had left it: There was still crime scene tape in a triangle around the door and the portion of the sidewalk right in front—also a seal in place at the jamb, which theoretically could be broken only on official business. No lights on inside the room or out in front of it. Nobody around.

Settling behind a thick-trunked evergreen, he used his black-gloved hands to pull his black wool hat down closer to his black turtleneck.

He was very good at staying so still that he all but disappeared. He was also very good at channeling his energy into a pervasive calm that conserved resources while leaving him hyperalert.

His prey was going to show up. That murdering madman had lost all his trophies—his collection was now in the hands of the authorities, and the CSIers were scrambling to tie him to multiple unsolved murders across the nation. But the sick bastard wouldn't come here in hopes of getting some or all of it back. The return would be about revisiting and mourning the loss of what he had put so much effort into acquiring.

Would it be reckless on his part? Absolutely, but then, that was part of the gorging cycle. The killer wouldn't be thinking clearly, and he would be desperate from his losses. And Veck would just cool his heels over the next couple of nights until the appearance was made.

As time passed and he waited, and waited, and waited some more . . . he was as patient as any good stalker. Although it did dawn on him that this could be disastrous, him being here alone. With a knife holstered on the back of his waist. And that damn gun—

The snap of a twig drew his eyes to the right, although not his head. He did not move or change his breathing or even so much as twitch.

And there he was. A surprisingly slight man weaving his way cautiously through the forest's crinoline of fluffy bushes. The expression on the man's face was nearly religious as he approached the flank of the motel, but that wasn't the only part of what identified him as the killer. His clothes were covered with dried blood, his shoes, too. He was limping, as if he had a leg injury, and his face had streaks gouged in it—from fingernails.

Gotcha, Veck thought.

And now that he was staring at the killer . . . his hand crept down to his hips and went around to the back. To his knife.

Even as he told himself to leave the weapon where it was and go for his cuffs, he didn't change course. There had always been two halves of him, two people in one skin, and in moments like this, he felt as though he were watching himself act, sure as if he were a passenger in a cab and whatever destination he was bound for was not going to be a result of his own efforts.

He began to close in on the man, tracking him silently as a shadow, shortening the distance until he was a mere five feet from the bastard. The knife had found its way into Veck's palm, and he really didn't want it there, but it was too late to resheathe. Too late to derail. Too late to listen to the voice that told him this was a crime that was going to land him in jail. The other side of him had taken over and he was lost to it, on the verge of killing—

The third man came from out of nowhere.

A mammoth man dressed in leather jumped into the killer's path, blocking his way. And as David Kroner leaped back in alarm, a hiss seethed through the air.

God, that didn't even sound human. And . . . were those . . . *fangs? What the fuck—?*

The attack was so brutal that with just the first strike at the serial killer's neck, the guy's head nearly came off. And it kept going from there, blood flying so far and wide that it speckled Veck's heavy black pants and turtleneck and hat.

Except there was no knife or dagger involved.

Teeth. The motherfucker was ripping shit apart with his *teeth.*

Veck tried to scramble back, but he slammed into a tree, and the impact sent him careening to the ground waaaay closer than he needed to be. And he should have run for his bike, or just plain run away, but he was transfixed by the violence . . . and the conviction that whatever he was watching was most certainly not human.

When it was over, the monster dropped the massacred remains of the serial killer to the ground . . . and then it looked at Veck.

"Holy . . . fuck . . ." Veck breathed.

The face had a very humanlike bone structure, but the fangs were all wrong and so was the size and that vengeful stare. God, blood was actually dripping from its mouth.

"Look into my eyes," an accented voice said.

A gurgling sound rose up from what was left of the serial killer. But Veck didn't glance over. He was transfixed by a stunning set of peepers . . . so very blue . . . glowing. . . .

"Shit . . ." he choked out, a sudden headache cutting out everything he saw or heard. Collapsing sideways, he went fetal from the pain and stayed there.

Blink.

Why was he on the ground?

Blink.

He smelled blood. But why?

Blink. Blink.

With a groan, he lifted his head and— "Shit!"

Leaping to his feet in shock, he stared down at the bloody mess that was in front of him.

"Oh . . . fuck," he cursed. He'd done it. He'd finally killed someone—

Except then he looked at the knife in his fist. No blood: Not on the blade. Not on his hands. And only specks on his clothes.

Looking around, he had no clue what had just rolled out. He remembered driving here . . . and parking his motorcycle . . . and tracking the man who was now dying on the ground.

If he was brutally honest with himself, he'd had the intent to kill. All along. But going by the physical evidence? It hadn't been him.

The problem was, all he had was a black hole of no info.

A moan from the serial killer snapped his head to the right. The man was reaching for him. Mutely asking for help as he leaked all over the place. How was he still alive?

With shaking hands, Veck grabbed his cell phone and dialed 911. "Yeah, Detective DelVecchio, CPD Homicide. I need an ambulance out at the Monroe Motel & Suites *now*."

After the report was logged and the medics were on their way, he yanked off his jacket, wadded it up into a ball, and knelt down by the man. Pressing his coat into the guy's throat wounds, he prayed the fucker survived. And then had to wonder whether that was a good thing or not.

"I didn't kill you," he said. "Did I?"

Oh, God . . . what the hell had happened here?

FIFTY-EIGHT

"He came to see you."

From Blaylock's vantage point on the bed, Saxton son of Tyme was showing him his very best side. Which, no, was not his ass. The male was shaving in the mirror in the bathroom, and his perfect profile was bathed in the soft overhead light.

God, he was a beautiful male.

On so many levels, this lover he had taken on was everything he could want.

"Who," Blay said softly.

The eyes that shifted over to meet his were all about the oh-puhlease.

"Oh." To dodge any further conversation, Blay looked down at the duvet that was pulled up to his bare chest. He was naked under the satin weight. As Saxton had been until he'd put his robe on.

"He wanted to know if you were okay," Sax continued.

Since *oh* had already been used as a reply, Blay spiced it up with, "Really."

"It was out on the terrace. He didn't want to come in and disturb us."

Funny, when he'd been on the verge of passing out after his stomach had been stitched up, he'd dimly wondered what Saxton had been doing out there. But he'd been in so much pain at the time, it had been hard to think too much about anything.

Now, though, he felt a terrible thrill go through him.

Praise the Scribe Virgin, it had been a while since he'd had this old familiar tingle—although the time lapse didn't diminish the sensation. And the rush that followed to ask what had been said was nothing he could act on. It was disrespectful to Saxton, for one thing. And it was pointless, for another.

Good thing he had plenty of ammunition to shut himself up with: All he had to do was think of Qhuinn coming home a week or so ago, his hair a mess, his scent clouded by some man's cologne, his swagger all about the satisfaction he'd grabbed on the run.

The idea that Blay had thrown himself at the male not once, but twice—and gotten shut down? He just couldn't bear to think of it.

"You don't want to know what he said?" Saxton murmured as he drew the sharp blade up his throat, skillfully avoiding the bite mark Blay had given him a half hour ago.

Blay closed his eyes and wondered if he was ever going to get away from the reality that Qhuinn would fuck anyone and anything except him.

"No?" Saxton asked.

As the bed moved, Blay popped his lids. Saxton had come over to sit on the edge of the mattress, the male blotting his jaw and cheeks with a bloodred towel.

"No?" he repeated.

"May I ask you something?" Blay said. "And now would not be a good time to be your charming, sarcastic self."

Instantly, Saxton's stunning face grew grave. "Ask away."

Blay smoothed the duvet over his chest. A couple of times. "Do I . . . please you."

From out of the corner of his eye, he saw Saxton recoil and just about died of embarrassment.

"You mean in bed?" Sax demanded.

Blay flattened his lips out as he nodded, and he thought maybe he might explain a little more, but as it turned out, his mouth was dry.

"Why would you ask that in a million years?" Saxton said softly.

Well, because there had to be something wrong with him.

Blay shook his head. "I don't know."

Saxton folded the towel and put it aside. Then he stretched an arm over Blay's hips and leaned up until they were face-to-face.

"Yes." With that, he put his mouth to Blay's throat and sucked. "Always."

Blay ran his hand across the male's nape, finding the soft, curling hair at the base of his neck. "Thank God."

The familiarity of the body poised over his was nothing he'd ever had before, and it felt right. It felt good. He knew every curve and corner of Saxton's chest and hips and thighs. He knew the pressure points and the places to bite, knew exactly how to grip and roll and arch so that Saxton would come hard.

So, yes, he probably shouldn't have had to ask.

Qhuinn, though . . . anything about that male unpeeled him and left him raw. And for all he had learned to bandage himself up on the outside, the wound remained just as bad and deep as the moment it had been made—when it became obvious that the one male he wanted above all others was never, ever going to be with him.

Saxton eased back. "Qhuinn can't handle what he feels about you."

Blay laughed harshly. "Let's not talk about him."

"Why not?" Saxton reached out and ran his thumb back and forth over Blay's lower lip. "He's here with us whether we do or we don't."

Blay thought about lying and then gave up the fight. "I'm sorry about that."

"It's all right—I know what I'm in." Saxton's free hand sneaked under the duvet. "And I know what I want."

Blay groaned as that palm rubbed against what immediately became a thick erection. And as his hips lifted and he spread his legs for Saxton, he met the eyes of his lover and sucked that thumb into his mouth.

This was so much better than getting on the Qhuinn roller coaster—this he knew and he liked. He was safe here. He didn't get hurt here.

And he had found a deep, sexual connection here.

Saxton's stare was both hot and serious as he released what he'd found, pulled the covers off of Blay's body and freed the knot on the tie of his own robe.

This was very good, Blay thought. This was right—

As his lover's mouth found his collarbone and then drifted lower, Blay closed his eyes—except as he began to get lost in the sensations, what he saw was not Saxton.

"Wait, stop—" He sat up and took the other male with him.

"It's okay," Saxton said quietly. "I know where we're at."

Blay's heart cracked a little. But Saxton just shook his head and put his lips back to Blay's chest.

They had never spoken of love—and this made him realize they never were going to, because Saxton was indeed clear on things: Blay was still in love with Qhuinn—and probably always would be.

"Why?" he said to his lover.

"Because I want you for however long I have you."

"I'm going nowhere."

Saxton just shook his head against the tight abdominals he was nipping at. "Stop thinking, Blaylock. Start feeling."

As that talented mouth went all the way down, Blay hissed in a breath and decided to take the advice. Because it was the only way to survive.

Something told him that it was only a matter of time before Qhuinn came forward and announced that he and Layla were getting mated.

He wasn't sure how he knew that, but he did. The two had been hooking up for weeks, and the Chosen had been in there again the day before—he'd caught her scent and sensed her blood next door.

And though this conviction could have just been a mental exercise to depress the hell out of himself, he felt like it was so much more than that. It was as if the fog that normally obscured the coming days and months and years had grown unbearably thin and the shadows of destiny were showing themselves to him.

Just a matter of time.

God, that was going to kill him.

"I'm glad you're here," he groaned.

"Me, too," his lover said sadly around his erection. "Myself as well."

FIFTY-NINE

The following evening, Payne paced around the front of the Brotherhood's mansion, going from the dining room through the foyer and into the billiards room and back again. And again. And again.

Her male had departed from the house in the middle of the afternoon to "take care of some things." And though he'd declined to inform her what they were, she'd very much enjoyed the slightly naughty smile on his face as he'd tucked her into the bed they'd fully used during the night—and then left.

No sleep for her after that. None at all.

There was too much to be happy about.

And surprised about.

Pausing in front of one of the French doors that opened into the courtyard, she thought of the photograph he'd shown her. It was so obvious he was of blooded relation to Butch—and thereby the king. But neither Manuel nor she was interested in risking a regression. No, she very much agreed with him on that. They had each other, and considering what they'd already overcome, there was no reason to chance a bad outcome.

Besides, the information would change nothing: The king had opened his house to her male even without a formal declaration of blooded affinity, and Manuel was going to be allowed to have contact with his human mother. Further, it had been decided that he would work here, with Doc Jane, but also with Havers. After all, the race needed more good doctors, and Manuel was superlative.

And as for her? She was going to go out and fight. Neither Manuel nor her brother was exactly thrilled with the danger she was going to face, but they were not going to stop her. In fact, after she had spoken to Manuel at length, he seemed to accept that that was a part of who she was. His only caveat was that she get the very best weapons—and her brother had insisted on seeing to that.

Fates, the two of them seemed to be getting along. And who could have ever predicted?

Moving to the next window down the line, she searched the darkness for headlights.

Where was he? Where was he . . .

Manuel was also going to talk to Doc Jane about the physical changes he'd experienced—changes that, given the way Payne glowed whenever they made love, were likely to continue. He was going to monitor his body and see what happened, and they were both praying that all she did was keep him healthy and perpetually young. Only time would tell.

With a curse, she doubled back, crossed the foyer . . . and entered the dining room.

Down at the third window in the row, she glanced up into the heavens. She had no interest in going to see her mother. It would have been wonderful to share her love with those who had brought her into the world. But her sire was dead, and her *mahmen*? She didn't trust the Scribe Virgin not to imprison her again: Manuel was a half-breed. Hardly the pure stock her mother would have approved of—

The pair of glowing eyes mounting the rise upon which the compound was built made her heart race. And then there was the music—a thumping beat curling in through the glass.

Payne tore out of the dining room and ripped across the mosaic depiction of an apple tree in full bloom. She was out through the vestibule and into the dark night a moment later—

She skidded to a halt at the top of the steps.

Manuel had not come back unaccompanied. Behind his Porsche, there was a massive vehicle of some sort . . . a huge, two-part vehicle.

Her male got out from behind the wheel of his car. "Hi," he called out.

He was all smiles as he came up to her, put his hands on her hips, and brought her against his chest. "I missed you," he murmured against her mouth.

"Me, too." Now she was smiling as well. "But . . . whatever have you brought?"

The elderly butler stepped out from behind the wheel of the other vehicle. "Sire, shall I—"

"Thanks, Fritz, but I'll take care of it from here."

The butler bowed low. "It has been a pleasure to have been of service."

"You're the best, man."

The *doggen* was positively beaming as he danced into the house. And then her male turned to her.

"Stay here."

As a stamping sound emanated from inside the big contraption, she frowned. "Of course."

After kissing her again, Manuel disappeared around the far side.

Doors opening. More stamping. Creaking and a rolling sound, followed by a rhythmic thumping. And then—

The whinny told her what she had not dared to hope for. And then his beautiful filly backed down a ramp and was brought around to her.

Payne clasped her hands to her mouth as tears formed. The horse was mincing with grace, her sleek coat shining in the light that bled from the house, her strength and vitality returned to her.

"What . . . whatever is she here for?" Payne said hoarsely.

"Human men give their fiancées something as a token of their love." Manuel smiled broadly. "I thought Glory was better than any diamond I could buy you. Means more to me . . . and hopefully, to you, too."

When she made no response at all, he held out the leather lead that was clipped to the horse's bridle. "I'm giving her to you."

At that, Glory let out a tremendous whinny and pranced as if she agreed with this change in ownership.

Payne wiped her eyes and threw herself at Manuel, kissing him deeply. "I have no words."

And then she accepted the lead as Manuel went all robin-chested with pride.

Taking a deep breath, she—

Before Payne was conscious of moving, she sprang up into the air, mounting Glory as if the pair of them had been together for years, not minutes.

And the horse needed no heel, no permission, no anything—Glory leaped forward, clawing her hooves into the pebbles and taking off at a dead run.

Payne wound her fingers through the long black mane and balanced herself perfectly upon the strong back that surged beneath her. As the wind hit her face, she laughed in pure exultation as they took off in a streak of joy and freedom. Yes . . . yes! A thousand yesses!

To set upon the night.

To have freedom to move.

To have love waiting upon her.

This was more than just being alive. This was to *live.*

As Manny stood by the horse trailer and watched his girls take off together, he was out of his damn mind with happiness. They were a perfect match, the pair of them cut from the same cloth, and both were whole and strong and tearing through the darkness at a gallop that most cars would have trouble keeping up with.

Okay. Maybe he teared up just a little. But what the fuck. This was an incredible night for—

"I saw this."

"Jesus *Christ*—" He grabbed his cross and wheeled around. "Do you always sneak up on people?"

Payne's brother didn't answer—or perhaps couldn't. The vampire's eyes were locked on his sister and her galloping horse, and he seemed as moved as Manny was.

"I thought it was a stallion, though." Vishous shook his head. "But yeah, this is what I saw . . . her on a black Thoroughbred, her hair in the breeze. I didn't think it was the future, though . . ."

Manny turned back to his girls, who were far off down the retaining wall and making a fat turn to return toward the house.

"I love her so damned much," Manny heard himself say. "That's my heart right there. That's my woman."

"Word."

As a powerful accord weaved between the pair of them, Manny felt like he was home in so many ways; and he didn't want to think too much about that for fear the fragile blessings would fall apart.

A moment later, he glanced over. "Mind if I ask you something."

"G'head."

"What the *fuck* did you do to my car?"

"What, you mean the music?"

"Where did all my—"

"Shit go?" Diamond eyes met his. "You gonna live here, you're going to start listening to my tunes, true."

Manny shook his head. "You're kidding me."

"You saying you didn't like the beats?"

"Whatever." After a harrumph, Manny copped, "Fine, they didn't absolutely suck."

The laugh was just a liiiiiiittle too triumphant. "Knew it."

"So what was it?"

"Now he wants names." The vampire took out a hand-rolled and lit it. "Let's see . . . Eminem's 'Cinderella Man.' Lil Wayne's 'I Am Not a Human.' Tupac's . . ."

The list went on and on, and Manny mostly listened as he went back to watching his woman ride while he rubbed the heavy gold weight of his crucifix.

He and Payne were together . . . that Butch guy and he were going to church together at midnight . . . and Vishous hadn't stabbed him. Plus if memory served, Payne's twin drove that black Escalade over there, and that meant payback was going to be a shitload of Black Veil Bride, Bullet for My Valentine, and Avenged Sevenfold getting loaded into that SUV's sound system.

Just the thought made him smile.

All in all?

He felt like he'd won the lottery. In each of the fifty states. At the same time.

That was how lucky they *all* were.

More titles in J. R. Ward's sizzling Black Dagger Brotherhood series
Available now from Piatkus:

DARK LOVER

In the shadows of the night in Caldwell, New York, there's a deadly turf war going on between vampires and their slayers. There exists a secret band of brothers like no other – six vampire warriors, defenders of their race. Yet none of them relishes killing more than Wrath, the blind leader of the Black Dagger Brotherhood.

The only purebred vampire left on earth, Wrath has a score to settle with the slayers who murdered his parents centuries ago. But, when one of his most trusted fighters is killed – leaving his half-breed daughter unaware of his existence or her fate – Wrath must usher her into the world of the undead – a world beyond her wildest dreams . . .

978-0-7499-5522-9

LOVER ETERNAL

Within the brotherhood, Rhage is the vampire with the strongest appetites. He's the best fighter, the quickest to act on his impulses, and the most voracious lover – for inside him burns a ferocious curse cast by the Scribe Virgin. Possessed by this dark side, Rhage fears the times when his inner dragon is unleashed, making him a danger to everyone around him.

Mary Luce, a survivor of many hardships, is unwittingly thrown into the vampire world and reliant on Rhage's protection. With a life-threatening curse of her own, Mary is not looking for love. Her faith in miracles was lost years ago. But when Rhage's intense animal attraction turns into something more emotional, he knows that he must make Mary his alone. And while their enemies close in, Mary fights desperately to gain life eternal with the one she loves . . .

978-0-7499-5527-4